CRUSADER'S VALOR

To David,

Enjoy Hagan's Adventure.

Crusader's Valor

A historical novel
by
LEVI MECHAM

Adelaide Books
New York / Lisbon
2022

CRUSADER'S VALOR

A historical novel

By Levi Mecham

Copyright © 2022 Levi Mecham

Cover design © 2022 Adelaide Books

Cover art image by Levi Mecham

Published by Adelaide Books, New York / Lisbon

adelaidebooks.org

Editor-in-Chief

Stevan V. Nikolic

All rights reserved. No part of this book may be reproduced in any manner whatsoever without written permission from the author except in the case of brief quotations embodied in critical articles and reviews.

For any information, please address Adelaide Books
at info@adelaidebooks.org

or write to:

Adelaide Books

244 Fifth Ave. Suite D27

New York, NY, 10001

ISBN: 978-1-956635-34-8

Printed in the United States of America

To Charity. Thank you for all your long-suffering support.

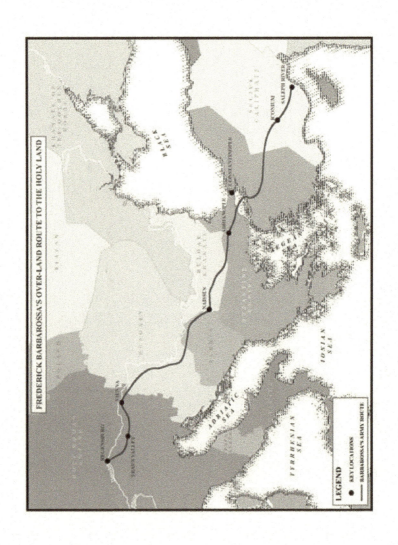

Contents

Prologue,	*9*
Chapter 1,	*15*
Chapter 2,	*22*
Chapter 3,	*32*
Chapter 4,	*39*
Chapter 5,	*46*
Chapter 6,	*52*
Chapter 7,	*62*
Chapter 8,	*67*
Chapter 9,	*71*
Chapter 10,	*85*
Chapter 11,	*92*
Chapter 12,	*102*
Chapter 13,	*115*
Chapter 14,	*120*
Chapter 15,	*122*
Chapter 16,	*139*
Chapter 17,	*144*
Chapter 18,	*155*
Chapter 19,	*165*
Chapter 20,	*175*

Chapter 21,	*187*
Chapter 22,	*196*
Chapter 23,	*204*
Chapter 24,	*221*
Chapter 25,	*243*
Chapter 26,	*250*
Chapter 27,	*257*
Chapter 28,	*264*
Chapter 29,	*271*
Chapter 30,	*279*
Chapter 31,	*282*
Chapter 32,	*303*
Chapter 33,	*309*
Chapter 34,	*317*
Chapter 35,	*331*
Chapter 36,	*335*
Chapter 37,	*340*
Chapter 38,	*342*
Chapter 39,	*348*
Chapter 40,	*351*
Chapter 41,	*360*
Chapter 42,	*362*
Epilogue	*367*
Historical Note	*374*
About the Author	*377*

Prologue

Levant
July 4, 1187

His mouth felt as dry as the desert around him and his swollen tongue threatened to choke him. The smell of smoke, sweat and blood filled the air. Around him lay scores of dead and dying men. A horse lay nearby, its eyes open, yet unseeing. The scene was familiar as was the smell; it was the scent of battle, yet it now smelled only of loss.

Sir Louis de Beaumont knelt among the debris of war; hands bound in front of him. As he sat on his heels, he remembered another time. He was kneeling then as well. The hall of the Cour de la Commanderie had smelled of smoke also, but it had the sour smell of incense rather than the acrid brush smoke that pervaded his senses now. He had been only eighteen. It was late autumn and there was a chill in the air that cut through his armor better than any sword could have. He remembered the sweat that beaded on his forehead and ran into his eyes despite the weather, betraying his nervousness to the onlookers. Sir Ridefort himself had been the one to knight him, he should have been proud to have been knighted by the Grand Master of his order, but he could not summon the respect he had once felt for the man.

He knelt now because he and other men were prisoners after a lost battle. There was no question, defeat had been complete. With this loss the Christians would no longer have the men to wage war in the region. They had lost. They had lost Jerusalem. How had it come to this?

An-Nasir Salah ad-Din Yusuf ibn Ayyub, or Saladin, had been consolidating power in Syria, Egypt and the Levant for years. As the Christian power declined the Arab's, under Saladin, grew.

Tensions had been high between Saladin and the Christians for some time, but Louis pinned the tipping point on the death of the King of Jerusalem. When Baldwin died, Guy de Lusignan became King through his marriage to Baldwin's sister, Sibylla. Guy had been a member of the knights Templar, as well, before becoming King. Another man I should be proud of. Louis thought. Instead of pride he felt shame. Guy had only been king for one year and he had already led his army to its own destruction.;

King Guy of Jerusalem had sallied forth with his army of twenty-thousand to meet the united army of Muslims under Saladin's command and had completely underestimated the enemy. When they had begun their march many of the men were sure of their victory, Louis wasn't, however. Guy had marched the army through the desert during the hottest part of the day in heavy armor with little water.

The objective had been to march to Tiberias where the Muslim army had the countess of Tripoli trapped in a besieged castle. They had moved away from the life-giving waters at Sephoria to some to the rescue of the Countess, despite Her own husband's adamant pleas for the army to stay in the relative safety of spring-fed valley. Raymond III, count of Tripoli loved his wife, but he had had the same doubts of a Christian victory as Louis had. Far more than the safety of his lady wife was at stake.

Louis was of low-rank among the Templars, and couldn't easily approach the Grand Master, with any objections; let alone the King. It wouldn't have mattered if he had complained, Raymond had voiced his concerns as did others but Guy and his cadre of followers ignored them.

Louis took a petty delight in seeing the King sweat along with the rest of the army as they marched. The tyrannical rule of the sun humbled all equally, it scorched the land below and made the chain-mail on his back so hot that it felt as if it would melt.

Dust filled the air from the men and horses as they marched around and in front of him, it invaded his eyes and mouth and formed a crust where it had stuck to the sweat on his face. His eyes felt dry and the brilliant light that was reflecting from almost every direction, was blinding. Louis heard yells of excitement ahead and lifted his gaze, squinting as he did so. The sound of the energized men seemed foreign among the weary soldiers.

There seemed to be a haze in the air, but a small hill blocked his view of much else as the column marched up. The men farther up the hill were the ones causing the commotion.
Louis spurred his horse forward. He crested the hill and saw light reflect off the distant waters of Lake Tiberias, shining like a jewel in the desert sun. The fear of death went rushing out of him in one great sigh of relief.

But fear came rushing right back when he crested the hill completely and saw what stood before the lake.
Saladin had placed his army between the King's army and the cool waters, the brush around the lake was ablaze, filling the air with dark smoke.

Trapped.

There was nothing behind them, or to either side but Saladin had trapped them all the same. They needed water, without it they were dead.

With one stroke Saladin had claimed victory. He had the defensive position, superior numbers and rested men.
The smoke burned Louis' already dry throat and eyes. The burning brush confused and disoriented the men as they blindly charged the enemy. The battle could not have gone much worse..

Louis had been in the second of many cavalry charges that broke upon the enemy spearmen like water over so many stones. The clash of steel and the terrible cries of dying men and horses rose to deafening intensity as Louis and his unit closed on the enemy. The Muslims stood their ground, stalwart, letting the horsemen ride into their waiting spears. Louis had been lucky. Unlike many of his allied knights, he had found a break in the spear lines and had smashed into the surprised footmen in front of him with bone crushing momentum sending men flying. The advantage of momentum, however, vanished when the press of numbers around him became too much for his mount to push through.

He heard his horse, Fermete, cry out in fear and pain as a spearman stabbed the frightened horse viciously in the neck. Fermete reared and Louis struggled to keep his seat while simultaneously slashing at the surrounding men. Even know, hours after the battle, the memory shook him.

There were too many spearmen and as he slashed at his left side, a heavy iron headed spear found his right. The chainmail that he wore under his tunic had slowed the spear, causing a painful but relatively superficial wound to the ribs. The blow, however, was enough to remove him from his already precarious perch. Louis landed hard on his lower back, but adrenaline brought him to his feet despite the pain and shock he felt. As the men pressed in around him on all sides, he looked back at the already closed formation of spearmen he had broken through.

The few knights and horsemen that remained on their mounts had no hope of reaching him. He slowly knelt, bringing his sword in front of him point down in the dirt. He kissed the cross in the center of the crossguard as he said a quick prayer and then lifted the sword again, holding it in front of him by the blade, an offer of surrender.

Maybe they would give him some water. Of all the lands and titles he would eventually inherit, water was the most precious that he hoped for.

What gave him solace was that Saladin's victory today would spell his own defeat, eventually. Uproar in Europe would follow the news of Saladin's success and armies would come with numbers twice that of Saladin's.

Here he was, kneeling in the harsh sun, waiting as he had so many years ago before his knighthood. What was odd was that he didn't feel as nervous now as he had when he was kneeling in la Commanderie being knighted.

So thirsty. Were they going to let them die of thirst out here in the sun?

He realized, as he knelt, prisoner, that he would probably sweat if he had any water left in his parched body. He felt weak with thirst and fatigue. He looked down the line of prisoners to the right and left of him and made another realization. All the surrounding men were knights Templar like himself, or Hospitallers, holy orders, both.

No footmen, spearman, or horsemen knelt with the knights in their solemn ranks and no other knights. Louis thought that strange and moved to remark as much to the man kneeling next to him, but stopped as a file of men came marching into view. As they neared, he could see that they had a somber cast to their eyes.

The column made a left face, turning to walk just in front of where the knights knelt and as the soldiers filed past, Louis made the assumption that this was their execution force. He absently wondered which one would be the one to kill him.

The Column finally came to a stop and Louis' silent question was answered as he looked up at the large man in front of him. Black cloth obscured the bottom half of his face, as if he were ashamed of what he was to do. The heavy dark skinned man didn't look at Louis as he walked slowly around to stand behind him.

A murmur rose from the waiting knights as they came to the same conclusion as he had. The Hospitallar next to Louis broke down and sobbed a tearless grief-filled lament.

It surprised Louis to not feel anything he thought he would in this situation. All he could think of was how thirsty he was, and why couldn't they at least give him one last drink. The ironic injustice of it made him smile.

Chapter 1

Traun Valley, Holy Roman Empire
Summer 1189

Hagan had been hunting for hours and had nothing to show for it but a few scrapes on his knees and a handful of berries, under-ripe and tasteless. He was now, reluctantly, returning home from his failed hunt, a task that was becoming all too familiar with the increase in pilgrims passing on the road only six miles away.

Hagan wiped the sweat from his forehead with his sleeve and swept a gaze around him. His head paused as a slight movement in the shade of a small evergreen caught his eye, he quickly identified the source of the movement as nothing more than a leaf caught in a spider's web. The gossamer strands glistening in the early summer sunshine.

The pilgrims and other crusaders moving through the area had all but decimated the countryside of the usual wildlife depriving Hagan and his family from the extra food that they depended on. The hunting that he did for small game wasn't necessarily legal.

According to the Baron food obtained on his land was his and if you hunted then you stole, therefore floggings happened off and on throughout the year since none of the poor families like Hagan's could manage without the extra food. Most years, the meager plot of land that the Baron let them cultivate did not provide enough food for his family and the taxes they owed. And with Baron Adelfried demanding more and more to pay for the Kaiser's crusade, it scared Hagan that his family wouldn't be able to pay and that he would be taken from his mother and forced into hard labor to pay for the debts, or worse, his mother cast into prison.

Hagan sighed as he continued his somber return home. He kicked at a small stone, sending it clacking off of larger cobble stones. He felt helpless, an insignificant speck, and the thought irritated him.

Just as he was about to kick another stone, a sound made him stop.

Hagan knew the sounds of the forest and instantly recognized this sound as being human made. A thrill of panic ran up his spine.

He wasn't supposed to be here, especially with a sling and stones in his pocket. There was no evidence of the actual poaching that he intended; a lack of it would not keep him out of the stocks. He slowly crept to the edge of the hill below which ran the main highway South from Salzburg. He saw the gleam of metal and the flash of the white and green of tunics through the thick brush that grew alongside the road and heard a nasally voice.

"I'm telling you Bercus I heard something."

"I hear lots of things." A deeper voice, who must be Bercus, responded.

"This was something big though. Wouldn't some venison hit the spot?"

"It had better be big if you are to hit it," Bercus laughed.

"Shut it, before you scare it away!"

Nasally voice said the last in a harsh whisper, and as Hagan listened, the thrill of panic he had felt became a torrent of fear. They were more than likely "pilgrims" on their way to the Holy land. This was just a nice way of saying "mercenary cutthroats". Men, who, he was sure, had a whole array of nasty things they would do to a boy in his predicament.

Even though they were just passing through they would more than likely turn him in to the local sergeant just to collect on any reward for captured poachers, or at the very least to curry favor with the locals hoping to get a hot meal.

Hagan told himself to calm down and think. They would probably just ruffle his hair and send him on his way. But did he want to risk that? He decided it would be best to avoid the two soldiers if possible. He slowly lifted himself from his concealment and crawled back from the edge of the hill.

"What have we here?" Nasally voice said

Hagan cursed himself for his stupidity and turned around.

The two men were still at the base of the small hill and neither was looking in his direction. Confused, Hagan quickly ducked back down. He wasn't about to make it easy on them. Maybe it was a ruse. Maybe they were trying to lure anyone out foolish enough to think the soldiers had caught them.

Hagan heard a yelp and a rustling of bushes as the smaller of the two men; the one Hagan assumed had made the exclamation, bent and wrestled a girl from the concealment of the foliage.

Hagan made an involuntary gasp as he realized the girl was his younger sister Greta.

Blast it. Of all the days for Greta to disobey him, it had to be today. She must have followed him and quickly lost his trail once he had left the road then sat down behind the bushes to wait for him to come back. She had done it before, and he thought he had made it clear how dangerous it was.

Anger rose in Hagan as he watched the smaller man grab his sister by the hair and all but drag her across the fifteen feet separating them from Bercus.

"Look at this tasty little morsel!"

"I see a scared little girl Fonz"

Hagan began creeping down the hill through the thick foliage careful not to make any noise. He wasn't sure what he would do, but somehow knew that if the situation required, he would do...something.

Greta struggled and screeched her protest as the man pulled her. She reached up, suddenly, and scratched deep furrows into the back of the hand that held her hair. The man, Fonz, let out a high-pitched squeal of surprise and pain but unfortunately didn't let go of her hair as she fought to get free. Instead, he brought his other hand down in an open-handed slap across her face. The blow was full forced and knocked Greta, violently, to the ground.

Hagan got to the edge of the clearing and could finally see without an obstructed view of the situation.

Bercus stood, clothed in a dingy green tunic and chainmail, laughing and holding the reins of two tired and hungry looking horses behind and to the left of Fonz and Greta. His sister had a cut lip and even as Hagan watched, blood dripped down her chin. She stared uncomprehendingly, dazed. The fight had gone out of her.

Rage made Hagan's blood boil. He couldn't think past the hatred he felt for these two poor excuses for men. Pulling a smooth stone from the pouch at his side, he quickly fit it, with trembling hands, into the soft leather fold formed in his sling. He forced himself to take a deep breath to calm himself. It would do him no good if he missed his target because of his trembling.

Amidst his laughter Bercus called "I can help you if you are not strong enough to handle her!"

Hagan exhaled and whipped the stone quickly around his head in a practiced motion and then let it fly directly at Fonz's head.

Fonz, hearing the thrum of the sling as it cut the air, looked towards Hagan just as the stone reached him. It took him in the left eye and sent him reeling backward. Greta curled in a ball, in reflex, as Fonz clutched protectively to his wound with both hands and fell screaming on the ground.

Hagan didn't need to watch the stone strike its target, years of experience with the simple weapon told him his aim was true. Hagan knew that speed, and surprise was his one and only advantage. He had moved as soon as the stone left the sling and sprinted towards Bercus.

As if in affirmation, Hagan heard Fonz mewl like a dying animal and wanted to look and see the situation of his sister, but knew it would be a mistake, perhaps his last.

Bercus had turned towards him recognizing the threat, the moment of surprise already gone, and was even now drawing his sword. Hagan was big for his fifteen years, but the man before him stood a full head taller and had arms that seemed like tree trunks. Hagan realized in that split second that his best chance would be to get inside the effective reach of the weapon.

As Bercus swung a vicious overhead swing at Hagan's head, Hagan slid to one knee letting his momentum carry him forward, left hand reaching up and grabbing Bercus' forearm, slowing if not stopping the swords progression entirely, as his right hand sought and found the cobblestone that would now be his weapon. Hagan pulled the stone back and brought it forward with all of his strength against Bercus's left knee.

The crack of bone and the pop of cartilage testified to the effectiveness of his makeshift weapon. Hagan stood, still holding the sword arm, attempting to push Bercus off balance. The soldier, however, encircled Hagan's head with his left arm. The vise-like pressure on his neck and head increased until he thought for sure his neck would break. He soon began to lose control of the soldier's sword arm and knew that once he did, the man would run him through.

Hagan began swinging once more with his right arm, trying to make contact again on the already broken knee. He found it on the third swing, and Bercus let out a low grunt of pain and quickly tried moving his wounded leg out of the reach of the stone as it continued to seek his knee for a third debilitating blow. As he did, he was forced to step backward and as the weight settled on the injured knee it buckled and with a cry of pain Bercus tumbled backwards taking Hagan with him.

Hagan now lay facing Bercus, struggling to get free of his powerful grip. The soldier brought the sword against Hagan's back. The blow, although lacking the leverage to do serious damage, felt like a hot iron as it struck his relatively unprotected back. Hagan let out a scream muffled by Bercus's chest as the man drew back for another swing.

Hagan heard a loud crack and waited for the pain that would follow, instead he felt Bercus's muscles relax. He slipped his head out from under the man's heavy arm and quickly scrambled away, laboring to suck in the breath that the big man's arm had deprived him.

Greta stood over Bercus with a thick branch in her hands looking down at the unconscious man. Handfuls of her golden hair had pulled free of her braids and now stood out in all directions. Her cheek, already swollen and red looked painful, and a dark trail of congealing blood ran from the corner of her mouth to her chin. She looked up from Bercus' motionless body and seeing Hagan as if for the first time, dropped the branch and ran the few steps between them. A wave of emotion hit her and she buried her head in his shoulder, crying.

They embraced for a few seconds, then the full impact of what he had done hit Hagan. These could have been knights. It was sometimes difficult to tell the difference between a knight and a man-at-arms on an errand for some Lord. The tunics though. Crusaders then.

"We've got to get out of here." He said.

As he grabbed Greta's hand, preparing to run back to the village, he heard the thunder of running horses. The sound of hooves on the hardened packed dirt of the road struck like a dagger in his heart. He looked back over his shoulder and saw six armored horsemen wearing the same white and green tunics as Fonz and Bercus...and they were coming straight for them.

Chapter 2

Sir Aldrich was in a surly mood. He and his men had been riding for hours, stopping in every hamlet and beer house on the road, inquiring about the two cowards that after only two weeks of marching in the Holy Army of God stole two horses and deserted. The only comfort that Aldrich felt was that by all accounts they were catching up to the damned idiots and would soon have their heads; figuratively, unless they resisted.

Aldrich raised a corner of his tunic to wipe the sweat from his forehead and silently prayed that the scoundrels would resist.

Ahren, Aldrich's sergeant, turned in his saddle "care for a drink sir?" and leaned over to hand a water skin to Aldrich.

Aldrich drank as their horses slowly crested a rise in the road. Sated, Aldrich turned to hand the skin back, but Ahren's attention was directed at something in front of them and he ignored the waterskin. Aldrich looked as well and saw two men, clothed in dirty white tunics with green crosses on them, lying motionless on the ground. While a man and woman stood holding each other. Aldrich tossed the water skin to Ahren and kicked his horse into a quick cantor.

The two men, wearing the green cross marking them as Flemish crusaders, were most likely the men he was looking for. Had they attacked each other?

The man and woman were actually a boy and girl Aldrich realized as they came closer. They turned towards the cavalry as the horses drew near.

The boy looked about sixteen and had a look of resigned fear on his face. The girl was younger, maybe thirteen. She had a red, swollen cheek and a bloody lip. The tears she cried left cleaned rivulets down her dirt-streaked face.

Aldrich pulled his big dappled grey to a stop.

"What happened here boy?"

The skinny youth held himself with a pride nonexistent in most peasants, and the reluctance to speak seemed caused more by fear of disciplinary action than humility. It surprised Aldrich to see strength in the boy. Aldrich was proud of his talent or instinct that he'd gained from years of military campaigns on a dozen battlefields, it told him that this boy could be dangerous.

Aldrich led men. He was a knight, yes, but the Emperor had entrusted him to command in battle because he'd said that Aldrich's "greatest ability was to gauge men." He could see their fears, their worries. He could inherently know, with indescribable comprehension, when a group of men were close to breaking and when they would push on despite incredible odds.

A breeze kicked up dust from the road and cooled Aldrich's sweating neck. He took solace that he was not the only person afflicted by the heat as the boy stood sweating in front of them. The youth reached up and pushed brown sweat soaked strands back off of his forehead.

"Sir Aldrich Kortig has asked you a question boy! I advise, you answer!" Ahren's voice thundered behind him.

Aldrich turned to his other banner man, Obert.

"check the men."

Obert spurred his horse to obey, and reaching the first of the still forms, dismounted.

Aldrich returned his attention to the Boy who had now positioned himself between Aldrich and the girl. Apprehension radiated off him like stink off a three-day carcass but the fear didn't reach his eyes.

"Give me the truth boy, for I will know if you are lying."

"My lord, I uh… " He cleared his throat and continued.

"They came upon my sister here on the road and uh… Well they hurt her, mi lord."

Aldrich didn't doubt it, men that would steal horses and desert the Army of God would undoubtedly do God knows what to a pretty girl like this.

The boy shifted his weight from one foot to the other, scared to continue the story.

"And?" Aldrich queried impatiently.

"Made me mad mi lord."

Realization suddenly hit Aldrich.

"You did this to these men?" He asked dumbfounded.

"Ye… Yes mi lord." The boy choked, terrified now.

Aldrich understood that this boy, seeing the common uniform of the empire's holy army, must have thought he and his men were there to seek justice for their fallen comrades, and yet the youths stood before him awaiting his judgment. That kind of courage was rare, even among men with the experience of many battles, the violence of which threatened their very lives. He knew of few men that, when faced with almost certain death, would wait to receive it as this knobby youth had. Upon closer inspection, the boy wasn't as skinny as he had thought. Sure he needed more food as most of his class did, but his shoulders were broad and his muscles, although lacking the girth given by proper nutrition, were ropey and strong.

"What is your name Boy?"

"Hagan Egger, my lord." He replied.

Obert stood from his examination of the second man and called, in a voice that had a hint of an accent unfamiliar to Hagan: "One knocked unconscious and one dead sir."

Sir Aldrich raised an eyebrow, as he turned to face Hagan once more. The look on the youth's face was one of surprise as he stammered:

"I didn't mean to kill him my lord...honest. I just wanted him to stop."

"I believe he has stopped." Aldrich paused. Thinking of the absurdity of the situation.

"You mean to tell me you overpowered two trained soldiers with nothing but your hands?"

"No, sir..."

Aldrich looked askance at Hagan, assuming that he was about to witness a lie.

"I used rocks.... and I suppose a tree branch was involved." Hagan finished.

Aldrich let out a booming laugh of surprised mirth at the boy's candor.

Adlrich's sour mood had suddenly rebounded. This peasant boy, to his great relief, relieved the drudgery of his task and freed Aldrich to pursue his other, more important tasks.

Hagan looked confused as he asked: "Mi lord, are you not angry that I have killed one of your men?"

"Ah, they were deserters boy, you did me a favor! After chasing those curs for a day and a half through this heat, I was ready to do worse to them." Aldrich exclaimed and on an impulse said:

"Hagan, I find myself in need of a squire. What do you say? You are a little older than a normal apprentice, how old are you, Sixteen, Seventeen?"

Aldrich wasn't sure why he made the offer. The boy was a peasant and there were plenty of qualified noblemen that would, with his reputation, pay him to take their boys as squires. The only thing he knew was that he couldn't explain it, it went back to that instinct that he had about men he supposed.

"I'm fifteen my lord" Hagan said with a growing smile on his face.

"Right then, it's settled, you will become my squire. I must warn you, we are on our way to battle the heathens for Jerusalem. Can you stomach that? This journey, I fear will tax our courage greatly before the end." Aldrich said seriously.

Hagan blurted out: "Oh yes my lord" then hesitated as his smile faded.

Aldrich, noticing the sudden unease, said: "well, what is it?"

"My mother and sister, mi lord…they would have no one to watch over them if I left, what with my father dead and all. I could never leave them as they are. Who would care for them?"

"You are Adelfried's subjects aren't you? This is his land is it not?"

"Aye, mi lord." Hagan replied.

"I will speak to the pompous ass and see if he could use more maids. It's the least he could do as he deems his own neck too valuable to risk it in this holy endeavor."

Aldrich's blunt speech about his liege lord shocked Hagan. This man must be powerful indeed if he felt safe in speaking like that.

Aldrich turned to Ahren and said "Then there is the matter of the reward, unless I'm mistaken."

Ahren nodded.

"Of course." He untied a purse from his saddle, and with a wink, tossed it to Hagan.

As Hagan reached to catch the purse muscles stretched in his back and pain lanced out causing Hagan to grimace and a sharp exhale of breath to escape his lips. He looked in the pouch and forgot his pain entirely. He gazed at the incredible amount of wealth inside. The amount could feed his family for a year, more if he wasn't there.

"Well, boy? What do you say?" Asked Aldrich

Hagan smiled from ear to ear, as he said: "I am your man for anything you would ask of me."

Aldrich nodded in acceptance of the oath.

Hagan turned to his sister who also looked, dumbfounded, into the purse at the small fortune.

Aldrich had interpreted Hagan's grimace of pain as the result of stiff and bruised muscles and exclaimed in surprise as he saw Hagan's back. The wool shirt was laid open, as was the skin underneath. Blood oozed from the wound, soaking the entire length beneath.

"Heaven above, why didn't you say you were wounded boy! Obert, see to him, let me know when he is well enough to ride."

Turning to the three mounted soldiers that rigidly sat their horses behind him, Aldrich began giving orders.

Within an hour the men had caught the stolen horses, tied up Bercus and were now burying Fonz's body.

Obert had built a small fire off the side of the road where he boiled water with which to clean the wound. He then pulled from his saddle bags thread and a kind of hooked needle that Hagan had seen being used by leather workers.

Obert saw Hagan's look of apprehension and, grinning said: "we could always burn it closed."

Hagan grimaced.

"The needle's fine." He responded.

Obert nodded and said "I thought you'd say that" and sat down behind Hagan to begin his work of closing the wound.

He stiffened as he felt Obert's hands on his back. He was nervous that the pain would be plain to read in him and these men would see weakness in him. He felt a prick and then a tugging. The pain stole a gasp from him, but he kept it to only a gasp.

Hagan, had a million questions all fighting to get out, and focused on those. He had no experience speaking to nobles or men of means. He did not understand how to start a conversation or even if he was allowed to.

"Sir, uh, I mean...mi
   lord." Hagan began tentatively.

"You can just call me Obert. No sir, or my lord, or any of that tripe needed with me." Obert interrupted. "Reichsritter Aldrich, however, is an Imperial Knight and beholden to no man but the Kaiser. You'd be well advised to show him the respect he deserves though he's not the type to demand such from his men. I suspect that's why so many freely give it"

Hagan nodded to himself, "Obert, is he sure that he wants me? I mean, I am...nothing. I wasn't a page, nor am I noble. It's all so sudden. "

Hagan gasped again as another stab and tug tormented his back. Obert paused in his stitching as he said: "In my experience, Aldrich does nothing by accident. His meeting with you may have been chance, but he knew beforehand what he wanted in a squire, and it seems that what he saw in you met his needs."

"But I've never even been to a tournament; I don't know the first thing about armor or weapons. The most fighting I've seen is outside Master Claus's beer house when the men get too drunk and rowdy." Hagan said.

Obert looked over at Bercus's unconscious form. "it seems to me that if that's true you have a knack for it that few men are born with." There was a pause in their conversation when Hagan flinched from an especially painful stitch.

Then Obert continued: "You are old to begin your training, especially without being page first, but if you prove a fast learner, then we could use you where we're going."

Aldrich walked over and sat across the small fire from the two, metal clinking as his bulk settled.

Hagan realized that the knight wasn't nearly as big as he looked when astride his warhorse. He wasn't a small man, but Hagan had definitely seen bigger. Aldrich's chainmail coif was down from atop his head and, for the first time, Hagan could see the full head of dark brown hair, plastered to Aldrich's head by sweat.

Aldrich considered the two and then said:

"Don't worry Hagan, Obert is no seamstress, but he gets the job done. He's stitched me up many times and nothing ever fell off."

Obert frowned and said: "I'm not sure that that inspires a lot of confidence, sir."

"I was giving you a compliment."

"That you were sir, but I was talking about you. How many times have I had to put you back together?"

Aldrich was about to say something, paused, then nodded.

"right." A slight smile slowly spread across his face.

Obert continued: "After all sir, we don't want our youngling here thinking you go about cutting yourself every time you draw your sword, when, in point of fact, it's more like every third time."

Aldrich assumed a look of reprimand and said: "That will be quite enough out of you Obert!"

Hagan suddenly realized that the warm show of friendship was most likely put on for his benefit. And what's more it surprised him to realize that he was grateful. His tension and nervousness had abated somewhat during the friendly banter.

Aldrich, a faint smile still on his lips, turned to Hagan. "You can still say no. If going into battle with the likes of us is too frightening or you are not wholly committed to the cause, then I would have it out now and have done with it. We..." He made a general motion, enveloping himself and his men in the gesture. " Have made vows. We have made certain commitments to God, and he in turn will bless us. I will have you make one as well before you commence on this crusade with us."

It startled Hagan at first, the sudden change in conversation, but soon he realized that the vehemence in Aldrich's request expressed true conviction and not flippancy. Hagan nodded toward where Bercus just now looked around blearily.

"Had they taken such a vow mi lord?"

Aldrich's expression changed to one of slight confusion.

"Well, yes. More than likely, they had. But they weren't sincere about their vow to God, they couldn't have been."

Hagan looked into Aldrich's eyes as he asked: "How do you know that my vow would be any better? I know little of God mi lord."

Hagan, who realized that he sounded ungrateful and argumentative gave a look of horror at his words and began apologizing profusely.

"I'm sorry mi lord. Forgive me, I don't mean to sound unthankful." he said.

Aldrich waved it away.

Aldrich saw a child's honesty in the question even though the comment hit him like a blow. The boy was right. It made little sense for him to ask for a vow, before he had gained a belief for himself. The boy had to want to make it. His own faith would hold him to the path better than any threat.

Aldrich smiled at Hagan and said: "We shall teach you of God then, and as you learn of him for yourself and know more of his will for you, then you may make a vow."

Hagan nodded.

"Thank you my lord, I will do my best to learn."

"Good!" Aldrich boomed. The smile broadening even more across his face.

He then looked over at Ahren and another of the men-at-arms as they pulled the bound and gagged man to his feet. Upon being forced to put weight on his bad leg, however, he instantly cried out in pain around the gag and fell back to the ground, whimpering.

Aldrich, evidently not familiar with the extent of Bercus's injuries, looked at Hagan in surprise and asked:

"What, in heaven above, have you done to that man?"

Hagan refused to make eye contact with the knight as he slowly responded, voice stuttering once again with trepidation. "Well... uh mi lord one of the stones was... rather large."

Chapter 3

Damascus

The dungeon smelled of urine, feces and rotten meat. Guy de Lusignan sat unmoving in the shadows. He had gotten used to the smell, the abusive nature of the guards and he had even started stomaching the food, but what he could not get used to was the disgusting dirty clothes he wore. The brown sack cloth made him itch. He was sure that lice infested it. It had probably had three men die in it before it became his, Guy reflected sourly.

I am a king! How had he been laid so low? Guy banished the thought before the anger could fully take root, as it had so many times in the past months. He could do nothing in this place, and it did him more harm than good to be angry here. He would retake Jerusalem and regain his rightful throne. All he had to do was…

A jangle of keys rang out in the silence as the door at the top of the stairs was unlocked. It didn't feel like it had been long enough for the visit to be a mealtime and they rarely came for his waste bucket until a day or two at least.

It tempted Guy to lift himself up off of the low bedroll to view the visitor as he made his way down the stairs, but decided against the obvious show of desperation. The creak of the door echoed through the prison, followed by multiple footsteps. A low murmur rose as those in the cells around his whispered. Light shone on the far wall of the cell suddenly and danced in time to the torchbearer's steps as the men turned down Guy's corridor.

Despite his wish to show defiance to his heathen captors, Guy was afraid. They may have finally come to kill him.

When captured after that cursed battle at Hattin, he and Lord Reynald de Chatillion were taken to Saladin himself. Saladin had given him water. After the torturous day he had, the water had been a kingly gift. Guy could remember how wonderful the cold felt as it trickled down his parched throat. Knowing that Lord Reynald's throat was much the same as his, he had passed the cup to him before he emptied it completely. Reynald grabbed the cup with two trembling hands and had finished it with greedy ambition.

"I did not give it to you!" Saladin shouted. His face a sudden mask of intense rage as he stepped closer to the kneeling Lord. Saladin had drawn his sword and struck with it in the same fluid motion. With great strength and obvious skill, the king had removed Lord Reynald's head from his shoulders. Blood sprayed from the sword as it continued its arc, splattering hot, and thick on Guy's face.

Wiping his blade on a clean white linen offered him by a servant, Saladin turned to him as if the murder had not just happened. To Guy's everlasting shame he had flinched and trembled with fear, thinking his life was also forfeit.

"The only reason you are still alive is the fact that kings do not kill kings." Saladin said in his thick Syrian accent.

As the men came to a stop in front of his prison cell, Guy was afraid once more. There were three of them. The two in front were guards. And despite the uncertain light cast by the torch, he could see well enough to make out the scar running down Saladin's right cheek. If the rumors were true, Saladin had received it from an assassin that came for him as he slept. The twelve-year-old boy who sent the killer was the rightful heir to the empire. He saw Saladin for what he was....a usurper. The knowledge did not save the boy's life, however. He was found dead shortly after the failed attempt on Saladin's life. No one could link Saladin to the death, or perhaps they just weren't willing. The empire was soon Saladin's to command, and with its armies, he captured one Christian city after another. Acre, Jaffa and now Jerusalem. They had all fallen to this man. With each victory his Army grew.

The man with the torch pointed at the far corner of the cell and said something in his native tongue. Although it was unintelligible to Guy, he knew that he wanted him to kneel facing the corner. As he had every few days when it was time to collect his waste bucket. Guy was loath to obey with Saladin looking on. Being a king kept him alive. However, as the man yelled again and gesticulated angrily to the corner, he thought he might wear out his good graces as it were. With all the grandeur that his current state allowed, Guy lifted himself proudly to his feet. His chain hobbled feet clanked as he shuffled slowly to the corner. Guy was feeling proud of how adeptly he had crossed the floor and was lowering himself to his knees when Saladin's deep voice rumbled: "That is not necessary."

Guy paused and then straightened. He hated himself for how grateful he felt to Saladin for not making him kneel. He turned as Saladin strode into the cell, alone. The disregard for protocol showed the supreme confidence he had in his control of the situation. Saladin now had the same look of bored contempt on his face as he did that fateful day in the tent as he slew his friend.

"I see no reason for you to stay here."

Saladin's voice was deep, and even though he spoke quietly, the words resounded through the hushed silence of the prison.

"If you but swear to me, you will not take up arms against me, I will let you free. Your beautiful wife is said to still wait for you, I'm not entirely sure why. My men tell me that Sibylla sometimes comes to ask for your release." He paused and strolled to the other side of the cell. He spoke slowly, methodically.

"Such loyalty is uncommon among your women I am told. Does she wish for your release in a hope of reclaiming her kingdom? It is hers you know, never really yours."

Guy was afraid to respond, as he hadn't received permission, and assumed Saladin's monologue to be rhetorical. Saladin's promise of freedom, however, inspired hope in Guy. Saladin turned and sauntered around the cell as he spoke.

"I met her brother, you know. King Baldwin, he was a king to be sure. Allah cursed him with the leprosy for our sake's I believe. Had he, instead of you, still been in command I'm afraid that Jerusalem would still be Christian." Saladin turned and looked at Guy, his face suddenly disgusted.

"You are a waste, and I see no point in you remaining, as I honestly see you as a liability here rather than an asset. At least free you would have to to feed yourself." He said it without malice. It was a simple statement of fact and it hurt all the more because of it."

Guy's anger rose with each barbed insult. The anger never completely replaced his fear, however. Guy bent weakly and slowly lowered himself to the floor. Kneeling, and with head bowed, Guy quietly said: "I, Guy de Lusignan, vow never to come against you or your armies."

Saladin had stopped in his circuit around Guy and listened to the solemn statement. When it was complete he nodded, as if something he had already known was confirmed and walked from the room. He stopped on the other side of the open door and said: "I shall go tell the lady Sibylla the good news." He then said something to one guard in Arabic and walked away. The guard walked into the cell while the other left with Saladin to light the way.

His guard unfettered him and drug him from his cell.

Bright sunlight temporarily blinded Guy as he stepped out into open air for the first time in months. Forced to close and shield his eyes from the glare, he stumbled down a step as the guard led him into a courtyard. As his sight returned, he saw his wife astride her white mare leading a black charger into the courtyard.

It surprised Guy to see her. If what Saladin had said was true, she had still been supportive of him while in prison, perhaps more than she ever had been before. Maybe there was some truth to the assertion that Sibylla was doing so, just to get her throne back. It made sense.

Their marriage had been controversial. He was an interloper to those already living in the Latin East. He didn't belong. Not in the East and not with the beautiful heir to the Kingdom of Jerusalem. He had his brother to thank for the betrothal. His brother Geoffrey had convinced the princess of Guy's charm and handsomeness. Enough that he was sent for at his home in France. Guy jumped at the betrothal to a future queen.

He was born to a relatively low station in the nobility and his marriage to the princess created quite the stir, especially given Sibylla's promise of engagement to Baldwin of Ibelin.

The Ibelin brothers, Balian and Baldwin were now among the foremost noble families in Palestine and Sibylla had spurned them with her engagement to Guy.

Her continued support was a great relief to him. She either still loved him or, the more likely, she needed him to be free to maintain his claim on the throne. Guy wondered how long the barons would recognize his legitimacy if he were not there to enforce it. He had, only gained his throne through the support of nobles like Reynald de Chatillon, who was now dead. She needed him free. Guy told himself. If the barons had pushed her to remarry, then he would still be in prison.

He was truly her only hope for regaining the Kingdom of Jerusalem. Saladin didn't see him as a threat. Why else would he have let him go? Sure he had sworn an oath not to wage war with Saladin, but an oath to a Saracen was no oath at all. Saladin couldn't truly believe that the vow would stop him from attempting to regain Jerusalem could he? Whatever the motivations Guy was sure that Saladin had just underestimated him. He would show that fool who he was and what he was capable of.

Sibylla smiled emotionlessly down at Guy as she handed him the reins. Guy took them without a word and lifted himself into the saddle, cursing the sore muscles caused from lack of use. They were completely out of the city before Guy finally turned to Sibylla and smiled.

"We will regain our kingdom." He said.

Saladin watched as Guy and Sibylla rode out of the city. One of his top advisors and generals, Taki-ed-Din stood next to him.

"Why do you release the Christian King?" Taki asked. He was often dumbfounded by the generosity that Saladin showed to those he had conquered, but Taki didn't realize that this was not an act of compassion.

Saladin turned to the shorter man and smiled.

"King Guy has done more for our effort since his coronation than my entire army. We are not the ones that defeated the Christians. They defeated themselves. And Guy will divide what little remains of the Christians for us.

Chapter 4

Traun Valley

Hagan felt Greta tighten her grip around his waist as the horse hopped over a puddle in the road. They weren't used to riding horses. Especially horses bred and trained for war. When Sir Aldrich had told them to take the horse back to the village, Hagan had been uneasy. He was excited certainly, but also afraid that he might make a fool of himself. His lack of experience was only part of the fear, however. Anyone that saw them would instantly be suspicious. Riding a horse as nice as Lord Adelfried's with a full purse at his belt was enough to get his head chopped off for sure, Hagan thought.

When he voiced his doubts to Aldrich, the knight took a small piece of parchment from his saddlebags and scrolled on it with a piece of charcoal from the fire. He then took a piece of wax from the same bag and, heating the end, pressed it into the bottom of the parchment. He then took the ring off his right hand and pressed it into the wax.

"There". He said.

"That should keep you alive until we see each other again."

And handed the note to Hagan.

"What's it say?"

"You can't read. Right, well, one more thing you will learn then." He said it as if he had merely forgotten, as if he was surrounded by people who could. The thought made Hagan feel sheepish. He knew there would be no reason for Aldrich to assume that he could read. For a peasant such as him to read was surpassing odd. He felt foolish nonetheless. "It says that you are under the command and protection of Sir Aldrich Kortig."

Now Hagan and Greta headed back home on the horse. Hagan touched the note in his pocket to make sure it was still there. How suddenly his life had changed. One minute, he was cursing his bad fortune, and the next he had become what he had always dreamed of being. With luck, he might become a sergeant of arms or perhaps even a knight. No, not a knight. He wasn't sure how difficult it would be for a squire to be raised to a knight, but it seemed too much for him to hope for, and he'd learned early in his life not to dare hope for anything that he wanted. You can't be disappointed if you don't hope for the impossible. But it had happened. The impossible had happened. To him. The thought threatened to tear a giggle from his mouth. He hadn't felt this way since... before dad died.

Greta tightened her grip again. Hagan glanced ahead, expecting to see something in the road that would make the horse do something unexpected. There was nothing. He realized she was hugging him. The show of tenderness was uncomfortable because of his wounded back but Hagan said nothing as he knew his sister had wounds that, although not physical were perhaps worse than his own. Reaching down, he patted her hand.

"You okay?"

"I am, thanks to you." Greta sniffled and Hagan realized she was crying.

"I've never been so scared. I was sure that the last thing I would see was that ugly man. Then when you came... it was like you were an angel. Like God had sent you to protect me." Hagan felt her embrace tighten even more as she rested her head against his back.

"I'm sorry for everything mean I've ever done." she whispered.

Hagan smiled to himself as he pulled the horse to a stop and straightened slightly in the saddle, pretending to have heard something.

"What's wrong?" Greta asked. A note of fear not long suppressed rising now in her voice.

Hagan signaled for silence and whispered "Did you feel that?"

"What?" Her voice pitched low to match his and her eyes searching for signs of danger.

"I think the earth just moved with your apology." Hagan turned and smiled at his younger sister.

As realization seeped past the fear, a scowl darkened her pretty face.

"I'm not sorry!"

Laughter erupted from Hagan as she slapped his arm and leaned away, folding her arms. A hint of a smile played across her face, despite her best efforts to remain serious.

Hagan's smile faded.

"I've never been so scared either." He said.

Hagan left unsaid that it had been for her welfare that he feared. His mind had been surprisingly clear after he decided to help his sister. There had been very little other than anger, and fear for Greta. He had always imagined that, when faced with a situation such as the one they had, he would be too afraid to do anything. He had had a strange understanding of men with power. Soldiers, noblemen, knights even squires had been beyond any influence of his. But now he saw them for what they were...men. Some were worth respecting, others were not. The same was true of every common born man He'd ever known.

Greta's resolve crumbled at Hagan's confession and she enveloped him in her arms again. He nudged the horse forward.

As they crossed the bridge over the tiny Traun River Hagan saw master Kronig step from the mill house. As far as mills went, Hagan had been told that Kronig's was small. Even so, it was impressive to him. The stone building was half on land and half in the water. The huge wheel that the river turned rolled two large round stones against each other inside the building, which ground wheat into flour. The mill was the reason the village of Traun existed. Kronig's mill was the oldest building in Traun, followed closely by Claus's beer house. It was a well-known saying among the villagers that Kronig's flour brought people to visit, and Claus's beer made them stay.

Master Kronig looked up as he heard the horse's hooves clomp over the wooden planks of the bridge. He looked on with confusion playing across his face until surprise replaced it as he recognized the riders.

"Where'd you get that horse there Hagan?" Kronig called.

"A knight gave him to me." Hagan responded.

"Sure he did." Kronig laughed "you'd better not let too many people see you. Horse theive'ns nasty business. I've seen more than one man lose his head over it.

Greta turned to face the miller.

"Honest master Kronig, a knight did give it to Hagan, and he's to be a squire."

Hagan assumed that Kronig's look of surprise was because of Greta's bruised face, and not the words she spoke. But when he responded he didn't remark on her abuse.

"I wish that were true girl, I really do. I liked your father. He was a good man. But you aren't going to live long with that as your tale."

Hagan pulled out the note that Aldrich had given him.

"This is proof." Hagan held the note out.

Kronig grunted in annoyance as he stumped down the small decline to the edge of the road. Sighing, he took the note.

Annoyance changed to interest as he looked at the parchment, then to disbelief as he saw the mark left by the ring at the bottom.

"I may not know what all this scribbling means, but I recognize the imperial seal when I see it." A smile spread across Kronig's pale face as he looked up into Hagan's. "Well done, boy. Your father would be proud." There was sincerity in Kronig's eyes.

He gave the note a final look and handed it back to Hagan. "Best go straight home now. Don't go show'n off. Some people aren't as easy to impress as I am." Master Kronig patted Hagan's knee and turned, walking back toward the mill.

Hagan nudged the horse into motion and tucked the note away. Rather than staying on the road, Hagan decided not to ride down the center of the village. Instead, they left the road and rode around the western side of the village and came to their tiny hovel on the northern side that was reserved for the peasants with no trade skills to speak of and who's only value to the Baron was that of strong backs for planting and harvesting.

Greta was off the horse and inside before Hagan had lowered himself to the ground. Hagan had always competed with his sister to be the first to share any news, but this time he felt reluctant. He knew that this news would take him from his family, and despite the money Aldrich had given him, he worried for their well-being. Would his mother be happy? Would she try to keep him from going?

As he entered he saw his mother sitting in the only chair, her mending forgotten in her lap. Greta had captured her attention. Greta knelt on the ground in front of her talking almost too fast to be understood.

Hagan watched his mother's reaction from the doorway as Greta told the story. There was a look of fear as Greta told of the two soldiers finding her. Then of disbelief as she heard of Hagan fighting the two men. She did not interrupt Greta, but looked to Hagan, perhaps wanting him to deny the story as the imaginations of a child. Hagan's silent nod, however, enforced his sister's words. She turned back to Greta, eyes wide as she heard of Hagan's injury. She rose from the chair signaling Hagan to come closer. He did so and turned, showing her the ruined shirt and the bloody stitching down his back.

Greta continued her litany. She told of Sir Aldrich and his men and ended with "And Hagan is to be his squire!"

Hagan turned as he felt his mother's gentle hands pull away from his back. Her hand pressed to her mouth, and tears were in her eyes.

"Oh Hagan." She said pulling him into an embrace.

Hagan suddenly realized that Greta had forgotten to tell of the reward that Sir Aldrich had given them. It surprised him that his mother had felt joy for him when his departure might mean the very worst for her. He pushed her away gently and pulled out the pouch of coins holding it in front of her. With a smile he said:

"Aldrich gave this as a reward for our deeds and says that he can talk to Baron Adelfried on your behalf."

Seeing the purse, she tentatively opened it and looked inside. As she saw its contents her smile deepened and tears fell from her eyes in earnest. She knelt and Greta and Hagan followed as she prayed. The act of piety was not unfamiliar to Hagan, but was rare at least it had become more so since his father's passing.

After the prayer Hagan went back outside to take the horse around behind the cottage while Greta told the whole story again more slowly.

Hagan hoped that no one had noticed the horse outside their house. The few people who visited them did not have horses; especially not so fine an animal as the one he now led. The beautiful beast would not escape suspicion by even the smallest child, and Hagan berated himself for leaving it out front.

As he led the horse around the edge of the rough stone walls, he saw movement out of the corner of his eye. He turned, seeing Gunther Schmidt hurrying down the muddy road in the opposite direction. Had Gunther seen? Of all the people that would be sure to turn them in for theft, Gunther was lead among them. Hagan gritted his teeth and bit back a curse as he pulled the horse out of sight.

All he could do now was to wait and see.

Aldrich had said that he would go to Lord Adelfried's keep and return to the army by way of Traun, allowing Hagan to join their party. Adelfried's keep was near to Traun, but if Aldrich dined with Adelfried, they may decide not to leave until morning. Hagan hoped Gunther wouldn't stir up trouble before then. He turned the corner once more and looked down the now empty street.

Chapter 5

Aldrich strode through the arched doorway of Adelfried's large hall. He was halfway across the room before the herald had finally finished announcing Aldrich's arrival. The presence of a herald at all, was proof of Adelfried's nature. The Kaiser himself only used the like on special occasions or when he was hearing petitions. The hall in which he stood was large compared to others of Lords with similar stature, but small for the herald's harsh voice. Aldrich frowned as the last of the recitation reverberated through the room and turned a menacing eye on the herald who quickly backed to the wall.

He turned his attention back to the fat man sitting at the end of the hall. Aldrich couldn't believe the audacity of this man. There he sat, like a king awaiting his subjects. Adelfried motioned for him to come closer, a twirling motion with his hand. Aldrich held back a scoff and closed the twenty feet that separated them. The fat man sat with all the laziness of a cat, and none of its grace. Despite the expensive clothes that he wore, Aldrich noticed sweat stains at the armpits and around the neck of his shirt. His face seemed to contradict the rest of his body. While his body was laden with rolls, his face was relatively thin. And when he finally spoke, his voice seemed to match his face, high and thin.

"To what do I owe the honor Sir Kortig?"

While the words were respectful, the tone was not.

"Kaiser Frederick Barbarossa will march through these lands in the next day or two, and I am to remind you of the worthiness of our cause. This will be your last opportunity to show your support....voluntarily."

Aldrich wasn't sure if the Kaiser would eventually force Adelfried to lend troops or not. He knew that Adelfried frustrated the old Emperor. His and other lords casual lack of support for both the crusade, and for the Emperor himself seemed constantly to stab at the Kaiser. He hadn't, however made any official decision on the matter.

Adelfried shifted uncomfortably at the implied threat.

Aldrich was only a knight, and was technically of lower status than the Baron, but Aldrich was an imperial knight who served the Kaiser directly. His service to the Kaiser allowed him some freedom in such matters, but only if he were under the Kaiser's orders. Adelfried apparently thought he was.

"Well, Sir Aldrich. I have given the required taxes to support this endeavor. I don't see that I owe the empire anything more than that."

Aldrich looked around the hall, noting the stained glass in the windows, the expensive tapestries hanging from the walls and the gilding on Adelfried's chair.

"I wonder if your taxes took into account your obvious increase. Your crops have done well it would seem. If an Imperial clerk was sent to investigate, what would he find I wonder?"

"Nothing out of the ordinary, I assure you."

The confidence implied in the words did not however reach the fat man's eyes. Aldrich saw fear and guilt there despite the other man's obvious reluctance to look at him.

"Well, I am sure the Kaiser will be happy to hear that from you personally as he will be here shortly."

"The Kaiser is coming here?"

Aldrich let the question hang in the air.

Adelfried's face paled but managed a weak smile.

"Surely his grace has better things to do than come here. Perhaps if I sent him a dozen or so servants to help with the difficulties of travel his eminence would be more comfortable and would not need to seek more... amenable lodgings." Adelfried finally said.

Aldrich was not a subtle man, as he was often told, but this idiot's attempt at appeasement while trying to save face was laughable.

He adopted, what he thought was, one of his more political faces and replied.

"Servants would be appreciated, but soldiers are what are needed. I think a man with your holdings could see his way clear of say fifty men-at-arms, but half that number should serve if you were to grant a favor."

The words hung like a giant stone in the room. No one seemed to dare move for a time as the meaning of them sank in.

The Baron moved as if to protest, but thought better of it.

"What is this boon you would ask of me?"

"I have taken a boy, one of your commoners, to be my squire." Aldrich rested his hand on the pommel of his sword and continued.

"His name is Hagan Eggar. You may count him as one of the twenty-five. The boon I ask is for his mother and sister to be cared for while he is away. Surely you have need of a couple scullery maids?"

Adelfried looked confused.

"Why don't you just take them with you and let them wash your small clothes. I'm sure even you need that from time to time."

Aldrich ignored the mocking jibe.

"A battlefield is no place to have a family. Their presence would distract the boy and that could get him, and I killed."

"That would be a pity." Adelfried mumbled.

Aldrich continued as if not hearing the Baron.

"It will tax him enough training and fighting on this campaign. Is it a deal?" Aldrich punctuated his question with a raised eyebrow. Adelfried didn't respond and sat considering his options.

He really didn't have many, Aldrich thought. If he truly believed the Kaiser would visit as it seemed he did, then he would have to appease Aldrich and the Kaiser. Aldrich wasn't sure, however, if the frustration that the Kaiser felt towards the Baron would culminate into a visit or not. If the Baron took his chances and ignored Aldrich's implied threats, then nothing may come of Aldrich's bravado.

The Baron looked up finally and nodded his head slightly in acquiescence.

Aldrich nodded his head and spoke in a somewhat sterner tone.

"The men are to be volunteers from your garrison Adelfried. I don't want a bunch of untrained louts who you have pressed into service."

After a brief hesitation, Adelfried lowered his head and nodded again.

"Good man." said Aldrich.

"I will send the two women to the keep. They will arrive in a day or two. The rest of the soldiers will meet up with the army as it passes on the road to Salzburg sometime tomorrow afternoon. If I do not see them, the Kaiser might like to have that visit after all." Aldrich turned making for the door, then stopped and turned back. His voice was low, but it cut through the hall just as easily as did that of the herald's.

"Make sure the Egger women are well cared for, I would hate for the favor you grant to turn into a debt you owe."

Aldrich finally bowed as custom dictated as he said: "thank you for your time lord Baron, I shall speak well of this meeting to the Kaiser upon our next meeting."

Then he turned for the door once more.

Aldrich had ordered Ahren and Obert to remain outside the hall, but they remained close enough to come to Aldrich's aid had he needed it. And From the look on both of their faces they had been close enough to hear the conversation.

Although they had both, presumably, heard the same thing, the expressions they had were as different as the two men were. Ahren stood with a pensive yet slightly troubled look on his face. Obert on the other hand, looked as if he had just been struck by a large fist to the gut. His eyes were wide, and his mouth gaped. Obert recovered before Aldrich reached them and, with his mouth now closed, he turned with Ahren to follow Aldrich down the steps and out of the keep. Ahren waited until they had reached the courtyard before he asked:

"Was that wise, sir?"

"Wise? No, perhaps not. But I couldn't resist. The man is a leech and does not deserve the respect I am duty bound to give him." After a pause he continued.

"Leeches do, I suppose, serve a purpose. I hope he serves his or mark my words, he will be torn from the flesh of this empire."

A stable boy stood holding their readied horses. Aldrich's three men-at-arms sat mounted behind, ready.

In a low voice Obert said: "In keeping with your rather apt metaphor my Lord, he would make a rather large smear wouldn't he."

Aldrich couldn't help the snort of laughter that came from his lips, but he quickly schooled his face as he pulled himself up into his saddle. He turned in the saddle the smile still in evidence on his face and said:

"Indeed, he would."

Ahren was shaking his head at the comment as he mounted, but Aldrich could see that even he had a hint of a smile on his face.

The sun cast a pink-orange hue to the sky as the six men passed under the portcullis of Keep Adelfried.

Chapter 6

Hagan smiled at his mother who sat across the tiny table from him in the only chair. He and his sister sat, as they always had, on wooden boxes. They ate slowly as they talked of the day's events and the plain food soon sat forgotten as their talk turned to the future. What wonders would he see? What stories would he have to tell? His mother told some of what she knew of the holy land. Most of the things Hagan had heard before, but he enjoyed listening to her. The firelight sparkled in her eyes as she spoke. They seemed to be lit from within somehow.

Hagan tried to fix her and his sister in his mind because he was boiling inside with apprehension about leaving them with the strong possibility of never seeing them again. His mother was beautiful with long auburn hair that nearly reached her waist. She was thin and almost frail looking, but Hagan knew better. Her frame was thin, but her muscles were strong for a woman, made so by years of hard work to provide for her children alone in this harsh world.

Hagan looked at Greta who sat as if spellbound, waiting on every word. She too had long hair, but not so long as her mother's and it was blond instead of auburn. Greta's frame was not as slight as that of her mother's having inherited the strong build of their father.

He knew she had heard most of this before, but she sat just as he was...captured. It hit him all at once that he may never see them again. He liked to think he would, but the truth was not as easy to take as the lie he had been telling himself. There was a good chance he would die. Or Sir Aldrich could stay in the holy land for the rest of his life as so many knights had. Would he ever be allowed to return?

A knock on the door cut off the story and drew a gasp of surprise from Greta. A gruff voice followed it.

"Open in the name of the Baron."

Another round of knocking sounded quickly behind the comment

Hagan crossed the small room, his hand finding the comforting parchment inside his pocket as he slid back the lock and opened the door.

A man wearing the green and blue tunic marking him as one of the Baron's men stood outside. He had a coat of chainmail under his tunic and a steel cap protected his head. Light shown off of the man's face from the torch he held, revealing a large nose, one that had been broken in the past, and bearded cheeks. Hagan looked past the man and saw another man, dressed the same way, holding Hagan's horse. Hagan's teeth clenched as he also saw Gunther standing at the edge of the light cast by the torch. The man spoke in the same gruff voice as before as Hagan's mother and sister came to stand behind him.

"We found this horse behind your house. Who does it belong to?"

"It is mine. A knight gave him to me today and..."

"Sure he did." The man laughed. "You stole it from a knight you mean?"

Frustrated, Hagan pulled the note from his pocket, but was thrust roughly to one side as the man pushed past him into the room.

"What is this?" The man exclaimed. He had seen the coins laying out on the table.

Hagan kicked himself for his carelessness.

"It looks like today is my lucky day!" The man exclaimed.

For the second time that day, Hagan felt angry. He started to speak, but was again cut off by the man.

"Arrest him Bern."

It startled Hagan as he looked back to see the other man, Bern, standing in the doorway. He had tied up the horse and stood watching his companion fill the purse with the coins.

Bern reached out with surprising speed and pulled his arms behind him with such force that it felt as if his arms would pull free from his shoulders. His already wounded back burned as if on fire. The pain tore a ragged breath from his mouth. Among the pain and surprise he could hear his sister crying as his mother tried to explain. What was she saying? Through the fog of pain he heard her say he was to be a squire and that he had a note to prove it.

The thought was like a splash of cold water. He felt the crinkle of parchment in his right hand and realized that he had the note in his hand.

"I have the note!" Hagan yelled.

Bern turned and slammed him face first into the hard stone wall of their cottage.

"It's in my hand. Please, it's true." He mumbled into the wall.

Hagan prayed that they could understand him. The pressure subsided slightly as one of the man's hands let go and grabbed the note.

. Bern's other hand remained, however, and was large enough to wrap around both of Hagan's wrists.

Hagan waited for the man to read the note. Surely they would let him go after reading it.

"Look at this Ham, his writing is worse than mine."

Hagan's head was turned away from the man Bern called "Ham", but he heard him cross the room. Boots clopping on the stone floor. There was a short silence followed by a chuckle. He suddenly felt his head pulled back by the hair and then roughly turned. Ham held the parchment up to Hagan and said:

"Surely this was not the best you could do."

The charcoal had smudged from the sweat of his palms making the note a big black smear. Hagan's heart sank. These men could do with him as they pleased. Sure, sir Aldrich might be put out when and if he found out, but little more would happen.

Hagan opened his mouth to protest, but before he could get more than a word out, Ham shoved the note into it then balled his fist, pulled back his arm, and punched Hagan in the face.

Hagan felt the room reel and saw black spots swim across his vision before...nothing.

As he woke, Hagan could hear women crying and water was dripping on his face. Why were they crying? His fuzzy brain tried to understand.

He tried opening his eyes but found that only his right did so. It was dark. He felt something stuffed in his mouth forcing him to breathe through his nose. He was outside, he realized, in the forest just North of the vegetable garden and it was raining.

He turned his throbbing head to the right toward the sounds of the sobbing and saw his mother and Greta. Both women lay with their hands bound in front of them. It was difficult to make out details in the faint light cast by the small torch, but Hagan could see that Greta's skirt was torn revealing her leg to her hip. And his mother's face was bloody and beginning to swell.

Hagan felt the coal of rage within burst into flame once more. He flexed his arms and felt the cords wrapped tightly around his wrists. He looked around wildly moving only his eyes for fear of alerting the two men that he was awake. He heard them then. They were off to his right somewhere in the dark and he strained to hear the whispering men through the falling rain.

"I still say we take the money and kill them. No one will miss them, and we can split the money." Hagan recognized the voice as belonging to Ham.

"What if their story is true? What if someone misses them?"

"No one's gonna miss these, especially no knight. Look at them Bern. You think a knight is gonna take that boy as a squire? He killed some poor fool and took his silver and horse. Tell me I'm lying. Why else would he have all he has? I'm sure the Baron would hang them himself if he knew, we're just doing him a favor. And so what if we get paid for our troubles?"

There was a long pause before Bern answered.

"I'll off the boy, but you gotta kill the girls. I don't like kill'n girls."

Hagan cursed his luck. How could they have landed in the same situation twice in one day? God himself must wish him dead. He would be blessed indeed to escape this time.

Hagan took two calming breaths as he slowly turned his head and opened his eyes just wide enough to see out of. Through the rain and darkness, He could make out the outline of the two men. They stood close to one another; Ham was slapping Bern on the back, clearly happy with his decision. As

Hagan watched, the dark outline of a man stepped out from behind a tree close to Bern and Ham.

"If you would be so kind as to disarm yourselves, I would be grateful not to have to do it for you."

The two men jumped and whirled at the voice from the newcomer, drawing their swords.

"Who are you?" Ham managed to get out. Surprise made the words come out in a choke.

"Ahren Faust, banner man to Sir Aldrich Kortig, Imperial knight."

Hagan was suddenly ecstatic inside. Was his befuddled brain playing tricks on him? Was Ahren really there?

Bern and Ham stood on the balls of their feet with shoulders slightly hunched and swords half raised as if expecting violence at any moment.

"I couldn't help but overhear you talking about murdering my lord's new squire and his family. Again, if you would be so kind as to drop your weapons, I'm sure we will sort out who should be executed and who shouldn't be."

From what Hagan could see Ahren stood calmly facing the two men, sword still sheathed at his side. Didn't he know that these men were dangerous? Why was he just standing there?

Ham and Bern looked nervous. They stood there for a moment, weighing their options. Ham shifted his weight and lowered his sword. He sprang forward suddenly; striking at Ahren with a vicious side arm swing intending to fell Ahren like a lumberjack would a massive oak. Ahren reacted with incredible speed. He slid to the right at the same time he drew his sword, twisting his body so that his sword was between him and the incoming strike as it left its sheath.

Bern stepped forward, lifting his sword high, just as Ham brought his sword back for another blow. Ahren flicked his wrist bringing the sword around in a lightning fast and surprisingly powerful arc towards Ham and at the same time the rest of his body spun. Hagan couldn't see any more as Bern's massive body blocked Ahren now. Hagan heard a howl of pain that sounded like it came from Ham.

Hagan sat up and worked at getting the gag out of his mouth with his bound hands, but continued to watch what he could of the fight. Bern's arms finally dropped to his sides, letting his sword fall, followed shortly by the rest of his body. The hilt of a knife stuck out of his chest.

With Bern out of the way, Hagan could now see Ham as he knelt on the ground holding what was left of his right arm. It ended just below the elbow. The blood that oozed from the wound glistened wetly in the torchlight. Ham's cries of pain changed to whimpers as he slumped to the ground. His groping left hand did little to slow the stream of blood as it ran out of him.

Ahren bent and took the belt from Bern's corpse and looped it around Ham's arm and pulled it tight. Ham looked at Ahren with unfocused eyes. He shook, teeth chattering, as if he were cold.

"He will most likely die, but we will leave it in the hands of God." Ahren said. The statement seemed like a familiar one for Ahren, and Hagan wondered how many times in the past he had said it or something similar.

Ahren bent and pulled the dagger free from Bern's chest. Hagan noticed that it had taken the big man right above the chainmail and was more in the throat than in the chest. He wiped it clean on the dead man's tunic along with the sword and came to free Hagan.

"Sir Aldrich sent me to find you and tell you we are staying the night at Master Claus's beer house." Ahren said as he finished removing the gag.

The village didn't really get enough travelers to justify a full inn, but Claus usually kept a few rooms ready for guests who needed to stay the night.

"A good thing I did too." Ahren continued.

"From what I heard, you wouldn't have lasted another ten minutes. How have you stayed alive this long? I'm not sure if I should view you joining our company as a blessing or a curse."

Ahren cut the cords around Hagan's wrists with the same dagger that killed Bern seconds before.

"You are extremely lucky to have survived both of today's excitements. But, by the same token, you are extremely unlucky to have found yourself in them in the first place. Lucky for you I don't believe in luck." Ahren smiled at his wit as he helped Hagan to his feet.

As he stood, Hagan felt as if the world was moving beneath him and nearly fell.

Ahren steadied him until the feeling passed then went to help the others.

As Ahren neared the women, Greta's sobbing grew louder, and she began struggling to get free.

"It's ok girl. I won't harm you." Ahren said in a calming voice.

Greta didn't seem to hear as she kicked her bound legs out pushing herself slowly backwards. Ahren turned his attention to the older of the two women and quickly set to work freeing her.

Hagan made his way to Greta's side.

As he came closer, he saw that her face had fresh bruises on it. Her nose had dried blood running from one nostril and smeared across her left cheek. The look of terror in her eyes was the worse thing Hagan had ever experienced. His heart sank as the probable atrocities committed to his sister, and possibly his mother, became clear to him. Hagan knelt; or rather fell, to one knee next to her, tears mingled with rain on his cheeks. She jumped at the sudden movement, but stopped struggling when she recognized her brother. Her attempts at screaming around the gag, faded to shuddering sobs as she looked up into his eyes.

Hagan lifted her head into his lap and untied the gag.

Ahren had finished freeing his mother and quickly cut Greta's bonds while she lay sobbing in Hagan's arms.

Hagan was afraid to ask what had happened. He feared that his mother would confirm what he suspected.

He hadn't lived a sheltered life. From time-to-time women would go missing from the baron's fields, only to appear hours later in much the same state that his sister was now in. He had always felt pity and sorrow for the poor women, but now... now he felt more.

Hagan shifted the weight of his sisters trembling form to his mother as he lifted himself to his feet.

Ham sat slumped against a tree. Rain had matted his stringy brown hair to his head. Lines furrowed his brow and his mouth hung slack as if he was too tired to notice the pain.

Hagan stared at the man then walked toward him. Ahren reading his intent, followed close behind.

"A man's life is an easy thing to take. Sometimes it takes more strength to let a man live than to kill him out-right." Ahren said. Hagan had reached Bern's corpse and bent to pick up the dead man's sword.

"After all, God's judgment will be far worse than anything we could inflict on him here." Ahren continued.

Hagan took the last two steps in a run and brought his right foot forward in a swift kick to the man's groin.

Ham's half-closed eyes widened abruptly and a fresh groan escaped his mouth. Then his eyes rolled and closed as he slumped unconscious to the ground.

Ahren paused, and then ambled up to Hagan's side, where he stood panting from rage. He held the sword in trembling hands, poised above the man's neck.

"Perhaps I was mistaken. I somehow doubt that God would have taken that exact approach."

Ahren slowly brought his hand up and laid it on Hagan's shaking hands. For a long moment Hagan stood there. Head reeling from injury and the absolute anger boiling inside of him. The torch had fallen in the mud and petered out. There was no pause in the downpour and very little light illuminated the scene but for the occasional flash of lightning, quickly followed by a crash of thunder that echoed on and on off of the mountains in the distance.

He lowered the sword.

Chapter 7

Hagan awoke with a start. As his sleep fogged brain cleared, the night's events came rushing back to him like a bad dream. The bruises and sore muscles were all too real. He sat up with a wince and looked around the cottage. He slept on the ground behind the door on a mat of straw he wove himself, while his mother and sister lay on a cot on the opposite end of the small house. The cot, usually reserved for his mother alone, was now being shared by the women. It surprised Hagan to think of his younger sister as anything but a girl, but if anything qualified her for womanhood, the events of the past day did. The curtain, used to give his mother privacy while she slept, was open, allowing Hagan to see the two as they continued to sleep.

The night had been a long one. Normally they would have all been up, preparing for the day, but the terror of the previous day had left them all sapped of energy.

After returning to the house the night before, Ahren had ridden to Claus's beer house to tell Sir Aldrich what had happened. Aldrich had sent the three men-at-arms Carl, Horst and Manfred to guard the house while they slept. Hagan was very grateful to Aldrich for sending them, because, although he was tired, Hagan wouldn't have been able to sleep until he felt the comforting prescience of the three men outside.

Hagan saw a shadow of feet under the door followed by a rap of knuckles on worn wood. He stood quickly and opened the door. Obert stood outside. His eyes seemed to search Hagan from head to toe. Taking stock of the injuries. With a crooked smile that belied the worry in his eyes he asked:

"How do you feel Hagan?"

Hagan shrugged the simple act a chore to his sore muscles. He did his best to smile, but felt that if he opened that window to his emotions, they might all break free of his grip. How would he look to these brave men if he broke down and cried in front of them?

Obert seemed to recognize the struggle Hagan silently fought and nodded a nod that seemed to say everything Hagan needed to hear. Hagan let out a shuddering sigh and then looked around. The sun shone high in the sky. It looked to be only an hour till noon. He had never slept so late.

"We had feared that maybe you were all poisoned and would never wake." Obert said.

Looking past Obert, Hagan saw Aldrich, Ahren, and the three soldiers standing in an unorganized circle. They were talking. Aldrich saw Hagan and made his way toward him.

"God has blessed you indeed!" Aldrich cried as he clasped Hagan on the shoulders.

"It is rare that a person finds himself in such poor circumstance as often as you seem to and yet acquits himself as well as you have. I should never have left you alone. Forgive me."

The combination of praise and request for pardon startled Hagan. Was he still dreaming? This nobleman had just asked him for forgiveness.

"It is I that should ask for forgiveness my lord." Hagan said as he lowered his eyes in shame.

"I feel that I have been nothing but a bother to you and your men."

"nonsense! You brought the pursuit of two fugitives to an end and provided me with an opportunity to flex a little of the emperor's muscle in the execution of those two louts that attempted to do God knows what to you last night. The Baron needed a reminder of the Emperor's authority."

"The man died then?"

"He did." Obert said. "It is rare that a man recovers from such a wound. He bled out during the night."

Hagan had expected to feel happy at the death of such a person. He had been seconds away from killing him himself just the night before. Upon hearing the news, however, he didn't feel happy. The man's death did nothing to change what he and his friend had done. He did feel better, but not that the man was dead.

Ahren's words came back to him. "God's judgment will be far worse than anything we could inflict on him."

Hagan realized that he believed those words, and he felt calm. A calm that only God could have granted in such a situation. He resolved to defend good people as Ahren had the night before. If that meant that he go to the Holy Land, then so be it. He would do God's will.

He raised his head slightly and nodded to Aldrich. Aldrich clasped Hagan on the shoulder again and said.

"I wished to meet your mother, but I must be going. I will not force you to leave them so soon after this ordeal. I will give you a day. Obert and Carl will stay with you. You will have to leave tomorrow morning to catch up with the army."

Aldrich was moving now towards the horses where the others waited.

"I sent a message to the Baron telling him what happened and he shouldn't expect your mother and sister for a fortnight. That should give them time to recover some. I'm afraid some things you never fully recover from, however."

He said the last under his breath, as if only wanting Hagan to hear, then mounted his war horse that pranced wildly from side to side in the road's mud.

Aldrich sat his horse with supreme confidence, an ability that Hagan wished he could copy, as he muttered the simple phrase: "Good luck."

Then wheeled his mount and rode away down the street followed by Ahren, Horst, Manfred and the bound and angry looking Bercus.

Hagan looked after his retreating lord with a respect and... love that he had never felt for someone other than his family. The kindness and help this knight, this stranger had shown to him and his family was more than anyone had ever given them. Aldrich Kortig was a man worth serving.

Obert stood next to Hagan, and they both watched the small group of men follow the road to the right and disappear from view.

"He's impressed by you. He told me you were the most promising pupil he's had in a long time." Obert said.

The sudden revelation stunned Hagan. He had thought himself a poor pupil. How could he have impressed Aldrich when in one day Hagan had gotten in more trouble than he had in his entire life? More trouble, even than in the lives of all the boys in his village.

Obert continued. "your deeds yesterday morning were... impressive. You were able to overcome two grown, trained men. That's difficult for any man. Let alone an untrained farm boy."

"Ahren made it look easy enough."

"Ahh, well Ahren was the last pupil that showed such promise I think. The only reason he hasn't become a knight in his own right is because he doesn't want to leave Aldrich. Aldrich could find a sponsor for him, possibly even with the Kaiser himself like Aldrich, but serving alongside Aldrich has its own advantages. At any rate I think last night made clear how good of pupil you will make."

"I did nothing last night. Nothing except being knocked out and almost killed."

"Ahren said you refrained from killing the man that savaged your mother and sister. That shows that even though you were angry, you were still thinking. That is a quality that many warriors do not have. Being calm when reason says you should be scared-blind will save your life more times than a good shield. Mark my words."

Obert's tone changed. "Now, I don't tell you these things for you to become proud and thick-headed. I tell you them so you realize your potential if you work hard. If you strengthen not only your muscles but your brain you will do great things God willing."

Chapter 8

Constantinople

Isaac Angelus Emperor of the Eastern Roman Empire sat under the large awning that covered the expansive balcony on the southern side of the palace's third story. The palace of Blachernae was not as artful or elegant as the Great Palace to the southeast, but Isaac liked the quiet surroundings of Blachernae. Besides, he would have never dared meet the man, who had just joined him on the balcony, in the Great Palace. There were too many eyes and ears there. Many people believed that dealing with the Infidels was sacrilege. Isaac however found it preferable to dealing with certain westerner pigs who called themselves Christians.

The tall man bent at the waist and bowed low, respectfully. Upon straightening he gave his name, which Isaac forgot almost instantly. Their names were always so difficult, and he had long since given up trying to learn their language. No matter. The man's name was of little importance.

Isaac waved to a servant who brought a drink for the traveler.

The man made an appreciative sound as he lowered the cup of water from his lips. Despite the long journey through the heat of the desert that the man had just come from, the kufeya that covered his head was a clean bright white, free from the stains of sweat and travel. His own clothes were hard enough to keep clean in this heat without the added challenge of travel.

Isaac motioned again, and a servant brought out a chair and sat it two arms' lengths to his right. Despite the chair being purposefully shorter than his own it discontented him to be eye-level with the tall Arab.

As he watched, the man slumped ever so subtly in his small chair allowing a clear difference to appear in their heights.

He allowed a small smile of approval to appear on his lips.

Maybe he is as smart as he is tall, Isaac thought. If he was, it would be a novel approach. Isaac himself usually only sent messengers with enough brains to relay the message, not to interpret it and form judgments.

"Salāh al-Dīn Yūsuf ibn Ayyūb has sent me as embassy and sends you his best regards." the tall man said.

Ambassador then, not messenger. Saladin must trust him implicitly to have sent him with authority to act for him. He had limited authority to be sure, but authority nonetheless.

After a pause, it would never do to appear too eager, Isaac spoke.

"How was your journey?"

He did not care about the Ambassador's journey, but what he did care about was who this man was. He needed to know who he was dealing with and how best to handle him. Angelus would not have survived long as the emperor if he did not know how to be political with people.

"It was blessedly uneventful your grace."

The ambassador looked out over the courtyard and the innumerable buildings beyond.

"and I find your city to be one of the most beautiful and yet impressive that I have ever visited."

Angelus merely nodded in acknowledgment of the compliment.

Uneventful is not how Angelus would describe the journey from Jerusalem to Constantinople. The terrain was some of the most unforgiving, and the time of the year did not make for an easy journey through the desert. Even if he didn't have to deal with the roving bands of brigands, Chrsitian and Muslims alike, that preyed on unwary travelers in the region, he still would have had a difficult journey. This man did not expound on the hardships of his journey for fear of looking weak, or maybe he just wanted to get to the point. Angelus would oblige him.

"Your Sultan was a bit ambiguous in his letter, but I gather that he is worried about the Germans. Why should their campaign against your people concern me?" He said.

"Has any crusading army brought anything but bloodshed and grief to your great empire? The Franks have no love for the Byzantines, this much is well known. "

The Arab's Greek was surprisingly good, but Isaac strained a bit to make out some more thickly accented words regardless.

"I admit that I was angry at having received a request, nay a demand, for passage through my land from them, but the campaigns from Europe never would have begun had your people not ripped Christian lands, my lands, away from my empire for centuries. What could possibly be in my interest in keeping the Germans from passing into Anatolia? They are a strong force. It is unwise to give them a target in Byzantium. I have not the resources to confront them and the rebel Bulgarians."

The man forgot himself momentarily as he straightened and looked directly into Isaac's eyes. The Emperor's candor took him a-back.

Good, Isaac thought. It was better to put an opponent off balance, whether in politics or sword play.

"The past conflicts between our Empires are...regrettable. What if I could assure you of your empire's stability long after the Germans have come and gone?"

Angelus couldn't help but wonder how he could offer something that his own country-men had, in his estimation, not yet attained. Syria had been a cauldron of boiling pitch for centuries. Faction after faction came and went. Caliphs, Allah's chosen leaders meant to bring about the destruction of all non-Muslim peoples, rose and fell. Infighting and assassinations upset the region in an almost continuous maelstrom of warfare. Betrayal and greed plagued the Syrians. At least it had. Sure there were still reports of corruption and dissention among the Syrians, but Saladin successfully united the Syrians as no one had before. His rise was, so far, short lived. Saladin's empire had not yet proven itself with centuries of relative stability like The Eastern Roman Empire, his empire.

The ambassador's words piqued his interest however, this was what he had secretly hoped for when Saladin contacted him. His candor with the ambassador revealed nothing more than he was sure they already knew. The actual state of his empire was considerably less stable than he hoped anyone realized. Byzantium, Rome's Eastern Empire, needed a reprieve from the constant assaults of Muslim Turks and protected trade routes to the East so he could re-deploy troops to the west to put down the Bulgarian and Serbian rebels.

"Continue." Isaac said.

His exuberance threatened to betray his show of taciturn demeanor. This treaty is what he had hoped for. A way out of the German quandary, and security in the East.

Chapter 9

Hungary

The Jutland mare didn't seem like the type of horse that a knight would take into battle. At least this one didn't. It lumbered along, hooves clopping at the same steady rate no matter how hard he kicked. The horse had squat looking muscular legs with a thick chest and short neck. Aldrich's horse was a huge, powerful animal, one full of energy and majestic pride. It even had a name. Abelard.

Hagan's looked like it belonged in a field. It had embarrassed Hagan a little, at first, at having such a horse compared to the beautiful animals that the other squires had, the plodding pace of the docile mare was soon appreciated, however. His backside had become raw after just the first day.

When he thought back, it seemed impossible that it had already been a month with the army and yet his rear-end had never been so sore. The first week had been the worst, jouncing along in the saddle all day long had made his rear so tender that he could not walk, and each morning the mere thought of getting back in the saddle would almost bring him to tears. The others laughed at him and teased him but Hagan didn't see much in the way of amusement in his pain.

They all promised that it would get better, and after that first week or two he had seen that they might be right. The pain lessened slightly and his stiff muscles loosened. He blessed Aldrich's wisdom in giving him the horse. He must have known that Hagan would be sore, and that the calm animal would make his experience less painful.

He rode better after heeding advice from what seemed like most of the army. The improvement in his skills seemed to lessen the pain as well and after the first month his rear only ached slightly rather than unbearably so. Aldrich must have noticed Hagan trying to rub the soreness out of his rump one day.

"Once you can ride better, we will fit you with a good horse. This mellow bay will suit you for now, but you will need to train with a war-horse before long. One that won't take half a day to catch up to us after we charge." Aldrich said.

Hagan only nodded, a smile splayed on his face. They still intimidated him, the huge chargers that Aldrich and the others rode, but the thought of riding one himself excited him. Aldrich was a rather well-known knight, both on the battlefield and in tourneys, and had, according to Obert, gained quite a lot of booty over the years. Enough to out-fit his entire retinue with horses, weapons and armor, something few knights could do.

Each evening the army would stop and set up camp. The tents strung out for miles and it was amazing, all of the people, fires and the noise. He had never heard so many voices at one time in his life. People laughed, grunted, yelled, sung. It was a hornet's nest of sound all the time. He thought the noise would calm down once night fell and men found their beds, but he didn't sleep for the first two nights because of it. He didn't know if everyone got louder at night or if it was just the fact that he was trying to sleep that made it seem worse.

He heard everything. Snoring, the rumbling throats of 20,000 men was loud enough to scare away every animal in one hundred miles. He even heard the awkwardly uncomfortable sounds of men and women having sex. Many of the camp followers, sculleries and laundresses were actually wives of soldiers in the army and some were just women trying to make a little extra money by...em keeping the men's morale up. All the hangers-on wished to pilgrimage to the Holy Land, and by accompanying the army, they reduced the risk of being accosted by bandits.

His insomnia didn't last long, however. Every night, after setting up the camp and getting the cook fires started, he would begin his weapons training. The long rides each day coupled with the intense workout, followed by a hearty meal usually helped him fall asleep almost as soon as his head hit the pillow these days.

Weapons training was something that he hadn't received as a youth as many other squires had, and he had the bruises to prove it. Despite the late hour the summer evening sun was still hot enough to roast Hagan as he stood with his training weapon in his hand.

Sweat beaded his forehead and his light rough-spun shirt hung heavy with sweat from his shoulders. The further south they went the later into summer it became and the hotter it got.

Hagan reached up with one hand to wipe the sweat from his brow before it could reach his eyes, and in that instant Carl struck. Swinging the wooden practice sword with impressive strength, Carl delivered a ringing blow to Hagan's left arm. The move to block the sword with his arm rather than parrying with his own sword was an instinct that proved more difficult to overcome than he imagined.

Even after the countless hours of drills, where Hagan stood in a row with other 'incompetents' and practiced forms. Waving their swords around at imaginary foes in a set of common sword strokes didn't look hard when Hagan had first seen the rows of trainees. He soon learned how heavy a sword became after only fifteen minutes of the drills and remembering all the different strokes to repeat instantly upon command was progressing at a snail's pace.

He had first held a sword, the night that Ahren had saved him and his family from Adelfried's men and at the time he hadn't given the weight of the sword much thought.

Later, when they had handed him his first sword, he commented how light it was. Ahren said that it would feel heavy soon enough.

Ahren was right. The sore muscles in his back, arms and shoulders screamed the truth of it. This sword was heavy.

Obert moaned from behind Hagan as if he was the one with a sore arm.

"Why are you holding your arm?"

"It hurts!"

"It wouldn't hurt if you used your sword rather than your arm to block. In the meantime, Carl could have finished you half a dozen times. Maybe I should give you a rock instead, you could probably defeat half the army if you had a good stone and yet basic swordplay eludes you."

That wasn't fair, he was new to this, while most of the squires had been training at some degree or another for years before getting to this point. And he had gotten better, at least now he could block eight times out of ten. They couldn't expect him to learn it all over-night could they? Even so, Hagan was disappointed with his own lack of progress.

How could he not be with everyone berating him for his failures? He kept up with the intense routine of chores, and training, but just barely. And while the other new recruits had seemed to learn swordsmanship quicker than himself, he had excelled at archery, which all the rest of the squires teased him about, it being a peasant weapon and all.

Archery wasn't nearly as important for a knight in training to learn as swordsmanship. As a matter of fact it was really only taught to teach the knights-in-training how archers could be used effectively on a field of battle. Still, Hagan had a knack for it. He had been a peasant after all, lower than a peasant though, because Hagan only ever had a sling to hunt with.

Obert walked toward him loosening the belt around his waist as he did so.

"This will help I think."

Hagan frowned. He would get a beating? Surely not in front of everybody. He braced for the blow, but it never came.

With a grin Obert grabbed Hagan's left arm and tied it to his side, using his own belt to secure the wrist.

Hagan sighed and looked around while Obert worked, wondering if he was the only person in the army that couldn't figure out how to use a sword.

"Can't I just use a shield? If I block with my arm anyway, can't I just put a shield on it and be better for it?" He asked hopefully.

Obert didn't even pause as he tightened the belt painfully around the wrist.

"No." He said. "You have to learn to defend that side of your body when you have no shield."

Hagan laughed morosely to himself as he remembered what Ahren could do to multiple armed and trained men. He decided that Obert knew what he was doing and this could save his life someday. Embarrassment coursed through him but he was willing to try anything.

Obert stepped away and brought his outstretched arms together beginning the bout once more.

Hagan noticed the difference at once. He felt extremely vulnerable on his left side and as Carl circled, Hagan felt the pull of the belt as he unwittingly tried to pull his hand free.

Carl swung a vicious side stroke at the vulnerable side but a jarring block met it from Hagan's wooden sword. The successful block surprised Hagan. He had never made such a block against such a determined swing before. Carl's Strike had been so swift and powerful that it should have gone through any kind of defense that he put up. At least it always had before.

Hagan noticed that he wasn't the only one surprised. Carl had hesitated before bringing his sword around for another strike.

Hagan wasn't sure if the block had made him bold or if the useless left arm made him more decisive, but he was surprised again that his sword was in motion, and not to defend. One of the myriad strokes and swings that had been drilled into him in the past month had somehow become action without him thinking about it.

In his mind the move was simple, clean, but he supposed that to anyone else it would look like a lumberjack cutting down a tree. There was nothing fancy about it; he had brought his sword back and then forward again, twisting his body to give the blow more force.

Carl had seen the move, but had been a fraction too late as Hagan's wooden blade slide past Carl's and slammed into his exposed side.

Carl let out a yell that was a mixture of frustration and pain and backed away quickly lowering his practice sword.

Hagan couldn't help but smile as Obert yelled something that might have been in another language and clapped him on the back. Then he used that same hand to push him forward saying: "Again."

This is how Hagan's world was now. He had little time to think which he supposed was a good thing, because when he had the occasional moment all he could seem to think about was his mother and sister. He worried for them. Aldrich had assured him that the Baron would treat them well, but Hagan wasn't sure. After all, it was because of them that two of his men had died.

Hagan felt a sharp crack on his right bicep and winced. Rather than ending the bout however, he advanced on Carl. His arm swung the sword in a high arc aimed at Carl's left shoulder. He knew that Carl would block the blow, but that was the point. Before his blow collided with Carl's, Hagan had already picked his next target and swung. It forced Carl to give ground as Hagan rained blows down on him. Despite his retreat Carl looked as if he was blocking the blows with ease. He even had a crooked smirk on his face Hagan saw.

Hagan was tired. Physically yes, of course, but he was even more tired of the berating way people looked and spoke at him. Even in his village he wasn't treated this way. He thought now that he was a squire to a knight he would have more respect, not less.

Hagan kept on; swinging with all the strength he had left in his tired right arm wishing he could use his left. I'm no cow to be hobbled he thought. As he attempted another downward stroke with his right arm, he pulled with his left. Sweat had gathered around his wrist allowing the hand to come free. And with a savage roar Hagan used his left to help his right in swinging the sword back up, a blow meant to cleave an opponent in two starting between the legs.

Carl had seen the strike coming and meant to knock it aside as he had done several times before, but did not account for the added strength that Hagan's left hand added. Hagan felt as the wood smashed into Carl's thigh then continue upward. Carl's sword deflected it enough not to cause all the intended injury, but the strike would nonetheless be painful. The sword continued up with all the reserve strength Hagan had. It next smashed into Carl's chin, the blow sending him reeling to the ground.

Sound returned to Hagan's ears as the roar died on his lips, and he heard...nothing. Silence, except for the beating of his heart in his ears and the sound of his own breath, Hagan heard nothing. He slowly turned to look at those that were watching and saw surprise and awe on their faces. Obert made as if to speak but paused then looked toward Carl.

Hagan felt a shock of fear as he realized what he'd done to Carl. He fell to his knees beside Carl.

Obert came and also knelt beside the still body and lifted one eyelid and looked into it. Then held his hand on Carl's chest waiting for it to move.

Hagan held his breath as he waited for Obert.

After what seemed like an eternity Obert smiled.

"He's alive. He may not want to be when he wakes up, but I think he'll be fine. Remind me never to make you angry. I think it's time that I took over as your sparring partner. Carl, while loyal, is not the best swordsman. I think you've learned all you can from him, and after today he probably won't be too eager to spar with you."

Obert lifted himself from beside Carl and turned to Manfred who had been standing behind him.

"Manfred, take Carl to his tent, and have someone stay there with him until he wakes."

Obert turned back to Hagan as Manfred began gathering men to help complete Obert's orders.

"It's a good thing this happened in our evening session or Carl would have had to spend a whole day catching up to the army."

Hagan nodded. He had had the impression that an army of this size would move incredibly slowly, but so far he had seen the opposite.

"Well, with Carl out of it, I think we can be done for the night. Why don't you run off and Ask Ahren if Aldrich needs anything before you sup?"

Hagan smiled and then caught himself. It wouldn't do to let everyone know that he was happy that he injured Carl. Well, that's not exactly why he was pleased but that's how it would look, so he returned a furrow to his brow and nodded. As soon as he was out of sight he bolted towards the part of the camp where Aldrich's tents were.

It was a good thing that the army was well organized or he never would have been able to find anything. Lost in a sea of people. The order and discipline that the army followed truly impressed Hagan, even while on the move. Outriders and scouts came and went all day at the front of the army, always returning with reports and instantly being replaced in the field by fresh men and horses.

The baggage train that held all of their supplies formed the center of the moving mass while guarded front and back by row after row of marching soldiers. Depending on the width of the road several columns of men would also form on each side of the supply train. Scouts even rode beside the army, cross-country parallel to the line of march, in case an ambush was set that the forward scouts had missed.

When the army was on the move, units of every kind made up of one hundred men each walked in time to a steady drumbeat. There were units of archers, spearmen, swordsmen, and each marched under a different banner representing different noble houses. Some smaller houses didn't even have enough men to form a full unit and were grouped with men from other houses. These mixed units marched with little armor and without matching uniforms behind the several banners that made up their units.

Adelfried's men were in one of these. The lack of training in the mixed units was obvious when compared with the disciplined, well-armored units provided by the wealthy houses. When the army wasn't marching however, the mixed units trained. Unless a capable Sergeant could be found among the unit itself, command of the unit was given to an imperial knight who had no holdings of his own to speak of or a sergeant like Ahren, a man beholden to no house but loyal to the empire. The commanders were hard on the men; many seemed determined to have the best unit on the field.

Hagan watched such a unit as he walked past. This was a unit of spearmen. Hagan had always frowned at the prospect of being a spearman. It had always seemed to Hagan to be the least glorious of weapons. And yet Aldrich had said that the spear was perhaps the most important weapon on the battlefield. "If you have spearmen and know how to use them" he had said. "You can keep enemy cavalry out of the fight. And if you can do that, you can control the battlefield."

Hagan watched as the men formed ranks. The instructor bellowed "left quarter!" Hagan watched as the unit responded. The four rows of about twenty-five men each turned. The man in the center rotated his feet a quarter turn, but his action seemed to cause a wave that rippled out from him. Each man down the line adjusted himself to match the direction that the man beside himself had adjusted to. The men on the ends of the rows had to run five or six steps to form the straight line facing the direction the instructor called. The entire maneuver took less than five seconds, which to Hagan seemed amazing, but then the instructor bellowed obscenities at the slower participants before calling "about face!" All the men turned to face the opposite direction, the spears lifted to point straight up in the air as the men rotated in what was obviously a well-practiced move.

Some spears however did not lift high enough and struck the steel-capped heads of the men in front of them before finding their proper places between the men's shoulders. Hagan heard low chuckles rise, presumably from the men who'd made the mistake, and before he was out of earshot he heard the now familiar sound of a brawl erupting. Such fights were getting less and less frequent, and when they happened, it was always among the mixed units, but in the short time that Hagan had been with the army he had seen so many that he didn't even care to watch anymore.

Punishments were harsh for the men who brawled, but Hagan believed that they only helped slightly in reducing the fighting. As the men worked together and even suffered together they form, if not friendships, bonds that quelled the fighting better than the threat of punishment. These men did not like each other. In fact, many of the smaller houses were all but feuding one another.

The air was finally cooling down, and the sun's last rays were stabbing through the trees in the distance and illuminating the tendrils of smoke that rose from the hundreds of cook fires scattered around the camp.

Hagan rounded a group of tents and saw Ahren sitting at the cook fire outside their group of tents.

"Done early?" He said as Hagan closed the distance.

"Carl got hurt."

Ahren's eyebrow raised ever so slightly, an uncommon show of surprise for the warrior, so Hagan continued.

"He should be okay. Obert says he'll have to catch up to the army when he wakes, but he's going to be okay."

"When he wakes? You knocked him out?" The surprise clear in the man's voice.

"Well, if Obert hadn't tied my hand down, I wouldn't have been so angry. I didn't mean to." Hagan finished, lamely. He didn't mean to argue, but it really wasn't his fault. Was it?

"You did." The warrior's voice sounded like a thunderclap to Hagan despite his calm demeanor.

"In that moment, you did mean to. You will need to learn to control your emotions Hagan, or they control you. Emotions on a battlefield can be dangerous. Some say that the Berserkers of the north have the right of it, that a warrior becomes stronger when he is enraged and that he doesn't feel pain, but he also doesn't think. I have seen the berserker rage before, it is terrifying, but it almost always leads to their death. Emotions kill more men on the battlefield than arrows. I know you can think in times of danger, we will exercise that".

Hagan nodded. This conversation frustrated him. They wanted him to succeed at the sword, and when he did, he got in trouble.

"Can Obert do it? Turn off his emotions I mean." Hagan finally asked, trying to steer the conversation away from himself.

Ahren glanced up from the fire, obviously a little surprised by the question.

"It's not turning off your emotions, which you will learn, and yes he can. Don't let his pleasant nature fool you. In battle Obert is as fierce a warrior as any and he does not let the flurry of death surrounding him cloud his judgment, which is a skill that few have, and one that we will help you cultivate."

Ahren shifted on the rock that he sat on, moving his sword to a more comfortable position, then continued.

"Aldrich is in a meeting with the Kaiser and will not need your assistance tonight."

Hagan got excited. He hadn't had a free night since he'd started his journey with the army, what would he do? There were the merchants that followed the army, selling the things that weren't provided by the army. Things that a person overlooked until one found himself lacking. Things like fresh meat. Well, maybe he was being generous with the word fresh.

Hagan's heart fell as Ahren reached into his saddlebag and pulled out a tome. Ahren, and on occasion, Aldrich, had been teaching Hagan to read and write. Hagan did not understand why he had to learn it. They said it was important for every great knight to know how to read and write, but Hagan was at a loss to come up with a good reason. He supposed that he could bore his enemies to death by reading them passage after passage from the books as Ahren sometimes did.

"So it looks like we will have an extra-long lesson tonight, Horst is making a stew and it won't be done for a while." Ahren said

What more could go wrong, Horst was cooking? Of all of them Horst was the worst, and yet he did it the most, as if they hoped that through practice he would become some great cook.

Hagan was sure that they would be well into their return trip home before Horst would learn how to use salt.

Hagan sighed and sat down on the ground next to Ahren pulling his knees up to rest his chin and awaited the coming tedium.

Chapter 10

Aldrich sat, listening to one arrogant wind bag after another express his undying support for the Emperor and the crusade, while also placing themselves above all others in the large circular pavilion. Each one seemed to somehow, come up with new ways of saying the same things, but no one really had any good advice of how to handle the new information coming in about the Byzantine Empire, which was the whole reason for calling the council together.

Most of the men in this meeting didn't truly care about the crusade, however. They didn't care about the Empire or the Kaiser; they were on this campaign to ensure the sovereignty of their current lands, which was a topic of unease lately. Ever since the Kaiser stripped his own cousin, Henry the Lion, of his lands and declared him an outlaw, for not bringing an army south to reinforce him during his last Italian campaign, the nobles seemed more eager to appease during this campaign. Which was good, but ass-kissing always grated on him like a rough stone dragged over a dull blade. He felt himself responding physically to the incessant grovelling.

Aldrich suspected that the men who were most adamantly loyal in public were the least loyal in truth however, and that they viewed the decree against Henry as an overreach by the Kaiser not his privilege under the law.

Aldrich couldn't help but sigh as Duke Otto Wittelsbach stood and began his oratory of self-grandeur and piety while throwing in the occasional declaration of loyalty.

Aldrich's eyes wandered from the speaker and saw, for the briefest of instants, the Emperor looking directly back at him. Otto's rotund body swayed and undulated in rhythm to his gesticulations, passing back and forth in the space between them, blocking the Emperor from view momentarily.

When the pontificating mass moved out of the way once more, Aldrich was again met with the Emperor's gaze, a smile was half hidden by his long white beard. That beard had still been red when Aldrich had first become a knight in service to the man. The beard for which the Italians had named him.

"I wonder..." The Emperor's voice instantly quieted Otto's speech, and the rest of the tent grew still as they waited for their leader to continue.

"I wonder, was my beard still red when we came in here?"

A sudden rift of laughter opened, and the pavilion's canvas seemed to billow with the force of it. Aldrich thought the laughter a little much for the joke, but wrote it off as part of the noble's appeasement.

"Don't take it too personally Otto" Frederick continued. "we all are to blame. Bear with me a little longer. I want to know what Sir Aldrich Kortig has to say about the Byzantine situation."

Aldrich's half smile disappeared as he stood abruptly. It caught him off guard, but in politics as in battle it paid to pay attention and to organize and prioritize one's options quickly.

"At Nuremberg, the Byzantines promised his Grace free passage across the Bosphorus and markets that we may refresh our stores while we march through their lands. I do not trust them however, and the fact that we have yet to see any evidences of their promises being fulfilled makes me think we should step warily."

Otto stood, his chair squeaking loudly at the sudden relief.

"They have never been our allies by any means but they are Christians. They would support us in this venture if for no other reason than that." Otto said. His voice was a wheezy grumble, and he had to pause often, even in the middle of a sentence, just to gather the wind to continue.

Aldrich shook his head.

"They betrayed our grandfathers at Nasau. We should not rely on their promises being kept; I believe that to do so would be foolish. If they do not grant us passage, then the fate of the Crusade may be forfeit. If we are forced to start our campaign with the destruction of a Christian city to reach Jerusalem, then I fear for our souls. We must make it past Constantinople and we must do it with as little bloodshed as possible. The more Christian blood we spill the harder it is for me to justify this crusade and I believe that God sees it that way as well."

It surprised Aldrich to hear a chorus of scattered applause as he ended his short speech. He nodded respectfully to the Kaiser before sitting once more.

"As ever Sir Aldrich, I appreciate your candor." The Kaiser said at the end of the applause.

"I agree that we can't, wage open war with Byzantium, regardless of my long held desire to do so. His eminence the Pope, has made his wishes concerning our dealings with fellow Christians known, and we are not to harm them. Wayward as they might be, they are Christian. We need to ensure that the Byzantine promises are remembered, however. I will send a council of envoys, I think."

"The land between here and Constantinople is full of danger, I volunteer to lead a thousand men to guard the ambassadors on this most important mission. " Lord Henneberg said. Lord Henneberg was possibly the oldest person Aldrich had ever known, and he had been the oldest person he had known for the entire fifteen years that he had known him.

The Emperor looked down at the old man with kind eyes.

"I would have once entrusted such a mission to none other, but we old birds have to allow some of the young lads an adventure from time to time, otherwise they become unruly and spoiled." The tent billowed with laughter once again, and when it finally died away the Emperor continued.

"I would ask Sir Aldrich if he would take this task on his capable shoulders."

Another round of applause erupted. The nobles were in obvious support of the nomination, probably because it meant that none of them would be, Aldrich thought.

The Emperor looked at Aldrich with eyes full of wisdom.

In his prime the supreme leader of the Holy Roman Empire Had broad shoulders, slim waist and a thick red beard that kept trimmed and neat. Aldrich remembered seeing him for the first time as a boy and being awed by his presence. Now standing in the uneven light set by the torches, Aldrich realized that his waist was not as trim as it had been and neither was his beard as red, as it so happened, the red was white; but he had an imposing and intimidating presence that seemed to have grown through the years.

Frederick made a sweeping motion with his hands as if indicating for everyone to rise.

"Let's adjourn for the evening, we all have an early morning ahead." And with that the meeting was over. Scattered conversations arose as men stood and filed out of the large pavilion and past the guards.

Aldrich rose from his chair and moved toward the door as well but stopped when he felt a hand on his shoulder. Aldrich turned. Frederick had that customary half smile on his face.

"Walk with me." He said.

Turning, the Emperor strode quickly for the side door to the pavilion reserved for his use. Aldrich ran a few steps to catch the old man, and as they exited, two sentries formed up behind them as they walked.

"I agree with your assessment of the Byzantines" The Emperor said once they had made it a discreet distance from all but the sentries.

"I must make a pretense of negotiating with the swine at least."

It surprised Alrdrich to hear his emperor refer to his nobles as swine, but tried not to let it show.

"Even if my suspicions that Isaac has betrayed our faith are correct." Frederick continued.

"I don't have the proof or good enough reason to raze his monolithic city to the ground. And even though Angelus doesn't answer to the Pope, we do. His eminence will not accept a Christian Crusading army sacking a Christian city without justifiable circumstances being evident. If Isaac Angelus is an enemy which I honestly hope he is not, but if he is, then I need his indiscretions to be irrefutable. I need everyone to realize his betrayal, so much so that I can turn his own people against him. They are Christian and many of the lands that he now has are held by but a thread. I believe that they will join our cause or at least rebel when taught of Isaac's betrayal. When faced with either losing the support of Saladin or that of his people, he will forget any allegiance to Saladin he might have, or lose his empire. After all, we are all beholden to the men in the fields in some regard or another, are we not?"

Frederick, as usual, had thought farther ahead than anyone, and had come up with a course of action. Not only a course of action, but an alternate course of action as well. Of course, it made complete sense to turn his own people against him. Aldrich had heard that the Serbians and Bulgarians had been giving Byzantium quite a headache of late. The rebels would be easily swayed if they were given the opportunity.

Aldrich waited for Frederick to tell him what part he would play, and a touch of nervousness waited with him. Frederick stopped beside a large oak tree. The Sentries had given them enough distance not to be intrusive, but not so much that they couldn't come to the Emperor's aid in a moment had he called for it.

Frederick cleared his throat.

"I need the ambassador to be escorted to Isaac's front door. And I need you to do it under the Imperial banner. Isaac's men will undoubtedly try to stop you if he has betrayed us, even kill you. There are many in their Empire that despise us more than they do the Muslims. The same is true for us I suppose, but we need them to see our crosses Aldrich. We need them to know us to be crusaders on a holy work come to pay homage to their Emperor and ask his assistance. And because of that I can not send an army with you, it must be a relatively small force so as not to instill fear, only respect." Frederick chuckled a humorless rasp that belied his age.

"I'm sorry my friend, that I did not put the noose you are to hang yourself with in a prettier box, but if anyone can do it, I believe you can."

Despite the danger inherent to a mission like this, Aldrich knew what his decision would be almost immediately. He believed that Frederick was correct, and that if they stood a chance of getting past Constantinople, this was it.

"You can count on me Sire."

"I knew that I could Aldrich. Count Rupert and Chamberlain Markward will go with you. I have also asked the Bishop if he would go, and he has accepted."

Aldrich smiled to himself as he realized that the Emperor had already known that they would send envoys to the Byzantines before the council met. He was also surprised that Herman the second, Bishop of Munster would willingly risk his life or freedom for anything. In Aldrich's opinion the Bishop was more interested in his own advancement than in God's will. Frederick must have noticed the look of shock on his face before he could conceal it.

"He may not have been told of all threats that are sure to be before you, but he seemed so eager to be the representative of the Holy Roman Empire in these negotiations that I didn't have the heart to tell him." A mischievous grin crossed the Emperor's face.

"Make sure he doesn't die before he sees Isaac, and everything will be fine. Take what men you think you'll need and leave as soon as possible."

Aldrich brought his fist to his chest in a salute and bowed before turning from Frederick's presence. The Emperor wasn't one for ceremony or speeches and neither was he. When there was action to be taken, he proceeded forward without wasting time on frivolous declarations or useless questions. As he walked away he heard Frederick say, "Godspeed my friend."

Chapter 11

The sound of Obert's chain-mail clinking woke Hagan, as it did every morning, before the soldier could say a word. The difference now was that the sky was still a deep dark and lacked the faint light that was usually present upon being awakened. Hagan had already sat up and turned toward the opening before Obert bent to peer through.

"Hagan, time to get up." He said in a low but insistent tone. He glanced around the inside of the dark tent at Horst and Mansfred's still sleeping forms.

"Wake them, do it quietly."

Hagan was confused, but when he woke Horst and Mansfred and told them to be quiet, they got up and began getting ready without a word.

Outside the tent, Aldrich sat waiting. Hagan doubted by the way his shoulders sagged that Aldrich had had any sleep. Although tired looking, there was an alertness to him, as if he waited for an ambush that would happen at any moment.

They were told to pack light. Hagan wasn't entirely sure what that meant, so he just followed Horst's lead, as they packed their horses with the essentials. Horst had obviously done this before, and donned his chainmail shirt with tunic, belted his sword around his waist and filled a small saddle bag with dried meat and bread, placing it in easy reach on his saddle, so as to be able to eat and ride, Hagan did the same. This was a common practice as the army didn't halt for a midday meal, but Horst had filled the bag intending it for more than one meal. Then Horst preceded Hagan once more as he packed nothing but a bedroll, then went to help Manfred pack two horses with additional armor and dried foodstuffs. They were apparently leaving the support of the supply train.

Hagan wondered where they were going, and why they weren't leaving till there was at least enough light to see. He grabbed the banner pole that proudly displayed the Holy Roman Empires Crest, A black eagle on a field of yellow. Below the Imperial crest hung Aldrich's personal crest which was a black boar on a red and white field. He stripped the pole of the banners to fold them and put them in his bag so they had them in case they needed them.

He had assumed that with all of this secrecy and with the need to pack light they wouldn't take the pole. He had to hold it from time to time as the army marched and the thing felt as if it weighed a thousand pounds. Strictly speaking the right to hold the banner was just that, a right, and it usually wasn't given to one so young and inexperienced as himself. But it turned out that that honor was only sought after when in battle, not when plodding along on an endless road in the heat. They could rest the banner pole in the stirrup or in a pouch on the saddle, but even keeping the thing from swaying with gusts of wind or the mere sway of the horse was painful after a few hours.

He realized that he had been holding his breath hoping no one would correct his assumption and let it out as Aldrich's banner came free and he began to fold it.

"Ahh good." Aldrich said.

Hagan's breath caught again as he froze, sure that Aldrich had found him out.

"I see you have anticipated me Hagan, place this above the Imperial Crest on the pole."

Aldrich took a folded banner from his saddle and touched his horse's flanks, bringing him close enough to Hagan to hand the banner down. Aldrich winked at him as he handed it down then straightened in the saddle.

So Aldrich knew but didn't want to embarrass him.

"We will raise our banners high for all to see, let them decide then if they are friends or foes."

Hagan felt a sense of misgiving at the knight's remarks, and not just because he would have to add even more weight to the blasted pole. He looked at the banner the knight had handed him and realized that it was the same green cross on a white background that marked them as part of the crusading army. That Aldrich felt that they needed to fly that banner showed that they were leaving the army as he had earlier believed, but more than that, they were doing so openly, as part of the holy army of God in a land rumored to be full of people opposed to them.

There had been a skirmish with some brigands and some of the armies out-riders not a week past. After which he had asked Obert how the brigands had dared attack them. Obert began by telling him about how the people here were supposedly Christian, but that was as far as the similarities in their two empires went.

They were technically in Hungary, but the Eastern Orthodox Christians in the country often associated more with the Byzantines than they did with their fellow Hungarian Catholics. They didn't even follow the Pope and spoke Greek of all things. Also, the Byzantines were trade rivals with the Holy Roman Empire and the populace that overflowed into Hungary still held a lot of the same hatreds for their German competition. The animosity among the Hungarian Eastern Orthodox was just a precursor to when they would, eventually, cross into Byzantium. Above all, it seemed they did not support the crusade as they had said they would. At least that had been the rumours he picked up here and there. They seemed to parallel the snippets he overheard from Aldrich.

No supplies had been freely traded with the army, and what merchants had come from the Byzantines did so with a guilty conscience and high prices as if they had been told not to trade.

As Hagan attached the green cross to the top of the banner pole, he noticed that this banner pole had only the two rings and lacked a place for Aldrich's Banner.

"How the devil am I going to put on Aldrich's?"

"Put mine on another. As my squire you may have the honor of carrying it."

Aldrich's deep voice startled Hagan. He hadn't realized that he had asked his question out loud, and despite his resentment for the heavy poles, he felt honored. He looked up from the banners at Aldrich who nodded down to him. He returned the nod with a bow.

The bow was not forced or unnatural feeling. The respect that he had for this man was real, of course he would carry his colors. Before it had been a chore, a thing that was placed on him because Ahren had been too tired or busy to hold the awkward thing, now it was his responsibility and he would not let Aldrich down.

Hagan looked at the surrounding men. They had all stopped their work temporarily and looked now at Hagan through the faint light cast by the watch fires. The looks on their faces were that of surprise and, what was surprising to Hagan, approval. He hoped that the light provided wasn't enough for the men to see his reddening face and he quickly turned back to his work.

Daily practice made packing camp a quick chore, and packing light made it even quicker. Aldrich and his retinue which comprised Ahren, Obert, Horst, Manfred and Hagan mounted and walked their horses quietly out of camp within twenty minutes of being awakened. The Sentry at the periphery of the camp made to challenge the group as they approached but thought better of it at seeing Sir Aldrich Kortig, Imperial knight and advisor to the Emperor. Aldrich trotted his majestic dappled grey past the guard. The sentry made a crisp salute, then stood at attention as the group passed.

They followed the road away from the army, heading east. Hagan hoped that he would get used to carrying the banner pole soon. After riding for only half an hour, the muscles in his back, just inside his right shoulder blade, were burning. Keeping the thing in his stirrup proved tricky as well, he was constantly knocking the thing out with his bouncing foot, or the resistance of the air catching the banner as he rode made the end slip off of its perch.

At least he had improved in his riding ability, he couldn't imagine what it would be like to fight with the banner pole and struggle to stay in the saddle at the same time. He felt confident now as he rode, that, he supposed, was the benefit of riding most of the day every day. Oh, how sore he had been. He had gotten used to that, surely, he would get used to this blasted unruly pole.

Aldrich heeled his horse to a stop, and wheeled it to face back the way they had come. The rest took his lead and formed up behind him. Ahren leaned towards Aldrich asking what they were waiting for. At least Hagan assumed that was the question he asked, that was but one of a hundred different questions that Hagan had.

Aldrich turned in his saddle and regarded those that sat their mounts behind him. His expression relaxed slightly as if he made up his mind about something, then he turned his horse to see at them all comfortably.

"We are to accompany envoys from our emperor to Constantinople, where they will sue for peace and passage across the Bosphorus. Relations with Byzantium are...strained to say the least, and our mission is a dangerous one. I don't want any of you feeling obligated to stay. No one will think worse of you if you stayed with the army."

Obert let out a loud guffaw.

"We won't think worse of you, just a little annoyed at having cowards for friends." Aldrich gave Obert a frown of disapproval but stopped as he saw the smiles on everyone's face. No one here would leave him because of a little danger. Aldrich simply nodded his head in thanks to the men around him and turned his horse back in the direction they had come when Obert asked:

"Who are to be the envoys if you don't mind my asking?"

"Chamberlain to the emperor, Lord Markward, Rupert of Nassau, and the Holy Bishop of Munster."

Obert had a stunned look on his face, as did most of the others. Even Hagan knew that such men as these deserved more pomp and ceremony than what they provided. Why, compared to the men listed the men here, accepting Aldrich, were a disgrace. Hagan suddenly felt self-conscience. He should have taken better care of his tunic. The bottom was all frayed, and the stain of mud splatters decorated the entire length.

The expressions on the men's faces was not lost on Aldrich.

"I believe that you men are of equal or even of surpassing quality to the men we are to guard, and I wouldn't take one hundred men in place of any one of you." Aldrich paused, and a smile touched his eyes as he continued.

"But it just so happens that it has been arranged to meet two hundred heavy cavalry a mile down the road. I did not say I wouldn't take them if they were offered in addition to you. They will appease the need to make a statement, I think, yet not be so many as to offend Emperor Isaac unduly."

Hagan heard horses coming closer along the same road they were on, and Aldrich turned his mount in that direction.

Hagan was able to make out movement, then shapes. Soon he made out a group of men three or four times the size of their own coming closer through the night. A tall, angular looking man with broad shoulders led the group. He sat his horse well and when he drew within range of Aldrich, the two men saluted each other, then went beyond the customary greeting and extended right arms clasping each other's forearms. This man was obviously a Knight, and probably Count Rupert of Nassau, personal friend to the Emperor. As Hagan watched, one man with similar features to the first drew reign to the left. Aldrich again clasped this man's arm and said:

"Henry, I am glad you chose to come along on this adventure."

"Henry smiled and said, I'm always up for a good adventure."

Rupert and Henry were followed by only four men, probably squires or sponsored knights.

Next out of the darkness came a man dressed in fine dark robes. The cross hanging from his neck was big enough for someone to use as a weapon and despite the warmth of the summer night, he wore a thick red cloak that hung far down the sides of his large bay horse. Hagan watched as the Bishop looked around him with obvious distaste, it seemed as though he was angry. Hagan wasn't entirely sure why. The bishop, like himself, didn't look comfortable on a horse, and guessed that that coupled with the early hour was enough to make the holy man foul-tempered. He was also obviously disappointed in not seeing more men. Hagan knew that this man was a Bishop and a man of the cloth, but he also knew that he would have a hard time liking him.

It surprised him to see six or seven men following the scowling Bishop. Two of them looked like servants, while the rest looked like guards and even in the dark Hagan was impressed by their gleaming matching armor and clean tunics. He made a mental note to try harder at polishing Aldrich's armor. Even with their perfect uniforms and weapons however, the five guards didn't look like hardened soldiers. They had a rigid look, not the ready stance that Aldrich had. From what Hagan saw, the guards probably served the same purpose to the Bishop as his red cloak, for show and little more.

The last man didn't seem to be a part of either of the first two groups. He wore rich clothing but his face seemed the type to smile easily, his slight nervousness, Hagan attributed to humility, not lack of confidence and a single attendant accompanied him.

"Is this all the men you are bringing Kortig?" The Bishop questioned.

Hagan noticed the Bishop's omission of Aldrich's title. His voice was deep, but it sounded forced to Hagan's ears. It reminded Hagan of a boy trying to make his voice like his father's and overshooting the mark.

"No, your grace. I have two hundred knights waiting a mile or so down the road. Don't worry we will bring you safely to Constantinople."

The Bishop seemed annoyed not to have a target for his frustration. He had put considerable energy into his anger about being accompanied by so few men and didn't want it to go to waste.

"Why must we leave at this ungodly hour Kortig." He said finally, hitting on a new target for his annoyance. Hagan didn't like how the Bishop continued to neglect Aldrich's title, however he unwittingly wanted an answer as well.

"His Eminence the Kaiser wanted us to leave as soon as possible, and it makes it harder on whatever spies are about. I am always for making it harder for the enemy to know what our next move is."

"Spies?" The Bishop said, a look of abject horror on his face.

Aldrich didn't seem in a particular hurry to soothe the Bishop's fears and took his time responding.

"Yes, your grace. There are undoubtedly numerous spies in and around our army, they have most likely been put in place when Emperor Frederick was first talking of joining the crusade if not before. Spies are common among any army, but it doesn't mean you make it easy for them to get information."

Hagan was as surprised as the Bishop looked. How could people live such a lie? What kind of life would that be?

Obert had told Hagan about a group of killers in the mountains right in the path of where they were headed called Assassins. Their leader was a man called The Old Man of the Mountain. Not very original, thought Hagan, but he wondered if such men would infiltrate their army as Aldrich had said that spies had. Hagan consoled himself that the Assassins were still a long way off, past the Bospherus, and by the time they got across the whole army would be with them.

Aldrich smiled, reassuringly at the Bishop.

"Again, don't worry, we have the jump on any left in the camp, and we have few enough men with us it will be easy for us to keep information from getting out. Especially since we have only one pigeon handler. A man I trust."

Rupert and Henry nodded as if these precautions were expected. Markward had a passive expression that left little to interpretation. The Bishop, on the other hand, had a face etched with surprise and fear.

Why would a man of such stature react so strongly?

"Are you okay your grace? Do you wish to return to camp? I'm sure that Count Rupert, Henry and Markward are qualified to address Emperor Isaac if you are too ill to continue. It is yet a long way to Constantinople, and I would hate for you to suffer for it."

Hagan watched as the Bishop hesitated, thinking about Aldrich's offer, then said.

"No, I am quite well, thank you. I will be fine, I just wasn't aware that such treacheries were commonplace."

Hagan watched as Aldrich's shoulders sagged slightly at the Bishop's answer. Evidently the Bishop of Munster wasn't the most popular of traveling companions. Hagan noticed, as he looked around at the other men in the group, that many of them had felt the same disappointment that Aldrich suffered at the Bishop's participation.

"The road will be long and hard. We'd better get a move on if we are going to get a good lead on the army." With that, Aldrich kicked his horse, to lead larger group of men down the road.

As Hagan kicked his horse into the row of horses, he couldn't help but wonder if there really were spies or if that was just a story to get the Bishop to stay behind.

Chapter 12

The two hundred knights that made up the deterring force meant to keep the envoys safe, looked impressive. The units were made up of men from many different houses, but unlike the poor units that advertised a smattering of houses, these units only lifted the Green cross and the black eagle of the empire. The men were Imperial knights, just like Aldrich, devoted to the empire rather than any individual house and as Aldrich's small group of nobles came among the knights, Hagan noticed a great deal of respect being shown to Aldrich. Perhaps they were not just like Aldrich, Hagan thought. Many of the men, the size of houses on their massive steel clad chargers, seemed to be as shy as a beaten dog as Aldrich passed, saluting forcefully but with averted eyes.

As Aldrich's group neared the center of the knights, Aldrich pulled reign and stopped. The rest of the nobles and their men stopped well back. They seemed to expect this and allowed Aldrich plenty of room. He turned from side to side, surveying his men. The look on his face was a display of pride and approval.

"I know many of you are wondering why we are not in our beds and the rest have spread various rumours as soldiers are prone to do. We will not be storming the walls of Constantinople as some of those rumours have undoubtedly told." A smattering of nervous laughter showed that Aldrich had not been far off the mark.

"We are bound for Constantinople, however. Our mission is to protect the noble ambassadors and make sure they reach their goal safely. His Eminence, the Kaiser has entrusted in us the lives of these loyal men. The dangers are yet unknown, but I have every confidence in your abilities."

Aldrich paused to look over the men one more time.

"Haste is our friend, but we must be vigilant as well. Sir Faust, your unit will make up the out riders and scouts. Nobles to the center and dry rations at least until we reach Gran. Move out!"

Hagan watched as the knights jumped to obey. The company was so well trained and experienced that they were on the road again within minutes, formed up exactly how Aldrich had commanded. The noble entourage formed the center of the column, Hagan was pleased, however, that Aldrich and his retinue were not expected to remain in the center with the nobles the whole time.

Aldrich was often at the front of the column as it wound its way down the road, receiving reports of terrain and possible difficult spots ahead from the scouts. It impressed Hagan with how quickly Aldrich could make a decision based off of what Hagan thought was very little information. Hagan realized that his duty as standard bearer for Sir Aldrich was, in some ways, more important than was Ahren's as standard bearer for the crusading cross and the eagle of the Holy Roman Empire.

Many of the leading imperial knights had the same standards as what Ahren carried, but Aldrich's sigil, a black boar on a red and white field, marked his position for the rest of the army. Every knight could quickly see where their general was. This revelation helped ease Hagan's ill feelings towards the banner.

One day a scout rode up to Aldrich and told him that there was a copse of trees that came in close to both sides of the road about a mile ahead, and that a quarter mile past that a river was running deep from a recent summer rain. They would have to go upstream to a wider spot where the water was shallower to cross. Aldrich gave a pensive frown at the news, then inexplicably lifted his right hand, giving the signal to stop the column.

"Were you the only scout in the area?"

"No, Sir Engel went to take a look at the far side of the trees."

"He hasn't returned?"

"No." The word escaped in a question. Then a look of realization crossed the young man's face.

"Do you think there is an ambush waiting?" The scout said.

Aldrich ignored the question and instead responded with his own.

"How long since you last saw Engel?"

"Half an hour my lord. I continued past the trees to the river before returning, he should have made it back before me."

"Right. Faust! Call what men you can back!" The knight nodded as he lifted a new flag on the banner pole he held. Hagan was annoyed to notice how easily Faust made it look.

Aldrich had previously split his force in two and given loose command of the two halves to two men, Hoch and Rothschild. He turned now to Hoch, a tree trunk of a man with a large mustache and said:

"Hoch, stay with the envoys."

He then turned to the other man. "Rothschild, take half of your men and go around the east side of the copse, I'll take the other around the west side. Don't go in too fast or you might get caught in a bog before you realize the danger." Rothschild nodded his understanding then wheeled his horse to gather his men. Every man knew his place, and they separated quickly.

Hagan was sweating even more than normal as he rode between Obert and Manfred into what could be his first real combat. Soon, the only thing Hagan could hear was his heart beating in his ears. "I've got to calm down" He thought. It was all happening so fast. Just moments ago they were riding along, not a care in the world.

Okay, maybe he was the only one that hadn't had a care. Everyone else was experienced at this kind of thing and were expecting something like this. Closing his eyes, he took three deep, slow breaths, trying not to think of anything. When he opened his eyes, the trees were before him. Had they traveled so far so fast?

Hagan wiped his unprotected sweaty palms on his tunic. He looked towards Obert and Obert was looking back, with one of his all-too-familiar grins on his face, the one that said "you will survive, and I'll try not to laugh too hard at you."

Just as they were rounding the west side of the trees, Hagan heard trumpets blare and the thunderous crash of distant fighting, then men screaming. The sound did not last long however, and as they came out into the opening on the far side of the thick trees, a large group of horsemen were already riding away from Rothschild's men in retreat.

Aldrich drew his sword which was a sign for every man to do the same. As they rode closer to the enemy Aldrich kicked his horse into a faster gallop, and again all the knights following did the same. Hagan was surprised when his mare actually increased its pace to match that of the surrounding horses. It was the fastest that the horse had ever gone; he was sure.

They were passing the trees that the scout had mentioned. They were going by in a blur on his right. Ahead, Hagan could make out a large unit of horsemen riding toward them. Most of the enemy knights wore blue and as a group they resembled a lake in high wind.

Before they were able to engage the enemy, they turned as a group, apparently seeing the flanking maneuver moments before it was too late for them to escape. It surprised Hagan how difficult it was to match speed and changes in direction while riding so fast. He was grateful for Manfred and Obert as they helped guide him and his mount through the maneuver and realized that they had positioned themselves on either side of him for this reason.

Hagan looked at the group of fleeing warriors wonderingly, he had expected no one to be there. He thought Aldrich had been over-reacting, although his nervousness was proof that he had not wholly convinced himself of that.

Aldrich looked out at the fleeing men with anger in his eyes as their escape became clear.

"Who here has a bow?" Aldrich said as they slowed their charge to a canter.

Hagan's heart clenched. He had one, but was terrified to admit it. He had packed it on his saddle, hoping that he could get in more practice or at least use it to get some real meat from time to time. Knight's rarely brought such weapons into battle, however, even so Hagan hoped that someone else would have one.

"Hagan has one sir, and he was just telling me this morning that he wished he could get in some more practice with it."

Hagan wheeled on Obert, mouth agape.

"You'd better hurry before they get out of range. Just keep them running. They know we will not waste our energy chasing them. Now that they are in the open they have the clear advantage in speed with their lighter armor, but I don't like to see them lollygag like that. Speed them on their way would you?"

While Aldrich spoke, the company had come to a halt at the edge of a small rise that dropped down to the meadow where the enemy now, almost casually, left the battlefield. Hagan had dropped to the ground quickly with the bow strung and an arrow knocked, and as Aldrich finished speaking he ran to the front of the horses where he could clearly see the horsemen. He quickly stuck two arrows into the dirt in front of him and fitted a third to the string.

His nervousness was like a tangible thing. He was sure that his heart would explode with each successive thunderous boom that resounded in his ears. He was sweating terribly and only partly because of the recent exertions.

"Just get close." He told himself. "Close enough that you don't make a fool of yourself."

He brought his bow up quickly and drew, not even giving himself a moment's breath for fear that the enemy would be out of range soon. He half hoped that they would be, but didn't want to embarrass himself or the other knights, and so he moved as fast as he could.

He felt the cool breeze on his skin and adjusted slightly to compensate for its direction, then loosed. The arrow shot from his bow and began its path towards the unsuspecting men and horses.

Hagan had shot enough to have a feel for the shot as soon as it had left the bow and didn't bother watching it, instead he wasted no time in pulling another arrow from the dirt in front of him and loosed it in the same fashion as the first.

As the first arrow struck among the men, Hagan heard an exclamation from Obert, and a few of the other knights behind him, that seemed to mock those of the enemy riders. Hagan had loosed three arrows before the horsemen had realized their danger and had quickened their pace to escape it. He hadn't even intended to shoot more than the one recommended by Aldrich, but when he had felt the familiarity of the arrow leaving the bow, instinct took over and instead of mere fright to speed them on their way they received a stinging slap.

After firing the third arrow, he looked at the retreating men, unsure if he had caused any real harm to them or not, and saw one man lying on the ground, writhing. As he watched the second arrow fell among the men, and a horse screamed in pain and reared as the rider struggled to maintain control of his wounded mount. Hagan winced; he hated the thought of hurting horses.

Then the third arrow fell and bloomed like a flower from the right shoulder of the second to last man in the column. The force of the heavy shaft pierced the chainmail and almost unhorsed the man, but he held on, urging his horse onward to a faster pace and calling for those ahead to do the same amidst loud groans of pain that even Hagan could hear.

His gaze returned to the man who now lay still on the ground. An arrow protruded from his neck. Despite himself Hagan felt guilt as he looked at the man. This wasn't like when he killed before. Before he fought for his sister's life, but now he stood back and killed without a thought. He had gone about the whole thing so quickly. He hadn't even thought about what he was trying to do. He had even been concerned about being embarrassed if he failed seconds before. Was his embarrassment worth this man's life? Maybe the man he killed was a bad man, he thought reassuringly to himself.

Anyway, they had been planning on ambushing them hadn't they? How many of their men would that man have killed had he been given the chance?

Hagan became aware of a chorus of sound behind him, and he turned in surprise. Several of the knights were pounding their shields with their swords and those that didn't have shields slapped their thighs in a rhythm that was so loud, that he was sure the retreating enemy could hear. That was probably the point, Hagan thought.

He told himself that the men were celebrating a victory and, at the same time, mocking the enemy rather than cheering him. But as he walked back to his mount, that Obert held ready for him, Aldrich nodded deeply to him as did several others. He lifted himself into the saddle and while he replaced the bow where it belonged under his right leg, Obert grabbed his arm and asked.

"Was that enough practice for you, I see a few of them still over there if you'd like more?"

Hagan turned in his saddle and managed a weak smile.

"I think that will do me for a while." He said.

He had attempted to say the words with a bravado that he didn't really feel and they sounded weak to his ears.

Just then Rothschild approached Sir Aldrich with a unit of his men.

"I'm sorry my lord." The knight said.

"They seemed surprised by our numbers and were set to flee at the sound of a mouse fart. I was hard-pressed to keep them engaged as long as I did. I even fell back a little as if I was uncommitted so as to give the dogs some courage, but they lost a dozen men in as many seconds." Rothschild smiled.

"You can only feign cowardice for so long my lord."

"Indeed. Fatalities?" Aldrich responded

"None my lord."

"Did you take any alive?"

"Certainly, my lord. Three can still speak although I don't know that they will. They seem a somber bunch."

Rothschild was a peasant knight as they were sometimes dubbed. He didn't have any lands, and he wasn't born into riches or titles of any kind, but had gained his rank through deeds and service to the empire. Hagan liked him. He liked his straight-forward talk. So many of the knights, even some among the peasant knights, seemed to talk differently around Aldrich, smarter, but to Hagan they sounded foolish. Rothschild was real. He seemed plenty smart to Hagan without using more respectable language.

Rothschild turned, and with his unit, led the way back to where the skirmish had occurred.

Six or seven horses lay dead on the ground. Huge furrows carved in the ground around the poor beasts. The head of one was twisted under itself at such a terrible angle that Hagan had to look away. Then he saw the men. He hadn't recognized them as such at first, among the twist of horse flesh and tack as they were. It looked like the first strike that Rothschild made was with the lance which punctured through the lighter armored horse and men, like a plow into soft soil. After the knights broke through, they fought with the sword which spared the lives of the horses, Hagan was glad to see, but dealt lethal blows to the demoralized and scared enemy who was most likely trying to flee. Hagan wondered at that. He wondered if he could strike down an enemy as he fled and realized that he already had. The writhing man on the ground flashed in his mind.

Aldrich had tried to teach Hagan about morale in battle. He hadn't fully understood the effects until now. He had said that the worst thing that he could do as a commander of men was to let them think they might lose. His first obstacle as a leader was to keep his men assured of victory. As Hagan scanned the small battlefield, he couldn't see any bodies bearing the sigil of the crusading army and was amazed by it, but Rothschild and the rest didn't seem too impressed.

"They were ill suited for this fight." Said Aldrich. Looking down at one horsemen's corpse as it lay, hard leather and chainmail exposed in the summer heat. Flies had already begun congregating around the dead man's impressive wound, a slice in one shoulder so deep that it opened his chest.

Most of the knights in the company had chainmail topped in places by plate mail and full helms adorned their heads. These men had only skull caps and leather in place of plate mail.

Hagan followed Sir Aldrich's gaze down to the corpse and instantly felt bile rise in his throat. He closed his eyes and forced the vile tasting acid back into his stomach. He kept his eyes closed and willed the nausea to leave and slowly began to feel better when the smell reached him. The man must have lost control of his bowels when he died, the smell of human feces and blood wafted to Hagan just as he began to relax again.

He only had time to turn in his saddle before the vomit came showering out of his mouth. Through the sound of the convulsing spasms that worked to eject the contents from his stomach he heard a guttural curse in Italian and quickly opened his eyes. Obert sat next to Hagan. He looked back and forth, from the mess in his lap, chest and arms, to Hagan, then back again. The look on his face was one of pure disgust.

"I'm so sorry! I didn't mean to." Hagan began, while wiping his mouth with the back of his hand.

Obert's tanned face grew more and more pale as the surrounding men laughed.

How could he have been so stupid?

Hagan handed the banner to Manfred and dismounted. He began trying to clean Obert while he sat unmoving in his saddle, and simultaneously begged forgiveness.

Obert finally looked down at Hagan, a frown on his face.

Hagan steeled himself, waiting for the inevitable tirade that he was sure to receive.

"Step back." Obert said through clenched teeth before he too retched on the ground where Hagan had been standing seconds before.

Gales of laughter roared from the over one hundred knights as they sat their horses, forgetting the carnage that they had recently inflicted. The bodies piled like so much refuse, forgotten momentarily by the soldiers as they laughed.

When the merriment finally subsided and the last of the jibes had been made at Hagan and Obert, Aldrich took inventory of their loses during the battle. Hagan listened as Aldrich ask Sir Rothschild for the count.

"We lost two horses during the charge. Broke their legs the poor beasts, what with all the men and horses in their way. Sir Norst broke his arm when his horse caught a leg and flipped, but that's the worst of it. We slew twenty-three, and have taken enough of their horses to replace what we lost and then some, although I judge their mounts not to be the equal to ours. They should make fine enough replacements, and pack animals."

Aldrich nodded at the end of the report.

"You and your men should be commended. A fine victory, small it may be, but a victory nonetheless. If they mean to harm us again, they will undoubtedly be better prepared, however. I only wish I knew who sent them." Aldrich seemed to say the last to himself as furrows creased his brow.

Hagan remembered something and blurted it out before his mind could tell him not to.

"The scout?"

Aldrich looked up, his thought broken by the interruption, a confused look on his face. Rothscild turned in his saddle to look at Hagan.

"What's that boy?" Rothschild's raspy voice called.

Aldrich sat waiting for the response as well, the furrows on his forehead even deeper now than they had been.

"Well, my lord, I just thought maybe the scout that went missing might know something." Hagan said slowly, sure now that he shouldn't have broke in on their conversation, and probably shouldn't have even been listening.

"That he might." Aldrich said, smiling at Hagan then turned back to Rothschild.

"Did your men find Sir Engel, he should have been scouting this very spot."

After a cursory search of the surrounding area Sir Engel's body was found sitting at the base of a tree, hands tied behind his back, throat cut. The blood that ran down his chest was already black-brown and no longer glistened wetly. Flies crawled and buzzed in swarms. Aldrich seemed confused by the sight, but merely shook his head before giving orders to bury the body. He also commanded a messenger to fetch the rest of the company.

"I would like to get across the river before we make camp for the night, even so we will not leave these bodies for the flies. My father always said 'If you make a mess, clean it up.' burn the horses and bury their dead."

They buried the corpses and crossed the river before it turned dark. Camp that night had twice as many sentries, Hagan noticed, and Aldrich had sent out-riders to range miles in all directions the moment they had crossed the river. He had feared that the enemy they had faced was only a contingent of a bigger group and wanted to be sure that no one would attack them as they slept. Even so Hagan hadn't slept well that night. The indistinct faces of the men he'd killed kept coming to him as he closed his eyes. The sight of the burning mound of horses and the faces of the men he'd helped bury also haunted him. He wondered how he would handle bigger battles if this was only a small skirmish; which, by all accounts, it was.

Chapter 13

Greta's fingers felt like over-stuffed sausages, stiff and numb from the hot water. Her hands had been working, as they had every day, for hours in the stinking grey water. She wasn't sure she'd call it water anymore. It was more like a... sludge. Yeah, a sludge. A gross mixture of old food and grease that she had scrubbed and scraped off of the dishes. Even with the brush, however, most dishes were so difficult to clean that the task would have been impossible if not for the hot water. The heat was good at loosening stuck food, but it was hard on her hands.

Greta looked around her to make sure that Milda wasn't near before taking her hands out of the sludge for a rest. Both were red and wrinkled, sore to the touch.

The only pain that was worse than her hands was the pain in her lower back. Greta was tall for her age but she still had to stand on a wooden crate to reach the bottom of the basin which, while on the crate, was lower than her hands hung normally. Therefore, she slumped most of the day, as she straightened, pain lanced out from the small of her back which relieved slightly as the muscles relaxed.

"So glad to see you've finished with all of those pans. After all the floors don't scrub themselves do they, dear."

Milda's low, raspy voice struck deep into Greta's heart. She was sure that the fat woman sat looking at her through some hidden hole in the wall, waiting for Greta to stop her torturous labor. At the first sign of rest Milda would descend on Greta teeth bared in a ghastly mockery of a smile. Milda's words often seemed kind, but Greta had learned that the woman was never kind, at least not to her.

"I'm nearly done Mistress Decker." Greta said. Her small voice breaking as she responded.

"Maybe if you didn't waste your time daydreaming you would be done, honestly child I don't know why I put up with you."

Greta knew why. Sir Aldrich had all but threatened Baron Adelfried to take care of her and her mother while Hagan was gone. Unfortunately Milda Decker's idea of "caring" differed from that of Greta's. Milda always picked Greta for the worst chores, at first she thought it was just because she was new to the castle, but as time passed, she realized that Milda hated her for some reason. Harriet had come into the kitchens after Greta and there she sat on the chair in front of the butter churn. The butter-milk had long since been drained from the butter and yet the girl sat, completely at ease.

Greta decided that her best response would be to turn her attention back to her work, and so she did. Milda looked almost sad that the girl didn't choose to respond.

"When you're done, fetch the bucket and start scrubbing these floors. I want to be able to see my face in them."

"Yes Mistress Decker." Greta responded without looking at the loathsome woman.

If she saw her face she'd likely have a heart attack. She thought. Maybe I should clean them extra good just on the chance that it would happen.

Greta's mother had said to do her best not to upset Mistress Decker and if that meant keeping her head down and working until her fingers bled, then so be it. In some ways life was easier in the castle, but Greta missed the fields. She preferred working in the dirt, feeling the warm sun on her skin and hearing the birds sing in the morning to working in this dingy kitchen. They ate better in the castle she supposed and without Hagan it was the only way. They had been given quarters, a room ten feet by ten feet with no windows in a servants barracks just outside the inner courtyard.

Greta felt herself exhale in relief as she sensed, Milda move away. Her hands throbbed, her back burned, and as she worked, she thought of Hagan. She hoped that he was happy. Of course he was. He got what he had always wanted. She thought of how they had played like they were other people. She had always been a beautiful Lady; she had all the finest dresses and would dance around among the trees as they played, which had always made Hagan mad. He was always a knight and wanted to play battle.

Sometimes she would give in and try to play like he wanted her to. When she did, it never lasted long. If they were sword fighting, she could never challenge him enough to keep him interested. He would usually sigh in frustration and let her go back to playing how she wanted to.

Greta felt hands encircle her from behind and, looking down, she saw the familiar hands of her mother. The hug felt nice, something she needed.

"Happy birthday Greta." Ana said from behind her.

Her mother released Greta and stepped back to allow Greta to turn around and dry her hands, a huge smile on her face. She looked at her mother, Ana, and hoped that she would someday be as beautiful as she. She had a few small wrinkles at the corners of her eyes that her time in the sun had exaggerated, but that now were diminishing from being indoors so much. Her hair, although graying slightly was still a beautiful light brown, thick and strong.

Greta hopped down off of the crate and jumped to her mother's arms and enfolded her in a real hug.

"Oh, my goodness!" She exclaimed, being careful not to let her voice rise above a whisper. "I didn't realize it was my birthday." she whispered, not wanting Milda to hear.

"I have a present for you." Ana said and produced a small object wrapped in a piece of sackcloth.

Greta slowly took the object and quickly looked around the kitchen, convinced Milda would descend like the carrion eating vulture she resembled.

She removed the cloth to reveal a beautiful dagger with a leather scabbard and small belt. Greta was pleased, but a little confused by the belt. It was too small for her waist. Ana took the dagger and sheath and said "This belts out-of-sight around your leg." Ana knelt and handed the hem of Greta's dress to her to hold while she belted the scabbard to Greta's calf.

When Ana was done she stood, a smile on her face.

Greta was exhilarated, and the cold of the steel against her skin seemed to seep into her very soul and transform into a confidence and strength that she hadn't felt since Hagan left.

"How did you pay for this? It looks expensive."

Ana just waved her hand, "you don't worry about that." she said. Greta's face darkened slightly. "You didn't use some of the reward did you? We were going to save... it."

"no, no." Ana interrupted.

"I gave some things that belonged to your father to Ulrich and he was more than happy to make this in return."

Greta smiled and nodded then said "You'd better go before Milda sees you and we both get into trouble."

Ana kissed Greta on the top of the head and walked from the room. Greta turned back to the basin and eased her hands into the, now tepid, watery sludge. Even the foul liquid failed to dampen her spirits, and as she scrubbed, she hummed an improvised melody.

Chapter 14

Frederick sat in the cog's cabin, a candle lit and perched on the desk before him. The wax ran down one side, then the other as the rocking motion of the ship threatened to lull him to sleep.

Marching with the army was young man's work, he had realized and cursed himself for it. The writing was on the wall so to speak. He was old. He decided that traveling by ship along the Danube would suit his pride better than being carried in a litter or in a carriage. Despite his reluctance to leave his men, this form of travel had its advantages, lead among them was that the nobles that had plagued him with their constant requests and squabbles early on in the campaign, no longer had the access to him they once had. As a result however, they would submit all of their 'matters of business' to his steward at each port along the Danube. Therefore, the Emperor would receive a mountain of paperwork all at once. Most of the despatches tonight were reports of punishments for crimes committed by men in the army.

He hoped to put an end to the poor behavior with the set of regulations that he now worked on. He scribbled another line on the parchment then set it aside to await more inspiration, as he continued with more trivial matters.

Frederick was not a man to leave work undone, and the worse the chore, the harder he worked until it was done. He finished reading another missive from Count Engelbert of Berg petitioning for reimbursement for work done by his blacksmiths and scrolled his response at the bottom. His old fingers ached and the letters on the parchment were barely legible. He sent his scribe to bed hours ago believing at the time that subjecting the young man to this torture would be inhumane. But now he was second guessing his act of compassion. Count Engelbert would have to deal with the poor handwriting.

On these late nights, his friend and Chamberlain would sometimes write for him, but he was gone now. He wondered how Markward was fairing on his journey to Constantinople. Despite the chamberlain's quiet nature Frederick knew that he didn't want to go, but he convinced him that sending someone so intimate with the Emperor would show Isaac a degree of trust. Trust that they needed to build with the Byzantines if they had any hope of making it to the holy land.

Frederick placed the missive from Engelbert into a pile to his right and picked up the next parchment in the stack from his left.

He rubbed his thumb over the wax seal, feeling the emboss of a large cross surrounded by four small crosses. He knew the seal at once and slid his dagger under the wax breaking the seal and unfolded the parchment. Sibylla wrote in a flowing, elegant hand that also managed to be efficient.

He read quickly then re-read the message.

The candle on the desk guttered, dark smoke rising from the elongated flame. The sound of the planks creaking in time with the rocking of the boat was the only sound as he read.

When he finished, he let the parchment fall to the desk.

"God help them." Frederick said.

Chapter 15

The two hundred Imperial knights made slow progress after the skirmish. Aldrich was increasingly wary as they neared the Byzantine capital and as a result even more scouts were sent out. When the cohort of knights and nobles came to towns or cities in which a portion, at least, would have previously found lodgings, they now camped on the outskirts. The men slept in their armor, and they tethered the horses closer to camp.

From time to time Hagan would see a hint of annoyance at the added precautions among the men, but the subtle grimaces and sighs were few. The respect the men had for Aldrich outweighed any inconveniences and they seemed to accept the added security measures as necessary. Despite the added difficulties of the travel the men were in good spirits and they made relatively good time in reaching the Byzantine capital.

Aldrich looked up at the largest wall he had ever seen. He had been to Milan, Italy, France and almost every city and Castle in-between but he had never seen walls this tall. He tried not to look like a peasant child on his first trip to town but it was difficult to tear his eyes off of the huge square barbicans, towers that rose an additional twenty to thirty feet above the forty foot wall.

Massive stone blocks made up the base of the wall, the surface of which was smooth to make scaling the walls without equipment near impossible. Years of experience had taught him to look at how best to defend the city, and then how best to attack it. These defenses were far better than any city he had been to, he was forced to admit. Taking Constantinople would be very difficult indeed. Not impossible, but difficult.

Its intimidating size would also be its weakness. When under siege it was easier to defend when certain where the attacks would be aimed. The city was guarded on two sides by water, the same water that kept the Imperial army out of the holy land, but the western side was an immense expanse of wall that would be difficult to man, especially if the attackers struck at multiple points along the wall simultaneously.

Aldrich noticed, as he approached the huge gate into the city, that there were masons and carpenters working around the entrance. The sound of hammers and chisels rang through the air as stonecutters made alterations. Wood saws also joined the din as two carpenters cut a large wooden beam.

The Byzantine guide that had been sent to conduct them safely to the Palace noticed the direction of his gaze.

"It seems that they are repairing that damn thing every year." The olive skinned man spoke with a heavy accent, but his face spoke volumes. He had made the declaration with a crooked smile on his face, an attempt perhaps to cover his lie.

The masons were not replacing old mortar or stone; they were adding new, reducing the gate entrance to a third the original size. The carpenters were constructing heavy wooden lattices that could be moved into place behind the gates to help support them in the event of a siege. The preparations were obviously being made in lieu of the army's arrival.

Aldrich played the politician and returned the man's smile. "Cities of this size are constantly in need of repair, are they not?" He said.

The man had introduced himself as Spatharios Photios. He was a young nobleman and judging from his title he was the first sword-bearer of the palace guard. Despite the young man's rank, he seemed nervous. He jerkily nodded his agreement to Aldrich's statement then kicked his mount, moving ahead of Aldrich, and indicated for him to follow. Two more mounted knights fell in beside Photios, ostensibly to clear the congested streets for the diplomats, but Aldrich wasn't sure that was the only purpose that they served.

Aldrich glanced around to make sure that the rest of his small company hadn't gotten lost in the throng of people that came and went through the massive gates.

Peddlers hawking their wares yelled their distinctive choruses vying to be heard above the general din.

The Bishop was the first to catch his eye. He was wearing his costliest of robes, red and heavy. Aldrich wasn't sure how the man wasn't sweating buckets in the thing. His face was a picture of pious solemnity, gaze focused somewhere off in the distance as if nothing close to him warranted his attention. It had offended the Bishop that a more important dignitary than Photios hadn't been sent to meet them at the gates.

Aldrich had to admit that it could have been taken as a well calculated slight. An entourage of their prestige should have been met by a member of the Imperial family, or at least a Palace official or chamberlain, not this young knight that no one had even heard of.

Aldrich hoped that the Bishop would be over with his sulking before they reached the palace, his attitude could prove embarrassing. He was sure that the Bishop was naïve about their precarious situation, and a show of outrage at this minor insult might be enough to disillusion them of any hopes they might have entertained for peace.

Ahren followed close behind the Bishop, eyes darting among the peasant rabble that flowed through the streets, as if any one of them could be a hidden killer, waiting for the perfect moment to pounce. Count Rupert and his cousin were behind Ahren. They, in their expensive clothing, looked out-of-place as they stared first at one marvel, then another. He noticed that they both gazed at the huge walls with an awe comparable to that of his own, although he hoped that he hadn't let quite so much astonishment show.

Aldrich had known Count Rupert before now, they had served in two campaigns in northern Italy together, but he hadn't personally known Henry Walram, the younger Count of Diez, Rupert's cousin. Walram's father, who was also Henry, was even now delivering an ultimatum to Saladin on behalf of the Holy Roman Empire demanding that he relinquish Jerusalem, but he hadn't met the younger Henry until this expedition.

As Aldrich got to know the young count he became more and more impressed. Henry was more than what Aldrich had come to expect from the sons of important noblemen. He was patient and respectful. He could lead men, but could take orders as well, and that was a rare quality.

Rothschild and Chamberlain Markward brought up the rear of their entourage. The burly knight contrasted starkly with the skinny academic. Rothschild seemed to be in the middle of some joke which, judging by the chamberlain's reddening face, was not in the best of taste. Rothschild laughed heartily at the conclusion and slapped the smaller man on the back, nearly knocking him from his saddle. Two more knights dressed in the livery of the Eastern Roman Empire rode behind their column. All-told eight byzantine guards accompanied them along the busy streets, that number was a little high, that combined with the Bishop's perceived insult and the preparations at the gate gave Aldrich a sinking feeling in the pit of his stomach.

Aldrich whistled and motioned for Ahren to join him. He was a little surprised at the reaction of the guards. The knights to either side of the column stopped and turned at the sudden movement and as Ahren moved towards the front with Aldrich; Photios wheeled his horse, a look of confused apprehension on his face.

Aldrich hadn't stopped to wait for Ahren. He kept moving forward as if he hadn't noticed the sudden disarray among the guards. Photios offered a sheepish grin before continuing. The intent was clear now; they were all but captives. The Byzantines must be well and truly the allies of Saladin. The knights to either side started forward again as Ahren fell in beside Aldrich.

"Rothschild is probably telling Markward that we're two farts away from having all out war on our hands." Aldrich said in a lowered tone so as not to be overheard by the knights guarding them. He shouldn't have feared. The throng of peddlers, peasants and tradesmen as they milled through the streets made far too much noise for the guards to hear anything below a yell, but it paid to be cautious.

Ahren's stony exterior broke slightly by the comment and his lips formed a crooked smile.

"There's no sense in them taking more captives than is needful." Aldrich said, getting to the point as soon as he could.

"Take Rothschild back to camp, I'll make up some excuse for you, although I don't think they will need one. Unless they are fine with arresting us right here in the street, peace banners flying and the Cross painted on our chests, they'll let you go. So long as they get the important ones."

Ahren's expression turned even more somber than normal, the contrast was dramatic.

"I won't leave you if I can help it. I would prefer being in prison with you, then being helpless."

"What do you think being in prison is like? That's all you feel is helpless. Besides, I don't think the Serbians and Bulgarians will long abide a ruler that imprisons Christians as they attempt to heed God's call. Between them and the pressure from the Kaiser, we should be out in a month."

Aldrich truthfully put it at more like two months, but he hoped the lie would appease Ahren.

They rode under an arch-way that connected two buildings, one on either side of the street. There must have been a walkway running atop the arch for children stood along it looking down at the group as it passed under them.

Ahead Spatharios Photios looked back over his shoulder, and seeing Aldrich watching him, quickly turned forward again. Aldrich began to feel almost as insulted as the Bishop, they should have sent someone better at deception than this. Did they really expect him not to notice that something was amiss? He supposed that they might not care, after all what could he do?

"Tell Rothschild to pack up the camp and move them farther from the city. I don't want them caught unaware if Isaac decides to rid himself of some Imperial knights in the offing. You'd better get going. Tell Obert I'll be back soon or he may desert, you know how he gets when there's nothing to do. Good luck sergeant."

Ahren set his jaw, hesitated for a few heartbeats, then lifted his fist to his chest in a salute. Aldrich returned it crisply, the sound of his mailed fist striking his breast plate could be heard above the noise surrounding them and made Photios look once more over his shoulder as Ahren turned his horse and started back in the direction that they had just come.

Again, the guards stopped, unsure if they should stop Ahren from leaving the column or not. Ahren paused next to Rothschild and spoke briefly with him before the two of them made to leave the column back towards the gate. One guard in the rear held up his hand, halting the two. The man was a well-armoured knight, as were all those that accompanied them, and Aldrich's long experience with war told him that this man, at least, knew how to fight.

At seeing the trouble, Aldrich turned to Photios. "They're just taking a message back to camp, I realized that my first choice in a camp location had everything to do with proximity to the city and nothing else. If these clouds turn into rain, I would prefer they set camp on higher ground."

Aldrich hoped that the smile he displayed was a disarming one. He had always had a hard time with lying so he had made up a lie with as much truth in it as possible. He was regretting his choice, and higher ground would be better in case of rain.

Photios had an unreadable expression on his face. Aldrich knew what the Spatharios was thinking.

First, the loss of Ahren and Rothschild as captives was weighed against the undesirable display of publicly arresting them all, then he would review the orders he was given in his head before coming to the same conclusion that Aldrich had.

Aldrich watched the young man as he went over his options. Photios took what seemed like an eternity to say anything and Aldrich worried. After all, he didn't know what orders he had been given, for all he knew he had been ordered to bring all of them to the palace dead or alive. If that was the case, Aldrich was sure that he Ahren, Rothschild and even Count Rupert and his young cousin would make a good accounting for themselves. If they defeated the eight guards flat-out, then the city's walls would still encircle them. Escape would be next to impossible after such a confrontation with the guards.

"It's of little import I suppose, would you like me to call them back?" Aldrich said. Hoping that his casual manner would put Photios at ease.

"No, it's fine, let them go." Although he was talking to Aldrich, he intended the words for his men and they backed their horses in a well-practiced arch, swinging like a doorway, a maneuver that was more difficult than it appeared. The street lay open before the two men as they kicked their horses back towards the gate and freedom. Ahren looked back over his shoulder one last time as Aldrich silently offered up a prayer and turned his horse to follow Photios once again.

Aldrich was amazed to see another inner wall that was even taller than the wall around the outer city. He couldn't imagine the wealth it must have taken to construct. As he looked at the immense walls, he realized that his initial assessment of the city's weakness was still valid as the wall stretched far in either direction out-of-sight. And unlike most castles with curtain walls this city's gates weren't off-set, making the job easier for an attacking army. The enemy, once past the first gates, could march straight for the second gates without first marching down the length of the occupied walls, being fired upon the entire time. For all its splendor it was just a city. That was until the palace came into view.

The palace was more like a complex of buildings rather than just one, but each was greater than the last. A massive hippodrome rose to their right as they entered the complex and huge pillared structures closed in on all sides. In his time in the Imperial army he had seen Rome, Sicily, and Venice and the architecture was similarly beautiful here.

Fluted columns fronted most buildings and huge domes could be seen capping several large structures, the sheet metal used to shingle the domes glinted brightly despite the overcast sky. Seagulls spiralled in the distance, a reminder of their proximity to the ocean. For the first time Aldrich could smell the ocean above the smell of the city, a salty, fishy smell that he found nauseating. The few times Aldrich had been on the ocean he had gotten extremely sea sick and now the smell alone was enough to cause his stomach to flip.

There were no longer peasants or peddlers, and only a few tradesmen wandered the streets among other diplomats and nobles. Men walked from building to building along cobblestone paths wearing rich robes that made the bishop's look like rough spun. Some nobles strode leisurely, servants shading their every move from recalcitrant rays that broke through the clouds. Others rushed carrying scrolls and looking harried.

This is where Aldrich needed to make his scene that the Emperor needed to help convince the rebels of Isaac Angelus's nefarious intentions. Somehow he had to let the people of Byzantium know that, Christian Crusaders of God were being opposed by their leader. He needed to act quickly before they moved farther into the inner circles of the Byzantine Hierarchy. If they made a scene in front of no one but Isaac's inner cadre of supporters, then it would go unwitnessed for all intents and purposes. Aldrich spurred his horse to catch up with the Spatharios, invoking a similar jumpy response from the guards as before. He hailed the First Sword.

"What exactly are your orders Spatharios?" Aldrich queried.

The man looked taken aback by the question. He had clearly been chosen for this assignment for his skill at arms and possibly his loyalty and not for his ability in deception and politics.

"I am to bring you safely to the palace my Lord." The First Sword responded. The look on his face was one of feigned innocence.

As soon as he had engaged Spatharios in a conversation, Aldrich halted his horse, thereby forcing him to halt as well in order to continue the conversation. The column came to a halt behind them and Aldrich heard the Bishop grumble something unintelligible.

"What else?" Aldrich pushed.

"Uh... nothing, my Lord." The man stammered.

"You weren't told to bring the envoys to the palace even if they resist? You weren't told to convey us safely whether or not we wanted to come? The streets didn't look so dangerous that you needed so many guards. And why was the First Sword sent and not a dignitary of some kind?" Aldrich knew that none of his accusations were substantial and he sounded like a whiny child to his own ears.

Aldrich could see that with every successive question the First Sword became more and more uncomfortable. His hand was very noticeably resting on the pommel of his sword. Aldrich didn't want to be killed, he just needed them all to be taken, since he was positive they would be anyway, but he needed to be taken in full view of this throng of witnesses. Against their will ideally. Already Aldrich saw many of the passersby who were too busy to pay them any mind before now pause, intrigued by the motionless column and the argumentative stature of the two men at its lead.

Aldrich waited for a response, but the nervous soldier just sat his horse, eyes shifting but never straying far from Aldrich. Finally, Aldrich decided that he needed another push.

"Are we not your prisoners? If not, then maybe we should return to our camp and await a true member of the nobility to receive us."

Aldrich paused to let the statement sink in, before turning his horse suddenly back in the direction that they had come.

The response from the First Sword was instantaneous. The sword was out of its sheath and in front of Aldrich's face, effectively barring his retreat. The move had been so fast that no one in the column had time to react.

"Perhaps you would like to re-think that action." Spatharios Photios said in his thickly accented voice, all of his nervousness gone.

"Perhaps you would like to rethink yours?" Aldrich rebuffed and lightly tapped the end of his own drawn sword against the man's groin where it had been resting, unnoticed by the First Sword.

The Bishop blustered into action.

"Sir Kortig! What on heaven's green earth do you think you are doing? This man serves the man we have come to treat with. How dare you threaten him! Know you no honor?"

Aldrich could hear the clergyman continue in his customary fashion but his words were totally ignored. Aldrich and Photios continued in this posture for a time. Neither man making a move.

Finally, Aldrich winked at Photios before letting go of his sword. With his eyes fixed on Aldrich's eyes and not his hands, the Spatharios interpreted the sword hitting his horse and groin as it fell as an attack, while to all who stood away from the confrontation could see that Aldrich dropped his sword.

Spatharios Photios, acting in concert with instinct and intensive combat experience but little diplomatic restraint brought his sword forward. The blade bit into Aldrich's face, slicing deep. Aldrich had a split instant of cohesive thought where he hoped that the Spatharios would not be able to find enough leverage in the short distance between the blade and flesh to kill him outright. Then there was pain, searing and blinding all at once. He saw blood, red and dark and then just dark. The world windmilled as he tumbled from his mount. He smelled blood, tasted it. He even felt it running down the back of his throat before the blackness took him.

All was confusion. The guards around the envoys had all drawn their swords at some point in the altercation but Markward wasn't sure when. All he knew was that Aldrich lay bleeding on the cobblestone, and Count Rupert and Count Walram had also drawn their swords and were even now fighting two guards each. The bishop had his arms raised in total submission and cried incessantly for mercy.

Markward had to get to Aldrich. He dismounted and made his way as inconspicuous through the fighting as possible to the prostate knight.

Markward had never been this close to battle, but had seen men with horribly gruesome scars, and knew that it was possible for men to survive much. What he saw in Aldrich's face however convinced him that the man before him must surely be a corpse.

He made to turn away again and try to make sense of the surrounding turmoil when he thought better of it and knelt instead. He laid his head down on the cold steel of the chainmail, trying to hear a heartbeat above the tumult, but to no avail. He hadn't known Aldrich well, but the man was a legend among all German knights, and from what he saw during their journey he deserved the reputation. The man was a natural leader, one that would be sorely needed in the days ahead.

Above all the commotion, Markward heard yelling in Greek. Photios was trying to get control of his men who had engaged the two counts ruthlessly. Part of their ardor had probably come from three of their fallen comrades lying motionless, their blood filling the wide cracks among the cobblestones. Even as he watched the skirmish one of the Byzantine knights charged, driving a lance deep into Count Rupert's mount. The horse reared, screaming a horrible death yell, and sent Rupert tumbling to the ground. Even unhorsed, the warrior righted himself and was ready for more foes.

Markward forced himself to look back at Aldrich's face, despite the gory wound, one more time before leaving him forever. When he did, Markward noticed small red bubbles coming from the knight's mouth. On a whim the Chamberlain attempted to roll the heavy knight on his side hoping that maybe it would help the man, he was sure was dead, to breathe.

It took the small framed academic several attempts to get the armored knight up on his side, but when he did Aldrich let out a sudden raspy cough, spurting blood several feet. The knight took two shuddering breaths before coughing again, spraying more blood.

It amazed and terrified Markward. Aldrich needed help now or he would not live long. He continued propping Aldrich up while surveying the continued carnage before him. Rupert's left arm hung limply at his side but another foe was writhing on the ground, and a horse milled riderless.

Walram yelled epitaphs to the oncoming Easterners. They fought with the obvious tenacity of men already committed to their own death.

The First Sword looked on, a man helpless to curb the bloodlust before him.

Markward yelled as loud as he ever had.

"Spatharios! Sir Aldrich yet lives, help me."

The First Sword, upon hearing his title being yelled from somewhere behind him, turned. A look of confusion crossed his face as he saw Markward with Aldrich, and then the prone knight gave another racking cough giving proof to Markward's words.

Surprise flooded the First sword's face, and he quickly dismounted and dashed to the man's side.

"Lift him up to sit, I think the blood won't drown him." Markward yelled.

Photios stood for a time, that seemed an eternity to Markward, weighing whether it would serve him better to let this man die or not. Finally frowned and lowered himself down beside the Chamberlain.

Photios helped to lift Aldrich up gently to a more reclined position and his breathing noticeably improved.

Markward grabbed the First sword's tunic to get his attention."

"We need to stop them before peace between our countries is made an impossibility."

Spatharios held Aldrich's weight long enough for the Chamberlain to take his place and stood. His face was a mask of pure anger. Photios yelled with all the considerable power in his lungs for his men to stop their attack. Two of the remaining four men paused in their assault and looked toward their leader. Upon seeing the blood curdling rage in his eyes, caused by their disobedience, the men retreated several steps from the conflict. The remaining Byzantine combatants fought on, heedless or uncaring of their commander's demands.

The Spatharios stepped forward and drew his sword, and in almost a graceful motion, plunged his sword deep into the armpit of the man fighting Walram. Count Rupert was on one knee, seconds away from being dispatched but his opponent hesitated upon seeing his companion murdered. And turned his head in shock.

Photios slid his sword from the sheath of hot blood and bone as the man fell and swung the sword around in a powerful arc, sending blood flying from the sword as it cleaved into the other man's neck and jaw. The force of the blow broke chainmail links, bone and teeth alike. He fell like a stone to the ground. His leg twitched in death spasms.

The First Sword turned to the two German envoys, a threat in his eyes, sword ready.

"Do you two wish to continue? Or can we end the foolishness? Your man lives, but won't if we don't end this and get him some help."

"Are we supposed to believe that you now care for his life?" Rupert said.

"Of course not. To be honest, I don't really care what happens to you. I was ordered to take you, willing or no."

Photios jerked his head toward where Aldrich lay.

"What happened was…regrettable. But it doesn't change my orders."

Rupert still had his sword up, defending himself weakly. He finally sagged to the ground and dropped his sword.

Walram followed his lead, and dismounted before dropping his sword.

Photios motioned to his two men, and they ran forward and took the two men and bound their hands with restraints that they pulled from pouches on their sides.

Convenient, Markward thought.

"Where is your bishop?" Photios said as the counts of Nassau were being bound, hands behind their backs. Looking around, Markward too noticed for the first time that he was gone.

He scanned the bodies that littered the ground, hoping that the man hadn't been killed. He didn't see the red robe that the bishop had been wearing, but spotted the horse he had been riding. It had found a quiet corner away from all the dying men and horses. Without a horse, the overweight clergyman would not have made it very far.

Markward thought about not pointing out the horse to the First Sword hoping the bishop would, somehow, get free of the city, however Emperor Barbarossa's intention in sending the bishop in the first place made Markward reconsider. The Emperor wanted the bishop to be a beacon of Christianity. While the bishop himself may believe that his skills as a diplomat were the cause, Markward knew otherwise. If the Bishop could be taken publicly, against his will, it may prove invaluable to their cause. Markward looked around at the growing throng of witnesses that were appalled at the public display of force. Many hissed at the Spatharios. They were not made any happier with the way the First Sword handled the situation when he murdered his own men.

Word of this tragedy would spread, if the brave man in his lap did die, he would not do so in vain.

Markward called for the First Sword's attention and motioned towards the bishop's horse.

"That is the bishop's horse, I pray, find him. I fear he may be wounded."

The First Sword moved away, towards the horse and scanned down alleyways as he went.

Markward pulled his knife from his sleeve and lowered it to Aldrich. The tunic was soaked with blood and his hands were covered in it by the time he finished cutting the garment from the knight's body. He struggled to roll Alrdich's heavy frame, so he lay on his side to keep him from choking on his own blood. Markward stood. The once-white tunic with its large green cross, held out in front of him.

"This is how your emperor greets servants of God. This is how he receives messengers from Christ's army as it marches to the Holy Land!" Markward's voice trembled. He wasn't sure if it was fear, or anger that made his voice so, but either way, it was effective. The people nodded, covered their mouths with their hands, clasped their hands in prayer and some women were crying. Markward didn't want to push his luck, already the two guards, the only two left, looked back and forth, wondering if they should stop this blasphemous talk and risk upsetting the crowd or not. And Photios, in the distance noticed that Markward was addressing the crowd because he was in full retreat from his attempt to find the wayward bishop.

"All we desire is safe passage through your city to Anatolia," Markward continued" that we may return those lands to Christian hands and save our Christian brothers who, even now suffer under Infidel rule." He heard the First Sword's heavy boots approaching from behind.

"Your Emperor has…." Markward saw a brilliant light, felt a searing heat in the back of his head and then nothing.

Chapter 16

Hagan sat on a rock polishing a helm, Horst's helm to be exact. The rest of Horst's armor was mostly chainmail which Horst was, even now, tumbling in a barrel full of sand to polish it. Horst grunted as he rolled the heavy barrel towards Hagan. This was his ninth or tenth trip and despite the copious amounts of sweat running down Horst's face, he was probably only about half-way done. Hagan sympathized with him. It was Hagan's responsibility to polish Aldrich's armor, a task made more difficult by the amount he had. Aldrich, unlike most of the knights in the company, had several mail shirts and coifs, two helms and two pairs of boots. Obert said that it was so he could dress according to the station of those he was duty-bound to kill that day. Hagan wondered at the truth in that. Aldrich did, after all, seem to have mail shirts that he preferred on certain occasions, while others were his "every day mail shirts". Right now Aldrich was wearing his best. That is unless they had stripped him of his armor before imprisoning him.

Hagan looked up in time to see Ahren leaving the large command tent alone. He hadn't had a chance to say more than two words to his mentor since they had taken Aldrich and he wanted desperately to get some answers. Up to this point he had not bothered Ahren, Rothschild Hoch or any of the other knights with his concerns. They seemed too busy to be bothered with a boy's worries, but burn him if he didn't have to know what was going on. Hagan jumped to his feet, letting the helm fall and clatter to the ground, prompting Horst to stop and glare at him. Hagan ignored Horst and ran to catch up with Ahren.

"Do you think he'll be okay?" Hagan spluttered out as he came up alongside Ahren. He had felt emotion rise in his throat as he said the words and struggled to keep it hidden.

Ahren stopped and turned to him, a kind smile on his face. Despite the abrupt nature of the conversation, Ahren seemed to have been expecting it.

"He'll be fine, but he's not the one I'm worried about. Although they are completely different types of men, I worry most about Markward and the Bishop. They have never faced anything like this before." Ahren said with a relatively casual tone that helped put Hagan at ease.

"why would Angelus try this? Doesn't he know that Frederick will be here with the army soon?" Hagan said.

"Of course he does, but I think it is clear now that he has made some kind of deal with Saladin. Perhaps he is only meant to slow us down to allow Saladin time to prepare. He knows that Frederick will be reluctant to attack a Christian city, and maybe he thinks Frederick will give up."

"He won't will he?" Hagan knew that he was pressing his luck and that Ahren had already given him far more information than he was obliged to, but he needed more.

"Give up? No, Frederick will not stop before he reaches Jerusalem. Our emperor's resolve and faith in God is beyond question, but Angelus has quite the commodity in the envoys he has captured. Aldrich is one of Fredericks closest advisers, and I don't know that Frederick would be able to run his house let alone the empire for long without Markward. From this point in time it seems to be a stalemate. Frederick cannot move on the city for obvious political reasons and because Angelus may threaten their lives if he does, but he will not leave until he has received safe transport for the army across the Bosphorus. It could be a long winter."

Ahren looked down at Hagan, whose fears had plainly not been resolved, and smiled.

"It should give us plenty of time to teach you all the things we should have taught you and haven't had time to."

Hagan brightened visibly.

Ahren lifted the saddle at Hagan's feet with one strong hand and gave it to Hagan.

"ten times around camp should be a good start."

Hagan's temporary excitement vanished, and he grumbled as he lifted the saddle to his right shoulder, holding it in place with both hands, he walked away from Ahren.

"Hagan, a knight runs into battle." Ahren called after him.

Sighing, Hagan ran.

Ahren and Rothschild had returned shortly after Aldrich's party had passed through the gates of Constantinople, and moments after that the newly laid camp was being struck. Their camp, now, was a few days ride to the west, outside of a town called Philippopolis. Ahren began the men digging a shallow mote with stakes planted in the bottom to help discourage a surprise cavalry attack. They had placed one side of the camp against the river for protection so the mote only had to extend around three sides of the camp, even so it took the knights the better part of a week to complete. Now that the mote was completed the men took shifts working on building a palisade wall around the camp. He was convinced that if they stayed here much longer, they would have a castle.

As Hagan ran around the outside of the spiked trench and unfinished palisade, men stopped their work long enough to smile knowing smiles at him before continuing their labor. Their training must have been similar. Most of the knights wore light woolen shirts that were terribly stained from sweat and dirt. In this setting, Hagan was reminded of his youth spent working in the fields. The noblemen smiling back at him could have been farmers, or woodsmen. Hagan reached the river and turned to follow it. The palisades had not reached down to the water's edge yet and Hagan passed through the back side of the camp uncontested. His shoulders were on fire after just the first trip around the camp and it took everything he had to keep going after the second. His legs had burned as well and his fingers felt like they would lose their tenuous hold on the saddle. Hagan stumbled to a stop in front of the cook fire that Ahren now tended, and barely managed the words "I...can't" among huge gulps of air. Ahren stood up and walked around the fire and knelt in front of Hagan.

Hagan's head was down and sweat dripped from the tip of his nose as he struggled to catch his breath.

"Why can't you?" Ahren asked.

The question confused Hagan. "It's too heavy, I'm not strong enough."

"You focus too much on the pain, and difficulty. Instead, focus on your breathing. Too much breath can be just as bad as not enough. Time your breaths and your foot-falls. Once you have mastered the simple art of breathing, then we shall move on." Ahren stood again.

It disappointed Hagan. He wanted to learn more about fighting. "Why can't I just practice the sword? I mean...don't knights have horses?" Hagan jerked backward suddenly in surprise as Ahren drew his sword and swung it at Hagan's head, stopping just shy of cleaving his skull. The move was so quick that Hagan's response was sluggish and delayed in comparison, but once started Hagan's momentum carried him backward and, off balanced, he fell onto his back where he lay panting. Fear and confusion covered his face as thoroughly as did the sweat.

"The reason you need to learn to breathe first is because you can't defend yourself while on the ground panting, can you? Horses are a tool, not something that our lives should depend on. What would you do if you were knocked from your horse in battle? Would you roll over and die?"

Hagan managed a scared shake his head.

Ahren re-sheathed his sword. "Then prove it." He helped Hagan to his feet and lifted the saddle once more to Hagan's arms. "breathe this time. speed will come, focus on your breathing."

Hagan knew that Ahren expected him to continue his run now, but the thought made him tremble with fatigue. Hagan turned, despite his weariness, and jogged away.

Chapter 17

Markward awoke and instantly wished he hadn't. His head felt like a boulder had landed on it. He moved to lift himself from the bed on which he lay and the pain intensified. He forced himself to push through the pain and opened his eyes to look around the room. It was small, but suitably furnished. A wash basin sat on a table against the far wall. The walls and floor were austere, gray-tan stone. The bed that he had been sleeping on was quite comfortable, and Markward tried to remember if it rivalled his own bed in that regard. It had been so long since he had slept in his own bed that he couldn't make a reasonable comparison in his fuzzy mind.

Markward swung his legs out of bed and noticed that he wasn't wearing the clothing he had been. He now only wore a light shirt and loose, flowing pants. Not the expensive, heavy clothing he had been wearing. Markward almost felt cheated at the loss, but then remembered that it had surely been soaked with blood. Aldrich's blood. Was he still alive?

He stood and made his way, slowly, to the door and hesitated before opening it. Surely it was locked. He tried it anyway. The bolt on his side of the door slid free easily, and it opened when he gave it a tug.

He was perplexed at seeing a large room. Tapestries hung from the ceiling, covering the bare walls. A large table sat in the middle of the room and comfortable overstuffed sedan chairs were situated around the room.

Count Walram and Count Rupert sat in a pair of these and looked up at hearing his door open.

Both were dressed in nice yet comfortable looking clothing similar to that of his own. Rupert had his arm in a sling made from a pristine, white scarf. His good hand went to his injured arm instinctively, protecting and steadying it, as he and his cousin stood at Markward's doorway.

The strength of these two men amazed him. Not just physical of which both were blessed in abundance, but of the type that few men truly possess. They were co-counts of Nassau, a very lucrative and important district and the fact that both had equal responsibility to manage, defend, and reap benefits was something that would pit two lesser men against each other regardless of their relationship, but in their case, it only made their loyalty to one another stronger.

Walram, the younger of the two by six years, stood a few inches shorter than his kinsman and had dark brown hair, with a red beard while Rupert had sandy colored hair. Rupert's beard was the same color as his hair. Well, it had been once, the light brown was fighting a losing battle to gray invaders.

Walram beamed at seeing him, something he did often, as evidenced by the deep smile lines around his eyes and cheeks. Rupert began slapping his hand against his thigh, a form of applause among knights, whose armored hands and legs create quite the raucous, however when neither are covered in metal the sound is somewhat anti-climactic. Walram, whose hands were uninjured, clapped his hands together loudly and yelled,

"Well done Markward. Well done indeed."

He felt foolish. Embarrassed even. Were they mocking him? The thought flew through his head and was gone almost as instantly as it had come. These men were not the type. They were sincere in their show of appreciation. Markward racked his brain. What had he done? It was difficult to remember clearly, but he remembered Aldrich's blood-soaked tunic in his hands.

"Is he alive?" He said in a rush upon remembering the gruesome scene.

"He is. All thanks to you." Rupert said.

The burly knight grabbed Markward with his one good hand and pulled him into a hug. Walram laughed and clapped Markward on the back.

Rupert released him, and Markward was stunned to see an unfallen tear wetting the man's eye.

"You have done us proud my good fellow." Rupert said.

"What have I done?" Markward sincerely didn't know why these two men, whose feats far eclipsed those of a simple Chamberlain, personal manager of Emperor's affairs or no.

"You saved Aldrich, you saved us, and you did it with style." Walram said jovially.

"Your little display, which led to your bump on the head, got the town stirring. I'm sure that there's not a beggar in the most squalid corner of this place that doesn't know the story of how Isaac Angelus' men attacked and arrested Christian envoys. Envoys wearing the crusader cross and accompanied by a bishop of the church."

"The Bishop?" Markward remembered. "Was he found? Is he all right?"

"Yes. He's fine." Rupert assured. "He's in his room." He motioned with his good hand towards a door on the opposite side of the large room from where they talked and continued.

"He stays in there, sulking, most of the time. I don't think he's too keen on everyone knowing how he was found."

Markward raised a questioning eyebrow.

"Let's just say he must have left us all in search of a privy and never found one." Walram explained.

"Photios was more than willing to offer up that little tidbit to us upon delivering him here."

"Where is here?" Markward asked.

"They have us, for all intents and purposes, prisoners, but a suite in the palace is far better than a dungeon I suppose." Rupert said it while looking around the large room, as if he could find some secret way out that had previously escaped his notice.

Markward had to agree. The suite was downright opulent for what he had been used to of late. Accommodations while traveling with the army had been, at times, uncomfortable to say the least. They were being treated with respect in accordance with their station at least.

"Have you ever been a captive before?" Markward queried the two counts. He knew that it was commonplace for nobility to be captured during battle and then ransomed back to the opposing force. It was often a source of pride among the higher classes to be ransomed for a large sum. The prospect confused Markward, but these two men, who were also knights, might be able to explain it to him.

Both men nodded.

"We were both taken at the battle of Legnano." Rupert said. A scowl had formed on his face.

"That was a bloody day, to be sure." Walram spit on the floor in disgust of the memory.

"I was also taken captive at the siege of Alessandria. I was only sixteen. Just a squire. We had tunnelled under the wall and broke out into the city. They were waiting for us though.

Hundreds of men died on both sides, but they had the advantage and used it well. The fighting continued for hours, long after the hopelessness of our attack was clear to everyone. We were, finally, cut off, surrounded and taken prisoner. I'll tell you, my captivity was not so leisurely spent when I was but a mere squire. They had us work, building up the defenses during the day, and we slept in the mud at night."

Rupert squinted as he looked around the room once again. "I think they're still worried about pushing Barbarossa too far. If it wasn't for our obvious resistance to their invitation, Angelus could claim that we are guests of his."

Markward jumped at the sudden entrance of Spatharios Photios followed by two guards.

"Chamberlain Markward. It is good to see you up." The statement was devoid of all sincerity.

"I have been instructed to retrieve you and the rest of your diplomatic party upon your awakening." For a moment Photios looked sheepish. "I do apologize for that hit on the head. You were causing an unacceptable scene though." his stern demeanor never left, and he waited for Markward to accept the fact that he had deserved the violence.

"That is quite alright First Sword, I fully understood the danger I was in after of violence you had shown over far less of a scene." The response caught Photios off guard, and he stammered.

"Well, um. Sir Kortig is expected to survive." He glanced sidelong at the two counts. "As I'm sure you have been informed." The First Sword furrowed his brow and paused, collecting himself for what he was going to say. "I apologize for what happened. I realized in the instant what I had done, and have had no peace since." He only met Markward's gaze at the end of his statement, but in the warrior's eyes, he saw honesty, and regret. This apology was true, made from guilt, while the one made moments before had been superficial and fake.

"It was not I that had my face nearly cut off. Your apology is ill aimed First Sword."

"You all suffered from my moment of carelessness. I ask you all, if not for your forgiveness, then for peace."

Markward realized that the real reason for Photios' guilt was probably in the realization that he had hurt far more than a fellow knight upon attacking Aldrich. He had instigated violence against a leader of a christian army set on advancing to Anatolia through any means necessary. The peace he wanted was more general and less individual.

"Convey us to your master and we will see what kind of peace can be salvaged."

Bishop Herman strode quickly to the front of the group, as if claiming the head of the dinner table, and shared an imperious look at those around him. "Quickly now, let's not keep his eminence waiting."

"By all means, lead the way." Walram said with a smirk at Rupert and Markward.

The Bishop's robe billowed in the salty breeze as he climbed the stairs. All of his embarrassment had seemed to melt away upon hearing the need for him and his diplomatic abilities once more. As he neared the top, Photios, who stood waiting, motioned with his hand and two sentries opened the massive double doors. They swung easily on well-oiled hinges.

The group entered an expansive room with marble floors and expensive tapestries on the walls. Tile mosaics patterned the walls, floor and even the ceiling. Despite its size and the expensiveness of the decorations, the room smelled of mildew. Markward hated the ocean, and this was just another reason why, every time he came near it everything smelled this way.

There was too much water in the air. It was like trying to keep a duck, swimming in a pond, dry.

Photios lead the way once more and as they passed through the room, the sounds of their shoes clicking on the tile was all that was heard. Some of the ambassadors seemed to be entranced as they walked. Count Walram had nearly stopped walking altogether as he tried to look at all the artwork. A large tile mosaic of Christ's face stared down at them from high up on the wall. Even the Bishop hesitated and stared back at the visage.

They were finally led to a large courtyard where a fat man sat in the shade of an awning.

"Our Eminence, Emperor Isaac Angelus has been detained in the south, but should return shortly. Photios explained.

This must be a steward or a relative Markward thought.

Photios continued: "This is High Chamberlain Nikephoros, he wished to meet with you and make sure that your... accommodations were adequate."

"Accommodations?" Markward asked.

They were close enough now for the fat chamberlain to hear and his high voice sounded like it should have come from a young boy.

"Surely while in Constantinople, such men as you did not expect to have to continue sleeping in tents?" Nikephoros said.

The fat man's skin seemed more transparent than merely pale, and his thin lips pulled back from yellowing teeth as his features attempted the semblance of a smile.

The Bishop was the first to respond.

"I, for one, am very pleased with them my lord."

"Good."

"My lord." Count Rupert said interrupting the bishop and getting a cold glare from the clergyman in return. "We have come to discuss transport of our Crusading army into Asia, among other things, and preparations must be made quickly so as to be ready when the army arrives." He continued.

"we may discuss such things upon Angelus's return." The fat man waved an incongruously flabby and thin arm, dismissing the question with the motion. "He shouldn't be long in coming, I assure you." Nikephoros paused and looked at them appraisingly. Markward knew that the interest in their well-being was all part of a show, an attempt to lessen the sting of the skirmish they had had with the cavalry unit and the fight in the street. "I do sincerely apologize for the horrible treatment that you received at the hands of Photios and his men." Nikephoros said, as if reading his mind. "You have already chastened most of them, and Photios will be dealt with." The last was said with an accompanying sneer towards Photios. "You have my apologies as well. Your man Sir Aldrich Kortig is being looked after by our best physicians."

"Can we see him?" Rupert interrupted. Nikephoros seemed flustered and annoyed by it, but collected himself and continued.

"Of course, in another day, I am told he will be well enough to be moved to your own suite. Now, I imagine that you and your men are exhausted, those outside the wall as well. Why not bring them inside? I'm sure we can find lodgings for so few."

Rupert's answer was immediate.

"No."

The direct refusal was a surprise to the high chamberlain who was undoubtedly expecting a more political response, if not an outright acquiescence to the suggestion. Courtesy for courtesy thought Markward, "Thank you, my lord, but it is a long road yet and the last thing I need is for them to expect a bed every time we stop." Rupert amended.

Markward nodded his approval, more to the attempt to dull the blunt response than anything.

The chamberlain's grotesque smile returned. It was plain that Nikephoros was no fool.

"Very well, Photios will show you to your rooms."

Just then, eight guards from the perimeter of the courtyard marched forward, as if they had been waiting for that very cue to act, and formed a column on either side of the line of ambassadors and statesmen.

It perplexed the Bishop.

"What is going on here?" He demanded, voice rising to a near squeak. No one made a move to answer him immediately, as if explaining their situation out loud would solidify it to an unwelcome degree.

The bishop fidgeted, rubbing his hands together feverishly as he looked from Rupert, then to Nikephoros and finally to the guards. "I demand to know what is going on!" He said, waiting for a response...of some kind... from anyone.

He was used to being obeyed, and confusion replaced the anger on his face when no answer came for the second time.

Markward watched as yet a third emotion manifested itself on the Bishop's face in as many seconds. Fear.

"We are duly appointed envoys of the Holy Roman Empire!" He squeaked. "I'm sure that Emperor Angelus would wish us the treatment that we deserve." He continued.

Nikephoros's grin never faltered. "Do not worry, my dear Bishop, you shall be treated exactly as you deserve." The words were chilling, but not nearly as much as the grin that accompanied them.

Sweat beaded the Bishop's forehead, and strands of stringy hair stuck to the corner of his gaping mouth as he swung his head, searching the people around him for any evidence of help.

Markward could stand it no longer and threw subtlety aside.

"You cannot truly hope to accomplish anything by detaining us. Frederick will attain the far side." He pointed to the East. "no matter how long it takes."

"Well in that case, I am pleased that we now have a few bargaining chips to keep him off our doorstep." The Chamberlain responded.

Markward stepped forward. The guard next to him made to draw his sword but was halted in the action by photios's reproving shake of the head.

"You would be well-served to let us go." His voice was soft, yet stern.

Nikephoros paused as if waiting for more before he broke out into wheezing laughter, followed closely by the guards. Markward noticed that Photios did not laugh.

"And why is that?" Nikephoros managed finally between stubborn chuckles.

"Because," Markward continued. "Emperor Frederick Barbarossa is not a man to take lightly. He is not a man you can bribe or threaten. He believes in his cause and will accomplish it no matter the cost. If you kill us, then he will level this city. He has the men to do it, he doesn't want to, but he will if he has to. If you hold us and refuse to allow Frederick passage across the Bospherus then he will lay siege and deprive your people of food. How long do you think this city can survive without food? How long do you think the Bulgarians and Serbians will continue to be subject to an impotent government? You will lose your empire over the decision you make right now by all means take me prisoner." Markward made a show of exposing his wrists, first to Nikephoros, then to Photios.

Nikephoros was no longer grinning. "Take them away!" He barked angrily, visibly disturbed by his counterpart's assessment of the situation.

Chapter 18

"Frederick! So good to see you. I hope the roads haven't been too bumpy." The King of Hungary was more square than round, and he shambled rather than waddled when he walked, even so, those who didn't know him might have made the mistake that he was fat under the tabard, he was hardly fat. The King took pride in, well...everything. But he especially took pride in himself. The limp was from an old hunting injury that had caused him considerable pain in his later years, though his pride made him try to keep that hidden. The limp was a part of him now, Frederick couldn't imagine him without it.

Frederick had sent messengers ahead of the army to inform Bela of the army's approach and had received a welcoming response from the King. Despite that, Frederick was wary of Bela. Hungary had long been the eastern-most bastion of the Western Roman Catholic Church, but Bela married his daughter off to Isaac Angelus only three years ago, and Bela had once been Kaiser Alexius. Educated in the courts of Constantinople, he had even been engaged to the Byzantine Emperor's daughter until the birth of a son effectively ruined his chances of becoming emperor.

Was Bela in league with the Byzantines? Could Frederick trust the father-in-law of a man who, reportedly, was in collusion with his enemy?

Frederick grasped the king's arm in greeting. "The roads are too bumpy for someone of my age I'm afraid, but I'm beginning to desire the bruising discomfort of the road over the stuffy discomfort of that infernal ship." Frederick pointed with his thumb back up the dock at the small cog moored at the end for emphasis.

King Bela had come down to the docks to meet the Emperor, a gesture of respect commonly shown to visiting dignitaries, even so it was not lost on Frederick. In Frederick's position it paid to be cognisant of the most subtle of political signals. Perhaps Bela would be a good ally. The King seemed genuine enough.

Bela shared a sympathetic smile with Frederick. "I despise traveling by boat as well, but my beautiful wife prefers it to any other form." Bela turned while speaking and took the Lady to his left by the hand and brought her forward. Frederick would not have described her, necessarily, as beautiful, as the King did. She had a long curved nose, similar to the beak of some bird of prey. Her face was square for a woman's, but despite her average appearance she flowed gracefully toward Frederick and curtsied to him while Bela continued with an introduction. "His Imperial Majesty, it is my honor to present my Queen, Anna of Antioch."

"My lady Queen, I was so sorry to hear of your father's demise at the hands of Saladin." The queen's poise faltered slightly at the comment. She clearly hadn't expected the Emperor to care of her father's death. Reynald de Chatillion was blamed by some for goading Saladin into war, which was a good thing for some, but as it had resulted in the horrific defeat of the army at Haifa and the loss of Jerusalem, sympathy for his death was undoubtedly rare. Frederick could imagine that such topics, among the social elite, would be casually ignored rather than confronted. Such things could be uncomfortable to discuss. And if they were confronted, then it would have come from a verbose orator, not an Emperor, followed quickly by a promise of retribution. Frederick had only met Reynald once, and was not as impressed in the Frenchman as he was in himself, but he was Anna's father, and Frederick knew well the feelings that the death of even a horrible parent could cause.

"Reynald may have been many things, but he was one of us. He was a husband, a prince, a Christian, and your father."

The queen's lower lip quivered slightly and her brow furrowed. She took her time responding, and when she finally did, Frederick could sense the emotion just beneath the surface. "My grace, I … thank you." She curtsied again.

Frederick turned back to the King who stood staring at his wife as if he didn't know her. The show of emotion, as subtle as it was, seemed foreign to him. He noticed that Frederick had returned his attention to him and quickly collected himself again. "Our messengers put your army only ten miles to the west. I have taken the liberty of sending guides to bring them to the great plains in the south. It is our most fertile land and abounds with wildlife, the best location for a host as large as yours."

"I thank you for your hospitality. Your contributions to the crusade will undoubtedly win you blessings in heaven." said Frederick.

Bela smiled and put his arm around the taller Frederick's shoulders "Come." He said as he turned to walk beside Frederick up the dock towards the city. "In that case we shall have to see what else I can give." He said with a wink.

"I do have a matter of which I would like to discuss. It involves your brother." Said Frederick.

Bela paused and turned to face Frederick once again, the joviality lost. "What about that traitor interests you my grace?" An anxious anger darkened his face.

Frederick lowered his head so the shorter king could hear the whispered response.

"Even now the fourth son of the late King Geza rots in prison. You cannot trust him to go free, given the past treacheries he has committed against you. Yet you cannot kill your brother and risk losing the tenuous support of his allies. He is an accomplished warrior. Would not his existence be better served on the crusade?" Frederick allowed the thought to fully impact the King. Bela looked pensive as Frederick continued. "He could serve penance for his sins, and a campaign such as this has a way of changing a man. Mercy, could win the continued support of his allies, while ridding you of him. Send a small army with him and claim whatever glory he will win for yourself."

Bela's mouth was now a wide grin. He visibly loved the idea. "You are more cunning than even your reputation gives you credit. I was sure the legend of your Grace's devious mind was exaggerated, but now I see that it was understated. Come, let's discuss the composition of your new Hungarian army!" Bela slapped Frederick on the back as they both turned toward the manor house.

They spent all day discussing the technicalities. Both men were excited for the bargain though for different reasons. Bela would lose a major thorn in his side, and Frederick would gain a competent commander and a small, yet well-trained army to strengthen his already considerable force. He also gained a measure of political strength as an endorsement from Bela gave him more sway over the various restless factions in the Byzantine Empire. At some point in the discussion Bela turned to a guard and ordered his brother released with the condition that he promise to accompany Frederick to the Holy land. Geza had apparently jumped at the opportunity, because he was brought to them dressed in rags and stinking soon after.

Frederick was impressed by the man, despite his bedraggled appearance. Geza was muscular, and while he was short like his brother, he was considerably more agile looking. Frederick recognized the stance of a man ready for anything.

"I would hear it from your own mouth." Frederick said, walking towards the shabby man. "Will you willfully accompany me on this venture against the heathen races who would dare challenge the will of God, and thereby have a chance to receive absolution of your sins?"

Geza looked at the King who motioned for him to answer.

"I don't care about my supposed sins, but I would rather die on the battlefield than in a dark prison." Geza took half a second to consider his next words, then said: "Especially when that prison is down-wind from my fat brother's privy." The guard seemed to have expected such a remark as his reaction was right on the heels of the insult. His mailed fist slammed into the back of Gezas head, but as quick as the guard had been Geza had judged the swing and allowed his head to lull forward just as the fist impacted the back of his head lessening the force of the blow. Frederick had noticed, as had the guard, who looked unsatisfied. The guard moved to inflict more lasting violence when Bela stopped him.

"Leave him be. Even his insults do nothing to dampen my spirits today. Take him away and bathe him, get him ready for the festival tonight." Bela's devious smile indicated to Frederick how Geza must feel about such things. The feast would probably be considered a special torture for the recently freed prince. A sentiment that Frederick shared. "Give him his own room to stay in while he prepares his army for march." Bela continued. "We cannot have our Hungarian general treated like a prisoner after all. Make sure you shave that thing off his face as well. I would hate for someone to mistake him for a bear and lop his head off."

The guard led Geza away.

Not long after, Frederick was shown to his quarters where he could rest a little and prepare for the feast. And before he even had time to test the feather bed's firmness, a page came to show him to the massive hall where the feast was being held. The more Frederick saw of Bela's manor house the more it impressed him. The hall was magnificent.

Just as Bela had heard of Frederick, Frederick had heard rumors of Bela's wealth but had realized that until now he hadn't truly believed them. It was said that Bela was more wealthy than Philip, the King of France, and Henry, the King of England. He had managed his kingdom well, and the opulence in this manor house was the proof.

Frederick sat by the King at his large table at the head of the dining hall where they now ate a feast commemorating his arrival to Hungary. The floor where the noble's table sat was raised several steps above that of the rest of the hall. Frederick could look down on the diners below. He picked out many of his own men among the crowd, as well as many noble pilgrims that accompanied the army on its crusade. He saw the prefect of Magedeburg, Widukind of Schwalenburg, and Adalbert of Grumbach sitting with Conrad of Swarzinberg. To the rear of the hall he could make out the immensely fat body that could only belong to Duke Otto Wittelsbach as he shook with laughter from an undoubtedly witless joke. Among them all, servants scurried, bringing food and drink. They attempted to sate the seemingly insatiable crowd. The food was excellent as was the wine. The cost of the entire banquet must have been considerable. Taken alone, the feast may not have been enough to convince the Emperor of Bela's wealth. Most Kings would sell half their family estate to please the caliber of men gathered in this room. Frederick had gained most of his success by being able to accurately read people, and the King hadn't seemed apprehensive by the extravagance being shown in the least.

Geza sat to Frederick's right and rhythmically sloshed the wine in his goblet from one golden rim to the other without spilling. He was flanked conspicuously by the same guard that was with him earlier. The feast was well underway and yet the prince had said fewer than two words to him. Frederick sensed a degree of respect from Geza despite his silence. The type of respect one sees after long years on the battlefield between two soldiers, perhaps even enemies, after their shared torment of battle. His thick black beard was gone, his clothes meticulously clean, and yet it didn't suit him. Bela, on the other hand, seemed to luxuriate with ease, the mantel of finery placed upon him seemed to fit his personality perfectly, The difference between the two brothers was striking in this regard, and it was obvious that Geza did not belong in the lavish hall. His black hair was neatly cropped, and Frederick could even smell a faint scent of flowers emanating from the prince, even so, this atmosphere unsettled Geza. Frederick wasn't sure, but it didn't seem to just be the newly acquired freedom that affected the prince. Geza shifted nervously looking at each of the guests individually, weighing them. He seemed fully prepared to fight any and all, but his courage had almost failed when presented with the few stunted conversations that Frederick had seen the prince forced into that night. Riding a sweat lathered destrier into a host of the enemy seemed more to the prince's liking than this affair. His tailored silks exchanged for armor, the smell of sweat rather than roses. Despite his obvious reluctance to speak, the Emperor could not resist.

"I get the sense that you don't care for this sort of thing." Frederick said, and waved at the luxurious festivities with a sweep of the hand.

A scoff of derision escaped Geza, the rude sound out of place among the finery, but well suited to the man.

"My apologies Emperor, I forgot myself." Geza said. His tone rigid and rehearsed, as if forced to say it.

Frederick was astonished. "My good man, you have nothing to be sorry for. I can see that this sort of frivolity does not suit a man such as you. A certain amount of your unease is expected from someone in your position, however I have never liked this type of thing much either. What excuse, then, do I have?" Geza lifted his gaze, a question formed across his brow. "I can't stand formal functions." The Emperor continued. "I'd much rather be with my men, drinking a stout ale and telling stories of past battles."

"But my grace, you are..." Geza hesitated.

Frederick finished the thought for him. "An Emperor?"

Geza inclined his head in response. "Just because I'm Emperor doesn't mean that I have to be a peacock as well." Frederick said the last in a conspiratorial, hushed, tone while signalling Bela with his eyes as the King stood to give yet another toast welcoming the crusaders into his country.

Geza realized that Bela's cloak did resemble the flamboyance of a peacock but quickly hid the smile before anyone could notice with his goblet. Emperor Barbarossa was not who he thought he'd be, Geza thought. Geza had always admired the man's reputation but doubted that such a man would be likable in person. It seemed to Geza that such a man should have been stuffy, dull, and precisely proper, at least on formal occasions while visiting with unfamiliar people. On informal occasions, as Geza was certain that tonight would turn into for more than a few men at the tables, he would have expected a man of Frederick's rank to be arrogant and condescending to a man so much younger than himself. Geza was a King's brother, and that may have afforded him some additional respect from the older man. Still, Geza had a hard time imagining the personable and down-to-earth, yet simultaneously intimidating man acting in any way that Geza had come to expect.

His brother had plainly been drinking a little too much. Evidenced by the slurred words that dotted his speech.

Geza was confident, however, that few were actually listening, and of those that were, most were probably suffering the same fate as the king. Geza's smile returned as he watched his brother attempt to remain regal as he ended his toast and sat back down. Bela never could stomach wine like a man should.

The Queen, who in the absence of such a distinguished guest, would be sitting where the Emperor sat, but who now sat to the King's left; leaned forward and whispered something in Bela's ear. Bela swore audibly and stood back up.

The quick movement forced a belch from the King, and there he stood in all his glory. The hall resounded with scattered laughter. Mugs of ale pounded down on tables again and again, forming the beginning of a crude applause. Bela frowned down at them and all those sober enough to think, quickly silenced.

"Bring out the gifts!" The King announced. Even his recent embarrassment could not dampen his obvious pleasure at flaunting his prosperity a little more. The gifts were mostly just announced by a herald, as they were too big or numerous to bring into the hall and ranged from sheep and camels to ships and wagons filled with supplies. One of the most unexpected gifts was a magnificent tent given to him by the Queen. It was large, had four rooms, and was double skinned for better insulation against both the heat and the cold.

When the announcements had finally ended emperor Frederick stood.

"What an honor it is to be among such Christians! Such generosity I have never seen." The Emperor turned to the King and Queen and said, loud enough for most to hear. "Your help rendered to the Army of Christ, will undoubtedly win you blessings in heaven." Then turning back to the crowd, "King Bela has graciously allowed Prince Geza the opportunity to bring honor to himself and to Hungary. He will lead a Hungarian Army of two-thousand to help in our fight for Jerusalem!" The men cheered before he was even finished and he was forced to say the last in a yell.

Frederick turned to Geza and motioned for him to stand. He came to his feet, reluctantly.

The crusaders were now banging their fists on the massive tables in a rhythm and chanting "Geza, Geza…" Frederick turned back towards his seat and could see both Bela and Geza. Both men were red-faced, but for entirely different reasons.

Chapter 19

Hagan longed for the days in Adelfried's fields. Back then he was ignored for the most part. Now, however, it seemed like every knight in camp had advice for him. As they passed him, while seeing to their various tasks, they would pause and say something like "saw your run Hagan, be sure to lift your knees. When battle comes, you will wear a helm making it hard to see. You wouldn't want to trip on a rock and skewer yourself with your sword would you?" Hagan would always nod and give a respectful little bow and say something like "Thank you sir, I will try to remember that." What was most annoying was that most of the advice was very good, there was just so much of it. It made him feel like he was hopeless, and that he would never be a knight. Never-mind that, Hagan just hoped not to "skewer" himself on his own sword.

There were worse problems to have, Hagan supposed, and as he carried a bucket of water up from the river in the dark for probably the hundredth time that night, he resolved to have a better attitude. Besides, he was a squire! His mentor and liege-lord was likely locked up in some dark, damp prison in Constantinople while he was stuck in this camp in a country full of potential enemies. But he had always dreamed of adventure. If anything qualified as an adventure, this did. It was disheartening, though, that adventure was not as wonderful as he had imagined. Most of his time on the trip so far had been work. He often wondered, while scouring the pots, or watering the horses, if squires were actually meant to ever become knights at all or if they were just servants that were given a false sense of hope to make them more willing. Still, he had made progress with the sword. Hagan was now at a level in his training where he was expected to wear a sword at his waist at all times, and as he shifted the bucket, awkwardly, to his free hand to relieve his tired muscles, the sword swung between his legs, tripping him.

As he fell, Hagan attempted, vainly, to keep the precious water from spilling. He pushed himself up into a kneeling position and lifted the bucket to test how much he had lost. It was almost empty. A stream of swear-words and curses escaped his lips. Words he hadn't even known that he knew. He had heard most of them from the knights as he traveled with them. He wasn't even sure if he was using them correctly. It didn't matter, it felt right. As he finally calmed himself he decided to carry what little he had left in the bucket to the trough anyway. There was no sense wasting the trip since he was so close.

Why did they have to have their horses up here anyway? It made much more sense to Hagan to have them down by the water where they could drink their fill when they wanted. Obert had told him never to keep your horses too far away from where you sleep. The idea was that if you were attacked you could mount up faster, which was life or death in such a situation. Hagan sighed as he stumbled on an unseen stone. Right now, life didn't seem to be worth it.

He up-ended the bucket over the trough and frowned at the depressing, small splash his efforts had made.

Obert sat at the fire nearby.

"You know. You'll get done more quickly if you fill the bucket to the top."

Hagan couldn't help but grumble as he turned back in the direction of the river.

He could hear the slow-moving water now as he started down the gradual slope to the water's edge. A glimmer shone off of the surface. A second, less detailed array of stars played out before him, dancing in on the ripples. Hagan dipped the pail into the water and looked up at the sky, it was huge, black but for the tiny pin-holes in God's curtain. He remembered a distant memory of his dad calling it that. "pin-holes in God's curtain." Hagan looked back down at the water as he stood with the full pail. He waded into the water to his ankles to fill the bucket and now the surrounding stones made it difficult to walk. He held the pail close to his body with both hands to keep it from tripping him again in his precarious position.

Hagan saw a dark shape on the shore to his left as he turned. It looked like a log, half fallen in the water, but he didn't remember one there any of the other times he'd come down that night. Hagan looked up the shore in the other direction and confirmed that this was the same spot. There was the rock he'd sat on two turns ago. He looked back at the log and stepped toward it. Light glimmered off of something and all at once the shape was no longer a log. Hagan recognized it for what it was, a lifeless body, face down in the water. The twig that jutted from his back was actually an arrow.

The tell-tale thrum of an arrow being sent on its deadly course rang like a trumpet in Hagan's ears and he turned toward it.

Half a second before Hagan felt the impact he saw the partial features of a cowled face disappear into the shadows, and then he heard the arrow break bone and spill blood.

Hagan looked up at the stars one last time, then down at the wound that would surely end his life. His distraught visage stared back from the bottom of the pierced bucket. White, trembling hands held the pail so tightly to his body that it might never be separated again.

Hagan looked up at the stars again and thanked God. His wits finally came back to him in a rush, and he scanned the shore for the murderer. He was gone.

"Murder!" Hagan yelled as he ran toward the camp in the direction the hooded figure had been moments before.

"Murder. Murder."

Hagan could hear the clank of metal and the rustle of canvas as men hastily armed themselves and ran from their tents.

Two knights came toward him. They were fully armored and had their swords drawn. The men had obviously been on patrol when they heard Hagan's alarm. Before they reached him, Hagan pointed in the direction the man had fled "a man, in black with a bow. He shot at me." The men understood and veered off to hunt the mysterious figure.

A group of men formed around Hagan. "what is it boy? What happened?" Hagan recognized the speaker as Hoch.

Hagan led the men to the dead body. Obert and Ahren arrived, swords drawn and ready. Hoch was bent over the body now, examining the arrow that stuck out between the shoulder blades like it held some great secret. It was clear that the man was already dead as his head was mostly submerged in the water making it impossible to breathe. Hoch gently rolled the body onto its side and peered at a face covered in mud. He muttered a curse as he began wiping at the mud, revealing the features of a young man. Hoch looked up at Ahren and asked "where is Sir Rolf Duerr?" Ahren turned to Hagan and was about to say something, then looked at the impaled bucket still being clutched in Hagan's unyielding hands like a trout in a hawk's talons, and changed his mind. Hagan had forgotten that he still held the pail, and slowly lowered it to the ground, embarrassed. Ahren turned to Obert instead. "He has patrol on the Western wall tonight I believe." Obert understood and gave a solemn nod in reply before leaving to retrieve the knight whose squire now lay cold on the ground.

Hagan recognized him now, and a wave of guilt washed over him. He couldn't remember his name.

"Why would anyone do this?" Hagan realized that his question sounded childish and tried to clarify "he's only a squire. Why not kill Rothschild or Hoch." Hagan winced and looked down at Hoch who still knelt next to the boy "no offense". Ahren shifted uneasily "It is much more difficult to get away when you kill someone in the center of the camp than on the perimeter. The intent is to demoralize and confuse, cause infighting and distrust. Most battles are fought long before the actual act of fighting." Ahren turned to Hoch. "We'll need to set perimeter fires and double the guards, at least until the army arrives."

Hoch nodded and stood "at last report they had entered Byzantium but were having...troubles." He looked back down at the corpse meaningfully.

Ahren nodded taking his meaning, but Hagan wasn't sure what they were talking about.

"Sir Hoch, might we discuss our defenses in my tent? I fear my stew might not be worth eating if I don't attend to it soon" Ahren said. It was clearly an excuse to get Hoch away from the others, but Hagan wasn't sure why.

Hoch rose and the two men started to walk away, then Ahren turned to Hagan and motioned slightly with his chin for him to follow.

Hagan looked down at the pail and picked it up, then hurried his step to catch the two warriors. It was interesting how he had hated the thing so intensely one moment and then loved it the next. That bucket had done more for him than any object ever had.

Ahren's tent was too small for any kind of meeting so they used Aldrich's command tent instead. They had set it up in anticipation of his return, and it was useful for meetings like this. They sent for Rothschild to accompany them and now the three men and Hagan all sat inside the tent. Hagan had just got done telling the story for the second time when Obert entered and pulled up a stool next to Hagan. Ahren looked at Obert with questioning eyes as if he were expecting a report, and Obert was expecting to have to give one.

"The spy eluded our sentries. The outer barricade now has twice the light and twice the men to guard it. Just as well really, with little else to do but wait for the army to arrive, they might as well stand outside the wall as opposed to within." Rothscild gave a single, ear-piercing, "hah" in, what Hagan assumed was, a chuckle; then he, loudly, began ringing the water that he had spilled in his beard while drinking.

Obert stared at Rothschild for several long seconds as if he were an animal he'd never seen before. Rothschild finally noticed that he was the object of Obert's examination and said "what?" with a confused look on his face and began searching his beard and chest for some overly embarrassing foreign material that could have caused the look on Obert's face. "At any rate," Obert continued "It won't be as easy to enter the camp, but not impossible. I think we need to go into town and ask some pointed questions of the populace. I know we've been trying not to make too many waves until the army arrived, but it might be a good idea to mingle with them a little to gauge how they feel about us, and even more important, how they feel about their own Empire."

Ahren nodded, as did Hoch. Rothschild looked up from whatever it was he had found in his beard and followed the example of the other two, nodding effusively, even though Hagan wasn't sure he even knew what he was agreeing to.

Hagan had noticed that Hoch and Rothschild often let Ahren and even Obert lead even though they technically weren't nobles at all or even knights.

Apparently serving under Aldrich had a degree of honor and prestige associated with it uncommon to the average knight. Ahren and, even, Obert, however, could not be knights and continue to serve under Aldrich. He being an Imperial knight and all.

Carl had once alluded to Hagan about some strange rule among the Imperial knights that said that an Imperial knight could not have knights in his retinue because a knight in the Emperor's service was subject to the Emperor alone and so were all that served under the knight. It didn't make much sense to Hagan.

Ahren was up and pacing now, as he was prone to do when expected to think and talk but the confined space of the tent limited his pacing to only three strides in each direction. He looked like a caged lion to Hagan. The subject of the conversation had moved on to why the attack had happened and what it meant.

"It seems fairly obvious that the murderer is Byzantine." Ahren said. "Or at least he was sent by the Byzantines, given that they have taken our emissaries captive. They fear all-out war with us, but are obliged to slow us down and make our crossing of the Bosphorus as difficult as they can." This time Rothschild's massive nodding head indicated genuine approval.

"What were you saying about the army Hoch? Are they having problems of this sort as well?" Ahren asked.

Hoch cleared his throat. He was the oldest person in the tent, even so, his back was perfectly straight, and he always seemed formal to Hagan. "I received a messenger today, informing me that the Emperor had encountered numerous difficulties. The guides they employed to lead them, after crossing the Hungarian border, have betrayed them on several occasions and led them through difficult terrain in the wrong direction. He also said that many of the servants and pilgrims are being killed at night when they stray from camp." Hoch shifted uncomfortably and continued "I believe I am at fault for the death of Sir Rolf's squire. Had I taken the initiative and fortified our defenses earlier the boy might still be alive."

"There was no way for you to know that someone would enter the camp so brazenly. Stalking past guards, watch fires, and over a palisade wall to kill a squire as he fetched water could not have been expected." Ahren said.

"Is it possible that the killer's target was someone of more strategic value, but his presence was detected by the boy?" Obert said.

"I wouldn't think so, since he had been shot in the back." Ahren said, then made as if to speak but hesitated before finally saying "unless he knew the killer."

Silence followed the statement as the men considered that. "What would be the motive for killing the boy then?" Obert said.

"He didn't want him to witness later as to who had been stalking around at night with a bow and arrow, wearing a dark cloak." Ahren said.

The nights were starting to have a bit of a chill, Hagan had noticed, and as a cool breeze wafted through the tent, he gave an involuntary shudder. He told himself that it was the breeze that caused it and not the topic of discussion. Until that moment everyone must have forgotten he was there because Ahren noticed his shudder and looked at him with understanding eyes "don't worry Hagan if the killer is a spy within our camp, he'll think twice about doing it again thanks to you and your bucket shield. We'll go into town tomorrow and you can get that bucket fixed" Ahren's eye's shifted to Obert and said "we'll use the opportunity to talk to the people as you mentioned before. Besides, I'm sure the quartermaster would like to try to buy some supplies as well."

"Try indeed." Rothschild grumbled. "These Byzantine merchants are closed up tighter than a maiden's…" Hoch cleared his throat again, interrupting Rothschild who looked hurt at not being able to finish his vulgar thought and listened as Hoch spoke over him. "Yes, well, we have no alternative. We must procure supplies quickly, one way or another."

"I say we just take the town, they are heathens who reject God's will" Rothschild said.

"It may come to that, but I don't think any of us here have the …standing to make such a decision. The Emperor is only a few days away, we can go hungry that long. Any hunting parties should have sufficient men as to discourage attacks." Ahren said.

Hagan felt his head dip, and his eyes close involuntarily. He jerked them open and snapped his head up to see Obert smiling at him.

Hagan expected a joke, some comment that would draw the other's attention to his childish behavior, but it didn't come. Instead, Obert merely said "Hagan, go get us some stew we should have ate hours ago then get some rest. You've had a hard night."

The others seemed to think this was a good idea and nodded their approval while they continued to talk. Hagan picked up the bucket and exited the tent. Everything went dark as he left the lighted interior of the tent, and it took a few moments to see. He noticed that several knights, stood guard around the command tent. They weren't standing so close as to hear what the men inside were saying, but the tent was the object of their protection. Hagan nodded to one as he passed, who looked at the skewered bucket, then nodded back.

After taking the stew, which was burned on the bottom of the pot and cold, Hagan laid down to sleep in his tent. He hadn't eaten. He feared his stomach would reject whatever he fed it. He hadn't realized how much tonight's experience had scared him. His hands trembled as he pulled the wool blanket up to his chin, and a shuddering sob escaped his lips as images and flashes of fear returned to him.

When Obert and Ahren returned from their meeting, much later that night, they found Hagan sitting by a crackling fire, poking at it with a stick.

The next day Hagan, Obert, Rothschild, Ahren, and half a dozen fellow Imperial knights rode into the town of Philippopolis. Ahren and the others were careful to choose the right number of men to go into the town. Not so many as to make the people worry that they were there to attack, but enough that they wouldn't tempt any group of questionable intent, whether they be town guard or ambitious citizenry, to...what? attack them? Hagan wasn't sure, but he supposed with spies in camp that had already tried to kill him, he'd welcome all the friendly company he could get.

Chapter 20

To Hagan the "town" was more a city. They had been through bigger cities on their way to Byzantium (Constantinople, although seen from a distance, was huge), but Philippopolis was far bigger than what Hagan had grown up in, and the size was still unsettling. People came and went through the gates, but he noticed that more people seemed to leave than were coming in, pushing carts laden with all manner of objects. They all moved to the side to let the knights pass, as was customary. They did so at a reluctant pace, which was customary as well for tired men and women, however, once they saw the green cross on their company's surcoats and shields their speed improved noticeably.

"Does it not seem that more people are going than coming?" Hagan asked no one in particular.

"Aye," Obert said. His eyes scanning the crowded road suspiciously. "The Greeks have never been overly courageous. Perhaps our presence near the city is too much for the sheep to handle."

"Perhaps." Ahren said. His eyes were squinted slightly in what Hagan had come to recognize as deep thought in the Sergeant.

An old woman sat by the side of the road, outside the city walls, yelling something in Greek, trying to sell some kind of dried meat. She must not have been permitted to sell within the city walls. She probably couldn't afford the taxes to pay for a space within. Her warbling cries, that undoubtedly announced what she sold, cut off when they approached.

She looked at them through squinted, suspicious eyes. Hagan looked around and noticed similar looks on the faces of most of the surrounding people, although the majority stole glances at the group and didn't openly stare like the old woman was. As Hagan rode slowly past her, he met her gaze. Most peasants were too scared to look into the eyes of anyone on horseback. Maybe she was just too old to care, or maybe she viewed them as an enemy to her country and felt obligated to share her disapproval with their presence, either way she was not afraid. The hunchbacked old woman bared her teeth, well he wasn't sure what was left in her mouth could be considered teeth but she bore them nonetheless in something that only a fool would call a smile.

As Hagan approached the gates to the city, he was struck with a sense of unease, much as he had been with the woman. The guards, little more than town militia, shifted uneasily as the group approached. Before they reached hailing distance, the older of the two men summoned a page nearby and sent him running on some kind of errand, undoubtedly to tell the guards superiors of their arrival.

Obert spoke to the two men in their own language, but Hagan noticed that no one stopped, or even slowed their horses as he spoke, so neither did he. The guards were too flustered to know what to do. He could tell that they wanted to bar the way, but that whatever Obert had said made them hesitate and look almost guilty. That none in their group stopped gave the guards little time to respond to the situation. The guard that sent the page away yelled something after them but did not move to follow or raise an alarm.

"What did you say" Hagan asked, after they had made it into the city a ways. "I Just told him we were brothers in Christ searching for fellow servants of the almighty to buy supplies from. A generous helping of guilt can be useful." Obert said, "He doesn't want to impede a servant of God any more than the next Christian."

Hagan looked around him at the City and realized that it had a lot in common with the old lady outside its gates. It was old looking and maybe it was just his imagination but it had an ominous feel to it.

The cobblestone streets were worn smooth in the center to the point of looking polished and the people watched the group warily from the corner of their eyes.

They came to a part of the city that was obviously the market center. People bustled around vendors who yelled, much like the old woman had, while the sound of tinkers, blacksmiths and various other tradesmen working came from farther up the street.

They reined in and dismounted as Ahren started handing out orders. He assigned two men to watch after the horses while the rest were to accompany him to procure a deal of some kind for food with some vendors. Ahren saw Hagan un-tethering the pail from his horse, "Obert, would you mind keeping Hagan out of trouble while he gets his bucket fixed?" It was said with a hint of humor, and with Ahren that was all you could expect, but it stung Hagan's sense of pride.

All the same, Hagan felt a little relieved at having Obert's company. He was sure that he would manage without the help, but he had wondered, nervously, how he would talk to the locals. He imagined having to use a lot of hand signals, but the repair that the bucket needed was pretty obvious. The point would have been an easy one to make. Still, the added security that Obert's presence would afford was a comfort, he had to admit.

The clack of their hard leather-soled boots became audible to Hagan as they separated themselves from the throng of people around the market and walked down the street towards the much less populated tradesman's quarter. They passed a blacksmith's forge, a leatherworker's shop and a carpenter's shop before seeing the sign of a barrel maker's shop.

"He'll probably be your best bet." Obert said. They crossed the street to an open work area. There were no walls around the shop and Hagan wondered briefly how the workers stayed warm in the winter before remembering that it didn't get very cold here and the fires that the workers lit to burn the inside of the barrels probably kept them plenty warm. Indeed, a sweaty man, with arms that looked like they would be better suited on a bear, stood and said something. One word from what Hagan could make out, and it seemed like the man was annoyed. He went back to work, not waiting for a response from them. Apparently the man was not hurting for work and could afford to be rude to potential customers.

Obert replied to the man and pointed at the bucket in Hagan's hand. The man was now shoveling glowing red coals into a barrel. He paused long enough to point at a corner of the shop where sat a huge pile of broken casks, buckets and barrels. Hagan's shoulder's slumped. Obert began talking to the man in a tone that Hagan recognized as the universal language of bartering.

From the barrel maker's non-interest in the negotiation, Obert wasn't making much progress. The man mumbled a reply and rolled the coal-filled barrel so that the coals scorched another portion of the inside. "He says we can take another bucket, for a price, and leave this one."

Hagan felt foolish, he didn't want to leave it. The bucket was like a sign. It was like God had reached down and saved him through the presence of this simple stave of oak. Finally, Hagan sighed, and nodded, but instead of taking the bucket over to the corner he went to a work bench instead and picked up a discarded mallet and a broken wooden stave. He heard the man behind him protest, but ignored him. He trusted Obert to make sure the man didn't attempt anything foolish. He placed the bucket on the edge of the workbench, open end down and broken side out. He then placed a rope around the bucket that was fastened to the back of the bench, he assumed for that very purpose, and cinched it tight to hold the bucket in place. Placing the end of the broken stave against the bottom of the stave in the bucket that had been nearly pierced by the arrow, the one that had saved his life, he dealt it three strong blows with the mallet. Each hit pushed the piece farther out of the constricting hold the rest of the staves forced on it, until the skewered piece fell free. Hagan picked up the stave and tucked it in his sword belt, then loosened the bucket from the rope and brought it to the corner with the rest of the broken material. On his way back to Obert he picked up a new bucket from a line of them along one wall.

The barrel maker had stopped his work long enough to watch and shook his head, confused by the young warriors actions. Hagan placed two pennies on the table. The man nodded then bent to his work once more.

Hagan was sure that Obert would tease him relentlessly as soon as they were out of the shop about the stave, but to his surprise Obert merely asked "what do you plan on doing with it?" "Not sure, I just feel... I don't know." Hagan wasn't sure that if he had a week to explain it that he would be able to do so successfully. "Like it's a part of you?" Obert said.

Hagan was surprised. "yes, that's it, more or less."

"Every man I know feels the same way about the object that saved them for the first time from certain death. For most, it's a shield, sword or chainmail, but for you it was a bucket. Doesn't make it any less important to you I suppose."

Hagan and Obert made their way through the crowded market towards where they had left the horses with the two knights. They found the horses, still tethered and unharmed, but the men were gone. Where had they gone? Hagan was sure that Ahren had given orders for the men to remain.

Hagan and Obert turned toward an alley at the sound of a muffled scream and saw the flash of a dirty white tunic with a green cross on it. Hagan didn't know what was going on, but recognized it as trouble instantly.

He ran to the sound and was relieved to hear Oberts chasing footsteps. Hagan edged around a cart and ran down the narrow alley.

At the sound of their footsteps on the cobblestone, one of the men that had been guarding the horses turned to face them. He had a slightly apologetic smile on his face when he noticed Obert and then looked apprehensively to his companion who hadn't heard them approach as he was still fumbling with his belt while holding a handful of a woman's hair in his hand.

No. A girl, not a woman. She couldn't have been any older than Hagan. She was struggling to free herself from the man's powerful grip, an effort that earned her a hard backhand from the hand that, until that moment, had been trying to free himself from his clothing. He let her fall, sobbing to the ground, and used both hands to undo his sword belt.

Hagan's blood was pounding in his ears. "Stop." His voice echoed around the alley and made the man jump in surprise. He turned to face Obert and Hagan, a scowl on his ugly, bearded face.

The ugly knight didn't know how to react. His duty told him to respect and obey Obert, if not Hagan, but his pride and lust refused to listen. He re-cinched his belt and squared his shoulders against Hagan, the scowl still present on his face.

"I was just having some fun, you two can have her after we're through. Wench deserves it, she slapped me."

"Undoubtedly for good reason."

"I did not accept such treatment from her, and if it wasn't for the respect I have for your liege, I would teach you a lesson too, squire." He said. His hand rested on the pommel of his sword now and Hagan could see the remains of several meals stuck in the man's bared teeth.

"Perhaps he's not the one that needs the lesson." Obert said. "If you truly respect sir Aldrich you would not be doing something so abhorrent to him and to God. Beyond that you are ignoring your duty and are instead indulging your baser instincts. This boy has more honor than you Sir Gerhard, and if he needs to teach you humility, then so be it, let the learning begin."

The man hesitated, unsure. Hagan realized that Obert never intended to fight the man, and that it was Hagan that was supposed to teach the lesson. He drew his sword, something that elicited a smile on the ugly man's face, he had apparently feared that Obert would fight in Hagan's place.

The man slowly drew his sword from its sheath and winked at his companion, who stood patiently watching the drama. The blond girl behind the ugly man whimpered as she dragged herself to the far corner, attempting to distance herself from further violence.

In that moment Hagan was reminded of another time when his sister had a swollen cheek and cried inconsolably. Hagan's fear of this well trained and experienced warrior vanished, replaced by anger.

"Breathe" Obert whispered behind him. Hagan let out a breath he hadn't known he had pent up. He also let the tension go out of his shoulders and thought of the rhythms that made up combat. These were things that Ahren had told him he must do to keep himself 'grounded' whatever that meant. Although the anger stayed, he could feel the techniques he'd been taught in his muscles, and they responded.

Hagan acted first, something that surprised the big man but delighted him as he laughed while easily parrying Hagan's strike. The man stepped forward and slammed his shoulder into Hagan sending him flying backward. Hagan's considerably smaller stature probably saved his life since the man followed the push with a swing of his sword that would have severed Hagan's head from his shoulders had Gerhard not pushed him out of the swords reach.

"You don't have to kill him to teach him a lesson." The man's companion said.

"If he wants to challenge my honor, then he should be prepared for the possibility of death. Though I shall think of sparing him if he apologizes."

The man's cocky nature sickened Hagan and he stepped forward. He saw what the man intended as soon as he made his move. A crushing downward two-handed stroke meant to obliterate Hagan. Hagan moved to the side from which his opponent swung, and his shorter height allowed him to sneak under the other man's arms before the sword cleaved him in two lengthwise. As he cleared the arms Hagan spun, bringing his sword around into the man's side.

Hagan knew that he should retreat after such a success. He shouldn't press his luck, but the man's side was still exposed. Everything seemed to be going slowly to Hagan as he watched the side of the ugly man's face grimace and contort in rage.

Hagan brought his right foot up and kicked out and downward, as hard as he could, into the back and side of the man's left knee. The kick buckled Gerhard's knee and forced him to kneel on it. His left arm swung out to force Hagan back, but Hagan was already too close to the big man and brought his sword up in time to block Gerhard's arm with it. Hagan felt the force of the man's blow cause his sword to bite into flesh and bone.

Hagan was surprised to see Sir Gerhard's face grow even uglier as he screamed. Hagan had no pity for the oaf and brought the pommel of his sword back, into the yelling mans dirty teeth, breaking several and sending him sprawling, to the ground. Hagan moved quickly to his right hand, still holding the sword, and stepped on the wrist then brought the heel of his other boot down hard on the fingers as they gripped the sword. The man screamed again even louder and almost pulled Hagan off of his feet as he dropped the sword and tried to jerk his arm free.

Hagan kicked the sword free then knelt on one knee next to the man and put the edge of his sword against the man's throat. "Do you yield?" he said.

The man's eyes widened as he felt the cold steel against his skin and nodded slightly in response.

Hagan was still angry, but feeling exhilarated at the same time. "Say it" he said. "I Yield" the man said through bloody lips. Rage painted his face dark red. Hagan wasn't sure what to do now. He had won the fight, but what was he supposed to do with the man. He decided Obert would take care of him. Hagan stood and walked to the girl curled in the corner and held out his hand to her. She slowly placed a trembling hand in his, and he helped her to her feet.

"Are you ok? um what I mean to say is. Are you hurt?" he said. She looked at him, not understanding, but replied in her own language. She lowered her head and curtsied low then walked away. "Wait." Hagan said. Then felt foolish since he didn't know why she should. "what's your name?" He turned to Obert, who was grinning broadly.

"Will you just ask her her name for me Obert?" Hagan said.

Obert repeated the question in Greek and the girl smiled slightly then said "Aella", still not wanting to look him in the eye. "My name is Hagan." he patted his chest and repeated "Hagan"

He saw the ugly man being helped over to the alley wall where he could sit while his friend could look at his arm. Hagan pursed his lips, "wait here" he said to the girl, Obert repeated it in Greek as he walked over to the two men. The ugly man flinched slightly as Hagan pulled out his dagger and bent to the man's belt and relieved him of his money pouch. He poured out a handful of coins and handed them to the girl.

She had a worried look on her face, as if she wasn't sure what she should do. Scared almost. Hagan smiled and said "it's yours" then motioned to the alleyway entrance signaling she was free to go. She giggled softly then remembered her manners and curtsied before running away down the alley. Hagan sighed.

Obert's laughter echoed loudly in the confined space of the alley. "Amor" He said, then laughed again. "Nothing buys a girl's affection like the sight of gold."

Hagan blushed. "I just thought she should have something to help relieve the pain she just went through" he said.

The man sitting on the dusty ground scoffed. Obert turned to the man "If I were you, I'd keep my mouth shut. You swore an oath, and this boy has more chivalry than you, likely, ever will." The man must have finally realized that his actions could, if reported to the correct individuals, result in his disbandment from the Imperial knights, or perhaps even stripped of his title. He lowered his head in an attempt to look humbled.

Hagan wasn't sure how it worked, but he was made very clear of the code of conduct that was expected of a knight and he was led to believe that the consequences for not following the code could be severe. The Code of Chivalry was something new to Hagan. He had grown up in a place where many men with power over others, used that power to hurt and steal more. A life of service was not what one thought of when they thought of knights, but Hagan was realizing more and more that a truly chivalrous knight was a servant. A servant first to God, then to the defenseless, and finally, to himself.

Hagan stood with the coin pouch still clutched in his hand. He lifted it and felt the weight. "It's yours if you want it. As well as whatever he has that you want." Hagan looked up at Obert with a dumbfounded expression. "Well, anything he has on him now, I'd say. Your prize for winning." Obert said.

"It was a fair contest, witnessed by two knights." Obert explained further.

Hagan was aware of the basic idea. A knight won his opponent's weapon's, horse, armor. But this hadn't been a true contest had it? He wasn't a knight. Maybe that meant Hagan was even more entitled to the reward?

His hand, still holding the pouch, was trembling. He felt strange, as if his brain was just realizing what he'd done and was rejecting it. He suddenly felt dizzy. Hagan braced one arm against the wall to keep from falling. Then he unceremoniously puked on the dust-covered cobblestones.

"Ancora! You do that a lot." Obert said.

Chapter 21

"As prisons went, this was by far the nicest" Aldrich thought. Their quarters were not the relatively lavish rooms that a friendly host would afford persons of their stature, but neither were they dark dungeon cells deep in the inner bowels of the palace. They were free to move around the suite as they wished, but all of their requests to see the emperor went ignored. They received food regularly, what Aldrich assumed was three times a day, and even had a change of clothes brought to them from time to time.

When Aldrich had awakened from unconsciousness, he had been extremely confused. During all of his many years of warfare, and almost as many injuries, he had never been unconscious for that long. A portion of his memory was gone. The last thing he could remember clearly was entering the city. He remembered the anticipation of being captives, and something about sending Ahren away with the rest of the men. The rest was spotty.

From what the others had said, he had confronted the First Sword about being led as a lamb to the slaughter and the first sword reacted...poorly.

Aldrich reached up and felt the bandage over his face. How did he look? His looks had never really concerned him before, he was an Imperial Knight after all, such frivolities were reserved for the upper ranks in society. It surprised him, however to feel a sense of sadness in the marring of his face. Such scars, so open and apparent to those he confronted would be a stigma against his character err he ever spoke. People jumped to conclusions about others based on how they looked. Everyone did it, him included. It was part of communication he supposed. That such an ugly visage, as his undoubtedly now was, would be a negative first impression for almost all people, regardless of how "open-minded" they professed to be, saddened him.

Altogether, despite his being wounded, Aldrich could not have asked for a more considerate captor. The time they had spent in captivity so far was almost relaxing. Aldrich heard the whiny voice of the Bishop and cringed, on second thought, his captors were inflicting more torture than they could have imagined by keeping them locked up where they had to listen to him.

Markward passed the open doorway to Aldrich's room followed closely by the Bishop. Even here the man wore his ostentatious red cape that swayed in time with his steps. "I will not live out the rest of my days rotting away in this prison." The Bishop said.

Aldrich squinted at the two through his one unbandaged eye and gritted his teeth at the complaining tone that seemed to always accompany the bishop's words. How did such a man rise so far? Called of God or not, the man was an overbearing imbecile who thought more of himself than any man should and Aldrich's patience for him had all but worn out completely.

Markward was the definition of patience, which was probably why the Bishop chose him of late to complain to. Even so Aldrich could sense the strain in his voice as he answered the red-caped buffoon. "I only know what you know my Grace. Angelus has returned from his campaign in time to meet Emperor Frederick when he arrives. If you are curious, then I invite you to ask the guards for more information."

The Bishop had in fact done that very thing several times each instance resulted in nothing more than embarrassing rounds of laughter and taunts made in the indecipherable language of the Byzantines. Given the Bishop's pride and the futility of the gesture, Aldrich was positive that the Bishop would be loath to attempt another query directed at the guards. Aldrich was also sure that Markward was subtly mocking the Bishop in bringing up the bishop's failure.

Aldrich only heard a guttural sigh of frustration and the Bishop's feet stomped quickly away, evidence that he recognized the mockery.

Aldrich heard the door open at the end of the hall and a guard call "The Emperor has demanded the presence of two representatives of your choice immediately." The accented words echoed throughout the suite and brought each room's occupants to their doorways.

The Bishop of Munster took the end of his long cloak in his left hand and strode toward the guards as if he were Jesus himself walking on water, God's gift to the world. He pompously assumed that he would be one of the two.

The guard, who had been one of the many that the Bishop's incessant questioning had annoyed, rolled his eyes and said, in thickly accented German, "Not you". The Bishop was taken completely off guard and struggled, visibly, with the thought of not being one of the representatives. He thought of himself as the leader of the group and most qualified to negotiate with the Byzantines. His eyes darted to several of the other emissaries, either searching for support, or noting who had witnessed his embarrassment.

He regained some composure and spun around with such force that his pectoral cross swung half-way around his neck and hung against his back, half obscured by the many folds of his velvet robes. Once again the Bishop stomped away in anger.

Chamberlain Markward and Count Rupert were ultimately picked once it became clear that he himself was not going to go. Aldrich hated these political maneuverings and tenaciously held onto the idea that he was a warrior, not a politician. Besides, he swooned every time he stood, and he didn't think it would make a good impression on the Greeks if he passed out in front of the emperor. This encounter with the Emperor Angelus could decide their fate better than any battle. However, they needed words now, not swords, and despite what his fresh scars would attest, he was better with swords than with words. Besides, his presence, after the foray with his guards, which he apparently started, might not be conducive to diplomacy for Angelus.

He and Walram migrated to the door and waited impatiently for Markward and Rupert to return. The Bishop, sullenly, stayed in his room but revealed his anxiousness through furtive glances around the door frame every time they made a particularly loud noise.

"why do you think he wants to see only two of us?" Walram asked

"He wants to remind us who is in charge. If he removes two from the presence of their only allies, they are likely to feel more intimidated than had all of us gone. I believe he allowed two instead of just one, because he didn't want to seem so insecure as to remove the emissary from all forms of support." Aldrich said. It still hurt to talk, and the words came out in a slur, but Walram nodded his understanding.

"why do you think they captured us to begin with? What threat are we?"

"I'm hoping that it was an overreaction by Nikephoros in the Emperor's absence. Even if it was, however, I don't think the Emperor can let us go now without getting something in return for fear of losing face with his own nobles. What I know of Byzantine government is that it is extremely prone to upheaval. Emperors come and go here, and it all has to do with how capable they perceive the individual, not necessarily with how capable they actually are. Public image is everything. Angelus cannot afford to look incompetent in the least." Aldrich said.

This was a conversation that they'd already had frequently, but they went through the motions, regardless. The familiarity of it helped calm their unease.

Walram made a scraping sound across the stones with his boot, then looked up in time to catch the Bishop peek his head out briefly.

Aldrich knew what would be the next questions, and he was not disappointed.

"How much longer will we have to wait until they release us?"

"Unless a miracle happens and Markward and the Count can secure our release, I think we'll have to wait another month at least. Emperor Frederick should arrive soon, but he will have negotiations to conduct. We are too valuable for Angelus to give up without getting something significant in return and he has the personality to want to get the most he can out of the situation. That means a lot of bargaining."

Walram slid the locking mechanism on his quarter's door back exhibiting a loud wooden sound. The Bishop poked his head out a few seconds later, then ducked back into his room as Walram watched, smiling.

Aldrich couldn't help but smile also as he realized that Walram was taunting the Bishop.

Time drifted on for what seemed like hours. All conversation died away and Aldrich sat on a small stool. The same stool, in fact, that the guards had previously used before the Bishop's mosquito-like annoyance forced them to seek refuge on the other side of the heavy door. Walram finally tired of provoking the Bishop and stood, slumped against the far wall and picked lazily at a loose thread in his tunic.

The door finally opened. Aldrich stood and Walram perked up in anticipation. Instead of their colleagues faces, however, Aldrich only saw the wretched face of the stooped old crone that brought their meals. He was sure she spit in their food. Walram told him once that he'd seen her do it. A reason for such disgusting behavior wasn't necessary for such a woman. She did what she was told all day long, cooked, cleaned probably for her whole life. The one enjoyment she had was making someone's existence worse by some measure. Exercising any amount of authority was sure to be a thrill.

Despite her attitude towards them, Aldrich pitied her. Their quarters were probably much better than what she had to go home to each night and the food she had to eat probably had worse things in it than spit.

Even so, Aldrich couldn't help but grimace as she screeched at them in her indecipherable tongue. The smell of her as she passed made all thought of food unappetizing despite the dull ache in the pit of his empty stomach proving that it was, indeed, past time to eat.

Escape from this deep within the palace would be virtually impossible, however the guards motioned for them to step farther away from the door and kept a wary eye on them as the crone went from room to room, presumably filling their bowls with the slop.

Eventually, she finished and made her way back out, mumbling and licking her dry and cracking lips constantly. She paused in front of Aldrich and looked up into his face then literally spit an insult at him and cackled to herself as she walked out.

The guard merely smiled at the woman's defiance and closed the door, leaving them alone once more.

Despite the probable added ingredients to their food, hunger got the better of them eventually and they left their vigil by the door long enough to eat. Not long after Aldrich returned, impatiently, to the stool by the door, the Count and Markward were pushed through the door. Aldrich didn't see any evidence of torture. That had been his biggest concern. If their captors had tortured the emissaries, it would show a level of resolve in Angelus that Aldrich was certain would cause war between the two empires and, ultimately, their death.

"They took us to the antechamber and made us wait all day. They didn't feed us nor allow us to access to a chamber pot." Count Rupert said after using his. "All a tactic to unnerve us for certain." Rupert talked as he ate the food that the old woman had left. Markward sat on a stool in the room and remained silent as he ate. He chewed methodically, his movements were efficient and neat. While Rupert talked with his mouth full and spilled pieces of food as he attempted to negotiate the more complex words, Markward refrained from contributing to the conversation while his mouth was otherwise occupied. Occasionally he made simple nods of affirmation.

"When they finally allowed us in to see the Emperor he tried to make us feel as if we were the least of his worries. He acted like he didn't know who we were at first and had that fat Chamberlain of his repeat our names and why we were there. I almost lost it at that point, which I believe now was what they wanted. Markward here saved me from making that mistake."

Rupert stopped putting food in his mouth for this part of the story and smiled bewilderingly at them as they listened.

"I never knew that words could be so deadly. Markward let loose a volley of words more fierce than any arrows. Insults flowed so smoothly among his sentences, like fish in a river. Angelus had gone through so much to put us ill at ease and Markward undid it all in a matter of minutes. He explained why we are here and reminded him that Emperor Frederick had taken up the cross in the name of Christ and counted on the support of his brother Christians in the defense of Christendom. He was very respectful to Angelus, weren't you Markward." Another nod in the affirmative.

"Even when you all but threatened Angelus with total annihilation." Aldrich raised his eyebrows at this. He knew that Markward had more strength in him than what was physically evident, but he couldn't imagine the skinny man being threatening in the least, even on behalf of an emperor and his army.

Rupert saw his look of incredulity and rushed on.

"yeah. He said something like God expected his sons and daughters to be obedient to his will and that if any of them chose incorrectly, they would be punished. The hand of God will be manifest through his army and will smite any who opposed him no matter how high their walls."

Rupert laughed then.

"When he was finally done he said 'we will await any message you have for our Emperor in our quarters, thank you for your time.' and he turned and started for the door. I was so surprised that I was left to follow at his heels like a child. The most astonishing part is that he let us go without a word. Maybe Markward succeeded in giving him something to think about after all." He laughed again and started stuffing his mouth with the disgusting food again.

Markward finally finished picking through his food.

"Angelus is scared, or at least nervous about his decision, as I'm sure any responsible leader in his position would be. He betrayed not only his faith, but that of the majority of his subjects as well. He must have made a pact with Saladin, it's the only thing that makes this all make any degree of sense. Even though Saladin is a man that he can not trust and in so doing, Angelus consigned his future to a path that is impossible for him to be entirely satisfied with. While he does not like our Emperor, he respects him and probably fears that Frederick will do just what I implied.

Aldrich was impressed. The passive, frail looking man had just intimidated one of the most powerful men in the world. He couldn't help but smile.

Chapter 22

Frederick winced as he dismounted. He'd never allowed his servants to hold his stirrup as so many nobles did, but perhaps it was time to swallow his pride and ask for the assistance. The ironic thing was that Frederick was certain the majority of those who demanded that their servants perform such tasks was because of pride. His pride forced him to continue mounting and dismounting alone, despite the pain it caused him, while theirs made the practice demeaning.

The lower legs and hooves of his charger were speckled with mud from the recent rain and he made a mental note not to slip in the stuff as he made his way to the group of people awaiting him outside of Aldrich's command tent. Such considerations had to be made when one reached the age he was. There was a time when he would have walked through this mud without a second's thought.

As Frederick approached the group of men, he attempted to identify the individuals as best he could while simultaneously navigating the treacherous ground. He made out Ahren, Sir Aldrich Kortig's second standing in the center while a giant of a man stood to his right. Frederick didn't have to see the face to know that that was Rothschild, one of his Imperial knights. To Ahren's left was a greying man standing as straight as a sword blade, his posture gave him away as Hoch, a senior Imperial knight who had proven his loyalty time and time again. A boy stood close behind Ahren with the Imperial eagle and Aldrich's boar hanging proudly from a long banner pole.

The sounds of the army as it added it's massive numbers to the comparatively tiny force of Aldrich's two hundred knights created a general din. Noise that threatened to over-power the senses. Individual sounds were hard to make out among the cacophony that infiltrated the Emperor's ears.

The men waiting, patiently, for him to approach dropped in unison to one knee. "No need for that. Get up." He called, motioning for them to rise. Even the boy had knelt while holding the banner pole. The loyalty that many warriors gave so generously, impressed him. Very few of his nobles could ever be convinced to show this kind of fealty and yet those who profited least from his rule were the most loyal. The men lifted themselves from the mud, a wet sucking sound accompanied the movement as knees were pulled free from sloppy clay. These men would die, if not for him, then for the idea of the Empire, and if not for that then for God. No matter their reasons, he could trust these men to do their duty. A simple act of kneeling in the mud was not what proved their dependability. Frederick was far too old to be so naïve as that. The men had a character that he could sense. He was good at judging men's character. These were the sort of men that Frederick was most comfortable with. Men like himself.

Unlike many of the prancy farts who reluctantly dismounted behind him, with help, into the mud, these men in front of him were warriors. They fought for God. They fought for glory, justice, honor, but most importantly, they fought for him.

Occasionally Frederick wondered if they fought for Aldrich instead of for him, but as he saw them lift themselves from the mud with pride in their eyes, he was reassured of their loyalty to him despite their love for their general.

"I had to hurry for I feared that you and your two hundred would take Constantinople to rescue Aldrich and get me excommunicated in the offing." Ahren allowed his teeth to show in an appeasing smile while those around him laughed audibly at the notion.

"The thought had crossed my mind." Ahren said.

"I'll be honest, I don't recall it ever having crossed mine." Obert said from behind Ahren.

Frederick laughed.

"Obert. You never cease to speak your mind. Good to know some things stay the same. Ever since we found your scrawny chicken legs in Italy, you've never failed to let us know what is in that head of yours."

Conrad of Swarzinberg and Duke Otto Wittelsbach finally picked their way through the mess and had drawn up behind Frederick to stand with the emperor and the rest of the nobles who had been invited to this meeting. He heard the Duke subtly yet impatiently clear his throat, a clear sign that the overweight Duke did not enjoy standing in the mud.

"Ahh excuse my rudeness. May I present Prince Geza of Hungary. He and his army has committed themselves to this cause." Frederick motioned for Geza to approach, past the frustrated and soggy Duke. Ahren's group saluted the Prince when he approached.

Frederick was not required to make introductions. Especially not to men of so low a station.

The Duke sighed as Ahren and the rest made uncomfortable salutations to the prince. They weren't used to prolonged involvement with high nobles.

Frederick smiled to himself at the Duke's discomfort behind him and decided his own discomfort could be prolonged for a little longer and continued making lengthy and tedious introductions of the nobles to Ahren and the surrounding men. After the fifth such introduction he finally decided that the Duke had had enough, indeed the obese man stood with his hands on his lower back, attempting to relieve some of the constant pressure he must feel there. Frederick's own back was sore, but couldn't resist taking it a step further.

"This, is Ahren, Sergeant to Sir Aldrich Kortig. He is a brave man and has proven his worth on the battlefield time and time again in my campaigns in Italia."

Ahren bowed his head in recognition of the high praise.

"It was on one such campaign that Aldrich found his second Sergeant, Obert." Frederick said,

Obert bent in half at the waist in a fluid bow, obviously made difficult by the armor he wore. The movement was foreign to the soldier, and he lost his footing in the slick mud, but escaped total humiliation by placing a gloved hand in front of him to halt a certain headlong plunge. He stood, chagrined, and shook the clay from his hand.

Frederick smiled at the failed attempt at a regal gesture but kept from laughing...barely.

He introduced Rothschild and Hoch then began walking towards the tent once more. "Now that we know one another, let us find a seat out of this dreary weather, and I'll ask Ahren to fill us in on what happened to Aldrich and our envoys." He said.

Ahren, Obert, Hoch and Rothschild moved to the side to allow the Emperor to enter the command tent.

Frederick sat as the rest of the men filed in. Chairs were a precious commodity in war and the lack forced most of the men to stand. Wittelsbach was a little forceful in his acquisition of a chair among polite company, but Frederick decided that the Duke wasn't entirely to blame as he had had to stand far longer than was comfortable for a man of his girth. The pain in his own back was such that he had to make a conscious effort not to squirm on the hard wooden chair.

Ahren told an efficient account of the entourage's journey after it left the army. He told of the unwillingness of traders or markets to sell their goods, a situation that worsened as they neared Constantinople. He gave a detailed description of the attempted ambush and the Imperial knight's resounding victory in the engagement. He told of the kidnapping of Aldrich, and the rest of the dignitaries, by the Byzantines. Ahren recounted the murdered squire and the attempted murder of another. Ahren ended by describing how the populace of Philipopolis had fled ahead of the army.

"The population does not seem to appreciate our presence, although not outwardly hostile, they are very reluctant to deal with us or provide information." After Ahren had finished, the tent was silent, waiting for their leader to speak.

Frederick raised himself from the chair, the thing hadn't brought the expected relief to his sore back and decided it was better to stand. He thought better on his feet, anyway.

"It is obvious now that we have been betrayed. I received Isaac's uncle, Alexios, in Nish a week ago and he promised me, yet again, markets, trade, and safe passage, provided that our intentions are peaceful." Frederick noticed several nods. The visit was well known among the leaders of the army, but the subject of their discussion was not. "I have yet to see any help," He continued "indeed, what I have seen has been far less than helpful. When I had mentioned the deception of our guides and numerous ambushes such as the one you described thus far, Alexios feigned innocence. He then informed me that Angelus was marching against the Serbians and that we should be wary of any attacks from that quarter. We shall be prepared for any attacks, though I doubt they will come from the Serbians.

Frederick turned to Ahren and the rest of the leaders of the Imperial knights and said. "I have divided the army into four divisions. My son will be in charge of the advance guard." He turned to the Duke of Swabia who acknowledged the honor and responsibility placed on him with a nod to his father. "The Hungarians and Bohemians have taken charge of the second. The third will be led by the Duke of Dalmatia" A tall man with long blond hair stood, and crisply saluted, pounding his fist on his chest. If Frederick hadn't known better he would have thought that the Duke was a glory-hog, but he knew that the Duke was only displaying the rigid formality that guided the man's every action, which is why he now led a fourth of the army of God.

"The fourth will be my own honor guard, of which you," He indicated the leaders of the Imperial knights. "and Aldrich, will be a part of. Count Rupert of Nassau's company will be my division's standard bearer. News that I'm sure will please the Count when he learns of it. With those preparations and open communication and wide scouting, I'm certain we can thwart any attack that the Byzantines can devise." Frederick shifted slightly, trying to relieve tension on some sore joints. "The army is sure to go into upheaval once news of the envoy's capture becomes general knowledge. Try to keep a hold of your men. We don't want to start an all-out war if we can help it. Keep the forays for supplies under strict observance to the rules of chivalry."

He glanced up at Ahren and asked "Any word from them?" referring to the captives in Constantinople.

Ahren took half a step forward again and appeared even more formal than normal as he responded.

"Reports from contacts within the palace say that they are being treated well, if not granted liberties to do much of anything. They are prisoners, but are not being kept in the dungeons as one would expect, if they had been kept there we would have been able to contact them. Perhaps that is why they have been afforded their own quarters in the palace. We haven't, yet, been able to acquire the help of any within to make contact with any of the members of the envoy, and we haven't dared approach the city with the few numbers that we had to parlay with Angelus as we would, likely, gain little and he would gain prisoners."

Ahren bowed his head slightly and stepped back to where he had been standing again, waiting for their leader to speak.

Frederick nodded.

"Thank you Ahren. Angelus hopes to keep us off balance as long as he can, wondering if he is friend or foe, hoping to put down our guard. I warned Aldrich of the possibility of the Emperor's betrayal before he left, but I hoped that I was over-reacting."

Frederick stopped and gave a slow, weary shake of his head. His soul would be responsible for any harm that would befall the group of dignitaries despite the warning and he knew that he had plenty already weighing against him.

"I have already begun corresponding with the Serbians and the Bulgarians." He said. "They have been increasingly unsettled with Angelus's rule and with their support, we may be able to pressure Angelus to capitulate."

There were thoughtful expressions around the tent, and several nods of approval.

As the meeting continued, pages were sent scurrying with messages, plans were discussed, and battle tactics were drawn up in the event that they were caught off guard and forced to defend their current position. Frederick believed that preparation was a key to victory, and he prepared for everything he could. It was determined that the army would need the city to maintain the army for any prolonged stay, so plans were laid for taking it if the inhabitants were 'reluctant' to accommodate them. The whole army would not fit inside the city, however, so plans for temporary defenses around the outer perimeter of the camp were also drawn up.

Frederick was pleased to see that Ahren and the knights had already made preparations for themselves and were working on expanding the defenses to prepare for the rest of the army.

Frederick left the general planning of the camp and other tactical matters to his generals. He himself was well versed in strategy and war, but he accepted that there were those that were more talented in the art than he, and he gave those men the autonomy that they needed to be efficient.

As Frederick listened to these warrior leaders, he couldn't help but miss his most trusted of generals and wondered how he fared in captivity.

Chapter 23

Word had spread of Hagan's defense of the maiden despite his embarrassment. He felt, after the incident was over and he had calmed down, that he had acted rashly and shouldn't have rushed into the situation. The outcome had been a positive one for him, but it easily could have gone a different way. The thought that if he had lost would have meant horrible injury or even death made him shudder.

He mentioned how he felt to Obert who said that battle is always a risk, but the decision to fight in such situations has long been a part of us. "trust your instincts" he said "but temper those with this" stabbing a finger into Hagan's forehead. Over-all Obert was pleased with Hagan's performance. It occurred to Hagan that Obert had probably hoped for such a situation to test him in, a chance to see how he would do in an armed fight that was somewhat controlled. After all Obert would have helped him had he needed it, wouldn't he?

When Ahren found out he seemed more interested in the other man's actions than Hagan's. Ahren made it clear to Hagan that what he did was completely honorable, but his anger at Gerhard's disgraceful actions clouded any praise he attempted to give to Hagan. Ahren made a report of the situation to Emperor Frederick himself and based on Obert's recommendation and Hagan's account of the events, the ugly man was disbanded from the Imperial order of knights. What's more Hartwin, Gerhard's friend in the alley, had to do sentry duty for two weeks straight. Obert said it was a minor punishment, but Hagan hoped that Hartwin wouldn't hold a grudge. The last thing Hagan wanted was an angry knight looking for revenge.

The rest of the knights slowly stopped giving Hagan pointers as he passed them on his daily runs, and they instead began simply nodding to him. It was a subtle change, but Hagan finally felt more accepted by the knights as something other than just a servant. For as long as Hagan had been a squire he hadn't felt much different than he had working in the fields. Sure he was treated with considerably more respect by the average person, but among the knights he was still the inferior worker. A tool to be used, then forgotten until it was needed again. Well, he wasn't really forgotten. He was always doing something, but most of the time it was some horrible task that any self-respecting tool wouldn't be caught dead doing. It was expected of course, even welcomed as he attempted to be the best squire he could. Yet he yearned for more. He knew that becoming a knight was too much for him to ask for, that was something that was well outside his reach. He wanted to be better. He wanted to do more. His thoughts had started down this road more and more of late.

Obert and Ahren now had Hagan running. Not running errands or messages, just running. He couldn't really understand it. He had started simple, only a few miles, but slowly his endurance grew and he was expected to run further and further.

His runs now circled the city since the army decided that since the people moved out, they might as well move in. Hagan approached a familiar puddle that stretched across the path and he braced himself for the effect that the cold water would have on his already damp skin. The air was cool, and the wind was blowing but the run had heated him, and after the initial shock, the water felt good.

Ahren insisted that he run the same amount of laps as he had before the army had arrived, never-mind that a lap around the city was five or six times the size of the camp. Hagan had doubted his own ability to accomplish the daily exercise with the increase, but to his surprise he not only did it, but he began to enjoy it.

Except for the occasional sharp pinch from his chainmail shirt as it pulled the hair on the back of his neck, his runs were tranquil. That was another addition that Ahren insisted on. Hagan had to wear his armor and sword. Ahren said that he needed to learn how it would be in battle so as not to be overwhelmed at the offset.

Hagan's breath steamed out like a blacksmith's bellows as he rounded the last leg of the run. He had pushed himself hard and was proud of the result. He'd made good time and couldn't help but give a wide smile of satisfaction to Obert as he came to a stop in front of him. His breath was coming out in gasps and he inclined his body forward in an attempt to breathe easier. Obert sat sliding a stone over his sword blade and didn't even lift his eyes from his work.

"What took you so long? The armor still needs cleaning. In this weather it will rust up on us in no time."

Obert lifted his sword and looked down the blade edge as he spoke.

Hagan's sense of personal triumph sank and for some reason the simple statement from Obert had caused a flood of anger to crash against him. Obert was guilty of giving similar commands to Hagan on a daily basis, but this one seemed almost like an insult to Hagan's intelligence.

It didn't matter how much it rained, there was no armor in the world that needed that much attention. Hagan knew that it was a way to keep him busy as the army waited for what Ahren called "the politics of war" to end.

Hagan knew that thanks to the Byzantines he had to clean armor more than normal, and perform a thousand other chores, just to pass the time and that was enough for him to want to assault Constantinople. He understood that thanks to the halt in the army's progress he was receiving training that most squires never received. Some squires were never given a sword, let alone the training to use it. When battle came, they just had to make their way the best they could, and according to Ahren most of those don't make it past the first skirmish. But still, this would make the second time in as many days that he had to polish that armor. In order to be part of Aldrich's retinue one had to do his part, and for Aldrich that included knowing how to fight.

Now that they had re-joined the army Hagan tried to mingle with the other squires more. He wasn't sure what he wanted from them. Maybe a friend, maybe someone his own age that he could talk to. Complain together about their shared troubles. He couldn't complain to Manfred, Carl, or Horst because they were the source of at least half of his chores. Obert and Ahren were even harder to approach with a normal conversation. In his mind, Hagan was still just a commoner they found in the field. While they were Lords in service to the Emperor himself. At that moment, however, Hagan's frustration strained against his sense of decorum.

He untied the leather laces at the neck of his chainmail and lifted the heavy garment up over his head. He knew better than to throw it on the ground, no matter how mad he was he knew better than to make that mistake, but tossed it on the log they used as a bench instead.

Obert glanced up at Hagan for only a moment, but it was enough for him to see the frustration on Hagan's face.

"What's the matter? You'd rather go back home and farm? Did you think this was going to be easy?" Oberts' voice was soft but serious and Hagan wasn't sure if he expected an answer or not. Either way, the questions succeeded in making Hagan feel foolish. He was still frustrated, but in those few words Obert had eroded Hagan's sense of indignation considerably.

Silence followed the questions for a space of time giving Hagan the impression that they weren't merely rhetorical.

Hagan felt the furrow between his brows soften and he sighed. He almost said the first thing that came to mind, a reaction to his emotions and frustrations, and undoubtedly unwise. He paused and attempted to cover his hesitation by adjusting his sword belt and scanning the log for the smoothest spot to sit.

He tried to push the emotion to the back of his mind as he ordered his thoughts.

"Sometimes I think of home and long to return, but all of those imaginings include me as I am now, or as I will be, not as I was. I can't imagine myself living the life I was to live before that day," Hagan hesitated again and looked up at Obert to judge his receptiveness before continuing. Obert was attentive at least so he continued. "I find this life more difficult in ways."

Obert's brow developed a questioning furrow of his own. "How so?" Obert said.

There wasn't impatience or condescension in his voice, just genuine curiosity. Obert, like most knights and squires, never had to do back-breaking commoner work to survive and therefore wouldn't know the difficulties of that life and could not compare the two. The revelation didn't seem to surprise him so much as pique his interest.

"There was an end to the work in the fields." Hagan explained. "We went home at night, and Adelfried allowed us the Sabbath to ourselves." Hagan wondered if he had said too much.

"I don't mean to complain my Lord. Forgive me. I'll go fetch the armor now."

Hagan moved to rise, but Obert reached out and put a hand on his shoulder.

"Perhaps we've pushed you too hard. We wanted you to be prepared for what is to come. War is upon us, on all sides in fact, though difficult to see. Ahren and I attempted to keep you busy to help keep you focused. Being a retainer of Aldrich's puts you in a difficult situation. You were older than most squires when they start, and Aldrich is the Emperor's best field commander. You will be expected to fight, if need be, and survive."

Hagan had known that Aldrich was a trusted General, but he sensed Obert's misgivings about his probability of survival. According to Obert's tone, Aldrich would be in more danger than what Hagan assumed he would be. For some reason he had expected the General and his retainers, himself included, to sit back and kind of oversee the fighting. He suddenly felt unsure of himself. The months of training and conditioning, even the fight in the alley had given him confidence in his abilities. Confidence that was perhaps unfounded. If he was thrust into battle tomorrow, he wondered how he would react. He somehow doubted that he would last very long. He wasn't completely naïve of battle. He remembered the attempted ambush at the river. While that engagement had been completely one-sided, he could see the results of the violence in his mind's eye. Bloody bodies, gore and the smell of awful that had caused him to retch. He suddenly felt like going for another run.

Obert saw the worried expression on his face.

"You are already better prepared than most of these poor bastards." He indicated the tents surrounding them and continued.

"I suppose we all need a rest every now and then. Why don't you take the rest of the day for yourself?"

Hagan felt foolish. Somehow Obert had turned Hagan's emotions upside down. Moments ago he had been ready to give Obert a verbal lashing. Now he felt like he should apologize for his immature behavior, and yet the excitement he felt at the idea of doing what he wanted for the whole day gave him pause. He went back and forth; the guilt struggling against the excitement. He looked up to see Obert looking at him with a question in his eyes.

"Did you not hear me? You're free. Go."

Hagan stood and picked up his mail shirt from the log and turned to Obert.

"Where's the rest of it?" He said, holding up the armor.

Obert's perpetual smirk turned into a full smile and he shook his head slightly. "over there." He said, pointing toward a pile of mail shirts and helms that reached past Hagan's knees. It looked like armor from more than just Aldrich's retainers and Hagan sighed as he picked up an unfamiliar helm.

"I'm not sure how this is going to help me stay alive, but I trust you."

If Obert wanted to play the guilt card, then he could do the same. He bent again and picked up as much as he could carry, careful to keep his worn tunic between his skin and the metal links of the shirts that would pinch his skin like ants if given the opportunity. He let his gaze fall on Obert before he turned and saw the little Italian smiling from ear to ear. He nodded to Hagan, and suddenly Hagan felt an overwhelming pride wash over him and despite the work that weighed heavily in his arms, he smiled slightly as he walked away.

"Hagan."

Hagan turned back to Obert and shifted some of the weight to keep from dropping it.

Obert lifted himself fluidly to his feet and sheathed the sword he had been sharpening.

"Leave the armor and come with me."

He began walking west towards the city square.

Hagan returned the armor to the ground where he'd just found it and hurried to catch up to Obert.

The city's shops and homes housed much of the army, but it was far too big for all of the soldiers to find refuge from the cold, windy weather. As a result, tents were arranged in semi-practical order throughout the city. The square was packed with dirty white canvas as was every dead-end alley and street. Pennants showing the various houses comprising the army's nobles waved in the breeze, where only months ago, shop signs hung.

The Emperor, in his wisdom, assigned groups of men the onerous task of removing rubbish from designated spots throughout the city where soldiers left it in smelly heaps, and cart it out of the city.

Hagan and Obert came to one such pile and disturbed a rat from its foraging. Despite the Emperor's rubbish carts, the shear number of people in such a tight location caused the piles to never really go away which gave the rats consistent locations to find food.

The rat turned its head and hissed loudly at Obert as he came closer. It hunched protectively over its find, a bone with a little putrid meat hanging from it.

Obert kicked at the vermin as he passed but it merely crouched lower.

Suddenly Obert's sword shot out and took the rat's head off.

Otto Wittelsbach, the rotund Duke from Bavaria, emerged from the building in front of them and began picking his way across the muddy street with the greatest of care. He was followed by six other men in expensive clothing. Wittelsbach reminded Hagan of a stalking heron, not for its beauty and grace but because his head swayed back and forth as he attempted to see past his belly while negotiating the puddle-strewn street. He stood for long seconds at a time on one foot, hands outstretched for balance which only added to the visage.

Obert paused and moved to the side to allow the Duke and the other nobles to negotiate their way past more easily. After the entourage had passed, Hagan noticed that Obert's gaze followed them down the street, a pensive expression on his face. He abruptly turned and began walking again in the direction they had been before.

It wasn't long before Hagan heard the thunderous gallop of hooves and the crash of metal. They were approaching the center of the town. The place where the market had been set up before. Only instead of a slew of vendors hawking their wares there was a list. A long fence, meant to separate and guide two opposing knights as they charged towards each other, dominated the center of the town square. Hagan sucked in a breath as he saw two knights in the middle of a mounted contest. Each of the warriors had a sword and the muscle to wield it. Although one knight was much larger than the other the advantage that he enjoyed was not readily apparent to Hagan.

Each swing resulted in a crash of steel that made Hagan clench his teeth. He knew from experience that, although armoured, the knights felt much of the blows that found purchase.

Hagan had, of late, been made to spar fully armoured so as to familiarize himself with the added weight. He felt like a lumbering bear in the gear, no a bear could see, he couldn't.

These men had clearly grown used to fighting in the garb, and what's more, they could do it on horseback. He noticed that the men didn't even have hold of the reigns. They guided their mounts with their knees which was made all the more impressive by the speed with which the beasts responded. Each knight swung, blocked and circled their mount for better position without a break in the fight. Each move and countermove had long ago been established in each of the fighter's minds. Neither seemed to have to think about what they were doing, they just reacted.

Hagan was so enthralled by the fight that he didn't realize that Obert had continued walking while he stood, mouth agape, staring at the spectacle. Hagan ran to make up for his curiosity and caught Obert just as he came to a stop next to Carl and Horst.

"Ah, Obert, Hagan. You made it in time to see Rothschild be humbled." Horst's smile led Hagan to believe that he didn't truly believe it would happen, but hoped that it would.

"I thought I recognized that mounted bear. You mean that someone actually dared spar with him? Must have been the only way to shut him up. Pray tell, who is it that I cheer for?" Obert said, turning his attention to the fight.

"Prince Geza. He is new and didn't ignore Rothschild's boasting as the rest of us do." Carl said.

Hagan was even more intrigued. It was rare that such a contest was seen by the likes of him. Geza was a Prince and Rothschild was one of the Emperor's most trusted knights. And as he looked around the courtyard it seemed that the rest of the men felt the same way as all eyes were on the two mounted combatants.

The bigger of the two was obviously Rothschild then, and the smaller man outfitted with the black shield was Geza. Rothschild let loose a barrage of overhead swings meant to weaken his opponent's defenses, when in point of fact it only seemed to weaken Rothschild. As Hagan watch the bear-like man's strength flagged. And he only barely protected his head from a reprisal swing from the prince.

"He's tired." Hagan said.

"Not quite." Obert said

Hagan was confused.

"He looks tired to me." He said after seeing a couple more half hearted swipes at the prince's head.

"Looks are often very deceiving."

Obert seemed sure of himself. Hagan looked past Obert at Horst who only shrugged and made a drinking motion with his empty hand.

Hagan laughed.

Obert only smiled but kept his eyes on the fight.

"Laugh if you want, but I'd say you will see what I mean in two or three more moves. He's drawing him in."

Hagan returned his attention to the courtyard. He thought he understood what Obert was saying about being drawn in now. During the whole contest Rothschild had been using his longer arms to force the prince to reach to strike at him. But now, with Rothschild's strength seemingly gone, Geza had pulled up closer to him and was striking at a more comfortable range. If Rothschild wasn't as fatigued as it appeared then being that close to the giant was dangerous indeed.

Suddenly Rothschild's shield shot forward with surprising strength and speed. The edge of it caught Geza straight in the visored helm.

Exclamations of surprise escaped the crowd of on-lookers.

Rothschild followed up the shield with an overhead swing which could have killed the prince, blunted sword or no but instead it was met by Geza's shield.

Remarkably Geza had reacted instantaneously despite the blow to his helm, and now Rothschild lay wide open.

Geza took advantage and struck hard with a side-swing that caught Rothschild's helm with all of the considerable force behind it.

The big man reeled backward in the saddle and lost his balance as his mount sidestepped.

The crowd was full of gasps followed by stunned silence, then applause. Hagan was amazed that anyone let alone someone so much smaller than Rothschild could have maintained his seat after such a blow, and yet he not only maintained his seat, but followed through with a decisive strike to the side of Rothschild's helm. The giant of a man leaned far in the saddle. The increase in pressure from his right knee steered the horse in the wrong direction, and Rothschild ended up on the ground, cursing.

Obert gave out a loud sharp bark of surprised laughter that was in contrast to the crowd's stunned silence.

"It appears I was not the only one to see Rothschild's play coming." he said.

Rothschild stood and removed his dented helm with some difficulty and cursed more. He had an upper lip that was seeping blood and a cheek that was already beginning to swell. He spit blood from his mouth and shook his head in disbelief. Slowly the angry look on his face faded, and he looked on as Geza climbed down from his horse and removed his helm which was also dented. The men clasped arms and complemented each other on the fight.

It was a good fight, and Hagan was happy to have seen it. Business began to go back to normal around the courtyard-turned-training yard.

Obert turned to Hagan.

"Your skill with the sword has improved considerably. Even to the point that all that will further your skill is experience. Your skill on horse-back is better than it was as well, though I don't see how anyone could be worse."

Obert smiled slightly to take the sting off the comment. But Hagan knew he was probably being truthful.

"What we need to do now is put the two together. Fighting on horseback is the one thing that separates us from the peasantry. No offense."

He was on a roll.

"Follow me." Obert said and began walking off in the opposite direction. Horst and Carl took up the que behind Hagan. They came to a large complex of buildings some of which were legitimate stables, while the rest had been converted to be such.

Obert entered one building that looked like it had been originally intended to store textiles.

Obert walked to the back of the building, past several beautifully groomed warhorses. He stopped in front of a massive black horse that stamped the floor loudly and jerked his head up and down agitatedly.

"When Gerhard was disbanded, the order naturally retained possession of several of his mounts and it was decided that you should be given one of them as compensation for your trouble with the degenerate. This is Wighard."

Hagan was surprised to say the least. Wighard was a warhorse the like of which Hagan would put under a great knight like Aldrich or the Emperor himself. He was not a horse for a simple squire with no real battle experience or prestige.

Fear accompanied the surprise. His proficiency on horseback had improved dramatically, but he had never ridden a beast such as this, and he had had enough trouble just leading Ahren's and Obert's warhorses let alone riding them.

These animals were bred for one thing, battle. That purpose did not lend itself to a docile, malleable character.

Obert and the others must have noticed his hesitancy.

"Go ahead. Let him get a good smell of you." Carl said.

Hagan held his hand out, slowly, palm down, to the imposing animal's head. Wighard's nostrils flared and then pushed the air back out forcefully. The sound reminded Hagan of a blacksmith's bellow.

Woosh. Hot and wet on his hand.

Wighard tossed his head back forcefully and neighed. Hagan couldn't help but smile.

The horse was simply magnificent and despite Hagan's self doubt he couldn't help but feel an increasing thrill of excitement inside him. He brushed the horse's thick neck with his calloused hand. The black of the animal's coat was so deep and shiny that he could make out indistinct contours of himself in the reflection as if he were looking down at a dark pool of water.

The physical contact seemed to sooth his nerves as well as that of the horses, and soon Hagan realized that the thrill he had felt was building with each passing moment. Joy mixed with fear. He was more excited than he had ever been. When he became a squire, he was new to everything in his new life. That coupled with his sadness at having to leave his family detracted from the excitement of it all.

Now Hagan was ready for the challenge. He knew, now, that he could overcome these obstacles as he had so many others lately. Confidence that he never felt in himself before bloomed inside him.

Hagan looked at Obert "can I ride him?"

"Well, that is what they are meant for aren't they." Obert laughed.

Hagan saddled the huge animal himself. He had had plenty of practice after all, and on horses less accepting of his existence than Wighard seemed to be.

Hagan led the horse out to the makeshift list. The melee between two famous knights had brought many on-lookers and much of the crowd persisted. Half a dozen less interesting contests had sprung up around the list but no one paid attention to any one fight. He was hesitant to mount the battle horse with so many witnesses. His excitement warred with the fear. Obert, Horst, and Carl caught up to him. Obert smiled at Hagan and grabbed the stirrup and held it ready for the squire. The act, traditionally, was a sign of respect. As a matter of fact, Hagan remembered a story about the Emperor refusing to do so for the Pope which led to some fierce reprisals by the Pope.

Hagan was touched. The fear he felt was now gone. It had been losing ground in the battle against his joy, but now with this smile and simple act of respect from Obert, the fear retreated entirely. He swung the reigns up over the horse's huge head and grabbed its mane while simultaneously putting his foot into the stirrup and launching himself onto the beast. Wighard's entire body tensed with the action, but Hagan was ready for any rebellious behavior and the horse seemed to know that.

He gave the horse a little kick with both feet and felt the animal's muscles respond instantly. Wighard's rear hooves dug into the soft dirt of the list and Hagan had to check the horse's exuberance quickly before the horse could take control. After the show of authority the stallion jerked his head forward and down in one last show of defiance before settling into the ordered trot. He was beautiful. The mane furled in the cold wind and the prancing steps seemed to be Wighard's way of bragging.

Many in the crowd were now looking at Hagan and the beautiful horse.

Hagan felt the strength in the horse. He felt safer because of it. Minutes before, he had felt fear or at least was worried by the horse's shear strength, but now the opposite was true. He began to feel the strength added to his own.

The horse he had been training on was not this. This was different. Hagan seemed to understand this animal. Its power and determination was an extension of his own now. The excitement now was nearly palpable.

He turned a beaming smile at Obert who understood the inherent question in the action and signalled for Hagan to go ahead.

"Enjoy yourself, but don't get killed." Hagan heard Obert call after him.

He maneuvered himself and the war horse through a maze of carts and soldiers toward the outskirts of the city and the surrounding camp. Once he was passed the final sentries, he kicked Wighard and was ready for the explosion of power that launched them forward into a full run within a few lunges of the animal's powerful legs.

The wind, which had already been cold, was now bitter. He didn't care. He had never felt this fantastic in his life. He could feel the horse's stride and began moving with him. The feelings of terror he had felt in the battle at the ford was foreign to him now.

Of course he had started to become more accustomed to riding in the months since then, but the confidence he felt while riding Wighard had been instant.

Eventually both he and the horse became tired, and even the cold air was not enough to cool their overused muscles. Hagan slowed Wighard to a walk and turned the steaming horse back towards the city. They made their way back to the stables slowly. Taking their time. Getting used to each other.

He found that the stall for Wighard had been mucked already and fresh straw had been added. Hagan smiled and led the tired horse into the cozy stall and unsaddled him. He then picked up a handful of straw and brushed the horse dry while he drank from a fresh bucket of water that had also been conveniently left.

The action soothed Wighard, as well as himself. And as he often had in the past while doing this exact same thing, Hagan lost himself in thought. Only this time he thought of what he would accomplish, not where or who he had left behind.

When he was finally done, and could yet again see himself in the dark pools of the horse's side, Hagan left the stables, energized.

Chapter 24

Spatharios Photios looked through the clearing at the tents and tried to estimate the German's strength. He knew that they had totally occupied the city, and the camp extended far outside of the city's bounds. The number of soldiers was almost impossible to determine. Regardless, the host was impressive.

As a tactician he constantly thought of plans, strategies and contingencies during a battle. His experience made him believe that Emperor Angelus would soon ask for what options were available to him in dealing with the stagnant army. The army that lay sprawled before him. Leaching the land of its sustenance. An army this size was hard to feed. And even with all the city's resources and the surrounding countryside supporting it, this army would have to move soon, or suffer hunger. And when an army gets hungry, they become difficult to control.

Photios knew that the Germans would have to be on the move soon or their pestilence would spread.

"Spatharios!" a man called from deeper within the cover of the wood. Photios turned, annoyed at the volume of the call. These men knew little of stealth.

Photios crawled backwards a few strides to be more fully concealed by the foliage before lifting himself from the ground and walked, bent-over, toward the man. The man, a Basilikos Mandator or imperial messenger began to hunch and pretend to use caution as Photios had displayed the apparent need. The messenger's attempt at stealth was laughable.

Perturbed, Photios grilled the officer after removing themselves further into the wood, and away from any German eyes that might see them.

"What can I do for you Basilikos?" anger etched in his tone.

The messenger made a clumsy apology before hastily spilling out his message to the Spatharios.

At the conclusion of the message, Photios swore and the messenger, accepting that as permission to leave, fled back to his waiting horse a short walk from where they stood.

How was he supposed to observe and report on the enemy's disposition when he kept getting interrupted and his position compromised with all of these Mandators running to and fro.

The latest message was more useless than the last.

"Await further instructions" was the gist of it. Sure there were the customary slogans that made each bureaucrat feel more important than he actually was, but the message was essentially that.

"Await further instructions" wouldn't he have done that regardless of this messenger's existence?

And risking the integrity of the whole reconnaissance in the process.

Regardless of the message, Photios didn't want to "Await further instructions". He needed to move their camp to the other side of the river. His camp was too exposed where they were, what with the German soldiers needing to search further and further into the countryside to provide sustenance for its masses.

Sooner or later he would be spotted, and he assumed that the Germans wouldn't be too keen to the spying.

Photios looked out at the sprawling tents and specks of soldiers walking around the camp. The only Germans he had known were those that he fought with in the street upon bringing them to the palace. If they were anything to judge the rest by. There would be no stopping this force. Not even Constantinople with its high walls would stand against this well organized and disciplined force. Photios shrugged and turned his back on the scene. He had to find a more suitable location from which to observe the enemy.

There was a bustle in the camp, and Hagan awoke to the sound of horses and steel. His mind jumped to the worst. He threw back the blanket and was about to grab his sword and dash out of the tent but Ahren stuck his head in and said "time to go Hagan, get up and get those lazy louts up as well." motioning to Carl and Horst's still sleeping forms. "Make haste. Prepare for battle." then he was gone.

Hagan was stunned. He had a sense that he was dreaming, but this was far too real to be a dream. Horst groaned to wakefulness at a particularly loud clash of metal from outside the tent. Carl slept on, so Hagan hurried out of bed and shook him awake. Horst saw Hagan's worried posture.

"What's going on?" came his gravelly, sleep filled voice.

Passing torchbearers turned the inside of the tent into a warren of confusing sights and sounds.

Hagan fumbled with his breaches while answering the inquisition with what little he knew. After that the other two hurried with as much haste as Hagan exhibited. Were they being attacked?

This scenario felt different from the one, months prior that sent him out with Aldrich and his two hundred. It was night then too, but that is where the similarities ended. As Hagan exited the tent, sword and sheath in hand, all was an organized tumult. Men jogged holding torches. Some were set to the task of lighting the braziers that were staggered around the camp. Men-at-arms, pages, and even camp followers led saddled horses. Hagan looked over to see Ahren and Obert, helping each other lace up the backs of their armor.

Hagan dragged his chest to a suitable place for him to don his own armor out of the way of the passers-by. As Hagan dressed, he saw the wooden piece of bucket reflect firelight from the inside of his chest. The very piece that had finally stopped the path of the arrow as it had sped through that dark night when fear hung like a curtain. On an impulse he bent and slipped the stave into his boot.

Once Horst and Carl were out and readying themselves, Ahren addressed them all. "We have been assigned by the Emperor to lead an assault on a camp three miles distant."

"It's about damned time!" Carl blurted out. Interrupting Ahren, but gaining a nod of agreement from Ahren regardless.

"Yes, well," Ahren continued. "We will be striking with surprise and force. No need for stealth as anyone with eyes will see the torches. What we need now is speed. We hope to cross the bridge through the town and circle round from the northwest. Hopefully, they will not receive word of our movements until it is too late. Now mount up!"

It surprised Hagan to see all of their horses were there. A stable hand stood nearby holding the reins to Wighard. His coat reflected the torchlight ominously. He appeared to have dancing fires all around his body.

Hagan went to the horse and greeted him with a quick scratch and pat on the neck before swinging up into the saddle. Once they were all mounted, they followed Ahren and Obert. As they made their way towards the gates of the town. Men on horseback waited alongside the road. They saluted Ahren and Obert as they passed and then fell into the column as they rode. More men and horses lined the road once inside the town itself. Some Hagan recognized as being part of the original two hundred that set out with them and the emissaries. The clank of metal sounded as each one pounded his fist against his chest in a salute when they passed. There must have been around two or three hundred knights in total that joined the column. Once across the bridge in the town, Ahren and Obert increased the pace of the horses to a gallop and the column followed suit. On the north side of town the torches had not been lit, and they had to go off of the light of the moon to guide their journey. He trusted Ahren and Obert and so it had to be down the line. Each man had to follow the man in front. A horse could easily step in a hole and break its leg in this dark.

Hagan's throat clenched. And his heart was pounding in his chest, ears, head. He felt like he would pass out for a second. Then he caught himself and focused on his breathing, the sound of the horses and Obert's back. Would he ever be over this fear at the moment before a battle? He doubted it, but he hoped that he would.

Photios was awoke from a dead sleep as a Basilikos Mandator rushed into his tent. The messenger was out of breath and took several seconds to remember to bow to the Spatharios as he lifted himself to a sitting position in his cot.

"This had better not be another useless damned message Mandator!" Photios exclaimed.

The messenger lifted his head from the bow and spoke.

"no Saptharios. Not useless."

Hagan saw Ahren lift his fist, and he pulled Wighard into a walk and followed Obert as they steered the column off of the road. The terrain was instantly worse and Hagan found himself hoping that the enemy was not far.

What? How could he hope for such a thing?

Hagan looked past Obert now and saw, in the distance, a faint glow of campfires.

There it was, the camp.

As he watched, being careful not to stray from Obert's chosen path, he saw more and more light seem to spring to life in and around the camp.

They had been spotted.

Ahren turned to Obert, "we weren't fast enough! We will have to risk a charge."

Obert nodded and signaled for the column to fan out.

Hagan went from just behind Obert to being third to the right of Obert in a matter of seconds.

"No loot until all are dead!" Ahren yelled as he drew his sword.

On that que the company drew their swords.

Hagan followed their lead. Light from the moon and the camp ahead glinted on his sword. The sound of two-hundred swords being drawn in the dark of night was eerie. He realized that despite the cold; he was sweating, and that sweat made him shiver. Maybe it wasn't the sweat at all. His heart and breath was soon almost all he could hear.

Hagan had made progress with the sword. As a matter of fact, Ahren had said that despite his late start he hadn't seen an apprentice learn as fast as he had. Once Hagan got the basics down, the rest seemed to be intuitive. He could now read an opponent and judge which response was best without thinking. He and Obert or Ahren would spar each night and hagan had won several bouts. Sure, it was only a handful out of what seemed like hundreds, but he was still proud of the progress he was making. All of this still felt like too much. It was too soon for him to be fighting in an actual battle.

Hagan forced himself to focus. He closed his eyes for a few seconds and concentrated on nothing but his breathing and steadying his pounding heart. Just when he thought he had control of himself Wighard shifted and took a few steps.

Upon opening his eyes he realized that the contingent was several paces ahead and picking up speed. Wighard desperately wanted to join the charge and threw his head several times in protest.

Hagan finally steeled himself, and letting out a shaky breath, kicked Wighard into action.

He felt Wighard's strength propel them both forward at a remarkable rate. Hagan helped in the process as well as he could and he soon saw the distance close. The enemy's camp took on definition and details became visible.

Suddenly Hagan heard an unfamiliar wailing. It was a trumpet in the distance. From his vantage point, still behind the main contingent and higher up the hill, Hagan could see an enemy cavalry unit was marshalling on the right flank. He veered towards them, anticipating the main contingent to do the same. Light was just visible reflecting off of their armor and weapons. Wighard lurched suddenly and then sprung forward. An unseen depression in the field forced the war horse to try to compensate. The jolt made Hagan feel like he was flying and then, just as suddenly, as if he were being crushed by a giant. The force subsided as the horse regained some more consistent footing. Hagan heard, through the thrum and woosh of his own heartbeat and breath, a distant commotion. The sound of combat. Horses screaming. Hagan looked ahead and could see the enemy in front of him. They were not yet moving more to the center of the conflict, but instead, they were retreating. The commander must have decided that it would be useless to try a counter strike.

They were moving off at a relatively slow speed. They were obviously trying to remain as a group, to gather and save all the men that they could. Hagan was closing the gap at an alarming rate.

Spatharios Photios swore. His men had not assembled as quickly as they should to his call. Men still donned armor, ran for their horses, and generally acted as if this was their first call to arms. He had to do something.

"Sergeant! Continue to sound the retreat and move the men to a safe distance." The man pounded his chest and blew the horn again.

Photios kicked his horse back in the direction that he had just come from, toward the camp. They had been forced to leave everything due to the speed of the enemy's attack. The only reason his whole force was not annihilated was thanks to the man that he had cursed earlier in the day for his uselessness.

Photios turned his horse among the tents and braziers calling to his men for order and speed. He encouraged them and drove them when they needed it. Photios paused in the middle of a tirade and listened. Above the general tumult of his men he heard the unmistakable thunder of heavy cavalry.

He wheeled his horse toward the intimidating site of hundreds of indistinct cavalry charging down the hill towards the camp. Their armor reflected, now and then, the fire from his own camp as the force moved closer to them.

"For your lives men! Mount up!" He bellowed. "The enemy is upon us!"

By now there were an additional twenty or so men around him. He sent them off towards the waiting assemblage of the contingent to the South East of the camp. There were several of his men now trying to form some kind of a last-ditch defense against the onrushing onslaught. Photios knew that their efforts were ludicrously underwhelming and was proved right as the front ranks of german heavy cavalry plunged through the unorganized band of horsemen. Horses screamed and men groaned. Photios turned his attention back to the men he could save. Two more men had formed up on him. Only two. He motioned sadly for them to proceed ahead of him. "Go!" He yelled. Him and his standard bearer lingered for as long as possible before following the last of his men to escape the camp.

Hagan glanced around. Ready to allow those with more experience lead the charge.

No one was there.

Looking back at the camp he saw that many of the tents were on fire and burning with gusto. The light created silhouettes of the men and horses between him and the flames.

Hagan pulled Wighard to a stop.

Where were they?

Hagan swung the shield off of his back. It was hard to see who was friend and who was foe.

Men on horseback were coming out of the camp now piecemeal. He focused on individual riders and tried to distinguish them. Helmets! Their helmets were different! The helmets coming at him were much taller with a point. These must be the enemy trying to catch up to the main body that was retreating. He was in their way; he realized!

Hagan held his sword tight and wondered if he should move. He didn't think he was capable of fighting one seasoned warrior on horseback let alone several. But if he left, he would be a coward. Wouldn't he?

The decision had to be made, and it had to be made now. No! He would stay and fight. Besides, from their stance, they were more concerned about fleeing than about paying attention to what was in front of them. He could be a surprise.

Hagan was now committed. He kicked Wighard into anticipatory action. The horse bounded forward, ready to meet the danger, seemingly excited for it.

Hagan was on the first of the unsuspecting warriors in seconds. He flicked his sword out at the last second so as not to be noticed as an enemy too early on. He needed every second's advantage he could get.

The end of his sword wielded the entire momentum of him and his horse, as well as that of the opposing man. The force of the impact jarred his arm. Hagan was expecting it from his experience in practice. This was worse. His arm flew backwards and something threatened to tear the sword from his grip and then suddenly released. He had little time to recover. His next foe was upon him. Although it appeared that he, again, had not been noticed.

The next man was on his left and so Hagan swung his shield slightly to make room for a backswing. He had to time the impact right with his swing or this time it would twist him from the saddle.

The man had just glanced behind him and had a moment of complete surprise when he turned to see an enemy right in front of him.

Hagan's aim was true, and the man's face split in two, the top half coming off with the helmet as they passed.

His attention now fell on his next targets, two men on horseback who had seen the violence and were charging straight for him.

No time to turn. He readied himself

He could only fight one at a time. Hagan stayed on his original course until the last second and steered Wighard sharply to the left. The war horse responded immediately and managed to stay out from between the two cavalrymen, sliding past the man on the left and exchanging blows as they did so. Staying to the left of the two made it so He only had to deal with one sword at a time, but it also was on his unshielded side. A prolonged fight would be lethal for him since it would allow the second man to circle around and attack Hagan's unguarded side.

He got past the two men and kept his head on his shoulders, which was a major victory to Hagan. After the contact Hagan slowed, and spun Wighard, ready for another charge. The two opposing cavalrymen had done the same. Hagan could see the men much better with flames of the camp striking their faces.

They were angry! Faces contorted in rage. They must have known the men he had just killed. Or maybe they just wished to unleash all their frustration at losing the camp so easily.

Their faces lifted in unison and looked past Hagan momentarily. They swore something at Hagan and turned to flee. Hagan glanced behind him and saw His compatriots charging through the camp.

Hagan kicked Wighard into action.

The magnificent beast flew over the familiar ground toward the retreating men.

Three short horn blasts. A signal Hagan recognized. It meant to press the attack.

Now with support, Hagan was more than willing to give the attack.

Oh, what a few minutes of time will do to one's perspective, he thought.

Wighard was catching the horsemen and Hagan was tempted to reign in slightly. He didn't want Wighard being too tired to fight.

He began to put some opposing pressure on the reigns, but Wighard pulled back. He wanted his head. He needed to run, to catch the enemy.

The horse's confidence fed his own, and so he gave the horse his head.

Wighard pulled ahead with no insistence from Hagan. They pulled up on the left of the enemy, only this time they were facing the same direction.

They had caught the enemy, and in full flight Hagan swung his sword down on the terrified horseman's back. With a cry the man swung off of the horse and pulled the path of his steed into that of his companion's. The man that fell became an obstacle for the other horse which lunged over the man. The tumult forced the other from his saddle as well. The horse, upon landing gave a horrible scream of pain and crashed to the ground, writhing in agony.

Hagan passed the scene and swung Wighard back around after they had passed. He could see now, that his fellow Germans were still half a minute away at the least and in battle, Hagan could have died a half a dozen times before they reinforced him.

Hagan was breathing hard, as was Wighard.

He reached down and patted the horse on the side of the neck. They had survived. And what's more, they had succeeded. Hagan was officially experienced in battle.

A feeling of accomplishment welled up inside of him. But then he saw the writhing horse and the writhing man. His sense of accomplishment seemed disturbing to him all of a sudden.

The horse had broken its front legs when it had landed in another one of those depressions after jumping over the writhing man's comrade. The man that writhed and screamed had a grotesquely broken leg as well, but the real horror was what his unsheathed sword had down to his face when he landed on it. He would not survive. But for some reason Hagan had an impossible time convincing himself to end the man's life.

Hagan dismounted and swung the shield back onto his back.

His conscience made him walk to the horse first. The animal was struggling so much that it was difficult for him to get close. He worked his way around to the head of the animal. A banner lay on the ground, possibly lost by the retreating company. Hagan picked it up and placed it over the animal's head. The darkness seemed to help it calm down. Enough so that he was able to get close enough to stand above the huge chest as is rose and fell. Steam came off of its body in long, streaming clouds.

His sword felt heavy as he lifted it up high with both hands and brought it down with all the force he had into the beast's chest, where it's heart should be. There was a tremendous shuddering scream that cut short as the animal's life ebbed away.

Hagan pulled the sword back out of the steaming corpse.

A handful of German knights on horseback approached. Hagan thought he recognized two of them, but couldn't remember their names.

They looked down at him and the surrounding carnage.

"Are those yours too?" one man asked. Pointing to the left.

Hagan looked. They had ended up surprisingly close to where he had initiated contact with the enemy.

He saw now that where he had struck the first man, was across the chest. The mail had attempted to save the man, but the force of the blow had broken through it and left a wide gruesome wound that the man did not recover from.

Hagan nodded.

The man on the ground had regressed to a low whimper that was somehow worse than the screaming.

"Shut that poor bastard up will you, Harman." The man said to the knight on the end.

The man only grunted in response and dismounted. He walked over to the suffering man and ended his life with a casual hack. It looked as graceful as chopping wood.

The man's plumed helmet fell free from the knight, the head, presumably, inside.

Hagan flinched at the action, but the silence was heaven.

Harman picked up the sword of the man that he had decapitated.

"This is one beautiful sword." Harman said.

"As if you knew beauty when it slapped you in the face. As a matter of fact wasn't her name beauty? You know the one that last slapped you in the face?" One of the knights jested.

Hagan walked back to Wighard. It was a testament to how hard the horse had run, or to his loyalty that he had not wandered at all once Hagan had left. The horse still held his head high. Proud.

Hagan scratched the horse's neck and hugged his nose. They had both done well. And now they got to walk away unlike these two.

The knights that had stopped were in the vanguard of the whole company.

One of the knights that Hagan recognized looked off at the retreating enemy, now far out of their reach.

The smaller eastern horses had proven that they had great endurance and they would outpace any pursuit at this point. In quick bursts, the larger war horses that the germans preferred could outperform, but not once they were past a certain distance.

"You have your bow with you? With your talent for carnage you could probably still bring down a few." the knight said.

Then Hagan remembered where he knew him from.

He was part of the unit at the ambush by the ford. He had also witnessed Hagan's barrage of three arrows into a retreating group of horsemen, a familiar situation.

"No," Hagan said. "I left it at camp."

A look of surprise brushed over another knight's face.

"Is this Sir Aldrich's protege? The one I have heard so much about?" The man had a slight accent.

"Aldrich's prote what? Use real words you damn fool!"

The knight known to Hagan only as Harman was back in his saddle now and smiling down at Hagan. Hagan was confused and felt uncomfortable. He felt like he was being teased.

Hagan tried to ignore the man by lifting himself into Wighard's saddle.

Harman continued his uncomfortable gaze.

Finally Hagan lost it. "What are you staring at?"

"A warrior who has proven himself beyond reproach this day. A good day." All the knights nodded in acknowledgment of Hagan's deeds.

Maybe Hagan was still frustrated by the stare, maybe he was still shaken by the suffering of his victims, either way he responded with a little more heat than he meant to.

"It wasn't a good day for them was it!" he said.

Most of the knights laughed. "No, I'd say it wasn't their best day!" one of them said.

But slowly they subsided as they noticed Hagan wasn't laughing.

"These men aren't Muslims! They are Christians! Why did they have to die? Politics!"

He was so angry. His face contorted. He felt like he would cry. He couldn't. That would be humiliating. The wave of emotion had broke upon him like a wave and threatened to founder his precarious raft of sanity.

The men grew somber. They couldn't return his gaze. Guilt, maybe, played across their down-turned faces.

Finally Harman spoke,

"It's always politics."

It took the unit several more hours of pilfering through the camp. Looting. It was their right after all. The men that abandoned this camp also abandoned their possessions that were in it. Possessions that could make their existence in this foreign land less precarious.

When Hagan had entered the camp, he was upset by the thievery.

Men scavenged the tents and came out with new cloaks, armor, and tack for their horses. Among a host of other things.

He found Obert and Ahren at the center of the camp. Obert wore a well made cloak that was fastened around his neck by a gold brooch.

Ahren had a new curved scabbard with a gold-inlaid knife handle sticking out of it.

Ahren saw Hagan first. The Five knights that had found him followed close behind.

"Hagan! I thought we'd lost you." Ahren yelled.

Obert looked up and grinned broadly.

They turned their horses toward him and closed the gap.

"Are you ok my boy?" Obert exclaimed as they got close enough to see the blood spattered across his face, and armor.

Hagan hadn't noticed that he was covered in the stuff.

He wiped at his own face and looked at his gloved hand.

The brown leather had a wetness that reflected red in the firelight.

"What happened?" Ahren asked.

His voice, a mixture of anger and concern.

Hagan explained his getting separated from the main force and explained his predicament in getting trapped between the two forces.

"He is talented." One knight said behind him.

Hagan cringed slightly at the compliment.

"There were four downed knights around him. One was carrying this."

Harman produced the sword for Ahren to see.

Early morning light was beginning to transfuse across the countryside and Hagan could see a heavy broadsword with great detail in the steel pommel. There were words etched with great detail in a language that Hagan had not learned the letters for. The engravings were flowing and there were designs that leant to the swords beauty but didn't take away from the efficiency. There were two jewels that were inlaid into the pommel. One on either side of each other. They were a blue-green color that reminded Hagan of a mountain lake in winter.

Ahren took the sword and looked at it in more detail. He handed it to Obert.

"Is this what I think it is?" Ahren said.

Obert took the sword and looked closely at the etched words, reading them.

Obert's eyebrows raised, and he slowly handed it back to Ahren.

"Yes, I believe it is. At least we know where the Spatharios went to." Obert said.

Ahren handed the sword to Hagan

"Unless I am mistaken, this belongs to you."

Hagan was hesitant to take the thing. He glanced over his shoulder at Harman. Harman merely smiled at him and nodded.

"Harman is the one that actually, uh finished him off."

"The victory was yours and trust me, you want to keep that sword. Take me to where you killed a leading noble of the Byzantine Empire and the First Sword lost his life." Ahren said.

Hagan blinked.

"What?" he sat in his saddle perplexed. "Who?" He stammered.

"The Spatharios of the Byzantine Empire. The First Sword of the Emperor's personal Bodyguard. I have met him. He is the one that escorted the emissaries to their prison. Photios was his name. At least unless I am mistaken. I need to see him, so we can inform the Emperor of your great act." Ahren smiled.

Hagan merely nodded and turned Wighard back in the direction from which they had come.

He led Ahren and Obert back out to the spot where he ended the horse's struggles.

Ahren and Obert took in the scene.

Hagan dismounted and led Wighard over to the headless corpse. Ahren and Obert followed suit and soon all three were standing around the body. With the additional light that the morning provided, Hagan could see that the man's armour was pristine. With his experience in polishing armour, Hagan respected the diligence needed in this set. The clothes were also of very high quality.

Ahren went to the helm and rolled it over with his toe.

"Ah, I see Hagan beat me to my revenge. This is him. This is Photios."

Obert picked up the corner of the cloak and pulled it back to reveal the expensive armor.

"You are rich now, Hagan." Obert said.

Hagan sighed and looked at Obert in an "I don't appreciate it right now" look.

"What? You are. Look at this armor. And the sword." Obert said.

Hagan just glowered at Obert. Still angry at the casualness of it all.

"It is what we do. It's how we survive. How else do you think most knights become knights, huh? They take it by the sword. Money is a part of this world. And if having it makes life easier? I want as much as I can get." Obert sighed and then continued. "You had better go catch one of those horses that you acquired so you can pack all of this stuff back with you."

Obert let the cloak drop back over the body before walking back to his horse.

Ahren was looking at Hagan now.

"I know how you feel. Killing shouldn't feel this meaningless. I get it, but the man is dead and you are not. He would have killed you had he had the chance. Do you believe me?"

Hagan thought of the contorted face in the firelight. The angry, unintelligible words that the man spewed at Hagan.

"Yes. He would have." Hagan said.

"Then take his spoils as penance. He won't be needing them."

Hagan finally conceded the point. He mounted up and went to retrieve the wandering horses. He was only able to catch two of the three that wandered the field. The third, probably the one that had slammed into Photios's horse, was in the wind. Far too gone to be tracked down and brought to heel in any reasonable amount of time.

Hagan returned to the spot where the corpses were and found that someone had removed the Spatharios's armor and clothing and had piled them up neatly next to a freshly dug grave. It gave Hagan comfort that at least they would be given burials.

He loaded up the spoils onto the trailing horses and set off toward the camp.

When he arrived, all were finalizing their own looting efforts and were gathering just to the northwest of the camp. Ahren and Obert nodded to Hagan as he came alongside them.

"Thank you for the help." he said to either or both of them.

They nodded.

"We don't do such gruesome tasks for everyone, so next time, you get to strip the corpse yourself." Obert said.

"And Bury it" Ahren added.

The words seemed harsh, but Obert's tone and the smile on his face made the strength go out of them.

Hagan smiled. It was the first show of happiness he'd shown that day.

Obert lifted the horn to his lips and sent two loud, long, blasts. The company gathered and formed in as Obert and Ahren turned their horses from the camp and rode back in the direction that they had come in the dark. Horst and Carl took up their original positions next to Hagan.

"What in good God's name happened to you!" Carl asked.

Hagan turned to them. Their faces were masks of shocked respect. Horst took in the blood on his face and armor, the sweaty horse, and the two that followed behind laden with booty.

"Looks like he found someone to fight." He said. A tone of sadness in his voice. "I will try to save some for you next time." Hagan said. The jab just came to him and was out of his mouth before he had even thought about it.

The two men's faces turned to surprise and then they both laughed. Carl reached over and slapped Hagan on the back.

"We would appreciate it, Hagan the mighty! We did not fare nearly so well as you." Carl said.

"Horst here nearly killed himself is all. I spent the whole time trying to get his horse off of him."

Hagan looked at Horst who didn't even attempt to deny it.

"What happened? Are you all right?" Hagan asked, concerned.

"Yeah" He said. "Didn't hurt really, sure I'll be sore in the morning, but when that damned horse hit that hole he flipped me off and then landed on my leg. Must have snapped his neck, because he was done. Not even a breath from him after. Here I am, just sitting there, waiting for my valiant hero to come rescue me, and all he did was curse and badger me for my stupidity. The same thing could've just as easily happened to him, I might add."

Hagan remembered Photios's demise.

"You were lucky." Hagan said.

"Lucky he had a good enough friend to come help him instead of going off and enjoying a good fight!" Carl interjected.

Horst rolled his eyes. "Will I ever live that down?"

The banter continued as they rode. The ride back seemed so different in the light of the morning sun. It seemed to take longer. The fear of whetting his sword on the stone of battle no longer hung over his head. He contemplated the night's events. Analyzed them. Played them over and over in his head until he was certain of the things he would have done differently and the things he was glad came about. He was glad that his training had kicked in. That he had not run from the fight, but instead charged, not just a single foe, but many. And above all, he was glad that he came out the victor.

Chapter 25

The smell of wet, and cold began to give way to the smell of smoke. They were getting close to camp now. The camp's fires and the torches of the night before left their lingering evidence on the surrounding countryside. There was even a subtle haze that hung low in the valley surrounding the river and town.

Upon crossing the bridge and making their way through the town, there were not as many men milling about. Not as many soldiers came and went.

Ahren and Obert noticed as well and flagged down a passing soldier.

"Where is everyone?" Ahren asked after returning a salute.

"Much of the army is massing to the South of the town." the man said.

"Thank you." Ahren said and turned to Obert.

The company made their way through the town and past the gates.

Ahren halted the company near the command tent and dismounted.

Ahren nodded to Obert and he as well dismounted with a grumble.

Ahren turned to Hagan next. "Bring the sword Hagan."

It caught him off-guard and had to move quickly to dismount and catch up with the two men as they entered the command tent.

Hagan had to blink several times and squint his eyes to help accustom them to the relative dark.

The tent had an old smell to it. Like the smell of many of the parchments and scrolls that Ahren gave him to practice his reading. There was the smell of sweat, probably himself, and dust. In the center of the tent sat the Emperor. His back was turned to them hunched over a scroll or parchment now.

The sound of scribbling reached Hagan's ears, he was probably giving orders of some kind.

Ahren said that that is why every good combat leader could read because often, things are lost in the verbal communication between messengers.

They waited patiently as the Emperor finished his scrawling and turned to them.

"And how went the battle?" His graveled voice croaked.

"They must have been warned of our approach. Upon arriving to the camp, the majority of the army had already mustered outside of it and were moving in a retreat, well out of range of our war-horses." Ahren said.

"We were able to catch many in their greedy attempts to save possessions or comrades. Around fifty were slain at our hands."

"How did we fair?" The Emperor queried.

"Lost two men Sire. Both in the charge on the camp. As you know it's tricky business crossing a dark field at full charge." Ahren said.

Hagan wasn't aware of the casualties. He supposed that with his own difficulty; it was only logical to assume that some would have an even harder time of it.

The Emperor nodded.

Ahren continued. "Hagan here was separated from the company and managed to kill four of the enemy, including the standard bearer and his liege lord Spatharios Photios, the presumed commander of the camp."

The Emperor grinned broadly and turned to Hagan.

"Indeed! A youth captured our first standard of the campaign! Outstanding young man, simply outstanding!" The emperor said, his voice no longer the hoarse croak it had been when they had entered. It seemed to have had life injected into it.

Obert removed the banner that Hagan recognized as the same he had covered the horse's head with as he ended its suffering and handed it to the Emperor.

He took it and again turned to Hagan. He lifted himself slowly to his feet and walked stiffly to Hagan. Was he supposed to kneel? He looked to Ahren for help. Ahren nodded and mouthed sword. Hagan slowly bent and knelt on one knee in front of the Emperor and as he did so he lifted Photio's sword in front of him. Offering it to the Emperor.

Hagan looked up into the blue eyes of the Emperor as he smiled down at him. Hagan wasn't sure what to say, but felt that he should say something.

"Sire, Accept the sword of Spatharios Photios, your vanquished enemy, as a token of my loyalty." Hagan said. It seemed right. Maybe. The old man still looked at him with quizzical eyes.

Hagan began to wonder if he did not hear him and that maybe he would have to repeat it all more loudly.

He was about to do just that when finally the Emperor spoke.

"My boy, you have done a great deed, one worthy of a boon from me. What would you have? If it be within reason," The Emperor chuckled softly to himself and continued. "I will grant it."

Hagan was astonished. He had no idea what to request. What if he asked for too much? But then what if he asked for too little. He thought for what seemed an eternity all the while one of the most powerful men in the world waited.

The anguished face of Spatharios Photios flashed into his mind unbidden. The thought made him queasy. Hagan looked up into the blue eyes once more. Eyes full of a rich life. Full of experience. Barbarossa had fought countless battles. He had certainly personally killed many people on the field of battle.

Hagan made to speak, but hesitated. The Emperor nodded his encouragement.

"I wish for nothing sire, save to continue being trained and serving Sir Aldrich." Hagan's voice sounded weak and almost pathetic to his own ears.

"Outstanding." Barbarossa said again but with an air of contemplation.

"You truly are turning into the perfect protege for Aldrich, pity I can't steal you from him. I'm afraid that is one man I respect too much to treat with such a treachery." The emperor's smile resumed its vigil.

"Very well. What is your name, boy?"

"Hagan Eggar Sire." He said.

"Very well Hagan Eggar you shall indeed continue your excellent training under these fine men's tutelage." The Emperor pushed a heavy purse into Hagan's hand.

"My lord, thank you." Hagan stammered out the words.

"Arise Hagan."

Hagan did so and then Barbarossa held the sword back out to him.

"You take this Hagan, I have far more beautiful swords than hands to wield them."

The smile stayed on his face as he turned back to Ahren and Obert. "An outstanding young man. Train him well." He said.

They both nodded their acknowledgment.

That business concluded; matters turned to the logistics of the army. It turned out that the Emperor was sending a large portion of the army to take a town called Berrhoe in official retaliation for the Byzantine's deception and capture of Aldrich and the envoys. Such an action could not go unpunished the Emperor had declared. He had to show force, if for nobody else than for his own men.

Since news of the Aldrich group's capture at the hands of the Byzantines became public, the army had been acting out and was becoming hard to control. They had begun taking villages and farmsteads in the surrounding area. There had even been a few castles that had fallen to the angry Germans.

Barbarossa's best option was to split the army and give them an objective that would be the right balance. Enough of a move that it would appease his own men, but not enough to set the Armenians and Serbians against him. He had wanted their help against the Empire that they were also fighting against. He had no desire to be the more threatening of the two.

They had ended up seated in the tent and Hagan got the impression that the Emperor felt the need to share his plans and devices with someone he could trust. With Aldrich and Chamberlain Markward imprisoned, he must have felt that the task had fallen on Ahren's broad shoulders.

Hagan bent in his seat and pulled out his stave. He looked at it thoughtfully and felt its comforting smoothness under his fingers.

The inside of the tent had grown comfortably warm and Hagan drifted as if he were on a raft in the middle of a lake. His head felt heavy.

The next thing Hagan knew Obert was standing above him shaking him awake.

"He may have a peculiar talent for killing people, but he does not have the same skill in conversation." Obert said.

The other two men laughed.

"We're done here." Obert said and offered him his hand.

Hagan looked around, startled. It all flooded back in and with it, embarrassment. He had fallen asleep listening to the Emperor speak. Of all the stupid things for him to do.

He quickly grabbed Obert's hand and let him lift him to his tired feet.

Hagan made his way out of the tent as quickly as his unsteady gait could take him. He still had the stave in his left hand.

Once outside, Hagan could see that it was still morning, but barely. His stomach grumbled upon the reminder of how long it had been since he had eaten. He could have asked the Emperor for a leg of mutton or even a nice roasted chicken, but no, he couldn't think of anything. What an imbecile he was. He had half a mind to go back into the tent and ask for something, anything. It didn't really matter what. Then He remembered the purse. He pulled it from his belt where he'd tucked it earlier. He'd forgotten all about it in the excitement of meeting the Emperor and then the subsequent discussion about tactics that had lulled his tired body into a dull complacency. He pulled the strings and opened the purse.

Gold glinted in the dark recesses! He'd never seen such wealth as this. He was rich! Well, maybe not compared to nobles, but compared to him he was certainly rich. Back home, this purse would mean never having to worry again. Him and his mother and sister could live comfortably for a good long time. Then there was the sword and armor and horses that he had just gained. His earlier unease about the battle was now completely gone.

Despite his frustration with himself over his non-answer to the Emperor, Hagan was delighted. He now had two new horses and an amazing suit of armor. For all intents and purposes, he was wealthy, and it had happened so suddenly that he still hadn't taken any time to think about how his life would change.

Chapter 26

Aldrich stared down at himself. At least he thought it was himself. The reflection that stared, sunken eyed, back at him didn't look like the man he had been a month ago. The scar stretched from just above his left eye down across it then formed a wide furrow down his cheek just missing his nose, thankfully, and split both of his lips. It finally ended as a pink scar on his chin. Altogether a gruesome thing indeed. The worst part were the lips. He had spilled more drink on himself since his wounding, a month ago, than he ever had in his infancy he was certain.

His face muscles pulled the massive scar in myriad different directions, each one forced crevices and cracks into the red and pink flesh where blood would begin to ooze once more. The stitches had been the only thing holding his face together for a while, and when they were removed he found that the increased movement in his face would break the tender pink scar open at the most inopportune times. Aldrich dabbed at one newly formed opening in his scarred face just as he heard the door to the main corridor open. He stepped out of his quarters and looked down the hallway, just as Chamberlain Markward and the two counts had done. A guard stood in the doorway.

Instead of entering fully and conversing with those within, as a civilized person would, he merely stood in the open doorway and yelled. "The presence of the representatives of the German empire is requested by, his eminence, emperor Isaac Angelus."

Aldrich glared at the guard. He hoped that his annoyance was fully transmitted to the man. Not just his annoyance with the man's casually rude demeanor, but his annoyance with the entire situation. His face for one. It hurt constantly and the fact that he was still here and not with Frederick across the Bosphorus was evidence of his failure.

His scowl seemed to have portrayed at least a portion of his frustration since the guard became noticeably uncomfortable under the gaze and took a step backward out of the doorway, trying, perhaps, to undo his abrupt intrusion. Still, the message was a good one. The emperor requested their presence. At this point Aldrich would have been happy with "demanded" but he "requested" their presence.

Only good could come from such a message, and from the look on Chamberlain Markward's face, he agreed.

Aldrich raised an eyebrow at him and instantly regretted it. He felt blood begin to well out of the wound above his left eye. He ignored it.

He started down the hall, passed Markward, Walram and Rupert as he made his way for the guard. The blood had found its way into his eye, and even now pooled there, hesitated. It took a great deal of concentration not to wipe the blood away.

"Return to the Emperor and inform him that we will make ourselves more presentable and be ready to meet him in an hour's time."

As Aldrich spoke the guard's forehead creased, and he stared at him with disgusted interest. Half-way through his statement, and as if on cue, the blood pooling in his left eye teared and dropped, continuing on its journey down his face. It traced the pink flesh of the hideous scar until it disappeared into his dark beard.

The guard just nodded and retreated further out the door closing it behind him.

"Good lord Aldrich! You didn't have to give the lad nightmares." Rupert said laughing as Aldrich came back down the hall.

"I did him a favor." He said, dabbing the blood from his eye. "After me, a vast German horde pressing down on his beloved city will taste sweet by comparison. A man must find his steel sometime or another."

Once again, the Bishop was dressed in his absolute finest robe and once again he waddled back and forth in front of the group as they made their way down the corridors of the palace to the same place where they had met with Nikephoros, that eunuch that so willingly imprisoned them all a month ago.

This time, however, no one sat in the gold-encrusted chair on the ornate patio. Instead, there was a young, handsome man who walked toward them. Servants shaded him with violet umbrellas fringed with gold tassels as he walked. He wore expensive silks that matched the umbrellas. He strolled with his hands clasped in front of him and as he came closer, Aldrich could see that his welcoming smile was anything but. The look seemed to more aptly describe a man in pain than that of a man attempting to put strangers at ease.

The sunlight reflected off of the man's darkened skin as he stopped earlier than his servant had expected. Emperor Angelus squinted as the sudden harsh afternoon light fell on his face.

The servant quickly realized his mistake and took a step backward to return his eminence to the comfort of the shade. Although the servant had realized his mistake and fixed it within a second's time, the blunder cost him an uncomfortable glare from the Emperor.

Angelus returned his attention to the Envoys who were coming to a stop themselves. The Bishop made a fluid bow. It was so low that it bordered on inappropriately submissive to the enemy Emperor, Aldrich thought.

The rest of the diplomats never made a move to kneel, bow or otherwise show any kind of respect to Angelus, a fact not lost on him. Angelus's squint returned momentarily, but this time it wasn't the sun that had caused it. The insult was far too brazen for him to neglect ordinarily, but Aldrich knew that the Emperor must be in a tight spot to have summoned them in person after such a long imprisonment without word one from him. They had come in good-faith to his door to treat with him. Brother nations in Christ. How did the man expect them to respond to him?

The Emperor visibly struggled to set his face again after the insolence, but he did so just as Nikephoros, the fat eunuch that they had met before made the introductions to the Emperor.

The sweaty, whiny voiced Chamberlain announced the bishop first, then the counts Rupert and Walram, then Chamberlain Markward, and finally Aldrich. He described their full titles and relationships to nobles of note, as if Angelus truly cared, but it was a show of respect. Too little too late. Aldrich thought.

When Nikephoros signaled to Aldrich and Angelus's eyes alit on the scarred face, Aldrich saw his eyebrows lift slightly in subtle surprise. He would have been told, undoubtedly, of the engagement in the street and how Aldrich had been wounded, but seeing such a wound in person was often shocking to someone not used to fighting long campaigns of bloody war.

Aldrich had, and the wound still surprised him almost every time he saw it hacked into what had been a familiar face.

Nikephoros had finished his recitation and stepped back, hands clasped behind his back and head slightly declined.

The formality that his servants and even his court chamberlain afforded him was unfamiliar to Aldrich. Everyone around Emperor Barbarossa respected him, loved him. But he did not expect them to gravel or simper as this man did his servants. As a matter of fact, he was certain that Frederick would chastise men that acted this way around him. There was a difference between respect offered and whatever this was, and Aldrich didn't like it. He felt his lip curl at the way the servants and followers around Angelus never made eye contact. They seemed to live in a different world.

Angelus began to speak. His voice was consistent with the rest of him, and although he had an accent, it was not as thick as that of Photios or the messenger he had intimidated earlier.

Come to think of it, Aldrich hadn't seen Spathario Photios since the incident and he wondered absently where they had shuffled him off to. Must have been cast out of court after the debacle with Aldrich.

"I would like to act as if nothing in the past few months has happened, but alas I cannot. We all know that I have kept you all here against your will, hoping to have a bargaining chip with your Emperor. There are a lot of unseen mechanisms that make up a functioning empire. And more in one surrounded by enemies. We have always been the bulwarks for Christianity against the heathen hordes, but there are things that must be done to ensure that those bulwarks stay strong." Angelus looked down at his feet before returning his gaze to the group and continuing.

"I do not ask you for forgiveness, as I would not give it had I been in your place." He looked pointedly at Aldrich.

"I do ask that you don't judge me too harshly as all was done with the noblest of intentions. I suppose you will be pleased to know that your crusading army has not made their presence an easy cross to bear since your capture was made known. For that reason, and myriad others, you will be released."

The perfunctory statement shocked Aldrich. He expected much more intrigue and attempts at leveraging information or ransoms from them. The revelation that he would free them was so unexpected after such a long imprisonment, it caught Aldrich off guard. He had been ready to thwart any attempts at bribery or deception. He couldn't help but wonder what angle the Emperor was coming from. Was this a trick?

Aldrich searched through the facts of the situation in his head rapidly and could see no reason Angelus would lie to them, although, admittedly, he was not as skilled at court politics as everyone else in his group.

Aldrich took a sidelong glance at the other envoy's faces. He could not see the Bishop's as he was still in front of them. Besides, he didn't need to wonder at his interpretation as the clergyman was, even now, all but kissing Angelus's rings.

"Thank you, your eminence. You are truly an honorable man…" The bishop assured.

The rest of the group's faces read the same way he felt his would if his features were readable anymore. It seemed that anyone with some sense accepted the situation with closely guarded optimism. They all wondered at the reason and what the catch must be although one wasn't readily apparent.

Aldrich decided to run with the offer.

"When may we leave?"

His simple question cut into one of a constant litany of praises and simpering affectations directed at the Emperor by the bishop. The particular one that Aldrich had interrupted was not important as all seemed overly ridiculous to Aldrich given their situation. Despite his opinion, bishop Herman glared back over his shoulder at Aldrich, offended, and Angelus's forced smile disappeared altogether at the straightforwardness of his question.

Damn politics. Aldrich thought.

Markward stepped forward.

"Sir Kortig has had a very difficult time, and I'm sure you understand the difficulties a man of war has at being away from his men for so long. We all desire nothing more than to continue on our journey with the goal of fulfilling God's will. I for one am indeed grateful that we can put aside our differences for so great a goal." Markward said.

The Emperor considered the words for a moment then inclined his head slightly in appreciation of them.

Aldrich caught an amused look from Walram. He had enjoyed Aldrich's rudeness.

Damn politics. Aldrich thought for the second time in as many minutes.

His face hurt.

Chapter 27

The snows had fallen heavy and wet early that year but then the cold had followed close behind. Not the cold common to every winter, but the kind of cold that hardens wet snow into thick ice. The winter so far had been one of the worst in Greta's memory. It only warmed up before a snowstorm which only added more layers of ice after the cold returned. It had been hell trying to keep the courtyards and walks clear of the ice. A hell that Greta shared with much of the castle staff.

Cold bit through her clothes and made her hands numb as she swept a long open-aired corridor for probably the hundredth time that winter. It led past the barracks to the servant's quarters and Greta was exhausted. It had been, at the very least, one hundred times this year, but her fourth just tonight. The moon had been out for what seemed like an eternity. She should would have been in bed hours ago if it hadn't been for the need to keep the inside of the keep cleared of snow. With the bitter cold turning everything to ice, it would be impossible to clear it in the morning after a few feet had fallen. Therefore, they had all been tasked with a sort of rotating vigil of the grounds, although hers seemed to be far more constant than was everyone else's.

Greta looked up the corridor towards her starting point and was too tired to care that the snow had already covered it with an inch or two of new snow. She sighed and leaned against the stone wall. Her cheeks were bitter cold. She touched them with her swaddled hands. The rough-spun that protected her fingers from frostbite was like rough stones being scraped across her tender face.

Greta pulled the cloth that she used for a scarf up over her mouth once again. It kept falling down as she worked, leaving her face defenseless to the bitter cold.

Her breath had made the cloth wet, and with it down while she worked, it was now colder up than down. She pulled it back down, frustrated. She closed her eyes and thought of Hagan.

She had wondered and imagined where he was at such a consistent interval that she did it now without any particular cue. No reason was needed to think of a distant land and people. Nor to think of her brother. She missed him still. She had assumed that she would slowly replace thoughts of him with reality. The here and now demanded her attention, but at the same time, her thoughts were her own and she luxuriated in the images that her mind conjured during her more arduous labors. Perhaps they were the only things that truly belonged to her. Everything else could be taken from her.

Was he okay?

Where was he now?

What people did he know?

When she let her imagination really run wild, she imagined Hagan as a knight riding a large destrier with beautifully embroidered caparison, the beautiful tapestries that hung from the richest of knights' horses, flowing as he rode. She knew that that would be a near impossibility. He was only a squire, but the imagery was the most exciting, nonetheless.

Greta felt white-hot pain as a hand slapped her freezing face. Milda Decker, shoes muffled by the snow, had been silent on her approach. And like a vulture, descended on her unsuspecting victim. She now stood before Greta, hands on fat hips, screaming. What she was saying, Greta wasn't even sure. All she felt was pain, fear, anger.

Milda just screamed, her words mostly unintelligible, but she could hear the occasional "lazy" and "stupid" laced throughout the tirade.

Suddenly Milda Decker pitched backward, arms windmilling upward as she fell and Greta was standing over her fist clenched. It seemed that neither one of them knew what had happened for a prolonged moment. Mistress Decker had been punched, Greta thought, by her, she realized.

Blood flowed from the fat woman's nose and her chubby hand rose to feel it. She looked at one sausage-like finger, now covered in red, to verify the wound, then up at Greta.

Greta wasn't sure what would happen to her after baron Adelfried found out, but she was certain it wouldn't be good.

Milda made as if she would scream an alarm and fear lanced through Greta spurring her to do something.

The knife on her thigh was out and pressed against the, now quivering, woman's throat in seconds.

Milda's eyes were wide with fear, but at least her mouth was closed.

Greta swallowed.

Now what? She asked herself.

She felt fear creep back into her heart. It attempted to uproot the control that the anger had asserted over her. She couldn't let Mistress Decker see any second thoughts she decided and pressed the knife harder into the fat waddle under the woman's despised mouth. Milda flinched with fear as the sharpness of the knife became clear.

Her brain rushed forward, thoughts and words came to her mind faster than she had ever experienced before. She went with them.

"What do you hope for?" She asked the woman.

Milda, who Greta had been convinced over the months was the devil, glared at her with a fierce anger that almost destroyed Greta's resolve, but the simple question made the glare falter slightly, replaced by puzzlement.

"Do you hope for life?" Greta asked.

Milda was afraid to answer since the knife was threatening to open her throat at the slightest provocation.

After a long, thoughtful pause, she nodded slowly rather than risk speaking.

"What makes your life worth more than mine?" Greta asked.

"I assure you that from my point of view it is not. So what makes you think yours is more valuable? Can you explain that to me?" She didn't really want a response and didn't remove the knife to allow for one.

Instead, she continued with her litany of questions.

"Did you think I would accept your abuse without end?"

Greta realized as she said it that that was exactly what she had expected her to do. Accept it. Do nothing but what you're told and accept it. Milda had undoubtedly had practice. No one gets as good at something as she was at tearing people down overnight. Milda had developed the skill on other girls before her and the other girl's acceptance of the abuse had bred a confidence in the woman that was galling.

The thought only heightened Greta's conviction that what she was doing to Mistress Decker would surely be met with horrible consequences. The Baron would hardly allow his staff to mutiny. Discipline had always been harshly doled out by the Baron, and she had no hope of gaining mercy from him.

"I have half a mind to turn this snow red with your blood." Greta's mind had recoiled when she had first imagined the phrase, but used it for that reason. Short of doing exactly as she described, she had no option but to intimidate the woman and make her believe that Greta was capable of such a thing.

"It would be easier you know." She said.

"Do you think anyone would suspect me? I doubt it. There are at least half a dozen other, more likely, candidates. See what not being nice gets you?"

Greta gauged Milda's expressions as she spoke. She was worrying in earnest.

"It is late. I wonder who would find your cold body first. I could find you first I suppose. No one would suspect the person who raised the alarm to be the murderer."

Greta's mind raced as she spoke. What had she done? And she was surely making the whole situation worse. Wasn't she?

Fear seemed to fill every corner of her body, but her mind seemed to, somehow, stay remarkably clear.

She knew Milda's character and if she let her go with an apology, the vindictive woman would seek Greta's imprisonment at least.

Greta pushed forward with her theory. The woman had to be more afraid of Greta than she was angry at her, and knowing the woman's skill at being angry, she would need more fear.

"In this shadow, though, you probably wouldn't even be seen until morning."

Milda whimpered pitifully

Greta decided to lift the knife from the woman's throat enough for her to speak.

"What should I do with you?" Greta prompted.

There was a hesitancy still to the woman's response. It wasn't born of fear, at least not enough to assure Greta that Milda wouldn't cry foul the moment she was released. She doubted that anything she was willing to do would be enough to scare the woman sufficiently to silence her.

"Release me child and I will never be harsh to you again. I was wrong to be so...so mean. Please forgive an old woman of her sins."

Greta wanted to believe her. She wanted it more than anything she had ever wanted. To believe her meant deliverance from this horrendous situation in which she found herself suddenly and a life free from Mistress Decker's heavy boot. The problem was...she didn't. The woman still had anger turned to rage behind her eyes. Greta was almost certain that if the roles were reversed now, Milda would open Greta's throat to the frozen air without a second's thought.

Greta imagined Mistress Decker's throat being cut by her knife. The image came unbidden to her mind's eye. The woman's sausage fingers jerking up in surprise to the gash, trying to hold in the precious life-blood that we all take for granted until it is stolen from us. Steam rising in the cold air from the wound, both from the heat of the newly exposed blood and from the breath escaping through her throat. Gurgling, gasping, coughing. Then death.

The image shook Greta. She could not do such a thing, no matter how much she thought she hated this woman.

Milda seemed to sense her reluctance and began to lift herself up onto her elbows. Greta lowered the knife, a feeling of hopelessness and fear overwhelming her. The fat woman inched away, scrabbling on her elbows, her girth jiggled and swayed with her movements and with each inch gained her look of subject fear turned to hatred and anger. She had lifted herself now to her hands and moved backward faster, confidence building in her as she moved unchecked by Greta. Greta signalled with her eyes for the woman to leave. Nothing was said by either woman, but everything was felt. Greta was certain that Milda would raise the alarm. The guards would search for her soon. The fear that the Greta had put into her would not extend further than Greta could reach. Even now, as Greta slumped and dropped to the frozen ground, she waited for the yell that would stir the guard to action.

She knew she should move. Knew she was condemning herself with her inaction. She couldn't move. Couldn't move. She missed Hagan.

Chapter 28

Hagan ran through the forest. Since that chaos filled night weeks ago, he hadn't been given nearly as many mundane tasks to perform. Maybe he had finally been deemed worthy to exit the ranks of squire and be accepted as a warrior. In reality, it hadn't been long since his first meeting Aldrich on that dust filled road especially not when viewed from a normal squire's perspective.

Most squires stayed in the service of their knight for years before they were either, shunted to the side like yesterday's refuse, or they died. Some went on to become men at arms and still fewer, those that were wealthy, became knights. Maybe his new wealth had changed his status with Ahren and Obert. Somehow he couldn't imagine those two being so affected by that.

Regardless, Hagan now ran for himself. He hadn't been given any exercise regime from Ahren as he used to so Hagan took it upon himself to work his muscles. As a result of his freedom, instead of making the same trek around the city and camp, he took dirt tracks to unknown locals and crossed country when convenient. It was convenient now, and he jogged through knee-high grass through a clearing.

He enjoyed the change in scenery if not the chill air. Back home this weather would be downright temperate by comparison with their usual winter, but Hagan was now used to the warmer climate and the sudden cold of the day made his lungs ache as he pushed himself up a hill.

The hill marked the goal he had set for himself and when he reached the summit, he bent in half and sucked in the cold air.

In between gasps Hagan heard the unmistakable sound of a horse's whinny. He looked around, searching for the source. A large copse of trees stood not a hundred yards off and through the thick foliage he could just make out a group of horses with riders.

The presence of Byzantine scouts was always a fear for Hagan and rightly so. Hagan reflected that he shouldn't be this far from camp and he cursed himself for his stupidity. Strictly speaking he wasn't supposed to leave the protection that the army afforded, but he so enjoyed the countryside during his runs that he had justified his wayward exercise sessions more and more as no sign of enemy scouts presented themselves.

Hagan dropped to his belly and crawled backwards down the slope of the hill, hoping that no one had seen his silhouette.

His breaths still came in gulps and the sound was painfully loud in his own ears. He knew that was ridiculous, no one could hear him. He was way too far from them to hear him.

If he just ran back the way he had come, how far would he make it until the scouts saw him? Maybe he could work his way back, using the trees and brush as cover. Maybe he should just find a spot here close and hide until it was dark.

Maybe they weren't even the enemy. They could be scouts from his own side patrolling the countryside.

Hagan decided that he needed a better look.

The grove that the horses were in extended up to the top of the hill that Hagan was on off to his right and he made his way over to them, careful to stay well down from the crest, using the hill as cover. Hagan was well versed at hunting and moving stealthily was second nature to him. The few times that he had gone hunting with Obert, the sturdy Italian commented on how ghostlike Hagan moved through the trees. He had to be able to provide food for his mother and sister and the quiet agility served him well.

Hagan crept now with all the stealth that his chainmail and sword would allow. He twisted through a particularly thick section of underbrush and moved through the grove toward where the horses stood.

He was careful not to allow a clear shot to open between himself and the group of mounted men, and he skirted a fallen tree. Based on where he had seen them from on top of the hill, they should be right on the other side of a thick tangle of branches and brush so Hagan, silent as ever, crawled forward into a gap in the bushes. There they were, Byzantines. Well, he assumed they were Byzantines. They weren't German that much was clear from their dark skin and hair. Their clothes were flowing and clean. These didn't look like the scouts that Hagan was so used to in the German army.

They sat, silent. They looked as if they waited for something.

Despite his ever-present fear, he was pleased with how close he had managed to get to these wary men, who silently waited with apprehension on their faces.

Hagan was about to crawl backwards and make his way to safety when he heard the approach of more horsemen.

Off to his right, Hagan saw what looked like a group of about twenty knights enter the grove. German knights. They wore the white tunics with green crosses of the crusading army. Hagan's heart leapt. Soon the knights would recognize the other horsemen as the enemy and charge and drive them off.

Then Hagan could extricate himself from the tangle without fear of his bloody demise.

Hagan smiled in anticipation. He felt like a child laying on the floor watching some puppet show. But these puppets were not made of wood, but of metal, flesh and blood.

These puppets might be made of wood, actually. What were they thinking? The enemy was right there. Surely, by now they could see them and recognize them for who they were. With each plodding step that the small company of knights took, Hagan lost hope that they would kick their horses and couch their lances.

Disbelief threatened to overwhelm him as he recognized the ungainly Duke Otto Wittelsbach perched on his over-encumbered horse, riding ponderously closer to the exotic-looking group of horsemen. The fat lord waved at the leader of the waiting horsemen and when he drew near they clasped arms.

What was going on? Whatever it was, it was suspicious. Why meet so far from Philippopoulos? If this meeting was on the level, then the foreigners would have come in to camp and met with the Duke there. Hagan was sure that Wittelsbach would not have left the comforts of his quarters if it hadn't been necessary.

He couldn't hear the conversation for the two talked conspiratorially, the Duke throwing furtive glances around the grove, sure that he was being watched and, in point of fact, he was. Hagan saw the sweat on the fat man's face despite the cold air, saw the nervous shifting and knew that Wittelsbach was betraying the Empire. He didn't know how but the guilt was plain.

Hagan pulled, slowly back into deeper shadows, no quick movements, until he was certain that no one would see him and waited.

Finally, the dark-skinned man dressed in flowing silk motioned to a subordinate and the man tossed a heavy purse to Wittelsbach who fumbled the sack and it fell to the ground. The Duke cursed and one of his men dismounted and retrieved the bag, handing it to him. He peeked inside the bag and nodded in acceptance, spoke a few curt words to the other man and pulled his horse's head around to head back in the direction he'd come from, leading his knights away.

The longer Hagan watched the less confident he was that the foreigners were Byzantines. The men he'd fought that night of fear and blood did not have the same armor and style of clothing that these men did. The silk clad man led his men in the opposite direction and was soon gone from sight.

He waited for an hour until he was sure that no one lingered and crept out of the shadows. The sun was going down in the east and he turned his back to it and ran back to the camp. He went over in his mind what he should do during the run. He had to tell someone, that much was obvious, but who. Accusing someone so powerful as the Duke would be very dangerous.

If the Duke found out that Hagan had seen his clandestine meeting his days would be marked.

By the time he reached the camp it was full dark and when he approached his tent, Ahren called out to Hagan.

"Running in the dark is dangerous."

Hagan mumbled and looked around him for Obert.

He had decided that he would tell Ahren and Obert and see what they thought of the situation. Maybe he was overreacting about the whole thing.

"Where's Obert?" Hagan said.

He must have looked as apprehensive as he felt because Ahren looked concerned.

"I'm here." Obert said from the darkness.

He came from the direction of their tents and sat down next to Ahren by the small cook fire.

"What's got you all in a lather?" Obert said.

Hagan sat next to the two men and told them of the suspicious meeting. In his haste, he'd left out details that weren't lost on Ahren and Obert.

"Exactly how close did you get to these men?" Ahren asked.

Hagan didn't say that he got close enough to smell them.

"Close enough." he said.

They asked how the men were dressed, and if he was sure that it was Wittelsbach. They asked if he was sure that no one saw him. Finally, after all of their questions had been answered, the two paused, thinking.

"Well? What do we do?" Hagan asked. His voice sounded calmer than he felt.

"Nothing." Ahren mumbled.

Hagan was stunned for a moment.

"Nothing?" He stammered.

"Yes, we can't do anything but watch him. And even that will need to be done with exceptional care." Obert was nodding as Ahren spoke.

"Wittelsbach commands a degree of wealth and power that few men in the Empire have. Men would kill you, me and Obert here, for only the possibility of pleasing the Duke let alone for any reward. The word of a squire, even one so reputed as you, would result in your death not his. You cannot accuse a Duke of treachery without firm, incontrovertible proof." Ahren sighed.

"We can tell Aldrich." Obert said. "But his hands are equally tied. I think even if the Emperor knew, and believed us, he still would not move against the Duke."

"Why?" Hagan had to ask.

"It is still only the word of a squire, Hagan." Obert said apologetically.

Hagan cupped his chin in his hands and looked into the firelight morosely, depressed by his ineffectual testimony.

"We'll keep an eye on our rotund friend and make sure he doesn't do anything too brazen." Ahren said, plainly trying to reassure him.

"Hey, you'd better get some food in you and make sure your stuff's all packed and ready for tomorrow." Obert said.

"What's tomorrow?" Hagan said despondently.

Hagan looked up at Obert and saw a twinkle in his eye.

"What's tomorrow? He repeated."

"Oh, nothing. We're just marching to the Bospherus."

Hagan was shocked.

"What do you mean? Is Aldrich…?"

"They have reached an agreement with Isaac Angelus. Aldrich is being freed." Ahren said. A wide smile painted his dark face.

Chapter 29

The roll of the deck under his feet threatened to toss him to the ground but Hagan managed to keep upright by stumbling awkwardly. Wighard snorted and tossed his head irritably at the motion. He had blindfolded and tethered the horse close to the rail to keep him from being able to cause too much damage to himself or anyone else.

Hagan sold his other horses to reduce the difficulties he would have in transporting them all. Keeping Wighard calm throughout the loading process had been difficult enough without dealing with an additional two horses.

Because he had sold the animals, he also had to sell the extra armor and weapons that he had pilfered from the dead body's of the men he had killed. Wighard could not carry it all by himself.

Hagan had kept only the best armor, that belonging to the Spatharios, and the Beautiful sword. Luckily the man had been close to his own size. The mail shirt was a little tight through the chest and shoulders, but it fit him better than the one he had already been wearing. Hagan had had the shield repainted to display the black eagle of the Holy Roman Empire. He wore it now on his back.

Wighard shifted again, stretching the cords holding him to the railing tight and Hagan wondered for the tenth time if they would hold against the massively muscled animal's strength, they did, this time.

Hagan looked out over the water. He could see the distant shore. Dozens of ships, all flying the colors of the Byzantines, on all sides. Some were headed back in the direction they had come, while just as many were mimicking Hagan's ship. The army was finally receiving the help that they had long been promised by the Byzantines. They were being ferried to the far side of the Bosphorus; the day had finally come.

Emperor Frederick did not hesitate and had the army rallied at the staging ground for the transport within days.

Angelus would not let the army pass through Constantinople, which would have been much easier for the army, but given the obvious animosity between them Hagan understood the desire for the army to cross well to the south of the city.

Wighard tossed his head nervously.

He patted the horse's neck and talked encouragingly. It didn't really matter what he said, just that he had a calm, reassuring tone. The trip across was taking a lot longer than he imagined it would.

He looked up the deck to where Obert stood comforting his horse as Hagan was Wighard. The horses had presented a level of complexity to the relatively short voyage that he had never really thought of until he was forced to. Luckily it would be a relatively short trip, but it still felt plenty long to Hagan's unaccustomed stomach. At least he wasn't down in the dark below-deck with the foot infantry that had been crammed into the hold as tight as they could be. He could only imagine what it must be like down there. Up here it was bad enough even with the refreshing salt-breeze on his face which seemed to ease the queasiness in his stomach slightly.

Hagan used Wighard's hard shoulder to steady himself against the unseen forces caused by an unanticipated wave.

He could see the far side now, but it seemed so far off. Was it getting any closer?

He focused on his breathing and stared out at the water, trying not to think of the pitch and yaw of the world around him.

He focused his thoughts on the same things he had thought of for months. His sister. His mother. What dangers and adventures awaited him on the distant land? He pictured himself in battle, vanquishing enemies on all sides. He even thought of the girl he had rescued in the market, not for the first time.

Wighard snorted and pitched his head once more.

Hagan let his attention return to the here and now and noticed that the land now took up most of the horizon. They were close enough that he could judge their progress as they approached land.

Above the white line of waves crashing into the distant beach, he could see the portion of the army that had already ferried across. He recognized the familiar pattern of camp being set up and tiny people moving to and fro. It would take at least all of today to ferry the whole army across, perhaps half of tomorrow, despite the efficiency that Germans pride themselves in, it was a slow process given the scope. The army was massive and Hagan was struck with pride. It wasn't the first time he had felt it, but it was the strongest. They had made it. Anatolia. They were crossing into the East.

The majority of the people from here on out would be enemies. The irony of the thought was not lost on Hagan. They had been, seemingly, at odds with everyone they had passed since Hagan had joined with the army and those were friends.

Well, countries they had passed through were obviously not all friends but they certainly hadn't been expected to be enemies.

The boat finally pulled into an open spot along a rough-built dock and the sailors scrambled to tie off and haul it in close to the wood planks. There were a few squat buildings close to the dock, but other than that Hagan couldn't see anything. It seemed like the three docks that had been built, at considerable cost, had only one purpose…to ferry undesirables across to keep them from entering the city. There were no merchants here. There was but one man who seemed to take advantage of the docks daily and that was a fisherman whose huts these surely were. He must have sold all of his fish early this morning to the first of the men across for he sat, contentedly, watching the soldiers disembark.

It took half an hour to get off of the boat and the dock. He nearly knelt down and kissed the ground once he was safely ashore. The injustice of it all was that he still felt queasy. He had heard that there were other crusading armies that were traveling most of the journey to the Latin East in ships. The thought seemed unbearable to Hagan.

Instead of kissing the ground he continued to follow Obert, Ahren and the others as they wound their way through the crowd. The same structure that the camp had since Hagan began this adventure was present here and they were able to find the land set aside for their tents relatively easy. When they arrived, however, a lone tent was already standing. A man sat on a stone in front of it sharpening his sword.

It was Sir Aldrich. Or was it? Hagan recognized the armor, clothes and sword, but he flinched when he saw the face. Harsh, haggard and scarred. He knew that it must be Aldrich, but his mind still rejected the harsh reality of it.

Despite the shock of seeing the scarred face, Hagan was suddenly overwhelmed with excitement at Aldrich's presence and yelled his name then pushed past Ahren and Obert. Aldrich stood, and they were soon all surrounding the knight clasping hands and laughing. Jokes, that had been saved for months, were told. For ten minutes all was excitement. The laughter soon turned to questions, at which point Aldrich held up his hand, stalling them.

"I will tell you all of my adventures, dull as they are, in due time, but first you must all set camp. Our conversation has waited months, it can wait an hour more."

As Hagan lifted himself from a crouch to obey, Aldrich looked at Hagan quizzically. The questioning look forestalled Hagan, and he waited.

Aldrich took another appraising look, impressed with the expensive chainmail and leather that protected Hagan's chest, arms and legs. He then looked toward Wighard, whose reigns Hagan still held.

"It seems that I have more to hear than to tell." Aldrich said. A smirk crossed his face, that may have been the closest he could now come to a smile. Hagan thought.

He returned the smile.

"See to the horses, Hagan, then we shall all catch up."

It was late before the camp was fully settled, much of the baggage came into camp piecemeal and soldiers and camp followers straggled in all afternoon and evening. The steady flow of people past their tents finally petered out once the sun went down and it was full-dark.

Hagan had to wait until the casks of fresh water were unloaded from wagons and a few casks were opened and portions divvied out for men and horses. They had been slow in coming, presumably because they were difficult to load and offload from the ships.

It was dark before he finally got the horses situated for the night. Their camp had long since been set and they had a fire's coals glowing strongly. Hagan feared that they had already all eaten and was even more afraid that Aldrich had told of his capture. And how did he get that ghastly scar?

Despite being so late back to camp, however, it seemed that everyone had waited for him. As he sat, wooden bowls were passed around full of Horst's famous stew.

Suddenly Hagan had a sense of belonging. One that had never been present inside him. They had waited for him. Hadn't just saved some food for him, as had happened often before.

"How on bloody earth did you get that God awful scar?" Obert blurted out.

He never had been one for subtleties.

Aldrich laughed and told the tale of his capture and of the fight in the streets. He mixed what he remembered of the event with what he was told happened since he was unconscious for much of it.

Everyone was excited to hear of the fight and were aghast when they learned of how Spatharios Photios had hacked at Aldrich.

He told briefly of their imprisonment in the palace. And when he was done, Ahren said, you may be pleased to hear that your wound was avenged err we caught sight of it.

Aldich looked a question at Ahren and waited for him to continue.

Ahren told of their attack on Photios's camp.

Hagan was embarrassed as the story included, of necessity, how he had become separated from the main force.

He was rewarded with pride, however, when Ahren got to the part of how he had "bravely attacked the fleeing knights".

Aldrich looked impressed, but didn't interrupt.

He explained how Hagan had been charged, in turn, by none other than Spatharios Photios and one of his men, and how Hagan had dispatched both.

Hagan felt embarrassed again.

It wasn't so simple. He had been terrified, and Ahren's story made it sound like there hadn't been a greater portion of luck than skill in his actions.

Hagan looked at Aldrich who was appraising him openly. A wry smile on his face.

"Well done Hagan, well done." He said.

Hagan couldn't hold his gaze and looked away.

"I was lucky." Hagan said.

"Luck!" Aldrich boomed loudly.

The vehemence startled Hagan.

"Blessed I'd say."

Aldrich crossed himself. Something that Hagan had seen Aldrich do only on rare occasions. Usually when a particularly ominous omen presented itself.

"You forget that God grants you the strength in your arm. He gives you courage when you need it, fear when it is necessary, and victory over your enemy. If that is what you mean by luck, then yes, you are very lucky."

Hagan felt that he had offended Aldrich and shuffled uncomfortably.

Aldrich continued in a softer tone.

"Despite all of that which God gives you, you were the one that was his instrument. He chose your prayers over those of the men you fought. And although you may not agree, God has seen fit to bless you with a surprising talent for killing. In our trade, that is a sought after talent indeed."

Was this a talent given to him by God? Would he give such a talent? He supposed that it was possible. God gave the wolf strong jaws and claws to kill with.

"Why would God give me a talent in killing?" Hagan said slowly.

Aldrich seemed to have expected the question.

"He gives us such talents to fight the evil in the world."

Hagan decided not to proceed with his questions though he had many. Aldrich and the others continued the conversation around him as he sat, pensive. Were the men he killed evil? For some reason he doubted it. They seemed no more evil than himself. They had been keeping the army from continuing on with the crusade which was contrary to God's will. He understood that but did that make them evil? He wasn't convinced.

Chapter 30

Greta lifted herself up onto one elbow as she heard footsteps coming down the corridor. Her body was sore and her joints had an unfamiliar cold ache in them that gave her new respect for the old men and women that she had grown up hearing complain about such pain.

The footsteps came closer. Was it time for her dinner? She had been locked away in an empty larder in the basement of Lord adelfried's keep since the altercation with that wretched woman Milda Decker in the snow and it had been increasingly difficult to keep track of time. Had it been ten days? More?

Greta Scrambled to the corner of the room and brought her knees up to her chest in a vain attempt to keep that pig Ludolf from being enticed.

The door opened suddenly and Ludolf stood there. A plate in his hand and a grin on his face.

Greta tried not even to look at him, but as he entered the room, all hope that he would drop the plate and leave was gone and a whimper escaped her lips.

He chuckled disgustingly. Everything he did was disgusting.

He dropped the plate on the ground where she had been laying moments ago and bent over her trembling form.

"I must apologize, my sweet thing, I can't stay today."

He ran his hand over her hair, almost gently. Then he grabbed a handful and lifted her out of her protective ball.

She screamed as he grabbed her breast roughly.

He laughed as if this was the greatest amusement one could have and threw her back down on the ground tearing out some hair in the process.

He lifted it to his nose and inhaled deeply.

Chuckling, he left her and locked the door again behind him.

The disgusting man had been more and more violent with each passing day. So far, this had been the worst he had done to her, but she knew that as her imprisonment continued, Ludolf would feel more and more free to do with her as he pleased.

She gingerly touched the spot on her head where he had yanked the hair from her scalp and berated herself once again for not running as soon as she had let that witch Milda go.

She might have made it out of the castle, and she might have made it out of the town but then she would have had to survive alone and the thought terrified her. How would she make it through the rest of the winter months without food or shelter? When Ludolf was at his worst she had to remind herself that this may well be a better scenario than the other. She may have already died had she left. The hard part was knowing if that would have been better or not.

She picked herself up off of the cold stone and walked over to the plate of gruel. They fed her the same thing for both of her daily meals and it was starting to be hard on her stomach and the tattered dress she wore was becoming loose in places.

She wondered how long she would have to stay down here. What were they waiting for? Would they kill her?

Milda wasn't noble, but she was a favored servant with special privileges. If she had threatened a nobleman or woman how she had Milda, she would be put to death for sure. Her situation was somewhat ambiguous, and the sad part was that she wasn't sure which outcome to hope for.

Chapter 31

What Hagan had once thought to be hard was, in hindsight, easy. He had learned the meaning of the word difficult. Winter had ended while the army waited outside of Constantinople and now spring had turned to summer. The army had passed through land that was so dry that Hagan could not have believed it had he been told of such a thing. The sand swirled in the wind. The black stones baked in the sun. To add to their misery, the Seljuk Turks that had unofficial dominion over these lands were hostile. They feared the size of the army so instead of arraying themselves for a proper battle; they rode around and behind the army, firing arrows at them regularly enough that the screams of dying men no longer startled Hagan.

His lips cracked and bled. His skin, where exposed, turned red with sunburn and blistered.

The distance between towns was so great that they were constantly low on food, and what's more, once they did arrive at a town, supplies were extremely hard to come by. The people in those towns had been warned beforehand and what food or supplies would have been present were squirreled away or sold to the Turks at a bargain.

The army scavenged whatever food they could find, leaving a swath of angry towns behind them.

It was hard for Hagan to feel any sympathy for the townspeople, however. They were supporting the same roving bands of men that constantly picked off stragglers and scouts and did everything they could to keep food from reaching the army.

The fervor that Hagan had grown accustomed to was all but gone among the soldiers. Men hung their heads as they walked. The well-organized machine that the army had been was now a mob of tired, thirsty and hungry men and horses. Conversation had gone away when the water had. Men couldn't justify opening parched mouths for frivolous talk.

The atmosphere felt heavy, oppressing like a wet wool blanket held over one's face.

That would have felt good though compared to this. Anything wet would have been a relief even if it stifled breathing.

Hagan walked leading Wighard.

Most men, that normally would have ridden, walked their mounts. There was no point tiring them unnecessarily besides, the footmen that were strung out throughout the long length of the army could only go so fast. Without the protection of the mounted knights the foot soldiers would be ridden down and massacred by the Turks. Or the savages would remain at a safe distance and lob arrows into the infantry at their leisure with those strange war bows that it seemed every horseman carried. The knights, that were also dispersed throughout the army, dissuaded the Turks from massing in any significant numbers.

Hagan stumbled on a stone. These blasted trails, for that's all they were, were miserable to march on. He could only imagine the frustration they were to the wagon teams. He was beginning to think that they were never going to get anywhere. This was all the same. The same dust. The same gray rocks. And oh, look the same scraggly bush that every man in the army had long ago given up on trying to feed to his horse. This place was hell. If ever there was one, this was it.

Obert had said that they were moving toward a walled city named Iconium. They would take it and supposedly replenish their rations there.

Every time he crested a hill, Hagan looked into the next empty expanse, full of dry drainages that spider webbed their way into the distance. And every time he felt his hope drop yet again.

Then, just as he was losing all hope of ever reaching anywhere, let alone eating a full meal again, they crested the last rise on their journey to Iconium.

The city stood in the far distance, its tan stone walls were hard to see against the distant horizon, but the unnatural straight lines gave it away.

The army's progress had halted on top of the plateau. Hagan assumed that it was to look out at the goal that they had almost lost all hope in attaining, but the raspy voices and pointing fingers brought Hagan's attention to a large dark patch in the otherwise light brown-gray of the desert topography,

What was that? He spotted Obert, Ahren, Horst, Manfred and Karl standing with Sir Aldrich.

Pulling Wighard to the side so as not to block the trail, he made his way over to where their horses stood tethered to one of the ugly bushes that dotted the wilderness. He tied Wighard off and went over to stand next to Obert.

Everyone looked out at the flat, seemingly endless plain of desert before them. But Hagan noticed that they weren't looking in the far distance at the walled city of Iconium. They too looked at the dark smear below them.

"I suppose our objective was obvious to them, but why didn't they form up before now? We could have decided this weeks ago." Ahren was saying.

Hagan felt foolish as he finally realized that the dark smear was an enemy army. Suddenly, with the knowledge, he could see the definite signs that it was true. Dust rose like a cloud above the shape, and an occasional glint of sun reflecting off of a sword or helm caught his eye.

"Because they wanted the heat, thirst and those God-forsaken arrows to do their work on us for as long as possible. They wanted to whittle down our numbers as much as they could before an engagement was forced. I only hope that they let us engage this time. For real." Aldrich responded. They all nodded.

That had been the biggest frustration for them all. The Turks would not fight. At least not how they should. As soon as a contingent went out to meet the archers, they would turn and flee, launching arrows the whole time. The only recourse was to hold tight in formation and do their best to ignore the barrage.

Luckily the bows that the Turks used seemed light and unable to send a shaft as deep as it needed to go, through tunic, chainmail, leather and padding. Most of the time the victim would merely curse and yank the arrow from his body. Sometimes, however, an arrow would strike home, finding minimally protected flesh and would elicit more than a curse. The army had been reminded, again and again, not to engage the enemy without orders. Hagan had asked why and was told that if the enemy found a weakness in our formation or a gap in our soldiers, then they would attack in force and divide us. Or if a group of knights gave chase, then they would soon be surrounded and massacred by the Turks.

"I must meet with the council now. Prepare for battle. I think the Turks will allow a contest today as we are within sight of Iconium. Strip the horses of all non-essentials. They have been through a lot lately I don't want them fatigued before ever we meet the enemy."

Aldrich turned and strode off toward Emperor Frederick's banner. Men parted to let him pass, saluting as he went.

Priests walked up and down the row of men as they stood looking down at the enemy blessing groups of men and absolving them of their sins. Apparently they didn't want to be caught off guard and began to do the ritual as soon as possible to avoid sending men into battle unprepared to meet God.

Obert and Ahren led the way back to the horses. They stripped their horses and Hagan followed their lead. Looking up, he noticed that he wasn't the only one. Several groups of men had also taken this que to begin the preparations. Ahren went to the tethered lances that dragged behind one of the packhorses and untied them. They fell with a clatter. Hagan's heart lurched.

He had practiced with lances. He'd even got to the point that he'd done it against Horst with blunted poles but he was hardly experienced. Obert pulled a fresh tunic over his head. Hagan looked at him quizzically.

"That one was so dirty one could hardly make out the cross. I want them to know who we fight for." Obert said, then he crossed himself.

Hagan only nodded his understanding and continued tightening the straps on his saddle. He had loosened them to allow Wighard breath as they walked. Hagan waited until Wighard exhaled and then pulled fiercely to cinch the belt to the warn mark on the leather. Hagan wasn't the only one that was feeling the results of not eating his fill, the girth strap was two holes tighter than it had been when they had entered Anatolia. Hagan patted Wighard's neck and then began pulling on his leather gloves. He surreptitiously retrieved the wooden stave from under the leg of his saddle and tucked it into his boot for luck. He lifted his coif to protect his neck, tightened the leather bracers that were on his forearms and untied his shield from his saddle.

It wasn't long before they heard a loud voice of a sergeant yell "prepare for battle".

The men that weren't already doing so began and the clangor of armor and weapons increased.

Hagan noticed that the entire army wasn't even to the top of the plateau yet, but they halted where they were and began their preparations and within twenty minutes the army had readied themselves and were forming ranks on top of the plateau. The baggage train remained on the other side of the plateau and were guarded by a company of spearmen and archers.

Duke Otto Wittelsbach stayed with the baggage sitting in the shade of one of the wagons, fanning himself with a pauldron. Hagan sighed at the injustice of it all. The man was a waste.

He didn't know what the Duke was conspiring but he knew that something nefarious was being conjured by the fat lump. They had tried to pay attention to the Duke's movements but it had been difficult to not become obvious in their subterfuge. Regardless of their efforts, no apparent misdeeds manifested themselves to Obert, Ahren, or Hagan.

Aldrich swore when he had been told of the meeting. He clearly understood the difficult situation instantly. He reassured them that he would discuss misgivings he had toward the Duke, with the Emperor, but more than that he could not commit to. He definitely couldn't discuss a supposed meeting that the Duke had had with the event's only witness being a low-born squire.

The Duke poured precious water over his head and belched. Waste of flesh, indeed.

Heavy cavalry formed both flanks of the infantry units and Aldrich and his men were on the far left. Page boys and soldiers ran back and forth distributing the lances to the mounted riders.

A rotund priest finally made it to where they sat their mounts and all the men within thirty feet of the clergyman dismounted and knelt to receive the blessing. The order to march was finally given, and they slowly moved down the hill.

The Turks had formed up far enough from the plateau so as not to give the Germans an advantage and so the army of God and the Holy Roman Empire marched to battle.

The plateau's slope was rugged in places. Rock outcroppings disrupted the orderliness of the unit formations and the army paused at the base of the slope to allow the units to reform. The Duke of Swabia, Emperor Barbarossa's son led this assault, and Hagan could see his standard waving high and proud in the distance to his right.

Hagan looked straight ahead and realized that the enemy was much further than it had appeared from on top of the plateau.

He turned to Obert and asked why they hadn't come down to the base of the hill before preparing for battle.

"The plateau is defensible. We left our supplies on top and behind because, in the event we have to retreat we can regroup on top and have our victuals to refresh us while we defend ourselves." Obert said.

"What victuals" Hagan mumbled.

Was it possible? Would they be defeated? Where would they go from here if they were? They were so far from anywhere. What they had on top was not enough to sustain them through much of a battle, or even days more of marching.

"Don't worry." Obert said. "We will crush them here. I have been in many battles and if these curs don't run at our first charge, then we will flatten them like a piece of soft led under a blacksmith's hammer. The only thing that we have to worry about are those damned arrows."

They had marched for almost a mile before the sergeants called a halt and the whole army came to a rippling stop. War horses side stepped and danced in anticipation of battle. The sound of beasts whinnying their excitement echoed from both flanks of the army.

Aldrich had been given command of the cavalry on the far left. Hagan had not trusted himself with Aldrich's personal banner during battle and so he offered it to Ahren who's right it had long been to carry. Ahren already had the Imperial standard and a horn that he would blow to relay different orders to Aldrich's men and so refused the banner. He had said something to the effect that Hagan had already earned the right and respect to carry it.

The added responsibility made Hagan terrified. The enemy would seek him out. It was a point of honor to safeguard a lord's banner and it was equally sought after by the enemy. They would do whatever it took to get that banner. Aldrich's honor was embodied in that piece of cloth. Hagan was also expected to remain as close to Aldrich as possible so as to give his men his position. If Hagan retreated, then the left flank retreated. If he advanced than they'd advance.

I wonder if I curl up in a ball on the ground would they do the same. Hagan thought.

Hagan turned in his saddle and looked at the knights that would follow the flag he carried. Thousands of eyes looked back at him. A shudder ran through him unbidden. There were so many.

His attention was caught by the man right behind him. Rothschild pursed his lips together and kissed the air between them and then bellowed with laughter at Hagan's uncomfortable smile.

"Most men are more worried about the men in front of them, in a battle, than those behind." Aldrich said.

Hagan turned back and looked to his right side where the knight sat his horse, calm and ready.

"I'm not." Hagan said. Which earned a raised eyebrow from Alrdich. surprised.

"I am less afraid of what they will do to me if I fail" signalling the Turks. "Then what they will do." and he pointed to the men behind him with his thumb.

Aldrich let out a surprised bark of laughter, as did Obert on Hagan's left.

Hagan did not laugh.

He had been serious.

He feared letting down the entire left flank of the army. A mistake by him could very well spell tragedy for the army. He could only imagine what would happen if he got lost like what had happened during that dark night when he'd killed Spatharios Photios. Only this time the entire left flank would follow his standard like dumb sheep to the slaughter.

Hagan sighed heavily.

"You have proven your honor and integrity in past engagements. All I ask is that you continue doing what you've done before. Just do it close to me." Aldrich said. A kind smile helped calm Hagan's nerves slightly.

He finally turned his attention to the enemy Turkish army in front of him and saw that it was all horsemen. There were no infantry. Thousands of men on horseback looked back at him. Grim-faced men with white cloth wrapped around their heads.

Was that for protection? Hagan wondered. It looked stifling to wear so much cloth.

Aldrich pulled his helm on and Hagan struggled to do the same with only one free hand. Finally he leaned the standard pole against his shoulder and pulled the great helm over his head.

There was a low trumpet call and the front two rows of the enemy kicked their horses forward. It was not a charge. They walked their horses slowly forward no real order apparent in their movement, but he did notice that the horsemen began to consolidate in the center. They were not tightly packed like a unit ready to charge. Suddenly Hagan heard a scream from the center of their own army. He looked and saw footman raise their shields. Arrows. The horsemen were launching arrows at the infantry. The center of the army where all the infantry stood tightly packed together provided a very target rich environment for the archers and they seemed to be drawn to it like moths to a flame. The Calvary on the flanks escaped the barrage for the moment. The enemy horsemen weren't letting the arrows fly in volleys, but each archer would loose as soon as he wanted and at what he wanted. Suddenly Hagan wanted to go. He wanted to charge and end the screams that increased from his right. Why do we wait? He wondered.

Aldrich waited. He wanted more of the enemy horsemen closer. There were very few German archers and the lack of return fire emboldened the horse archers. Good. Aldrich thought. They came closer.

Aldrich looked to his right. Yes, He was sure that the Emperor's son the Duke of Swabia, who commanded, saw it as well. How could he miss it?

Aldrich turned to Ahren on his right and told him to be ready to signal a full charge.

He looked back to the field. Yes, they were almost perfect. He looked to the distant right flank.

The Duke would probably wait for Aldrich to announce it. A hat tip to Aldrich's years of experience commanding men even though the Duke vastly out-ranked Aldrich. Sure enough, there was no movement on the right even though the horse archers had reached the perfect position. They would charge simultaneously from both flanks and hit the main line of waiting enemy horsemen behind the horse archers. That would allow the infantry to come forward and seek their revenge on the trapped archers.

Aldrich turned to Ahren and nodded.

Ahren put the horn to his lips with the hand not holding the Imperial standard and blew three loud quick bursts.

Abelard was ready and lurched forward under Aldrich at the sound. The incredible power of the animal still amazed Aldrich. The sound of hooves striking hard, dry ground sounded behind him as the left wing came forward with him.

He rode with the lance up. There was no point lowering it until they had closed with the enemy.

He glanced to the side to find exactly what he had expected. The Duke had also gone at his horn and the right flank was only slightly behind Aldrich's left. Aldrich saw the Seljuk horse archers confusedly turn and start back towards their own lines but it was too late. Aldrich was already passed the bulk of them and their own lines would not receive them as they would close in anticipation of the charge. The archers were trapped.

Aldrich glanced forward then to the sides to make sure he hadn't outpaced the rest of the cavalry. The objective of a good cavalry charge was for each knight in the front rank to strike the enemy's lines at precisely the same time. Then the successive ranks would hit the gaps that the others created. The danger to the front ranks was clear, but the danger to the following ranks of charging knights was mostly from their own men. If a knight fell the following knights would often be too close to avoid the sudden mound of thrashing steel and hooves. There were usually several knights lost when one fell.

Arrows flew from the enemy lines and Aldrich hoped that the charge would not stall behind him.

He looked forward and picked his target. A gap between two grimacing horsemen. He could plow through and allow the men behind him to cut down the men he passed.

He lowered his lance. His shield was strapped to his left arm, protecting that side.

Aldrich corrected Abelard's trajectory slightly with the press of his right knee into the horse's side.

Aldrich took a blow on his shield as he passed the front lines of the enemy but it did little to slow his momentum or distract him from his ultimate target.

Aldrich's lance dipped at the last moment and plunged into the horse's chest. The lance shaft snapped leaving a portion in Aldrich's hand. He threw it away. The impaled animal reared violently, trying to escape the torturous pain and fell sideways carrying the rider down with it. The felled animal cleared Aldrich's path and miraculously he remained horsed as he continued to move forward through the stunned Turks. Riders came at him from his right side but his sword was out as soon as he had dropped the lance and he knocked an incoming metal tipped lance up and away and as its holder came charging past, Aldrich slammed his arm forward striking the man full in the exposed face with his sword.

The man's head opened to the sword's freshly sharpened blade. Blood, bone and turban tumbled to the ground, followed quickly by the man's twitching body. A curved blade swung down at Aldrich but he slammed it away. The Turk brought it back for another swing but Aldrich slid the tip of his sword through the man's throat. He had been too slow and the surprise on his eyes was clear as he dropped the sword and reached for his gushing throat with both hands.

Aldrich caught the motion of a mounted archer draw his bow and in that instant he shifted the shield to cover his front just as the shaft struck. It made a loud thwack and the force of it slammed the upper rim of the shield into Aldrich's helm.

Anxiety started to grip Aldrich, and he forced the emotion to one side. Behind him he heard fierce fighting, but his men had not yet made it as deep as he had into the enemy ranks. He had assumed that the lightly armored horsemen would have broke before now. They're charge should have been devastating to the Turks, and yet, they fought on. Aldrich saw three more Turks bearing down on him from his right. On an impulse he turned and chopped a nearby riderless horse across the flank with his sword. The animal screamed in terror and launched itself forward right into the side of the closest Turk. Two of the horsemen went down in a sprawl of moving men and horseflesh. An enemy rider brought his sword down on Aldrich's shield which he lifted to plunge his sword underneath into the man's thigh. He pushed so hard that he heard the horse underneath the man scream in pain and then it was careening away in fear, as the other one had, taking other combatants out of the fight as it went. Suddenly Abelard shuddered under him, stumbled, tried to take another step. Another arrow was sent on its devastating path into the animal's chest. Aldrich saw this one come, but he was helpless to stop it. Abelard gave a gurgling moan of protest and collapsed under Aldrich.

Aldrich was clear of his dying friend in seconds and charging at the man that had sent the shafts. He would not give these dogs a stationary target to pin cushion. The man had put his bow on his back and switched to the curved swords that these nomads preferred. The man kicked his horse into motion but the beast only took two steps before Aldrich slammed his broadsword up to its hilt into the animal's chest.

Aldrich felt the animal pull to the side in surprise. He yanked hard on the sword and got it most of the way out of the wound before the horse had moved it out of reach.

Suddenly something struck him hard from behind. It had the force of a hammer blow to his back that knocked him to the ground. An arrow, had to be.

Aldrich tried to use his right arm to push himself back up but the pain in that shoulder was too intense. He heard a clash of metal behind him and felt a horse coming near through the ground. He rolled to his left instead and sat up from there.then scrambled to his feet. His right arm hung loosely at his side, useless.

He wanted to look round, see where his men were, but he needed to be armed first.

He used his teeth to uncinch the shield from his left arm and dropped it. He bent and picked up a dead Turk's sword. There he stood, too tired to charge the enemy, too proud to surrender. He looked over his shoulder and saw a Turk slumped in his saddle slide slowly to the ground.

As his body fell it revealed Hagan's face. It was covered in blood and it was contorted into a mask of pure hatred. Where was his helm? Aldrich glanced up at his banner. The boy still had it. And somehow was the first one to his rescue. How had he done it?

Hagan Had been ready to kick Wighard into action as soon as Ahren blew the horn, but there was no need. Wighard was excited and ready for battle. He had done this before. He probably had much more experience with this than Hagan did. The thought gave him comfort, small as it was. Aldrich was slightly ahead of Hagan and to his right. He used Aldrich's trajectory to check his own as he rode and he lined up his target. Because he carried the banner he wouldn't have a lance so at least there was that. He had been nervous about the prospect of having to use the weapon in an actual battle. Instead, he had the banner pole gripped in the left hand along with the shield grip. He found that the pole actually helped him lift his shield higher than he normally could for a sustained amount of time. He would place the pole in his stirrup and grip high on the pole so that the pole supported the weight of his shield as he rode.

As he picked up speed, he was glad that he had thought to pack the extra gaps between his new helm and his head with strips of cloth. It kept the heavy cap in place as he rode. The helm was very expensive. Most men had been jealous of it when they saw it. It was essentially just a skull cap which was like what most men in the army wore but it also had a nose guard and hinged cheek flaps that clasped under his chin. A chainmail curtain hung around the back of the helm to protect his neck. Hagan was proud of it and kept it spotless.

He was closing on the enemy. Arrows came intermittently from the enemy horsemen and he heard horses scream and riders fall around and behind him.

He saw a flash and flinched as an arrow slammed into his shield. It hit hard and before He felt Wighard take another step another had hit his shield. They wanted to bring down the banner he realized. He looked forward and saw his target, the man he'd kill turned and hit Aldrich's shield as he passed by leaving his back totally exposed to Hagan. He brought his sword in hard against the man's rib cage. His arm felt like it would pull from its socket as the sword was dragged through chainmail, muscle, bone and then spine. Then his sword was free, it had cleaved three quarters of the way through the man's abdomen. Hagan returned his attention forward and saw a horse and rider fly into his path. The horse had what could only be a piece of Aldrich's lance sticking from its chest. A great cloud of dust rose from its struggling body and suddenly Hagan was flying. Rather than slow and try to negotiate the thrashing animal, Wighard went over. He had leaped forward on powerful legs.

Hagan was not ready.

He had no hands to maintain a seat, and his body tumbled backward out of the saddle.

He landed among the dying horse and rider. A hoof slammed into his helm and jarred his head back as it was ripped clear of his ringing head.

Stars swam in his vision and he felt dizzy but he knew that he couldn't stay there.

He had kept a hold of his sword and used it to dispatch the rider who lay trapped under the horse. He had a moment's guilt at that, but he didn't want to leave a potential enemy behind him. Then he stumbled to where the banner lay. A Turk was dismounting to retrieve the fallen prize and Hagan slammed his shield into his back then slid his sword underneath it and up into the man's heart.

He bent and picked up the banner and then scanned the battlefield for Wighard. He saw him in the near distance kicking and bucking, fighting his own battle.

A Turk saw Hagan as an easy kill and spurred his horse toward him ready to end him with his raised sword. Hagan dropped his sword and stepped forward. Gripping the banner pole now with two hands he slammed it into the approaching rider's face.

He knew that the man would fall. No one could maintain a seat when being hit square in the face with that much force. He bent and picked up his sword again and without hesitating ran toward Wighard. A Turk on horseback was trying to grab Wighard's reins when Hagan reached the horse.

The man was shocked to suddenly feel his arm cleaved off at the elbow. Hagan finished him by stabbing his sword up through the man's throat and into his head.

Hagan wasn't prepared for the shower of blood that poured down on top of him but he kept moving.

He had to find Aldrich now. He couldn't believe he was lost again. Where was everyone, he wondered as he pulled himself into Wighard's saddle.

God please let me find Aldrich.

The prayer came unbidden to his thoughts, but it felt right. He scanned the battlefield once again, only this time looking for his liege lord and friend. He heard and saw melee all around him. The initial charge had cut deep into the enemy lines, but had stalled as the mass of dead and dying created obstacles that impeded the calvary's advance. A glance behind him gave him a fleeting view of several familiar faces, but they were still out of range to assist him.

Hagan checked a sword thrust to his right side and spurred Wighard forward. There was a void in the forest of enemy horsemen about twenty paces deeper into the thronging horde and Hagan knew it had to be Aldrich. An arrow smacked into Hagan's shield and Knocked the pole into his nose, stunning him briefly. That was the first thing he felt, but then he felt pain radiating from his left hand. The arrow had pierced his shield and went through his hand and into the banner pole.

Hagan screamed and then turned the sound into a war cry. He urged Wighard forward faster. The horse slammed into a

Turk's side and sent the smaller horse and rider tumbling to the ground. Wighard pawed at the man when he hit the ground and continued on. Hagan was almost there. Just a little further and he would be able to see what obstruction created the void.

The next Turk in his path lifted his bow and shot an arrow down. Hagan knew it was at Aldrich.

He gritted his teeth against the pain in his hand. The man's attention was still focused on where he'd shot the arrow and Hagan rode up beside him and slammed his sword through the man's back. It had plunged deep and struck the man's heart. He was dead while still in the saddle and finally he slumped to the ground.

Hagan looked down over the now empty saddle of the Turkish horse and saw Aldrich looking at him. An arrow protruded from the back of his shoulder and the scar on his face had opened giving an even more ghoulish cast to the warrior's face but he was alive.

Hagan pushed Wighard past the horse and past Aldrich and past Abelard's body.

Hagan had to maintain an aggressive stance or the enemy would realize its advantage and overwhelm them. The only reason he could think of why they were still alive was because of the speed with which it was happening. So much had happened in so little time. Hagan had killed four, six? He wasn't sure. But he knew that men were doing that up and down the line. The Turks had been stunned.

Hagan bellowed another war cry. He put all the frustration, fear, anger and pain into it that he felt. A group of men that were about to attack Aldrich from behind, were taken aback by the rage in Hagan's eyes.

He wondered what he looked like that would put such looks of fear and shock on their faces. He kicked Wighard forward and slammed into one man. The man tried to block a blow with a wood and leather shield but Hagan's sword cleaved deep into the shield and the momentum of the swing brought the shield down and the end of the sword split the man's face. He screamed a terrifying scream of pure pain and fell from his horse. As he did, Hagan's sword pulled free.

The other men had had enough and wheeled their horses away.

Hagan turned and searched for more enemies.

He saw the Imperial flag and then Ahren was through. He'd cut his way through the enemy and come to Aldrich's banner. Obert was there soon after that. More and more crosses could be seen as they forced their way through the enemy. Hagan saw Rothschild like a bear mounted on a horse swinging a broadsword, laughing. He was laughing!

Hagan scanned back. And felt another arrow glance off of his curved shield. He spotted the man and began to charge at him, but the man turned his mount and fled before Hagan could reach him. Hagan saw that that was happening up and down the line. Then suddenly something changed. It was something unexplainable. Like when the weather is about to change and you know it. The enemy's morale had been broken. Their resolve to fight had been used up and they turned and fled. Small bands retreated first, then larger groups until all were running. The German cavalry gave chase cutting down all they could catch.

Hagan sheathed his sword, dismounted, and went to Aldrich. The banner came with him of course as it was stuck to his hand.

"Are you alright?" Hagan asked.

"I have an arrow in my shoulder but I'll live. What took you so long?"

"I fell off my horse sir." Hagan said.

Aldrich laughed and sheathed his own sword then slapped Hagan on the back.

"I'm glad to see that you got back on." Aldrich said.

Obert rode up and dismounted. He hurried over to Aldrich. They clasped left arms, since Aldrich's right was suffering from the arrow in that shoulder.

"Can you ride, sir? I'd like to have you where you'll stay before I go about removing that arrow from you."

"I can ride." Aldrich said. He turned and looked down at Abelard. "He saved my life several times. I wish I wouldn't have gotten him killed."

Aldrich turned and looked at Hagan.

"You can put that banner down for now Hagan, why don't you start gathering up some of these horses you liberated." He said.

Hagan looked at his hand, remembering the pain now.

"I can't sir" Hagan said.

"Why can't you" Aldrich said somewhat more forcefully than Hagan had expected.

"An arrow sir. It pinned my hand sir." Hagan answered somewhat defensively.

Obert stepped over and examined the wound.

"I'll be damned! That is the first time I have seen such a thing." Obert laughed.

He continued to laugh as Obert reached out and wiggled the pole in Hagan's hand as if not quite believing that he couldn't release it.

"It may be amusing to you, Obert, but to me it is rather tender." He said through gritted teeth.

"Oh" Obert said. "Does that hurt" and he poked the tender flesh surrounding the wound.

Hagan's right hand swung up and cuffed Obert across the head, nearly sending him to the ground.

Aldrich roared with unexpected laughter but quickly quieted it due more to the pain from his wound than a sense of impropriety.

Hagan stood there, stunned by his own action. He hadn't even thought about it. His arm seemed to have responded of its own volition. The reaction was apt to how he felt after giving it more thought, so Hagan didn't apologize.

"Well, I guess I should know better than to poke a bear with a toothache." Obert said.

Chapter 32

The sun had set in an orange hue that covered the whole sky that evening. They had moved camp to be closer to the sealed gates of Iconium and the wounded had been taken there first, along with a third of the army so as to dissuade the garrison from sallying.

Despite Hagan's protests he was considered "wounded" by Aldrich and was taken along with his liege lord to the besieging camp early. Obert went as well to look after them.

Ahren reported to Aldrich the sad news that Manfred had died.

The news stunned Hagan. He had spent too much time with the man over the past months to not be affected.

Manfred had taken an arrow in the charge and they found his body on the battlefield. Hagan had wanted to stay and help bury his friend, but after Obert had removed the arrow from his hand, the pain made him relent. Obert said that it would be easier to ride if the arrow in his hand was out and so he had broken the end and pushed the arrow through the shield. Then, when he was finally, excruciatingly free of the shield, Obert pulled on the pole brining the arrow though his hand and free.

He had almost passed out with the pain and decided that he'd forego helping bury Manfred.

He sat, instead, looking out at the distant mass of bodies mill about the recent battlefield. The far distant mass of dark had turned orange with the setting of the sun and as dusk settled, the mass broke up and started filtering into camp.

They had plenty of food now. Horse wasn't as good as he had hoped, but it filled the void that everyone had felt for far too long. Fires blazed that night and the smell of roasting horse meat filled the air.

Obert had cut the arrow out of Aldrich's shoulder without too much trouble. Aldrich had cursed as he had done so, but Obert said that it hadn't passed far into the muscle having been slowed by Aldrich's leather jerkin and chainmail.

They sat together now, waiting for the rest of their men to return to camp. Obert had set about setting camp with what they had available and had forbidden Hagan from helping. He was glad, but felt awkward. It was Hagan's job to do the work as those of higher rank rested after a long day. He was ill at ease during his forced idleness.

He sat a few feet from Aldrich, shifting uneasily.

"I am indebted to you." Aldrich said, out of the blue.

Hagan was taken aback. Was he being sincere? He thought for sure he had failed Aldrich by not staying closer to him during the battle.

Hagan turned to assess Aldrich's face. He looked sincere.

"Uh. I don't.... Why do you say that?" Hagan stammered.

"Besides the fact that you saved my life?" Aldrich said, somewhat exasperated.

"Oh, umm. I shouldn't have lost you to begin with. It seems that I tend to get lost when I fight." Hagan said uncomfortably.

Aldrich chuckled. It was an easy, contented sound that Hagan couldn't recall ever hearing come from the man.

"Well, you found me when no one else did. For that I thank you." He said.

Hagan just nodded to him because he wasn't sure what to say.

"What happens now?" Hagan said and pointed toward Iconium. He mainly wanted to change the subject, but he was also very curious about what would be expected of him in the next fight. He'd never been part of a siege.

Aldrich grunted and looked at the dark silhouette that the city created, black against the setting sun.

"Shouldn't be too bad as far as assaults go. Frederick may give us a few days to rest after the battle. After all, we have the dead Turk's supplies, but he just as easily could decide to go in the morning so as not to give the enemy time to regroup. We still have to build ladders so I bet that we will have a little rest."

"Ladders?" Hagan said. "What do we build them with?" He looked around as if maybe he had missed something. There weren't any trees and as a matter of fact, they only had fires tonight because they were close enough to the city where there had been wandering goat herds whose dung they now burned. The herds must have been brought into the city in anticipation of their arrival, but they neglected to gather the dried pieces of fuel. That coupled with the scraggly bushes, they had fuel enough for fires to cook their tough horse meat.

"Lances," Aldrich said. "We lash them together."

Hagan nodded. That made sense. There had been plenty of lances broken during the fight that could now be used for the rungs, and the full lengths they had could be used for the sides.

Rothschild probably shouldn't try to climb one, but they would probably work for normal-sized people.

Hagan shifted uncomfortably and accidentally used his injured hand to adjust himself. A lance of pain shot through it and up his arm. The wound was slow to forgive his mistake and throbbed after. Hagan's face betrayed him and made his discomfort plain to Aldrich.

"Here." Aldrich said and tossed a water skin to Hagan.

Hagan nodded his thanks. He was parched. He unstoppered the nozzle and poured the cool liquid down his throat, then immediately choked and coughed. Burning. It burned. Aldrich laughed as Hagan struggled to breathe. It wasn't water. It was some kind of wine. It smelled very strong, unlike any wine he had smelled or drank before.

"That is something I picked up in Philomelium. Good, eh?" He laughed.

"I think it's still made with grapes, but who cares, it's strong enough to help with the pain." Aldrich said and motioned for Hagan to drink more.

Hagan hesitated but then took a strong pull from the skin. He was determined not to choke this time, and it went down easier but he still made a face as he pulled the skin away.

Hagan smiled as the burning in his throat subsided and a warmth spread down into his chest. He looked up at the handful of twinkling stars, the first of the night, and was happy to be alive. There had been several moments that day that he shouldn't have survived. His happiness increased as he took another long, successful, pull on the liquor.

Hagan sat with Aldrich, having escaped death earlier in the day, and felt content...until Ahren and the others came into view. Their heads were bowed with sorrow and fatigue. Hagan had almost forgotten about Manfred and berated himself. How could he feel happy at a time like this? One of his friends had just died.

He handed the skin back to Aldrich.

The knight took it and took a final drink before stoppering the top.

The very air seemed to have changed as the other men approached the fire. Their solemn faces seemed to darken the very sky as the sun pulled the heaven's few recalcitrant rays in its wake.

They prayed that night. Sir Aldrich had knelt first and motioned for the other men to take a knee around the fire. Aldrich prayed for Manfred and thanked God for the victory. He prayed for the army as a whole and for each one of them individually.

Hagan had never heard anyone pray as he did. The words were honest and clear. The thoughts seemed to be his own, as if Aldrich could read his mind and Hagan found himself in complete agreement with what was said. The prayer wasn't as the priests prayed; it was sincere, genuine and Hagan could understand it. The priests always spoke in Latin and while Obert and Ahren had tried to teach Hagan the language he had made little progress. A word here and a phrase there was all he was ever able to make out when the priests prayed. As Aldrich spoke, it felt like he was talking to God himself which, Hagan supposed, was the point.

After Aldrich finished all the men crossed themselves and began to relax around the fire. Words came slowly, everyone contemplated the day's events and what Aldrich had done as Hagan did.

They ate and as the hot food filled their shrunken bellies, their moods began to lift and words and conversations came more smoothly. By the end of the night the men had returned to themselves and laughed as they always did in each other's company. Hagan sat silently. He pulled the piece of wood from his boot and looked at it. He had carried the thing for so long that each grain was familiar to his touch. His mind's eye could picture perfectly each indentation and notch.

He slipped his dagger from the sheath on his belt and began to carve on the stave. The piece of wood, his good luck charm, would no longer be hid away under his saddle or tucked in his boot. Hagan smiled to himself as he carved.

Chapter 33

The hours and days melded together. Greta wasn't sure of much of anything anymore, let alone what time of the day it was or even what the season was. She had tried to count how many meals she had had but the inconsistency of the meal times had even robbed her of that ability. She never would have thought how hard it was on her emotions and mental state, not knowing where the sun was at in its repetitive sojourn. At one moment she would be relatively optimistic and coherent of thought, the next she would be trembling and sobbing in the corner.

Greta had imagined scenario after scenario of being rescued. Most of the imaginings depicted Hagan as the hero. He would always kill Ludolf. Most of the time in very painful ways. He would scream while she watched.

Hagan would sometimes have a whole army with him he would use to take the keep and kill Adelfried and all the staff. Including Milda Decker. That hag deserved it. Didn't she? Greta regretted not killing her. Maybe. She wasn't really sure. Nothing made sense anymore. All Greta knew is that she wanted to either be free or dead. Continuing on in this absurd existence was beyond her ability to imagine.

Greta heard the familiar heavy footsteps of Ludolf as he brought her food. A whimper escaped her throat. She would gladly never eat again if it meant that she didn't have to see that man again. If it meant that his groping hands would not touch her. If it meant that his disgusting smell did not fill her nostrils.

Keys jangled in the door and the man's large foot kicked the door open as it always did. He tossed the food down on the floor as he always did, not caring about feeding her, just using the food as a pretense to harass and rape her.

He grunted and undid the belt at his waist. She didn't move. He grunted again.

"Come here, you whore." he said.

"You know what I like."

She whimpered again and slowly raised herself to her feet.

He apparently wouldn't be appeased this time by a little fondling and abuse. He must have judged that today he had the time to rape her as he sometimes had before anyone would miss his absence.

Greta's legs quivered as she stood and she steadied herself against the wall. His leggings were around his ankles, and his hand was moving under his tunic.

"Take it off." He said.

Greta knew what he meant, and she despaired as her hands moved to obey. She tried not to sob. Ludolf would sometimes use her tears as an excuse to beat her. She slid the loose shift off of her slender shoulders and let it fall to the cold stone floor. She stood naked.

Ludolf grunted his approval and his breath came more rapidly. His disgusting face had a slack expression of pleasure on it.

A knife appeared from behind Ludolf suddenly. The blade whipped up to his throat and sliced deeply into the hideous man's throat without so much as a pause. Ludolf's hands left his groin and instinctively reached for his wound. He felt there, blood covering his fingers. His face, that had moments ago been slack, turned terror filled in an instant. His eyes were wide as the hopelessness of his situation became apparent to him.

As she watched, Greta saw a bubble form in the blood around his throat. The man collapsed to his knees and behind him, Greta saw her mother. She had a look on her face that Greta had never seen her express before. Pure hatred. She stood looking down at the struggling man, teeth clenched and the red dripping blade in her right hand. Her blade. Greta's little knife, the one that her mother had given her for her birthday had ended Ludolf. They had taken it from her when they had imprisoned her and she had wished for it ever since. It couldn't be her mother. It must just be another one of her imaginings. Her desire for rescue had made her see her mother cut the wicked man's throat. Sadness at the realization wrapped her in a heavy cloak.

Ana's angry scowl turned to one of pained love as she looked up and saw her bruised and dirty child standing naked in the cold room. She dropped the knife and ran to Greta. The apparition of her mother hugged Greta.

Greta in turn seemed distant. Her response was slow, and she seemed to not understand what was happening. She didn't hug Ana back and didn't look at her as she spoke soothing words to her.

Ana had to get her moving, regardless of the distant unseeing look that her daughter returned.

Ana ran out of the room and returned with her bundle of clothes she had brought for Greta. She coaxed her into them.

"I tried everything to get to you." Ana heard herself saying. She didn't even know if Greta heard her. Her eyes seemed to not recognize that she was even there.

"Greta." Ana said. She shook her daughter gently and looked into her eyes.

"Greta look at me."

Greta finally looked at Ana. Her expression still distant.

"Greta. I'm here and I'm going to get you out of here."

Greta focused on her mother's eyes finally. Her eyes glittered with a hint of emotion and the corners of her mouth turned up very slightly. Her hand rose slowly and touched Ana's cheek. Greta's head tilted slightly, inquisitive. Suddenly her brows furrowed and her chest heaved. Tears fell in streams down her face. Touching Ana's cheek had seemed to solidify the fact of her presence in Greta's mind.

Greta's breath came in shuddering gasps as she sobbed. Ana pulled her daughter close. She knew that they had to get moving. She knew that every moment that they spent here was a moment that they would lose on any advantage that they had. Once Ludolf's Corpse was found they would be hunted down. Their lives would be forfeit. Their only chance, slim as it was, lay in their speed. Their embrace felt like it lasted for far too long given their circumstances and yet not nearly long enough.

Ana forced herself to pull away from her sobbing child and led her from the room.

Ana returned to the storage room turned dungeon and found the key in Ludolf's pocket then locked the corpse inside. Hopefully that was the only key and the body would remain hidden for long enough for them to escape. Ana returned to Greta and guided her forward.

They stalked quietly among wine casks and grain sacks. Ana's heart was pounding so hard that she heard little over the rhythmic thumping in her ears. She turned left instead of right when they reached the top of the stairs that led from the basement storage rooms. The courtyard, barracks and gates were that way, and the normal path that servants took to leave the castle. There were also an abundance of people, guards and men at arms to recognize and seize them.

Ana coaxed Greta to follow her along a side corridor that paralleled the massive hall, that Adelfried hosted banquets in, toward the kitchens in the rear of the keep. Ana prayed that she would meet no one in the corridor or past the hectic kitchens in the side passages that led to the postern.

Ana turned the corner and could now hear the clatter and clangor of pans and cooking tools over the beating of her heart. She swallowed even though her throat was completely dry and grabbed Greta's hand. She walked down the poorly lit corridor as quickly as possible. They had passed two doors leading to the kitchen and were halfway to the third and final door when Ana heard the door behind them open. She didn't stop and just prayed that whoever it was wouldn't stop them, or better yet see them.

"Greta?" A voice asked.

Ana's heart sank and Greta's hand suddenly gripped her hand tightly. It was Milda's voice.

If they ran, they wouldn't make it far before the bitter old woman's alarm sent Adelfried's men in pursuit. Any advantage they had was gone. They were done.

Ana turned around and pulled Greta behind her as she did so.

Milda stood, framed by the light filtering down the corridor, the light from the still open door to the kitchen reflected off of her wrinkled face.

Milda looked into the kitchen and Ana was sure that she would yell the alarm. Instead, she closed the door.

She took a cautious step towards them.

"Greta, I had no idea. I didn't know…" She was speaking low and wringing her hands.

"I wouldn't have told on you if I had known they were going to give you to Ludolf." She paused. "He is a monster." She said.

Her voice had cracked at the mention of Ludolf and Milda had come close enough for Ana to make out tears starting a path down each of the old woman's cheeks. Milda had come to within an arm's reach of Ana and held out her hand.

"Please help me atone in some small measure. Let me help you." Milda said. Her voice was thick with emotion.

Ana had a hard time believing her. Not that the expression on the old woman's face wasn't genuine looking. Her tears looked real enough, and the woman's voice seemed contrite, but it was hard to see her as anything but a bitter old hag that deserved the knife stroke that Greta hadn't given her. For years she had abused her and her daughter. She had never seen a moment of compassion from the woman since being placed under her.

What choice did she have? Their fate was in this woman's hands regardless if Ana trusted her or not.

She nodded and Milda clicked her tongue in that annoying way whenever she was decided on something and moved past the two women in the corridor.

Once she got to the end, she stopped and looked down the next, presumably, to check that it was clear, then she motioned for them to follow.

Ana pulled Greta along and prayed silently to saint Rupert. She didn't pray often and she, honestly, didn't know much about the saint, but she had grown up hearing prayers to him. He had lived long ago in Salzburg which was not far. Maybe he had God's ear and would put in a good word for her and Greta.

Milda navigated them successfully into the small courtyard in the shadow of the massive keep tower. This small area was rarely visited by anyone during the day as its only function was to guard the sally port. The sally port was a small doorway through the outer wall and was guarded by a single man.

Ana hadn't thought for long about how she was going to get the guard to let them out but she was fairly certain that the dagger would again be needed. She didn't want to do it but her daughter's safety gave her a resolve that she never imagined she would be capable of.

Oh, Saint Rupert. She thought. Bless us now.

She felt the knife handle nervously through the cloth of her dress.

"Ah, Merkle! What a day it is." Milda said. Ana had never heard the woman use this tone with any of the kitchen staff.

The guard looked up and grunted at Milda when he saw her.

"I brought you your lunch deary." She said and shuffled through her pocket then pulled out a large sausage that she doubtless pilfered from the kitchens.

The man's demeanor perked up at the sight of food.

She handed the sausage over to him and he instantly took a large bite and chewed eagerly. Grease dribbled in his beard. "Still warm" he said delightedly.

"Now don't I treat you right?" Milda said.

The guard took another big bite and chuckled.

"Deary, do you mind opening this door for us? I don't want to be walking halfway round the castle in this mud."

He didn't even hesitate. He turned to the door, stuck the sausage in his mouth and fiddled with the locking bar. The door swung open on squeaky hinges.

"We'll be coming back with a load, love, so you won't have to worry about letting us back in. We're bringing a cart in from town after some errands." She patted his cheek as she waddled past. Ana and Greta followed her through.

They were through. They were free.

They walked for a time in silence. No one really dared tempt fate.

Finally Milda spoke.

"Do you know the priory at Graz?" she said.

Ana shook her head. She hadn't been that far south.

"Follow the road to Graz, but don't use the road. I assume that Ludolf is dead?"

Ana nodded.

"Good, but his death will make your journey harder. Stay off the roads. They will be looking for you. The priory is to the north of the town. Ask for my brother Odo. He's a good person. Far better than me." Milda looked at Greta apologetically.

"Give him this" Milda said and reached up to her neck and pulled a necklace that had been hidden under her clothing up over her head. It was a silver cross that hung from a simple sinew cord.

She handed it to Ana.

"He'll know that I sent you."

"Is he a priest?" Ana asked.

"A monk."

Milda pointed to the trees.

"You had better get going. They may sound the alarm any minute."

"What will you do?" Ana asked

"I have to make my way to town and find a cart to bring in through the main gates as well as two women to accompany me." She smiled at Ana. "God speed your journey." Milda clasped Greta's hands and brought them to her mouth, kissing them. "I hope that someday you can forgive me. I know that I will never forgive myself." she said. Then she turned and walked toward town.

Chapter 34

They came during the night, and by morning the entire army was surrounded. He hadn't been surprised by the tactic. As a matter of fact he had anticipated it. What had surprised him were the numbers. Dust swelled from the arid ground in massive columns.

Turkish horsemen darted forward in their customary way and launched savage barrages of arrows that made horses scream and men curse.

Frederick's obvious course of action was to fight his way through to the relative safety of the open ground beyond. It was customary for a sieging force to give way to a relieving force like that of the Turks. It was madness to do anything else. The preservation of the army was paramount to anything else and pinned against the walls of Iconium as they were was a recipe for disaster.

That's what logic told him. That's what years of experience told him. Hell, his generals were sure to tell him the very same thing in a few minutes. His heart, however, told him something very different.

He had to take this city, and he had to do it now. His men would sooner turn on him than go off into the desert again. Progress was forward. He could not withdraw and maintain the fragile morale of the men.

He was decided, now to coerce the rest. He threw the tent flap back ahead of his guard who took up positions just outside. The command tent was already filled. Aldrich stood near the front of the group next to his son. His son shared his name, and it appeared his abilities as a commander.

Not three weeks past Frederick Duke of Swabia had led a counter-attack on the turks that relieved the army of that horrible pressure that only the Turks could inflict.

The meeting went surprisingly well. Aldrich had helped make the point that they had wished that the Turks would fight in earnest and it appeared that they now, finally, had been forced into action rather than the frustrating hit-and-run tactics they had all become accustomed to.

He convinced them to, simultaneously, take Iconium and defeat the surrounding Turks. Only a few voices offered any kind of descent. They all wanted into the city as soon as possible.

He put his son in charge of assaulting the city.

"You will be with me" He said to Aldrich who merely nodded in response.

"You will help me with the cavalry and the command on the ground."

"Of course, Sire." He said.

"Hold back the charges until you are certain of catching the maximum number of their troops on their back foot. We don't want them to break us up and devour us a piece at a time." Frederick knew that Aldrich knew this and he didn't need the reminder, but many of the subsidiaries needed the reminder and it would give Aldrich additional authority later if he needed to reprimand any subordinates for disobedience.

Aldrich nodded once more.

Frederick called the meeting to an end and men left, talking excitedly.

Frederick pulled his son to the side before he left.

"If things go poorly for us, we will be depending on you to capture the city quickly so we may save who we can."

The duke nodded. "I understand, father. God Willing, we will lunch in the citadel."

Hagan looked out at the dust swallowed enemy. There were so many of them. He felt at his neck and grasped the cross that hung there. It was wooden, and smooth. He'd left the cross large compared to those formed from metal because he didn't want the wood to break. But the object was still small and delicate feeling in his hand. He stroked it and then raised it to his lips and kissed it. The stave. The pail. It had been changed and yet the importance to him remained the same. God saved him that day. Spared his life. Given him a reason to believe. His faith had grown from that moment of realization.

Strength seemed to course through him. He felt comfort. He tucked the cross back under his chainmail and looked over at Obert.

Obert looked back.

"This should be exciting." He said. A huge smile was on his face.

"Why are you so happy?" Hagan asked.

"Because today we will finally be able to pay those bastards back for all the damned arrows they've sent at us."

"What was the other day then?" Hagan said.

"Oh that." Obert chuckled. "That was a pittance, they ran off before we could really get satisfaction from them."

Hagan raised his bandaged hand to Obert.

"A pittance? I wonder what will happen to me this time if that was a pittance."

Obert laughed and clapped him on the back as if he had said something funny. Hagan didn't think he had.

The men had been arrayed for battle, separated into units and ready for fighting since dawn but were forbidden, as always, to be goaded into a charge by the enemy archers. Instead they waited, exposed to the enemy, waiting for the order.

To his left Hagan heard a curse as a group of Turks launched a volley into their ranks. A horse screamed and Hagan heard the clang of metal and the rattle of shafts as they fell among the men. One horse seemed to falter and the man astride it, a shaft protruding from his shoulder rode the beast to the ground before jumping clear as the animal rolled. He cursed loudly and yanked on the arrow in his shoulder. It seemed, as was common, the man's armor protected him and the arrow only stabbed shallowly into his flesh. Even so, it took several tries and help from a comrade to get the arrow removed. The man bent and stroked the animal's head as it died then began removing the tack from the beast.

He would fight on foot it seemed.

Hagan wore his shield on his back and held the banner in his left hand. He couldn't hold both the banner and the shield with his wounded hand, so he was even more exposed to the enemy's arrows than most.

Hagan heard horns blowing and distant shouts that spoke of excitement coming from behind him. He turned in the saddle but couldn't see far through the heads of cavalry and past the baggage train which clogged the space between them and the city walls.

A few others heard the commotion and turned, but most remained focused on the threat directly in front of them.

"They have begun the assault." Ahren said. "Won't be long now."

The now familiar flutter of fear passed over Hagan, but it wasn't as fierce as it had been the last time.

Men coaxed their horses to the side to make way for Aldrich as he came up to the front of the formation.

Aldrich nodded to Hagan.

"Are you ready for today? I won't have you being killed over that scratch on your hand." He nodded to Hagan's bandaged hand.

Hagan looked at his hand and back to Aldrich.

"I'll be fine Sir." He said.

Aldrich grunted a grudging acceptance.

"Well, if you need to move to the back, there is no shame in it. Obert can handle the banner but if you're determined to fight then I can't blame you. Just pace yourself. It's going to be a long day."

"We're not pushing through then?" Ahren asked from the other side of Aldrich.

"We're not, unless it's to break the horde into more manageable bites which is exactly what I have been commanded not to let happen to us." With that he kicked his horse forward and half stood in the saddle as he turned his mount, a grey beast that Aldrich had won in their last fight. The horse was slightly smaller than what they usually rode, but quite large for the Turkish lot.

"Men of Germany! Men of God!" He shouted.

The men around Hagan erupted with a cheer.

"Finally, we get revenge for the past month of torture!"

The cheer that followed now dwarfed the last. The men were all watching and listening to him now, despite the faux charge of a nearby detachment of Turks. The men had all gotten used to this tactic. It was a way to tempt knights into an unplanned charge, the very thing that Aldrich had mentioned.

All men, even Hagan, were tempted from time to time to charge out at the incoming enemy and chase them into the ground.

"Do not let your fervor for justice cloud your minds though. Remember discipline. Hold your formations and wait for your commands! I will personally burn out the eyes of any man that disobeys the command or charges early! No booty until after the fighting is over! Don't worry there will be plenty!"

At that, the men cheered again.

Aldrich turned his horse and backed into position once more, marking the end to his short speech.

Booty was a soldier's right Hagan was becoming more and more accepting of. They all risked so much, the least that they deserved was the spoils left by the dead. All too often, however, men would die while trying to secure a particularly expensive looking sword from a fallen enemy, or while rifling the pockets of a richly dressed corpse.

A group of Turks had, seen Aldrich give the speech and moved in for the kill. A commander of a force this large would have booty indeed.

They charged in until they were well within bowshot and took aim at Aldrich. A group of foot archers who were stationed nearby had prepared for this and sent arrows at the oncoming Turks with such force and accuracy that the Turks drew and loosed too quickly, sending their shafts wide, while several of their number fell. The survivors regrouped and wheeled away as another volley was sent in their wake. The cavalry cheered the archers as they went up and down the line protecting the horses where they could. It was obvious that the German army had far too few archers for this style of fighting and Hagan found himself tempted by the prospect of joining the archer's ranks.

Wighard tossed his head as if sensing Hagan's thoughts.

"Don't worry boy, I wouldn't leave you." He said and patted the horse's neck.

Obert donned his helmet beside him and Hagan took this as the cue to do the same. He had only his mail coif pulled up as most men had since the heat was so fierce that wearing the full helms, like what Hagan now had, was stifling. He'd traded his open-faced helm for a great helm. The old one was now dented and after how Manfred had died, he decided that a full helm might be a good idea.

The helm was large and cylindrical. It had two narrow eye slits, and it was polished steel.

He had been afraid that he would have difficulty seeing out of the thing, but it wasn't as bad as he thought. Due partly to the fact that his helmet fit him snuggly. It moved with him and didn't jostle as he rode which was nice. It had a large cross inlaid into the steel over the face of the helm.

Horns blared behind Hagan. They weren't German horns. Coming from the city then?

The army of Turkish horsemen responded almost instantly. Detachments advanced in organized units to harry the German lines as they never had before. Waves of arrows assaulted the armored German troops. Screams rose in abundance all along the front ranks. Sound that was at first dulled from his helmet, became a torrent in his ears. Arrow shafts clattered and barbed tips rang as they struck a resilient helm or shield, but all too many landed with the sickening thud as they drove home into a soldier's body.

"These devils don't like the idea of us taking Iconium, I'll tell you that much." Obert said to Hagan from behind the protection of his shield. Two arrows were stuck in it.

Amazingly, Hagan had, so far been untouched by the deluge.

He tapped his chest, where his cross lay hidden, and yelled his defiance over the noise of dying men. He put all his anger and frustration that had been pent up the whole time that he had been with the army. He roared his rage and Obert picked it up as well as did a smattering of other voices. Suddenly, it was the whole army screaming a deafening war cry that seemed to shake the very ground.

The onslaught of arrows seemed to falter as did the organization of the Turks detachments. Some of the enemy seemed to lag behind their comrades and their cohesion melted before the vehemence in the German's yells. Gaps formed in their attacking lines as only the bravest among them continued forward. German arrows whistled forward to strike down the stalwart few who pressed the attack.

The whole enemy army seemed to stall, then commanders yelled, and an organization began to take shape once more. Units gathered into their loose formations and started forward, a little more slowly this time. Turkish sergeants yelled threats in their indecipherable tongue, and the attack began again.

"They're piss'n in their boots!" Rothschild's booming voice called from somewhere behind Hagan and the men within earshot rumbled with laughter.

The German Infantry formed in the center of the defense as it had in the battle a few days before, but this time there were also a thin, two ranks deep, buffer between the cavalry units and the enemy. As a result Infantry now faced the enemy across the whole battle line, and it curved out of sight to Hagan's left.

As they were on the defense, Hagan understood the importance behind it. The infantry spearmen were an effective counter to the light Turkish cavalry charge. The German archers were also effective against their mounted counterparts. If a counter charge was ordered by Aldrich, the infantry would open practiced gaps in their lines that would allow the cavalry to rush forward to engage the enemy.

The Turks were still a way off, and not yet in bow range when Aldrich signaled for the Infantry to move forward. The sergeants called orders to their men, and the foot began to move forward.

Ahren looked a question at Aldrich, perplexed.

"We need room. We can't give our mounts their head crammed in like this." He told him.

If they could get enough space opened in front of them, then they would be able to have a strong charge which was their greatest weapon.

"But what about the foot?" Hagan blurted out.

Aldrich turned to him, his visor up, and reached up and patted his shoulder. The gesture was familial. Like something a father would do to a son when he was teaching him something important.

"They will be in no more danger there than they would be here. Trust me." He said.

"I do." Hagan said and instantly felt foolish as his voice rang back to him inside his helm.

Aldrich nodded and signaled for the foot to stop their advance. It gave the cavalry enough space to get their mounts into a dangerous charge, but it would take them only seconds to cross the space between.

Turkish horns sounded and the charging enemy kicked their animals into a full charge. This would be no faint. They were committed.

"When they stall at the infantry, we go!" Aldrich yelled then lowered his visor.

Hagan felt a trickle of sweat run down his cheek and heard the blood in his ears. With the exceptions of Aldrich and Hagan only the front rank of cavalry had lances, the rest would only be hampered in the tight area by the weapons.

This was it. A few enemy horses went down to the defending arrows, but the majority struck the infantry hard, and Hagan felt pity for those men. He couldn't help but think Aldrich had abandoned them. It seemed impossible that any line of defense would be enough against such numbers. Hagan saw many of the spearmen fall. But he also saw a number of horses collapse.

A few of the Turks broke through the infantry line and, instead of pushing forward towards the waiting cavalry, turned on the rear of the infantry ranks.

Hagan looked at Aldrich, waiting for the nod that would begin the charge, but it didn't come. More and more of the enemy collided into the ranks of the Infantry and a mass of horsemen were clumped together up and down the line, waiting for their turn to fight. The infantry were doing their best but losing ground.

Finally Aldrich nodded, and Ahren put his lips to the horn that sounded the charge. Hagan was ready and kicked Wighard forward. As ever, the charger bounded forward, pent up energy being released suddenly. Hagan drew his sword as they careened forward.

In those seconds that separated them from the infantry lines, Hagan saw the world slow around him once more. Spearmen, training having been beat into their heads from the start of their march till now, scrambled to clear gaps in their own ranks for the oncoming cavalry. More than a few, however, were too engaged in the fight to have realized the charge had been sounded. They seemed oblivious to the fact of their own cavalry charging hard on their rear.

Ahren had seen it as well and gave another call from the horn as they neared the line. The line became a blur as its cohesion collapsed. The line of infantry was replaced by small groups of men, the infantry that were too far from one of the groups would inevitably be killed by the enemy or run down by the charge. Turks flooded past the infantry as the resistance suddenly slackened and then gave altogether.

They were met by heavy cavalry at full charge. Lances destroyed the front ranks of Turks. They were unaware of the cavalry's charge until it was too late. It smashed into them.

Hagan had killed several men in the first minute of fighting. He'd steered Wighard to where he judged would be the best place to attack. Wighard slammed between two horsemen. One man was reaching down to jab at a spearman that was too surrounded or engaged in the fight to get clear of the charge. Hagan swung down with his sword with all of his strength. The weapon chopped through the Turk's thigh. He was sure that the man must have screamed in sudden pain as he tumbled from the saddle but Hagan couldn't hear it. At least he couldn't distinguish it from all the yells and noise around him.

Hagan turned to attack the man on his left and was relieved to see that Sir Aldrich had already done so. A slumped body fell from his saddle and Hagan was pushing forward. He swung left and right, having to constantly check attacks on his left side that he would normally use his shield to block.

Hagan hammered the edge of his sword into the back of the neck of one man sending the head rolling forward grotesquely. He couldn't reach the next man on his left so he instead chopped the horse's neck. The blade cut deep and the horse dropped on suddenly limp legs. Blood poured from the animal. Hagan felt bad for having done it but he would have felt worse had that man killed Aldrich or Ahren instead. The Turks began to put up a stiffer fight for the next few minutes until they saw how many of their comrades had fallen. Fear replaced the anger in their eyes, and one by one the horsemen fell back from the fight.

Soon Hagan found that he had more room and wheeled Wighard left and right to gain the upper hand on his opponents.

One man grabbed a hold of the banner, as Hagan fought another man, and tried to pull it from his grasp. He turned his attention to the would-be thief and saw him ready to swing his sword into Hagan's back. Hagan brought his sword around as fast as he could and severed the hand holding the pole. His sword continued on as the man screamed and blocked the oncoming sword. The hand wound had sapped the man's strength, and there was little force behind the swing.

Hagan felt a sudden fire on his right shoulder and back. He let out a ragged cry of pain. The man to his right, who had lost Hagan's attention, when the banner pole had been grabbed, had taken advantage of the distraction. Despite the intense pain that flared as he moved, he swung his sword back-hand, into the Turk's side. His sword cut through the leather armor and padding underneath, exposing a gush of red from the man's side.

He had a moment of respite from the fighting and spared a moment to look for Aldrich. They were, surprisingly, only separated by two riderless horses. Ahren was on his far side blade whirling in deadly arcs almost too fast to see, and too fast for the enemy to counter as one by one they fell to his skill. Hagan scanned his surroundings once more for enemies. They had all pulled back and were moving in an organized retreat. Fresher knights that had been in the rear of their detachment came forward and pushed past Hagan and Aldrich but Aldrich called them back.

"Ahren, signal to halt and reform."

A few short trills of the horn brought the men back and all across the line knights pulled back from the pursuit to reform at their original defensive lines.

Hagan slumped against the pole as he urged Wighard back to their original spot in formation past hundreds of dead bodies. Luckily most of them were Turkish, at least until they reached where the infantry had made their stand. Men moaned and dragged themselves along the ground or tried to extricate themselves from the piles of bodies around them. Several men were trapped under lifeless horses struggling for freedom as other men tried to extricate them from their grisly confinement. The wounded helped the wounded and as the cavalry returned many of the knights called for squires to go fetch surgeons for the injured infantry. Men ran everywhere carrying men off of the front lines back to the baggage train to be seen after.

Obert gasped from somewhere behind Hagan as they made their way back to their defensive positions.

"What in God's name happened to you, boy?" Obert called.

Hagan removed his helm with a grunt and hiss of pain then turned to eye Obert's expression. Obert's eyes were tightened into a scowl.

"Is it bad?" Hagan asked.

"Well, it isn't nothing. Why can't you ever come away clean and smelling like roses like Ahren and me? Why do you always have to go off looking to get killed? If you keep it up, you'll find what you're looking for."

"So I'll live?" Hagan said. Cutting off Obert's continued tirade.

Obert just grunted a reply that Hagan chose to interpret as being in the affirmative.

"I don't smell like roses because I don't stop to smell them during a battle as you must." Hagan said.

He turned once more to see his friend's expression. It had improved considerably with the calculated insult. Obert grinned and Ahren, Horst, Carl and Aldrich laughed.

"I can't help it, after smelling you lot who can blame me for trying to get the stench out of my nose. At any rate, I would like to wash out that wound and dress it before we go again. I dare say we will have the time before those bastards work up the courage again." He looked toward Aldrich who nodded his agreement. Hagan handed the banner off to Horst and followed Obert toward the baggage train.

Chapter 35

The monastery was small. Smaller than Anna had expected. It was not a long journey from the castle but taking the long way through the forest had slowed them and she was worried about being overtaken. The thought had crossed her mind that Milda had been playing a part and setting them up to be captured and hanged. But that theory didn't make any sense, and she discarded it.

If she had wanted them to be caught then she simply had to tell the guard that guarded the rear gate. Or easier still, she could have yelled the alarm and Anna and Greta would have been killed already.

Anna decided to continue with the plan that Milda had laid out if for no other reason than she had none. She hoped that Milda's brother Odo would help them, but she doubted it. What other choice did she have? She didn't know the country very well, traveling was not something that she ever did.

She was so afraid.

The truth was, if it wasn't for Greta she would probably just curl up in a ball and cry.

She pushed on. Odo would help them. Because if he didn't they were dead.

Anna stared out through the thicket at the stone building. It was on a picturesque hillside with high grass all around it that a few hobbled oxen grazed at near the walls. Anna had led Greta around the end of the priory keeping in the cover of the trees to where they could see the massive door to the main building.

They watched together. Anna was still reluctant to go to the priory. There were so many dangers involved. There could be men watching and waiting for them. There couldn't be more than a handful of places that they could have fled to, so it seemed likely that the castle's garrison would search all of them.

Anna and Greta sat for about an hour in the shade of the trees. Greta still hadn't spoken but Anna talked to Greta. She spoke of hopes and dreams newly realized after their acquired freedom. She was shocked to realize that the hope she spoke of began to take root in herself. If they could get away, then they could use the money that Hagan had given them and make their way to the Holy Land. Perhaps they could find Hagan.

She was under no illusions about the coming difficulty but excitement began to work its way through her mind. Anna was in the middle of describing how happy seeing Hagan again would make her when she realized that Greta was looking at her. Not staring through her as she had been all day, but actually seeing her and understanding her in her eyes.

"Hello my sweet." Anna said.

"Hello momma. Did I kill him?" Greta said. Her eyes were watery and as Anna watched a single tear escaped the confines of the eyelid and slid down her cheek.

"I did, love. I did."

Greta sat and thought about that for a moment then nodded as if to agree with some inner argument. She looked around seeing her surroundings for the first time.

"Where are we?"

"The priory outside of Graz." Anna said. "We are to find Milda's brother Odo."

Greta's eyes went wide. "Milda?"

"She helped us escape remember?" Anna said.

Greta was confused and her face took on a deeper seriousness as she concentrated.

"Maybe." she said and shook her head. "It's all fuzzy. I remember a guard?"

"Yes. We wouldn't have made it out of there if it hadn't been for her. I think she felt remorse for what she had done." Anna said.

"She has lied to me before mother." Greta said. Her eyes had a spark of anger behind them.

"I know dearest but there are few options left to us."

Greta saw the look of desperation in her mother and nodded her acceptance of their situation and of their being dependent on Milda.

It was becoming dusk and Anna decided to wait until it was dark before moving.

Maybe Anna was wrong. Maybe the death of scum such as Ludolf wasn't worth a search party. Maybe they would be free to leave with no fear of being chased.

Darkness finally fell, and they slipped from the trees as quietly as they could and walked to the door.

They knocked once and a muffled call came from inside.

They waited, and the door was opened a crack. Anna had rehearsed what she would say but when the door opened, she couldn't recall what she had practiced to say. She stammered out what she hoped sounded more like words than what they sounded like to herself and then stopped and started over.

"We need refuge, father." She managed to say.

She couldn't see the man's face, only a bulbous nose showed from the deep shadow cast by the man's cowl.

The silence stretched. Finally, the monk spoke.

"Refuge from what" His voice was deep.

"We seek safety from Lord Adelfried's men." Anna said. They had discussed what they should say, and this was not it.

Greta looked at Anna in surprise.

"They took my daughter and locked her in a storeroom and performed all manner of evil to her Father." She bowed her head and sobbed.

"I died every day that she was tortured. I prayed that God would help me rescue her from evil men and the path was made clear to me. I murdered father. To save my daughter, I murdered the evil man that tortured her and stole her virtue."

Her sobs were making her gasp, and she crumpled in despair to the cold ground. Surely they would not let them in and help them now that they knew the truth. They would probably send a messenger to the castle, and she and Greta would be dead by tomorrow.

Why had she told all? All she knew was that she couldn't lie. Lying to this man was like lying to God.

"I am damned." she sobbed more to herself than to the monk. She felt a big hand rest on her shoulder as she sobbed.

The monk had opened the door and crouched in the opening. He stroked her dirty hair and she could see his face in the dim light. He was smiling at her, tears in his caring eyes.

Chapter 36

Geza lifted his shield just as an arrow slammed into it. They seemed to have picked him out from the rest of his men for they shot at him twice as often as any single soldier that he now commanded. He'd have preferred to be on his horse rather than coaxing and encouraging his men as they fought for a foothold on Iconium's walls but he had experience in this type of fighting while much of the army did not. So here he was, yelling at sergeants to reinforce a flagging section of the assault. The Duke of Swabia had taken the larger part of the assaulting force to the main gates and would be attacking there in an attempt to gain command of the gates and thus, give the defending army a redoubt if things turned desperate. Geza's mission was to secure a foothold on the walls closest to the German camp. Benefits of success would be two-fold. First, they would relieve the camp of the constant barrage of arrows being shot at them from the walls, and second, they could install their own archers, as few as they would have to be, to rain hell down on the enemy within the city.

The second point of attack would also serve to string out the city's defenders to make both his and the Duke's missions easier...he hoped.

It felt like they had been fighting for hours already, but Geza knew that it had only been minutes. None of his men could get a foothold on the top of the wall, each man was cut down as he climbed the ladders. His men didn't have a chance against the defenders. The enemy had every advantage.

Geza cursed in frustration as another body fell from the top of the ladder and crashed into several other men waiting to climb. This one's head was gone. Men jeered in an unintelligible language from atop the wall. Geza poked his head above the rim of his shield and saw a man standing above, holding a severed head. He saw Geza looking and spit into the dust-filled air and hurled the head down at him. The bloodied orb rolled to his feet.

Geza slammed his drawn sword into his sheath and ran to the ladder.

"Out of my way! Let me show you bastards how it's done.' He yelled.

He wore a full helm and much of his voice reverberated back to his own ears, but the yell must have been loud enough for most of his men to hear over the fighting because men scrambled out of his way. One man must not have heard him and began to climb just in front of Geza. He shouldered the man off of the ladder and began to climb. Geza had a man in front of him and let the man shield him as they climbed. They were almost twenty feet in the air, probably two-thirds of the way up when the man above him was knocked unconscious by a falling stone. The man fell limply onto Geza and then slid past, almost knocking him off as well.

Geza shifted his left arm and raised his shield above his head. Most men didn't climb with their shields as they preferred to have their sword drawn as they climbed. Geza didn't understand the logic as you were exposed the entire assent. He moved up as quickly as he could, right arm and legs propelling him up the ladder. A heavy thud proved the shields effectiveness.

Suddenly, almost too quickly, he felt a sword slam down on his shield with the power of a blacksmith's hammer stroke. His shield arm tingled and went numb with the strike and it burned with the need to lower but he commanded it to stay up as he brought his feet up under him on the top rung. He still held the ladder with his right and waited.

The sword strike fell again, and Geza launched himself up. His legs pushed him explosively off of the top rung. His shield slammed into several men's faces who were unprepared for the suddenness of his lunge and fell back.

Geza drew his sword as he landed among the men. He was off balance, but so were they. He swept his sword left and right, feeling it make biting contact with poorly armoured arms and legs. Men screamed and suddenly he had his feet firmly under him and space to fight. He pushed forward quickly. Battle was all-too-often about momentum. He knew that if he pushed hard here, now, he could break these men in a matter of minutes.

He slammed his shield into a man armed with an ax and cut off his leg before he could recover from the shield strike. The man screamed and fell back then rolled off of the inside of the wall. Another man took his place and tried to charge Geza with a spear in his hands. Geza parried the thrust with ease and rammed the crossguard of his sword into the man's face. He followed through with a swing that beheaded the stunned man. Geza dispatched a man that approached from behind with a thrust to the man's chest. He glanced at his men's progress in their attempts to reinforce him. They would be another couple of minutes before there would be enough of them to make real headway. Two of his men now guarded his back as he held off the defenders from his side.

"Push them back!" Geza yelled.

He ran forward into two waiting defenders who hesitated. The sudden death of so many of their friends by his hand seemed to make them reluctant. Good, about time he got a little respect around here.

He laughed out loud at the thought and pushed one man off of the inside of the wall and slammed the edge of his sword into the other's neck. The cut opened an artery that sprayed blood in an arc.

The men he now faced turned and began pushing their way through their comrades in fear. Trying desperately to get away from this laughing blood soaked demon. Geza used it and laid into the fleeing men, cutting down one after another as they turned in terror. The press of men behind were unaware of the demon called Geza and so continued on toward the fight.

Men that were unable to break through the ranks of men decided that broken legs were preferable to Geza's wrath and jumped from the wall.

Men screamed, bled and died. He panted for breath as he fought.

Suddenly the mass of men before him fled. Sergeants yelled for them to stop, to fight, they cursed and swung swords on their own men but it was useless. The fear on the faces of men as they flung themselves from the walls to escape something terrible was too much for them. They escaped down the inside stairway and dispersed in screaming fright.

His men cheered behind him at the retreat.

Geza turned and saw his men still fighting defenders in the other direction. He had pressed far from his initial foothold and the wall top was now filled with his men who pushed Geza's lifeless victims off the wall to the city streets below making their way toward him. Several men caught up to where he stood, breathing heavily. They saluted him.

The cheers increased instead of decreased and Geza realized that they were chanting his name. But it wasn't coming from his men on top the wall. They were all fighting, climbing, or standing in front of him awaiting orders. The cheering came from the camp below. He looked out over the German army and smiled to himself inside his helm.

The cheering tripled in volume as he raised his sword.

The remaining defenders broke at the sound. The walls were his.

Chapter 37

"What should we do with you?" Abbot Muller said. He shook his head subtly as if to say that nothing could be done.

The man at the door to the priory was the abbot. Apparently he had long despised Adelfried and his un-Christlike behavior so accepting the two women's explanation was not difficult. But now they were in the chapel discussing what was next. They had told the abbot of Milda and how she helped them and that she told them to come find her brother and so Odo was sent for and now sat in his wool habit with them in the chapel.

"The Holy Land Father. I wish to go to the Holy Land. My son is there and we have money." She had gone back and forth whether she should reveal all to these Holy men but had decided their lives were in their hands anyway and the money might help them realize the possibility of the journey.

She jingled the pouch that hung from her waist as evidence of her words.

The abbot perked up and Anna felt a pang of worry at the sudden interest but it calmed again as the man's face lightened and became pensive.

They waited for minutes as the old man thought.

"Yes." He finally said.

He'd said it so low that those in the room with him barely heard him.

"Yes." He said louder.

"That may work. It will be difficult." The man looked at the women again as if appraising their strength.

"But you can do it with God's help." He stood up from the bench and his voice was no longer pensive. He had made his decision.

"Father Odo was petitioning me not two nights hence to go to the Holy Land."

"Indeed, I was." Declared Father Odo. His excitement was clear in his voice.

God had surely blessed them, thought Anna, She had not imagined that they would even be able to go themselves and in truth she hadn't even been asking the Abbot for physical assistance. She just needed advice. Maybe a map. A few night's refuge from Adelfried's search parties. But now it seemed that they would be given a guide and priest for their journey.

Excitement coursed through her and she turned to Greta and saw the same excitement in her eyes. They embraced and laughed at their new fortune of blessings.

Abbot Muller smiled at their joy and said "God has surely saw fit to soften my heart. When Father Odo came to me and asked for the priory's sponsorship in sending him to the Holy Land I was, I'm sad to say, thinking of the worldly and not the Godly." The Abbot came closer to the women and Father Odo.

"The Priory will sponsor this holy journey Father Odo and may God grant thee safety. He has surely saved these two souls and prepared me to help them."

It was that simple. Ana knew now, without a shred of doubt, that God was real, that he loved her and Greta. That comfort elevated her eyes to heaven as she clutched her daughter and prayed. No words formed in her mind, but she prayed with all of her rapidly beating heart. A prayer of thanks.

Chapter 38

Hagan grimaced as Obert poked and prodded. He was wet from the water that he used to wash his wound. It felt nice in the heat. It was about the only thing about his current situation that was in the least bit pleasant.

Another stab of pain lanced down from his back as Obert worked. Once Obert got a better look, he said that it was too deep a wound to just bandage. So here they were. Far more badly wounded men groaned and whimpered around them and it made Hagan embarrassed for being here but here they were.

In the distance, from the direction of the Emperor's command the dull roar of combat emanated. Hagan had heard it the whole time he had been sitting there. He wondered how they were faring. Hours had passed since fighting had begun. Would they be defeated here? Would they lose this war before they even really started? Hagan was unfamiliar with this scale of fighting and it was nearly impossible for him to comprehend the numbers of men involved in this battle. How many would it take to defeat them? He knew their army was massive, and that wasn't just according to his own skewed peasant view of it. The army was said to be the largest ever to set out for the Holy Land. What were they up against?

He knew only what the Turkish army looked like as it had materialized in the first light of morning. Dust clouded much of the army, and it wasn't until they had stopped and the dust settled that their numbers were seen. The city and the crusaders were surrounded. The numbers needed to accomplish that alone was remarkable.

Hagan had begun to view the Crusading army as an inevitable wave, so large that nothing would be able to stand against it indefinitely. But, as the clangor of battle sounded in his ears, he began to worry.

Frederick kicked his horse forward. Men fought and died two ranks ahead of him. His guard kept yelling at him to withdraw to a safer distance, but he needed to be here. He was too old to fight, at least to fight well. He wasn't too old to be a symbol, however. His men needed his presence. They needed to see the Red Beard.

A horse screamed out and thrashed the ground as it fought instinctively to relieve itself of the pain it had just been dealt. A spear jutted from its neck and the knight atop it fought on despite his sagging mount.

They had been fighting hard and no matter how many men they cut down it seemed there were always two more to take his place. There hadn't been so much as a breath of rest for his men for hours. He had tried to send in his reserve so that the men on the front could withdraw and catch a break, but the reserve served to pin most of the men against the enemy and there wasn't enough room to maneuver the tired men out. He told the sergeants to do their best, and that's all he could do.

There was so much about battle that was out of a general's hands. With his age came the wisdom to be patient, but he had reached the point in every battle when little more could be done. His men were committed. It was God's fight now. His will would see them through.

The only thing left was for him to encourage his men. So from time to time he would sally out from the protection of the ranks upon ranks of men that separated him from the enemy, and together with the knights that made up his bodyguard, engaged the Turks. He personally slew two men during one of the sorties but the skirmish was one-sided. He felt cheated and grateful that both men had been wounded before he reached them. Had he still had the strength of his youth he would have fought these Turkish devils all day long but now he wheezed at the exertion of striking the second man down. It had been a hard slash at the man's neck as the Turk lulled forward, blood dripping from his open mouth. An arrow had caught the man in the chest and he wasn't long for this world but Frederick had long ago learned to take every advantage that God gives.

The dead man's head lulled unnaturally far forward after the second stroke and his helmet fell from his head. Frederick grabbed the hair in his left hand and cut down a second and third time to sever the head completely.

His guards were, of course, pushing the enemy back around Frederick. They didn't approve of his sorties. He was far too valuable to be fighting, they kept telling him. Frederick wheeled his horse and lifted the severed head high. The men around him started screaming their warcry. His attack had worked. The men were at a near fever-pitch and the army, who had moments ago looked tired and sluggish surged forward. Frederick wheeled back around and threw the head at the Turks. His screaming men flooded around him and past him, and he and his bodyguard were protected once more by ranks of men as they pressed on for God and Frederick.

Once Obert had Hagan all stitched up, and both men had gotten a long draught of warm water they mounted up and rejoined Aldrich at the front of the line. They had had another charge, and so far the attacks had been working. Despite all their success on the battlefield, the Turks kept coming and when Hagan and Obert wormed their way through their men to the front, Hagan could see the mass of Turks closing in once again. It seemed their god forsaken arrows had finally run out and now the enemy had no alternative to fighting close in, to the waiting German's delight.

Men barked insults at the approaching horde and smashed their weapons against their shields in a welcoming rhythm.

Despite the exhausted look of many of the men, there was vehemence in the cat calls and jeers. The enemy couldn't continue this way and they knew it. Any army broke after losing so many men.

The German infantry, that had helped so much in the first attack were now only used to clear the dead and dying from the field as best they could. A dead body served as an obstacle for a horse, a field littered with hundreds of them made a charge impossible.

Nothing could be done about the dead horses however and so the charge would lose some of its strength as knights negotiated the corpse-strewn field.

Not a single word passed as Hagan and Obert took their positions in the line once again. The standard was handed back to Hagan, and Aldrich gave a solemn nod before raising his sword.

The Turks had closed once again to within striking distance and Aldrich was ready.

Hagan felt the familiar sweat break out on his forehead, underneath the helmet, caused less by the heat than by anticipation. Aldrich lowered it and a great cry of German voices surrounded Hagan. Wighard, as ready as ever, sprang forward with the rest of the host. Hagan's shoulder burned as he pulled his sword, but the pain was eclipsed by the fear and excitement that coursed through him.

The Turks were less excited to engage once again in what they could only assume would result in another devastating charge. Their advance never came on faster than a canter. Hagan veered left to miss a fallen horse as did Aldrich. Obert went right and passed on the other side of the fly-covered carcass.

Once past that obstacle Hagan didn't see anything ahead but the enemy and so he urged Wighard to greater speed.

Just when Hagan picked his man in the Turkish line he noticed that they didn't have swords out. Bows! They all had bows strung with arrows.

As one they lifted and too late the onrushing cavalry saw the impending volley. The air vibrated with the thrum of bowstrings hundreds at a time. Never before had Hagan seen so many arrows. Unlike the rest of the knights, Hagan's shield was on his back and little use to him. He heard calls. "shields! Shields" down the line, but any that had not been already ready would not escape being struck. Hagan could only lift his sword arm in front of him and lower himself in the saddle.

Shrieks, whistles, thuds. Wighard jerked suddenly and Hagan felt a hammer blow in his left shoulder that nearly made him drop the standard. Tingling numbness ran down his arm to his fingertips.

There was no time to think. Instinct pushed him onward. Wighard was clearly in pain and it was difficult to control the big animal. But he still had momentum and Hagan used it. No longer able to choose his target, he just had to gauge where he would enter the fray.

He was close enough now to make out facial features and almost close enough to see eye color when the line of Turks in front of him, put arrows to strings again, pulled, aimed and released in one motion.

The blow hit him right in the forehead. The force slammed his head back and suddenly he was falling, backward off of Wighard.

Chapter 39

Geza led the way down the steps on the inside of the wall and into the streets of the city. Pockets of the enemy lingered here and there but, for the most part, they had broken them. Geza ran around the corner of a building, followed closely by about twenty of his knights, right into a volley of arrows. One glanced off his thigh tearing a hole in his leggings and another clattered off his helm.

He heard several of his men swear angrily behind him. At least one of them gasped in pain. He didn't bother to see the damage done to his men. He barely slowed when the arrows hit and ran right at the bowmen. They struggled to fit arrows to strings as the blood-soaked demon charged them. Two men guarded the bowmen with spears. The spearmen jabbed at Geza as he approached but the second man ran as the first doubled over spewing blood from his mouth, a sword in his lungs. As the spearman went so went the bowmen.

Geza worked his way to the gates, using the sound of battle to guide him. The fight was still fierce here. Turks fought from the ramparts, and several hundred men stood between him and the gate. The doors were still closed, but Geza saw them tremble as the Duke and his men chopped at the stubborn obstacle. The Turks waited for the eventual entry of their enemy with nervous focus. None noticed him and his men behind them.

Through the forest of enemy spears Geza could see the gates move in succession with his comrade's axes and judged that it would still be some time before the Duke broke in. Not a weak spot could be seen from this side of the thick wood gate. Geza frowned when he realized many more men would die before those gates fell.

At least that was if they had to chop through the gate. Geza was tired. He was starting to feel it now, but there was nothing for it. Something had to be done, and he knew what.

He turned, finally, to his men that had just caught up. They were breathing hard through their helms and the few with open visors had a sheet of sweat running down their faces.

"Are you ready to win this city?"

They stared at the columns of men, hundreds of them, and looked back at their liege lord with consternation.

"We don't have time for a water break, someone is bound to turn and notice us standing here and then our advantage will be gone."

Geza turned back towards the enemy.

"Take courage, it will be over soon." he said and heard a deep voice behind him

"That's what I'm afraid of."

He knew they'd follow him, and he knew they'd fight hard for him. He had always tried to give his men something to believe in and as payment they had never let him down.

Geza started forward at a walk that quickened into a jog within a few steps. He heard the steps of his men behind him and smiled to himself.

They had crossed half the distance to the unsuspecting soldiers and Geza was thrilled that they had not been discovered.

As if on cue yells sounded the alarm, but Geza knew it was too late. He was the sower of chaos. Voices from atop the wall shouted down to the spearmen, who didn't seem to understand their comrades.

Geza was upon the rearmost of them before any of the spearmen had turned. He felt as if he were death, doling out the inevitable justice. Cutting down men as if they were wheat. He had killed two before the first of his men were with him. Although Geza and his men had better armor, weapons, and training then the men they fought, confusion was their greatest tool against the Turks. Men trampled each other in an attempt to distance themselves from the onslaught.

The sudden attack from within the city they defended caused near instant panic among the Turks. No thought to how many attacked them or how to counter the attack crossed their minds. They ran.

Geza with his small band of men cut through nearly two-score men before a path was cleared to the gate.

From the vantage point of the ramparts the true size of Geza's force could be seen and men yelled at the spearmen to return and fight. But reason fled with them. Geza and two other men reached the doors and lifted the heavy cross-beam. The doors swung open, and men cheered.

Chapter 40

The damned rats were at him again. He just wanted to sleep, and the cursed rats wouldn't leave him alone. There was one at his side now scrambling around. But other details started to seep into his muddled brain. The rasp of metal against metal. The weight of chainmail hung heavy despite his reclined position. Then the pain came. It was intense and brought him around to consciousness. He remembered everything in a rush. He felt his arm being lifted and groping hands were attempting to undo his sword belt.

He opened his eyes and saw the blackness of the inside of the helm around the periphery of his vision and there was the fletching of an arrow right in front of him; the shaft extended toward him and vanished.

Those rotten bastards had shot him in the head. He couldn't believe it. He had been totally surprised by the first volley and only luck had brought him through it, but the second volley had finished him off, and now the enemy were searching his corpse.

He felt far too much pain to be dead. He saw a second arrow shaft that must have been the source of the pain at his left shoulder, a fine companion to his earlier wound on his right shoulder. Hagan wondered about his predicament.

But if someone was rummaging through his possessions, then that meant that last charge had been pushed back. How long had he been out for?

Hagan didn't dare move and tried to slow his breathing as he thought about what all of this meant.

Were there allies nearby? No, he couldn't hear any fighting. Several men rode by on horseback, all Turks. Suddenly there was a commotion next to him and men talked excitedly, but unintelligibly. Then the banner came into his view. The standard that was his charge. The black boar was hard to make out under all the blood and dirt on it. It must have been buried under corpses and lost until now. Hagan did not like that thought. That meant that there were enough corpses for the banner to have been lost. It did not bode well.

Hagan's blood boiled as he saw two men arguing over the prize. A captured enemy banner was worth glory and honor. Honor that he had let them steal. Sir Aldrich did not deserve to lose his banner and because of him Aldrich would be humiliated.

A mountain of thoughts and options tumbled through his head and sweat tickled his forehead and ran down his face as he anticipated his next, crazy actions.

He would not lie here and play dead while the enemy made off with the physical manifestation of his and Aldrich's honor.

Hagan made the decision, and it was done. He had already come to terms with whatever consequences would come from his decision which would undoubtedly be death.

He lurched suddenly and seized the dagger that he kept in his boot and turned.

He caught the man that had been retrieving the sword belt off guard.

Hagan didn't blame him for trying to steal the beautiful sword and belt, after all, he had done the same but the man had to die. The man was testing the grip of his new sword with a grin on his face.

Hagan brought the knife across the man's throat without a second's hesitation and the grin turned ashen with realization and surprise. Blood poured from the surprised man's throat and Hagan had his sword back in his hand before the Turk slumped over.

Behind him, he knew that the man that had won the argument over the banner was mounting up once more and he had to act fast while surprise was still on his side.

Pain stabbed at several points around his body, his head throbbed and both shoulders but he did his best to ignore it as he turned to the man carrying the banner. He had, indeed, just mounted his horse that flinched at Hagan's sudden movements.

Hagan lunged as the horse jumped forward. His sword bit, but not enough.

The man rode several yards away and then turned to face Hagan. The man's horse was more reluctant however and was trying to bite its rider and it kicked and refused his commands. The wound Hagan had given the poor beast had driven it mad with pain.

Hagan moved forward and was happy that his legs were working. Men around him shouted, evidently becoming aware of the dead walking, and he wondered how he must look with the arrow protruding from his helmet and one from his left shoulder. He hoped he looked terrifying, any advantage he could get he would take.

The horse was slowing but instead of becoming more docile the beast was just becoming more dead. Blood was running down the animal's side from Hagan's surprise attack and it labored to breathe. The man finally got control of the beast and forced it into one last terrible charge. The Turk seemed to be in slow motion as he careened toward Hagan, Banner pole held in his reign hand and a short lance extended in the other.

Hagan knew the theory of defending from a charging knight's attack while on foot but hadn't ever done it before.

The man was on him in seconds and Hagan tried to time his move perfectly with the movement of the horse and rider. He forced himself to stand ready despite the overwhelming desire to turn and run.

He counted it out and sprang to one side just as the man braced for the impact to his arm. Hagan had timed it well, and he brought the sword up as he moved and sliced it into the horse's nose. The horse reared and Hagan dashed forward and chopped down on the man's body as he fell to the ground, once, twice. The first swing was enough. It had cut deep into the man's neck; the second was just because Hagan's blood was up, and he struggled to keep his head.

Hagan seized the banner staff and wrenched it away from the dying man's hand.

More and more men were noticing the commotion. Hagan looked around and saw only Turks. He counted only two men that were looking at him but they signaled others to come kill the stubborn flag bearer. He had moments, before more men were on him and he would be killed. He reached up and attempted to pull the arrow from his helm but it would not come easily so he switched his attention to his left shoulder. That arrow had only sunk a few inches into the meat before reaching bone where it stopped. Hagan gritted his teeth and pulled the arrow savagely from himself. The pain was intense but the constant weight of the arrow was gone and movement seemed better as he rolled his shoulder, experimentally.

The two men that had signaled the others waited for their friends before engaging him. They had seen how efficiently he had dispatched the previous man and decided that it would be best to take him in force. Hagan used the time to try to make heads or tails of his surroundings. He must be close to the front of the enemy ranks where he could break free and run to his own side. It was a miniscule hope, but it was something.

Hagan saw over his right shoulder the thinning of enemy troops as they returned to their lines after scavenging the dead. He saw in the distance the wall of the city. If only he were on Wighard. Wighard. Where was he? Dead he supposed. He remembered the thud of an arrow as they struck the horse's flesh and the stumble of the horse, then Hagan had been struck in the head and been knocked unconscious. As he looked around, there was no sign of his mount. Hagan was in a half crouch turning in circles and waited for the next man brave enough to come for him. He should surrender, he realized, but then what. He wouldn't be worth much. He didn't have much more than what he had on him or on Wighard's body wherever he had fallen. It wouldn't take them long to realize he wasn't worth any ransom and if they didn't kill him outright, then he'd stay a prisoner for years.

He decided this was better. He thought of his mother and sister and wondered what would become of them once they received word of his death. A mere thirty seconds had passed since he had killed the man who had stolen the banner but it felt like a lifetime.

Five men now encircled him and Hagan tried to keep moving backward toward the safety of the Germans. He hoped they were still there. It was possible that the Turks had gained a resounding victory after the last failed charge and there was no refuge to be sought. But Hagan refused to accept that because to accept that would mean accepting his own death and he would not go so easily.

Hagan kept a constant vigilance, turning his head and twisting his body to keep the enemy from flanking him. As the horsemen came closer, he would jab at them with the banner pole.

A small man charged in and swung at Hagan. But he had seen the man and crouched low. The Turk had started his charge at Hagan only a dozen feet away and the horse had only made two strides before reaching Hagan. It hadn't been moving fast and Hagan parried the man's stroke easily and jabbed the sharpened pole into the man's unprotected throat. He pushed with the pole and the body tumbled from the saddle. Hagan lunged for the reigns and pulled himself into the saddle despite the fierce pain that tore through his shoulders he managed it and swung the pole viciously to keep the men off of him, but one man, angered by the stubbornness of this thick-skulled German boy darted forward and brought his curved blade down on Hagan's head. The clang of the metal vibrated his ears and stunned Hagan.

He had to get away. If he gave them anymore opportunities, he'd be dead. He kicked back his heels and steered the small horse toward his friends, at least he hoped it was in the right direction. His senses were still reeling from the blow to his helm. The Horse responded admirably and from its back Hagan was relieved to see that only a handful of unobservant Turks separated him from safety.

Aldrich stared at the enemy as they plundered his men. It had been bad. The volleys of arrows at such close range had completely stalled the charge. Horses crashed into each other and reared as they were struck. Many men and horses went down in the first volley and created obstacles that were too close to avoid for a charging war horse and more went down. He had lost his mount before ever reaching the enemy and Ahren had pulled him onto his protesting horse and withdrew. The morale that had been so high minutes before had fallen to a depressing low.

Aldrich order the butcher's bill but the sergeants hadn't yet reported it to him. He knew poor Hagan had fallen. He had seen the boy fly back off his horse after being struck in the head. Horrible, Aldrich thought. He liked the boy. He had incredible potential and Aldrich cursed himself for having allowed the boy such an early baptism by blood. It was his fault that Hagan had died and Aldrich cursed again. He stared out at the opposing horde of Turks.

Suddenly a western style banner flew up among the enemy ranks. It was his, had to be. Those bastards had found it and were undoubtedly singing praises to their God for its capture. Then the flag wavered, fell. Then it was waving and swinging back and forth wildly.

"Bring me a horse!" Aldrich yelled.

Hagan crouched low in the saddle and swerved to avoid the reach of a Turk on foot who had seen the unexpected westerner barrel towards him. He hoped that the Turks would be slow to string their bows. He had passed all but three mounted men.

He was closing quickly on the three and had no hope, as battered as he was, to break through, they were no longer ignorant to him. He hauled on the reigns trying to buy time for him to figure out how to get away. The men's yells behind him changed to jeers as they became assured that he was well and truly trapped.

Hagan spun the horse, desperately searching for his path of escape. Despair became a tangible thing. It bit painfully into his chest and brought tears to his eyes. He had done more with his last few minutes of life than he had thought possible just minutes ago, but he had had a glimmer of hope then, he realized. None still lingered.

He whipped the horse around the other direction as the three horsemen blocking his escape slowly walked their horses forward.

He looked past the heads. To his right. Then he heard something and looked to his left. And saw it.

Hagan raised the standard high and yelled.

The yell was punctuated by screeching metal and heavy thuds as heavy horse met horse.

Aldrich had come. He'd launched another charge at the sight of the flag and had come in obliquely to the enemy lines. They were leery of being mired down in the enemy ranks by a direct charge and so swept down the enemy ranks like a long curved blade slicing into flesh. The three men that barred his escape had disappeared. One minute they had been there, the next they were gone. Carried away by the flood of steel and horseflesh. There had been brief seconds of realization on the men's faces as the sound registered and their doom became apparent. Those around Hagan had been caught totally by surprise and turned to run at the sudden crash of death. Beasts tumbled and men screamed as the Germans cut into the Turkish lines. Their light armor did little to stop the carnage.

The men that had been so confident as they jeered at Hagan's predicament now fled with all the speed they could muster from their tired horses. The fear that hit them was contagious and, as it does on so many battlefields, it spread quickly.

As his comrades passed, Hagan heard them cheer. The Banner was safe. The enemy fled. Morale was back, and Hagan was alive. And so was Wighard!

Obert came trotting up to Hagan, leading the sweaty, black war-horse. Hagan jumped down and ran to the horse. A long line of blood ran from his left shoulder down to the ground, and Hagan shot a worried glance at Obert, but the man just smiled.

"That's nothing for a horse like Wighard." He said.

Hagan hadn't realized how the loss of the horse had affected him until now.

"I'm glad you got him out of there, but what the hell Obert? Why didn't you pull me out of there?"

Chapter 41

Ana, Greta, Odo and a servant named Peter walked through the gates of Graz on the road south. This marked the farthest that Ana and Greta had ever gone from home. They all carried bundles on their backs and there was a mule that carried the rest of their supplies. Ana had tried to purchase a lot of the supplies herself despite the exorbitant prices, but Father Odo had bade her to save her money.

He was a truly charitable man. He and Abbot Muller had purchased everything needed for the journey and had insisted that Peter join their company since a monk traveling with two women alone might have been seen as odd.

Peter was almost as old as Hagan and had a similar build. His hair was black and his shoulders were wide. Ana had to agree that she would feel safer with another man to protect them from robbers and rogues that would prey upon defenseless pilgrims along their path.

The morning sun warmed her face as she looked out to the farms that lay below and the distant forests and hills that they would have to traverse. She was exhilarated as was everyone in their party. She thought of Hagan and prayed to God as she did every day that her son be alive.

Upon thinking of him, standing on the precipice of a holy journey, she suddenly knew that Hagan was alive. She didn't know how she knew, but she knew. It was an irrefutable fact in her heart and mind. Tears blurred her vision at the sweet revelation.

She turned to Greta who returned her gaze. The girl was beautiful. Her golden hair waved in the light breeze.

"He's alive." Greta said.

It shocked Ana that Greta too knew the unknowable.

"I know." Ana said and sobs shook her body as she cried and embraced her daughter.

"I know."

Chapter 42

The church had been a Mosque the day before and the prayers offered there had done little to stop the Christian army pouring into the city. The Turks had lost. It surprised Hagan when the battle had been described as a resounding success for the Christians. The losses had not been many, considering how many Turkish bodies strewn on the sunbaked ground.

The entire army was jubilant. Men sang and got drunk on the harsh Turkish alcohol. There hadn't been much in the city, at least by comparison with his homeland where there was even a beerhouse in the small town he grew up in, the German soldiers had found the stuff, anyway. And despite the Emperor's insistence that the army remain sober, men, after such a long fight and difficult sojourn through hell could not resist.

Women had screamed, men cheered, and houses burned.

The next day the mosque, a great building in the center of the city with a massive domed roof was ransacked and then converted to a church.

Hagan sat in the church, looking up at the ceiling far above. They had to scour the city for chairs. Turks apparently didn't use them nearly as much as Germans, and so, fifty or so chairs sat toward the front of the church. They were filled, and a few hundred spectators stood behind the chairs.

Hagan felt uncomfortable. Not physically, he was sitting in a chair after all but that was the problem. Why should he sit when there were so many that stood?

Aldrich sat next to him and sensed his unease and patted his knee.

"Don't be nervous." he whispered.

The words didn't make Hagan feel any better. As a matter of fact, he felt worse.

Aldrich had told the Emperor what he had done to rescue the banner and how he had rescued Aldrich the week before. So, he was invited to this ceremony where Aldrich had said that he would be honored for his heroism. That's all that he could get out of the man.

His body hurt. He was bruised and bandaged, sown and sore. It was all covered by his freshly repaired armor. The chair back dug in to his tender back, and he wondered if he could get away with standing and moving to the back.

He turned in his seat and glanced at the faces staring back at him. Still no sign of Duke Otto Wittelsbach. He had commented as much to Aldrich and so the knight had sent Carl and Horst to scour the city for the absent Duke. All of the other nobles were present, and Hagan worried at the development. Surely the man wouldn't try anything too terrible so close on the heels of the Emperor's victory.

He turned back, facing forwards.

Hagan was afraid that they would try to make him a knight as they had done after the battle where he killed Spatharios Photios. He did not feel any more worthy of the office than he had before. But could he refuse the Emperor in front of so many witnesses?

The Ceremony had started an hour ago. At least Hagan thought that it was the ceremony. Bishop Herman had been giving a sermon about sin and pride. Something about God's wrath and Hagan was hot. The place was stifling. They had all dressed in polished armor with cleaned tunics but with this many men the huge room stank of sweat, horses, and the oil used to clean armor.

The Emperor was speaking now and he began going through the list of heroes from the battle. One of Geza's men was called forward. He had been a survivor from Geza's savage attack on the walls and was presented with a beautiful sword that the Bishop blessed. Two more men were knighted from Geza's attack. Men cheered in the back of the church earning a sour glance from the Bishop. The Emperor's son, Duke Frederick, was next. The Emperor gave him a chest of gold and an embrace for his successful assault on the city.

Aldrich was called forward next.

Hagan's palms were sweating. Aldrich, it seemed was a stabilizing force against Hagan's nerves and a wave of anxiety rushed over him as the man left his side.

"Without Sir Aldrich's stolid defense of my right flank we would not have prevailed in our bloody fight. I am even more indebted to you Sir Aldrich." The Emperor turned and the Bishop handed him a scroll.

The Emperor turned back to Aldrich. "This scroll states that Sir Aldrich is now lord and steward over the Traun Valley and all its towns and fortifications." A gasp rang out among the spectators. Then shouts and cheers reverberated in the church.

Traun! Hagan's home would be Aldrich's? Hagan was still standing and cheering when the Emperor asked for Aldrich to kneel and swear fealty as a Count to the Emperor. Frederick helped Aldrich back to his feet and then kissed his cheeks and clapped as Aldrich bowed to the crowd and returned to his seat.

Frederick Barbarossa called Geza up. The hall was filled with cheers. The Bishop, Hagan noticed had given up trying to quell the noise, but instead smiled at the jubilance. The Emperor gave him territory in the new land that they took as a consequence of taking Iconium. It was a valley to the south that was said to have good crops. Geza smiled at the gesture and whispered something in the Emperor's ear that made the old man laugh before returning to his chair.

Next I'd like to call Hagan Egger of Traun!

The cheers were intense. Everyone cheered.

He never heard his name said like that. He stood nervously as he walked up to the front of the huge room.

The Emperor began to explain Hagan's virtues and valor to the crowd which erupted when the Emperor described his actions when he killed the Spatharios.

"I was ready to knight the boy then but he was determined to remain a squire so as to train under Aldrich. That kind of humility is quite rare. Then he saved Sir Aldrich's life on the plain when Aldrich had lost his horse. Wounded and surrounded by the enemy, Aldrich had little time and not much hope left I'd imagine. Hagan fought through the horde to rescue his mentor from certain death. Hagan was wounded, and yet he fought in the battle for Iconium. He was wounded again, and again he chose to fight." Grunts of satisfaction and agreement accompanied the Emperors words from those watching. Hagan stood there uncomfortably. He was sure the heat in his face was visible.

"He was struck multiple times by enemy arrows, lost his stead. When he rose bristling with enemy arrows and fought and killed for the standard, that was his charge, the enemy must have thought that Armageddon had come."

Men laughed.

He won the standard and with it our respect as a true warrior of Christ."

The room thundered with applause and stilled as abruptly as it had started. The Emperor had turned to Hagan.

"Kneel."

It was not a request. And despite Hagan's misgivings about being knighted, he knelt without hesitation.

"I knight thee Sir Egger. Protector of the weak. Be the strong arm of thy Emperor and they God. Arise a knight!"

The converted chapel thundered with applause. Hagan was surprised. It had happened so suddenly.

He rose, bewildered. He was a knight. The meaning of what just happened began to seep into his befuddled mind. He turned to the spectators and saw individual faces. Rupert and Henry sitting side-by-side. Rothschild bellowed in the back. Obert and Ahren stood bandaged and smiling. Hagan had done it. He had accomplished something incredible. He had become a knight. He had been accepted into their ranks and stood before them, applauded for his bravery, his valor. His life had changed so completely in the year since he left home. He reached down, with his bandaged hand, to the cross that he had fashioned himself and stroked it and thought of his mother and sister.

He understood in his heart suddenly that, somehow, he would see them again and his exhilaration renewed. He returned to his chair and clasped arms with Count Aldrich Kortig. His liege lord. Despite his pain, and anxiety for the perilous road ahead, he felt his smile would never leave his face.

Epilogue

The Army slithered like a lethargic snake down the mountain road, its tail far below in the distance. House pennants fluttered in the breeze that pushed its way into the mouth of the canyon. Aldrich looked out over the Crusading army with pride. Although these men had suffered much in the past month they marched on, following the will of their Emperor. How long would that stalwart determination last if, God forbid, he died?

Not long, Aldrich concluded. The high-ranking nobles would want to return to their homelands to consolidate what power they had so that they could make what gains they could while the voids were filled. Would any remain to continue on the Crusade? Technically, every man had made his oath and was duty bound to see it through regardless of the Emperor's hypothetical demise, but Aldrich suspected that that would not influence the minds of much of the Imperial Court.

He would be free to continue on, he realized. He was a Count now. No longer an Imperial knight and restricted by the codes that attempted to keep the order free from the politics that corrupted so many knightly orders. The first thing that Aldrich had done, upon being made a Count, was to perform the military benedictus on Obert and Ahren, raising them to knighthood. The men had been immensely loyal and should have been raised long before, but desired nothing more than to support him. They sat their horses next to him, as did the rest of his hangers-on, Horst, Carl and Hagan.

Aldrich turned and looked eastward. Across the mountains, and a finger of a sea, stood yet more mountains. In those it was said there lived a band of killers, specialized in the stealthy murder of high-ranking enemies. "Enemies" was a loose term. According to his sources, the Assassins reclassified their "enemies" based on whoever they were paid to kill. Their proximity to such a dangerous band of mercenaries coupled with Duke Wittelsbach's suspicious behavior made Aldrich feel perpetually on edge. Surely no Assassin would dare threaten the Emperor as long as he traveled with the army, as he had been doing of late, the lack of a convenient river, paralleling their path restricted the Emperor to travel by land.

Aldrich scanned the pennants and failed to see the oversized banner indicating the Emperor's presence. He did see that of the Counts of Diez, Henry and Rupert, and Aldrich made for them. The Co-Counts walked their horses up the switchback, their units of mounted sergeants, and spearmen trudged behind them.

"Aldrich." Henry yelled as he saw them approach, raising his hand in greeting.

"Henry, you look chipper this morning. Not even a morning trudge up a mountain can dampen your spirits?" Aldrich asked.

Henry just shook his head, smiling. The Counts steered their horses out of the line of march to continue their conversation with their newly made counter-part.

"I do not see the Imperial bodyguard in the line. Do you know where they've gone off to?" Aldrich said.

The bodyguard was made up of an elite unit of Imperial knights that Aldrich knew well, but he feared that they did not have the mindset to foresee threats from more subtle avenues. Avenues that he had heard that the Assassins employed.

He had warned the guard and had even warned the Emperor of the threat of the Assassins, but he was reassured that "all needful steps" have been taken to ensure the Emperor's safety. Aldrich had even, with as much tact as he could muster, informed the Emperor of the shady meeting that Hagan had witnessed.

The Emperor had patted his shoulder as a loving grandfather would an unruly grandson and shrugged off the implied deception of the Duke.

"He has had opportunity to end me countless times before, and I don't see what it would profit him."

"Perhaps the profit is purely monetary. Sir Eggar saw the transfer of a purse to the Duke." Aldrich used Hagan's new rank to instill a degree of legitimacy to the evidence.

The Emperor shook his head and scrunched his face in casual dismissal of the testimony.

"Undoubtedly some business deal that the Duke didn't want his rivals in the Court to witness, nothing more. You know how those wolves operate. Otto is many things, and one of them is a shrewd businessman, but what he is not, is a killer. His stomach turns when we hunt." The Emperor laughed. "His political ass-kissing is nauseating, but when you can get him away from all the pressures of the politics, he can be quite diverting."

Aldrich nodded and smiled weakly as the Emperor patted his shoulder again. He wasn't convinced, but he had played all the cards he had. Short of out-right confrontation with the Duke, Aldrich was at a standstill. He would need more proof of the Duke's corruption, but none had been forthcoming.

"He said he was too old to climb a mountain, and he's gonna go round and cross the river." Rupert said.

The river that Rupert referred to was the Calycadmus River, it was a longer detour and came dangerously close to the Silifke Castle. The smaller unit of Emperor and Bodyguard should be able to evade any enemy patrol and the danger of such an expedition would be small... normally. For some reason, Aldrich had a sinking feeling in the pit of his stomach. Was he just being paranoid?

"Do you know where Duke Wittelsbach is? I see his men, but not the Duke himself."

Rupert frowned at Aldrich's abrupt and nervous tone.

"He accompanied the Emperor." Rupert said.

"Apparently he is too fat to climb mountains." Henry said, snorting at his jibe, failing to pick up on Aldrich's concern.

"I think that's the reason why he pushed the Emperor so hard to take the easy road." Henry continued.

"Wait, it was Wittelsbach's idea?" Aldrich nearly yelled.

Henry frowned now too, Aldrich's mood apparent.

Ahren kicked his horse down the verge of the road, shale rock skittered in his wake. Hagan and Obert were close on his heels. Their turbulent passage frightened spearmen back from the torrent of men and horses. Aldrich spurred his horse to follow the knights as they careened down the mountainside and didn't respond to the Count's yelled questions.

The Emperor was hot. Oh, how equalizing the harsh rays of that distant orb were. Poor and rich alike, sweltered in its gaze. Perhaps he should have stuck with the army. Surely it would be cooler the higher they climbed. This path was easier though, and he suspected that mountain road would stall and it would take an eternity to get the whole army over. He was better off meeting them on the other side, where he could have the comfort that his age demanded.

He definitely had gotten soft.

His scouts returned and reported that the river was a mile or so ahead, but that they'd have to go up river half a mile to the ford.

Some water would feel nice, he thought. Maybe he'd go for a swim. Swimming on a hot summer's day was most enjoyable. Despite the incredulity of his sycophants, he often stopped his entourage for a quick swim at a river or lake along their path these many months while crossing this arid oven.

The river soon came in sight, and he thought he might just take a dip, or at least wade for a time. They stopped at the edge of the water. A worn track indicated that this was, indeed, a well-used ford. In the distance Frederick could see Silifke Castle atop its tree dotted hill, but no enemy had been spotted and the water did look extremely tempting.

"I have a mind to wade this ford. I wouldn't want to linger too long, with that castle looking on, but the coolness looks inviting, and it doesn't look more than waist deep."

"Indeed, my lord. It didn't even touch my stirrups when I crossed it." The scout said.

"Very well." The Emperor said, and he dismounted.

"Would you care to join me, Otto?" Frederick asked the sweating Duke.

"I feel that I should ride ahead with your men to make sure that that looming castle doesn't vomit a horde of brutes, sire." Wittelsbach said.

"I shall enjoy it alone then."

The Duke had been uncharacteristically concerned of enemy bands this trip and had made many scouting forays as they neared the river. Aldrich's revelation of the Duke's clandestine meeting surfaced in Frederick's mind. Looking around him, he scrutinized his surroundings. Was there some trap that he had missed? That his guards had missed? He was alone now, standing next to his horse, petting the animal's muzzle.

If this was a trap, then he was giving them every opportunity to kill him, standing here without guards, waiting for the knife.

Guardsmen splashed their mounts up the far side of the river and reconnoitered the area. Wittelsbach stopped his horse and looked back once he was on the far bank.

He stepped into the water and felt foolish all of a sudden. Was he really suspecting his most ardent supporter of treason? Ridiculous, wasn't it?

He pulled on the reins, coaxing the horse down into the water. The horse shied suddenly to one side, and he turned to see what had spooked the animal, and saw a boulder rise from the edge of the water, amongst the thick reeds that grew there. No, it wasn't a boulder. A man dressed in a tan, gray-brown mottled tunic and loose trousers was not four feet from him and moving fast. Brown linen wrapped his head and covered his mouth, leaving only the murderous eyes visible.

Frederick let the reigns fall and reached for his sword. Despite his age, he prided himself in his swordsmanship practices that helped him keep some measure of his once impressive fighting stature. He was old, however, and the man was close.

The Emperor managed only to draw his sword before the man was on him. The Assassin, for that's who this must be, had wet clothes. He must have been almost completely submerged, literally laying in wait.

The Assassin grabbed Fredericks wrist with one hand and chopped his throat with the other, just as the old man filled his lungs to yell. The escaping air came out in a gurgle, a hiss.

Frederick could not breathe. He grabbed at his throat instead of the man and dropped his sword. All he could think of was the need for air. Then his head was in the water, a hand on the back of his head.

Hagan pushed Wighard harder than he had wanted to, what with his recent injury, but the horse didn't seem to want to slow. He must have sensed his rider's urgency and plowed on. He had out-run the rest, who had grasped the severity of the situation and had flown after the Emperor. It was a good thing that the tracks that the Emperor's bodyguard had left were so obvious. He was able to follow their path with ease, even while moving so fast from horseback.

Pretty soon he came to where the group had merged with a well-worn track heading for the river that he could see now in the distance. As Hagan approached, he saw a group of knights wearing the tunics of Imperial knights dismounted and gathered around something at the edge of the river.

Hagan launched himself off of Wighard and ran to the group. A few men turned and reached for their swords but saw that he was a friend and turned back. The Emperor lay in their midst, and as Hagan drew near, he knew that he had been too late.

Historical Note

The Battle of Hattin, that takes place in the epilogue of this book, was a singularly devastating event to the Christian States in the Levant. After his victory there, Saladin trounced city after city along the coast and only took Jerusalem after securing most of the Christian city ports. A strategy that allowed him to efficiently cut off the Christians from sea bound reinforcements. Tyre was the only hold-out and was expertly defended by Conrad of Montferrat.

Guy de Lusignan was captured and held by Saladin, but was released much as it is described in the book. Saladin wanted Guy's divisive nature to form a rift once again in the Christian ranks and weaken Conrad's hold on Tyre.

Frederick Barbarossa was an impressive leader and had a keen understanding of battlefield tactics, but his greatest strength I feel was his ability to inspire. Frederick raised the largest and best organized army of the Crusade, and had he lived to reach Acre, he most likely, would have taken command of the Christian forces instead of Richard the Lionheart. His death, while odd and somewhat suspicious for the political atmosphere was probably only an accidental drowning and not the nefarious murder perpetrated by the Old Man of the Mountain's Assassins and facilitated by the Duke Otto Wittelsbach. I admit I piled way too much derision on to the poor Duke who was actually a Count and a close friend to the Emperor and who was known to join Barbarossa in his indulgent swims. Count Wittelsbach died before the third Crusade but I needed a scapegoat.

The envoys from Frederick were held as prisoners by Isaac Angelus as part of a treaty that he had with Saladin to keep the Germans out of Anatolia, a treaty that was made known to Barbarossa by a letter from Sibylla, Guy de Lusignan's wife. The dramatic fashion in which the envoys were captured was my fabrication, but the underlying machinations were very real and convoluted. Barbarossa used the imprisonment and the Byzantines ill treatment of the Crusading army as a tool to anger the already unstable Bulgarians and Serbians who helped push Isaac into capitulation.

Geza of Hungary was, indeed, being held prisoner by his brother-King upon Frederick's arrival and was released to lead an army on a Crusade. There is no mention of him leading a grand assault on Iconium's walls as I describe in the book, but I could not resist giving the Prince the triumph.

All the engagements in the book, and more, really happened, and the frustrating tactics by the Seljuk Turks were difficult for the westerners to combat. One battle, omitted from the book, was that of an ambush by the Turks on the army as it made its way across into Anatolia. The Turks were able to attack only half of the army at a time, while the other half struggled across the water in ships that were also attacked by Turk and Cumen galleys. It was suspected by the Germans, that the Byzantines had betrayed the army's movements to the Turks, thereby completing, in part, their duty to Saladin. There were simply too many engagements to include them all. The battle for Iconium, except Geza's escalade, happened much as it is described in the book and the Emperor gave an admirable defense against tough odds, trapped against the walls of the city.

Hagan's ready inclusion into the ranks of the more noble class was somewhat idealized as was many aspects of the book as I wanted to keep it light-hearted, but the opportunities he gained at being elevated to a squire were not unheard of. His elevation again to knighthood, also, happened from time-to-time, when a heroic deed such as that performed in the book was accomplished. Hagan, Aldrich, Obert, and Ahren will continue on, for their duty to their oaths have not been fulfilled, Acre and Jerusalem await.

The Crusade of Frederick Barbarossa translated by G.A. Loud was instrumental in my writing this book as was Steven Runciman's narrative histories A History of the Crusades volume I-III. I cannot forget to mention Crusading Warfare, 1097-1193 by R.C. Smail. And The Crusades: A History by Jonathan Riley-Smith.

About the Author

Levi Mecham was born and raised in rural Utah and has a strong connection with the outdoors as a result. He attended Utah State University while in High School and received his Associates degree at the same time as his High School diploma. In 2004 he left his home town for two years and lived in Buenos Aires Argentina where he learned Spanish while doing missionary work for his church.

Later, Levi attended Brigham Young University and earned a Bachelor's in Geographic Information Systems (GIS). Upon leaving BYU in 2009, Levi created a GIS department for an Engineering/Surveying company with headquarters in the Uintah Basin in Utah. Levi was head of this GIS department and supervisor of several employees for 12 years.

Levi's love for history and human geography has been lifelong. He sometimes reads several books at once to compare the historical facts between editions. He pursues ideas that are interesting for him until he has resolved his fascination. Relating inspiring stories from the past in an entertaining way is a goal that he loves to pursue. Levi currently lives in Idaho with his wife and three sons.

Levi Mecham

CRUSADER'S VALOR